SWEET MADNESS

"What's happened to you, Neal?"

He looked deep into her eyes. *"You* happened, Ginna."

A moment later, they were in each other's arms. After a long, deep kiss, Neal whispered, "I don't want to rush you into anything."

Any other time, with any other man, she would refuse to be rushed. But this was Neal—the man she loved.

The rain on the roof of the quaint old cottage had a silvery, music box sound. Off in the distance, thunder rumbled over the valley. Neal's kisses transported Ginna to another realm—somewhere beyond the fourth dimension. She lost track of who she was, where she was. But she knew whose arms were holding her, whose mouth moved temptingly over hers, whose warm body was pressed close to her own. She felt a sweet, languid weakness flow through her veins like a river of fire, kindling a longing so intense that she knew there could be no turning back.

Not this time. Not with Neal.

"Ginna, Ginna," he whispered between kisses, "I never knew I could feel this . . ." He paused, groping for the right word.

"This alive?" she said. "This free and crazy?"

"Crazy?" He chuckled, a low, sexy sound. "Yes, that's it. But what sweet madness!"

SWAN'S WAY

Becky Lee Weyrich

Zebra Books
Kensington Publishing Corp.

http://www.zebrabooks.com

Prologue

"What a delight to have such a handsome couple before me, Miss Swan, Mr. McNeal. You must both hold perfectly still now and look directly into my lens."

Slender, dark-haired, bearded Mathew Brady spoke to his subjects from behind the large, tripod-mounted box of his camera. He was a dapper gentleman in his black coat and doeskin trousers, topped off with a merino vest and silk scarf. Propped nearby was a handsome cane with a silver head fashioned like a tiny camera, a gift to the photographer from the Prince of Wales, who had had his own portrait done in this very room only five months ago, during his tour of America.

Of all Virginia Swan's extraordinary adventures on her first trip to New York City, this visit to Brady's uptown studio at 859 Broadway and Tenth Street to have her engagement portrait done ranked as the most unique. She didn't know what she had expected, perhaps a drab shop that reeked of chemicals and cigar smoke. She had steeled herself for such a place—something between a sweat shop and a mortuary. Instead, she caught the faint aroma of expensive Atwood's cologne, the same scent her fiancé sometimes wore. And imagine her surprise when she entered the reception room two floors below, through doors of beautifully etched glass, to find inside velvet tapestries, walls hung with silver and gold paper, banks of mirrors, crystal chandeliers that sparkled like stars in the mellow gaslight, and elegant rosewood furniture. The special "Ladies Parlor" was no less pleasing, with its green satin decor and fragile gilt-painted chairs. Examples of Mr. Brady's work hung every-where—portraits of statesmen, European royalty, freaks from Mr. P.T. Barnum's museum, along with likenesses of everyday people like herself.

Now she stood one floor above "Brady's Famous National Portrait Gallery" in the studio, her head firmly held in place by a metal support, waiting for the moment of truth, when Mathew Brady would uncover his lens and magically imprint the image of herself and her fiancé on his collodion-coated glass plate, stopping time for an instant and capturing forever the love that shone in her eyes for the man who would soon make her his wife.

Having her portrait done photographically was a new experi-ence for Virginia. But then she was finding these days that life after betrothal was full of new experiences, each one more exciting than the last. She was engaged, but more than that—*in love.* And love, she found, made all the difference in the world.

She rested her hand lightly on Channing McNeal's shoulder and smiled down at him. He looked especially handsome this morning, dressed in the high-collared, brass-buttoned, gray cadet uniform of West Point Military Academy.

It swelled her heart with pride to think that in another four months, he would graduate with the Class of 1861 and receive his commission in the United States Army, along with her eldest brother, Rodney. The entire Swan family planned to travel with the McNeals from their plantations in Virginia to upstate New York to attend the commencement ceremonies and the grand reception afterward, on the superintendent's lawn. There would be parties, too, teas, balls, and, of course, the traditional stroll along Flirtation Walk with her beau.

Following that auspicious occasion, the two new second lieutenants would return to Virginia for a visit at home and for the wedding—a double ceremony to take place at Swan's Quarter at which Rodney Swan would wed his childhood sweetheart, Agnes Willingham, while Virginia exchanged vows with Channing McNeal. There would be no time for a honeymoon, but that didn't matter to Virginia. Becoming "Mrs. Lieutenant Channing Russell McNeal" would provide more than enough happiness for her. Wherever her husband's orders took him, his new bride would follow, willingly. They would honeymoon, as they traveled to his first post, their first home together.

Whither thou goest, she thought, smiling down at her darkly handsome fiancé.

From behind the bulk of his camera, Mathew Brady peered out of his wire-rimmed, blue-tinted spectacles at the stiffly posed couple. "If you don't mind, Mr. McNeal, this is to be an engagement portrait, not a wanted poster. Do try to relax, won't you? You look as though you're staring into a hangman's noose."

Brady wasn't far off the mark, Channing thought. Actually he felt as if he were staring into the barrel of a loaded cannon, as he might well be, before long. The prospect of war did not frighten him. He was trained for battle. Something else far more unsettling was on his mind this bright March morning.

He had wanted everything about Virginia's visit to West Point and his furlough to New York City to be perfect. Perhaps his fiancée had missed the tension at the Academy, but her father had noticed the dissension in the ranks, immediately upon his arrival, and Jedediah Swan had not been cheered by what he saw. Since South Carolina's secession from the Union back in December, the cadets had become polarized, North and South. The atmosphere at the Point these days was explosive. Many cadets had already resigned to go South. The first had been Channing's own roommate, Henry Farley, from South Carolina, who left in November of 1860, even before his home state seceded. There had been many fights among the cadets, even one duel. On Washington's Birthday, one of Channing's classmates, a flamboyant but unstudious fellow named George Armstrong Custer, had led the singing when the band in the quadrangle struck up the "Star-Spangled Banner." Custer's roommate, Thomas Lafayette Rosser, had countered with a boisterous rendition of "Dixie." A near-riot had ensued. That was when Virginia's father had ceased holding his silence to state his opinion to his future son-in-law clearly, and succinctly: "I am raising a cavalry unit for the coming conflict, Channing. I expect *all* my sons will want to ride with me, should the North be so foolhardy as to invade our homeland. We men of Virginia know our duty and must answer the South's call."

A war was coming; there was little doubt of that. The only question in Cadet Channing McNeal's mind and heart was with which side—North or South—would he, a born and bred Virginian, cast his lot? He knew his own family's sentiments. They were Virginians to the pits of their souls, the same as Jedediah Swan. But Channing himself had other feelings, other loyalties. How could he fight against his own country? He had walked the hallowed halls of the Academy at West Point for the past four years in the very footsteps of Ulysses S. Grant, Class of 1843; William Tecumseh Sherman, Class of 1840, and Robert E. Lee, Class of 1829, a Virginian himself, yet rumored about the Academy to be the most likely candidate to lead the Federal forces in the "Southern rebellion," as his northern classmates termed it.

"Smile, dearest." His fiancée's soft voice interrupted his troubling thoughts. "If not for Mr. Brady, smile for our children and grandchildren. What will they think, if they see you scowling so in our engagement portrait?"

Mathew Brady gave a short bark of a laugh. "Ah, Mr. McNeal, she has you there! Think of the wonder of it. A century from now, your children's children will gaze on my work and see you both, just as you are today, flesh and blood, smile and scowl. Do you really want to be remembered this way? With such a lovely fiancée, it looks rather unseemly, somehow."

Channing glanced up at Virginia. His heart never failed to thunder with joy at the sight of her. Dark gold curls draped her shoulders and framed a face that was as perfect as the finest French porcelain. Lips as delicate and soft as the petals of the first summer rose and a pert nose that tilted up just enough to suit him. Her eyes, though, were her most bewitching feature. Dazzling now in the shower of sun from the windows, with tints of blue, silver, and gold. Looking at her, he couldn't help smiling. She was his love, his soul, his whole world.

"Yes, that's better," Brady said. "Now, hold that pose. Don't move a muscle."

Virginia held her breath. She felt almost wicked, having this portrait made. Her grandmother had railed against such modern voodoo, claiming that to have one's image captured, other than in a painting, was the same as having one's very soul stolen by the charlatan behind the camera. But if there was any soul-stealing going on in Mr. Brady's Broadway studio, Channing McNeal was the thief. She had been in love with him since before she knew the meaning of the word. He had been born and raised on a neighboring plantation. Often, it had seemed that he was the fifth son of the Swan clan, or she the third McNeal daughter. Soon it would be so, and the two families would be linked forevermore.

She had to force herself to keep from smiling wider when she thought ahead to the June day when she and Agnes would descend the elegant staircase of the main hall of Swan's Quarter to be married in the front parlor, while their assembled families and friends looked on. Virginia planned to wear her mother's wedding gown, the same handstitched satin and lace that Melora Etheridge had worn twenty-eight years ago, when she became Jedediah Swan's wife. On that day, the happy couple had planted a tulip poplar sapling. Now a towering monument to their enduring love, it spread its branches to shade the swan pond on the plantation's front lawn.

Channing and I should plant a tree, Virginia thought. *A symbol of our love for each other and a vow never to be parted.*

"*Done!*" Mathew Brady announced. "You are now immortalized, my young friends. I hope you will invite me to your wedding. I'm opening a studio in Washington soon, and I would dearly love to create your wedding portrait.''

"Oh, what a wonderful idea!" Virginia cried. "By all means, Mr. Brady. The date is set for the first of June. A new month for our new life together. Mother and Father will approve of our inviting Mr. Brady, don't you think, Chan?''

Channing stood and took her hand. His dark eyes captured hers, and the intensity of his gaze all but took her breath away.

"How could anyone not approve of whatever you want, Virginia?''

She fought for control, before she could speak. When she did, her voice was a bare whisper. "Then it's all settled, dearest. We'll have another portrait on our wedding day.''

A slow, lazy smile warmed Channing's dark features. "There can't be any wedding until I give you a token of my affection. Come along now, my love. We're going to buy you a ring.''

Virginia knew it was rather unseemly, but she couldn't contain herself. Besides, no one but Mr. Brady was watching when she threw her arms around her fiancé's neck and gave him a sound hug. He hugged her back, but, even as he did, she felt him sigh deeply. It was a worried sigh, and she knew, even though she had tried to keep it from him, that the possibility of the coming war was uppermost in both their minds.

Why now? she wondered. *When our lives should be so perfect!*

Chapter One

The discreet wooden sign on the rolling lawn read in elegant gold script, "SWAN'S QUARTER." Smaller lettering below the name of the former plantation identified the current establishment as a "Rest Home and Sanatorium."

Beyond the sign stood the old mansion. On the veranda, Pansy Pennycock, Elspeth McAllister, and Sister Randolph huddled together around the white wicker tea table, clutching their crocheted shawls close about their shoulders. They waited. They whispered among themselves. Nervous, excited, dry-throated bird twitters. All the while they talked, they watched the path that led out of the woods to the swan pond and up the hill, hoping to catch a glimpse of Ginna's lithe form.

Ginna always came on Mondays. *Always!* She came to laugh and chat and charm the inmates of the rest home. She came to hear how they had spent their weekend, to find out who might have had a surprise visitor, to inquire as to which of the three white-haired ladies had sung the loudest and most harmoniously at chapel on Sunday.

But this Monday was fading quickly, with yet no sign of Ginna. As the afternoon sun began its gentle descent, the three little ladies—two widows, one spinster, all mothers who had outlived their children—shifted uneasily in their cushioned wicker chairs, their hopes fading with the setting sun.

Why was Ginna late for tea? *Today of all days!* A day when the three friends were absolutely bursting with anticipation at the special news they had to tell. News of a mysterious young man who had arrived at Swan's Quarter since Ginna's last visit.

"She'll come," Elspeth stated, adamantly, staring out toward the clearing west of the sun-spangled swan pond. She cradled an antique china doll in the crook of her mahogany-skinned arm and asked, "Did you ever know her to miss a Monday, Miss Precious?"

Sister, who didn't hold with talking to inanimate objects, snapped, "That old rag of a doll won't give you any answers. Don't act foolish, Elspeth. She'll either come or she won't, and that's the long and the short of it."

"Oh, dear me!" Pansy's pudgy, blue-veiled hands fluttered like moths before the flame of her cinnamon-brown eyes, eyes focused on the line of woods. "There was that one Monday last January. We waited and waited and she never came until a whole week later. Remember, Sister?"

Sister had outlived all her six siblings, but still wore her nickname with pride and authority. She gave Pansy an arch look. "We had a blizzard, you ninny. The roads from Front Royal and Winchester were impassable that whole week long. Even the postman couldn't get through." She sighed. "Not that it mattered. No one ever writes to us, nowadays."

"It's not their fault, dear." Pansy always felt it her duty to apologize for everyone, even the dearly departed, as she added, "They're all dead."

"And likely better off for it. You call *this* living?" Elspeth's scornful voice trailed off in a weary sigh.

"There, there now, Els." Pansy patted her hand. "We still have our moments. Mondays at least are special—when Ginna comes."

A tense, watchful silence fell over the threesome. Six rheumy eyes searched the clearing near the pond. But something was

missing, something more than the first glimpse of Ginna. Elspeth would never have admitted it to Sister, nor Sister to
Pansy, but a change in the atmosphere always preceded Ginna's
arrival. It was a shifting of light, a modulation of shadow,
accompanied by a delicate breeze, flower-scented even in the
dead of winter. And, most amazing of all, the old tulip poplar
always materialized to cast its giant, ancient limbs over the
pond, announcing Ginna's approach. The tree, they all knew,
had been wounded in the war, then blown down in a fierce
storm back in 1924, over seventy years ago. Yet when Ginna
came, the tree materialized miraculously, rising tall and strong,
as if to banish the present and recall the past with its looming
presence.

"Tea's getting tepid," Elspeth said, through a scowl. "Miss
Precious can't abide cold tea. Shall I pour out?"

"Please," said Sister.

Fluttering again, Pansy simpered, "Shouldn't we wait,
dears?"

Ignoring her weak protest, Elspeth carefully tipped the heavy
vessel toward Sister's blue-flowered china cup.

The late afternoon sun glinted off a disfiguring dimple a half
inch below the old English *S* engraved on the right side of the
antique silver teapot. The dent in the metal was as much a
battle wound as any suffered by the men of Swan's Quarter
during the long-ago War of Northern Aggression. The women
of the Swan family had suffered their wounds as well, but they
had worn them deep inside, unlike their men and their teapot.

The war might have been decided well over a century past,
but all three ladies knew the conflict's history by rote. They
knew the teapot's story as well, although each one of them told
a different version of the bravely scarred vessel's travails. For
this reason, they seldom discussed the tale, because of the
disagreements the telling always precipitated. But today was
different. Today, Ginna had yet to come and there was little
else to do besides retell old tales.

"Juniper really should have wrapped the teapot in a crocker

sack or a quilt, before he tossed it into the well to hide it from
the Yankees,'' Pansy began.

Both Elspeth and Sister cut their eyes her way. Pansy met
neither of their gazes, but kept her dimpled chin tucked, as she
sipped her tea. They always scoffed at her story about the Swan
family's butler dumping the silver service down the well. Still,
it *could* have happened that way, she reasoned.

''Juniper would never have done such a thing, and you know
it. He was said to be a fine servant, a credit to his people.
Besides, that's the first place anyone would have looked for
valuables.'' Sister clucked her tongue and waggled a finger at
Pansy, who pretended not to notice. ''It was those crude Yankees who dented the teapot. And after Miss Virginia offered it
to them filled with a cool drink from the well. They imbibed
of that sweet Southern water, then tossed Miz Melora Swan's
prized teapot right here onto this very veranda, and it bounced
across the paving stones and got the dent in it. They rode off
just a-laughin' afterward. And that's the truth of it!''

Replacing her fragile cup with such force that the saucer
danced, Elspeth glared at her two companions. ''Neither of you
knows a blessed thing about it! You make up history as you
go along, to suit yourselves. If you're going to tell it, for pity
sakes, tell it right! My great-grandma was right here on the
place when the Yankees came that day. I got the true story
handed down to me through my own family. Great Gran told
my granny, and she told my mammy, who told it all to me,
just the way it happened.''

Sister and Pansy settled into a bored, but polite, silence. They
had heard it all before—a hundred times—but they pretended to
listen again, as they kept their eyes keened on the road, watching
for Ginna.

''Now, as you all will likely recall,'' Elspeth began, ''Colonel
Jedediah Swan rode off to war at the head of his own cavalry
unit and all four of his sons went with him. They were a fine
looking passel of manhood—big, fair-haired, square-jawed,
and strapping. The very steel and cream of the South. Back
here at Swan's Quarter, they left only Miz Melora and young

Miss Virginia, the prettiest belle in Frederick County, to look after the place and the hundred slaves.''

"Last time you told it, they had *two* hundred slaves," Sister interrupted, with a good deal of satisfaction at catching Elspeth in a mistake.

"Well, some of the sorry ones ran off with the Yankees. It was just my Great Gran and the other loyal ones that stood by the family. At any rate, Miz Melora Swan and her daughter, Miss Virginia, had their hands full taking care of all this land and this house and our people. It was early in the war—May or June of 1862—that the Yankees first showed up around here. Stonewall Jackson had been chasing them up and down the valley, trying to run the blue-bellies far away from the Shenandoah. But he'd lick 'em one place and they'd pop up somewhere else. Well, with the Yankees tramping all over and burning whatever they didn't steal, it was no easy task for Miz Melora and Miss Virginia, I can tell you. They had to be strong and stern to keep up their spirits and their faith. Those were no ordinary times.''

Pansy loved this part of the story and couldn't help interjecting, "And Miz Melora Swan and her daughter, Miss Virginia, were no ordinary women."

Elspeth nodded her approval. She didn't mind interruptions, when they added emphasis to her tale. "Right you are, Pansy. No ordinary women at all. They were the bravest of the brave. So when the Yankees came here on the twenty-fifth of May, back in 1862, and burned their fields and threatened to set their torches to the house, the women of Swan's Quarter stood right up to them, as bold as brass. Miz Melora ordered them off her land. She had made pretty Miss Virginia dress like a boy so the Yankees wouldn't be tempted at the sight of her. But one of them noticed that a golden curl had escaped from under her daddy's old cap and saw the tempting rise of her young bosom, even though Miz Melora had ordered old Mammy Fan to bind her breasts tight. That lusting blue-belly marched right up to Miss Virginia and snatched the hat off her head, freeing her long hair to tumble down like golden coins spilling from a money bag.''

"And they all laughed and those that had turned to go turned back to see Miss Virginia," Pansy added, too eager to wait, when Elspeth paused for a sip of tea.

"That they did!" Elspeth nodded, solemnly. "But Miz Melora stood her ground. 'Y'all get out of here now,' she warned them. 'My daughter is untouched and promised to another brave soldier.' "

"But they didn't listen, did they?" Sister asked, as she knew she was expected to, at this point in the telling.

Elspeth shook her head sadly. "They were no gentlemen, those Yankee devils. They closed ranks around poor Miss Virginia and stroked her hair and *touched* her." Elspeth leaned close and whispered that one word.

"And one even stole a kiss," Pansy added, breathlessly, her pale cheeks flushed to dusty rose at the very thought of such a disgrace.

"They shamed the poor girl," Elspeth said, with a sad nod. "And after she'd been so kind as to serve them cool water from this very teapot. Brutes they were, and some of them married men with children—*church goers,* mind you!"

"Tell what Miss Virginia did," Pansy begged. It was her very favorite part of the story, the part that purely made her swell up with Southern pride.

"Well," Elspeth drawled, lengthening the suspense. "You'll recall she'd just poured them water from this very teapot. She still had it in her hand. When the brute who'd snatched her hat off caught her about her slender waist and tried to press his randy body to hers, she hauled back and cold-cocked him with his very pot. He gave a fearful yell, staggered backward, tumbled down the veranda stairs, and landed in a heap in the dirt of the carriage drive.''

"Good for her!" Pansy crowed, clapping her arthritic hands.

"It's a wonder those nasty Yankees didn't shoot Miss Virginia and Miz Melora Swan," Sister said, with a shudder.

Elspeth's attention now seemed focused on something far

away, as her gaze searched the woods beyond the swan pond.
"They might have," she said softly, "but for an accident of
fate. The troop's captain, a member of General Nathaniel
Banks's forces that had just been whupped by old Stonewall
at Winchester, came riding up about the time that Yankee
bastard landed at the foot of the stairs. All the others—a dozen
or so—had drawn their pistols and had them aimed right at Miss
Virginia's wildly beating heart. But the captain—a handsome
fellow, even if he was a Yankee—yelled, 'Halt! Put your guns
away. Whoever harms a hair on the heads of these ladies will
answer to me.' "

"And they backed right down, didn't they, Elspeth?"

"That they did, Pansy. They put away their guns and left
the veranda. The captain ordered them off the property, down
beyond the entrance gate, out of sight of the house. They camped
there for the night."

"But the captain didn't join his men in camp, did he, Elspeth?" Pansy said, with a sly grin etching her thin lips.

"Sh-h-h!" said Sister. "That part of the story's a secret."

"Not to *us!*" Pansy insisted, through a pout. She loved
hearing this romantic part of the tale. It reminded her of her
own life and lost love. "Tell the rest, Elspeth. Tell it! Do!"

"Very well, but it's to remain among the three of us. Always.
Swear?" She clutched her doll closer and looked hard at the
other two.

"Always! I swear it!" Pansy crossed her heart, holding her
breath after she spoke.

"Very well, then. You'll recall that Miz Melora had told
the rude soldiers that Miss Virginia was promised and still a
virgin."

The other two nodded, blushing at Elspeth's use of such a
forthright word.

"Miss Virginia's mother spoke the truth. Her daughter had
been betrothed not long before the war broke out to a fine
young man who lived over at Belle Grove plantation. But she
never married. The start of the war put an end to their plans
and near broke Miss Virginia's poor heart. You see, the man

she loved had graduated from West Point and felt obliged to join the Union forces."

"*A turncoat in blue!*" Sister said, with disgust.

"A misguided young man," Elspeth explained. "But he did love Miss Virginia with all his heart and soul. They vowed to wed, once the war was over. It was Colonel Jedediah Swan who forbad the union, not wanting to divide the family and possibly meet his daughter's husband across the line of fire in the heat of battle."

"We know that," Sister broke in impatiently. "Get to the point, won't you?"

"*The point is,*" Elspeth paused dramatically, "that Miz Melora held more with love than with war. She saw the look that passed between her daughter and the captain—the pain and sorrow and longing in their eyes. It proved more than a mother could bear. So she told my Great Gran to prepare a feast of what little they had left to eat—one scrawny hen, a bit of bacon, a few dried beans, and some yams. Miz Melora invited the captain to dine with them. She even opened the last bottle of Colonel Swan's fine old French brandy, a surprise she'd been saving to celebrate the end of the war and her husband's safe return. She told Miss Virginia to put on the white satin wedding gown they had hidden in the attic, beneath a loose board under the eaves. They had a jolly evening with the captain as their guest. After dinner, Miz Melora told all the house servants to gather in the parlor. Then she instructed Brother Zebulon, a self-styled minister to the people, to perform a marriage ceremony. It was an odd affair, a combination of a Christian service and a broomstick jumping. Likely the Lord Himself had never seen anything to match it. However, what it lacked in orthodoxy, it made up for in sincerity."

Pansy and Sister giggled, picturing the scene.

"Actually, it was a wartime wedding, and not unlike many another back in those times. It was certainly good enough to satisfy all involved, especially the bride and the groom."

"And afterward?" Pansy said.

"Afterward, Miz Melora bid the happy couple a good night.

She sent the people back to their quarters, went to her own room, and left the newlyweds to their one night of bliss. At dawn, the captain kissed his bride and told her goodbye, before he rode away. His parting words to her were a vow to return, the minute the war was over, and marry her in proper fashion.''

"But by then, it was too late," Pansy said sadly, sniffing back tears.

"You're wrong, Pansy. It's *never* too late for love," Elspeth added, cryptically.

Just then, the breeze changed suddenly, bringing with it the scent of spring flowers. Clouds shifted and the heavens seemed to shine with more light. The three women sat up, staring off toward the woods, their senses keen with anticipation.

Ginna glanced at the fly-specked face of the clock over the dessert case. She was running late this afternoon. Her regular shift at the Rebel Yell Cafe had ended over an hour ago, but she couldn't dash off and leave that mess on the red countertop. Her last customer, a three-hundred-pound trucker named "Slim," had slopped his coffee, then topped off the spill with a blob of meringue from his lemon pie.

She glanced around. The lunch customers were long gone. Now the earlybird dinner crowd was beginning to file in. In another hour, the place would be filled again. She needed to leave *now*.

"Lucille," Ginna called, "I gotta go, or I'll miss the last bus. Can you take care of this for me?"

The other waitress, owner of the Rebel Yell, shook her red head, as she balanced a huge tray. "Sorry, hon, but I got five blueplate specials, three coffees, a water, and a tea to get out, and Cindy's late for work again."

With a sigh and another glance at the clock, Ginna gave a quick swipe at the counter, then another. Poor Lucille, she thought. What would she do if Cindy—never the most reliable employee—didn't show up? Ginna would stay if it wasn't Monday. But she just couldn't. She had a standing appointment for Monday afternoons, the one bright, exciting spot in her otherwise ordinary life.

"You go on, hon," Lucille called, as she served her customers. "I can hold the fort till Cindy shows up. I don't want you to miss your bus."

"Thanks, Lu!"

Her counter shining, Ginna whipped off her apron and slipped into the ladies' room. Staring into the mirror over the less than sparkling sink, she grimaced at her reflection and vowed to start eating regular meals. She had dropped twenty pounds in the past few weeks. Her face was drawn, all sharp edges and angles. She looked ten years older than her age.

"Starting tomorrow, it's three squares a day for you, Ginna Jones. Lots of potatoes with sour cream, chocolate éclairs, and Lucille's fried chicken. I think I'll start taking those vitamins the doctor gave me, too."

Still staring, she squinted at her image. Her bottle-thick glasses didn't help her looks, either. They magnified her eyes, so that she was reminded of a fish staring out of an aquarium. She reached into her bag for the contact lenses she had splurged on a few months ago. She didn't wear them on the job, for fear of losing one in some customer's beef stew or vegetable soup. Stowing her unattractive glasses, she quickly washed her hands and face, then popped in the delicate contacts. The drastic change in her appearance made her smile.

Quickly, she pulled the pins from the tightly coiled braid crowning her head. Her straw-colored hair took on the sheen of old gold, as she brushed it out, long, full, and wavy. Satisfied with the transformation, she grabbed her battered overnight bag from the waitresses' locker, then headed for the back door in such a hurry that she didn't even answer when Lucille called out, "See you tomorrow, hon."

Mondays were Ginna's treat, her fantasy, the only time she had all to herself. And, for some reason, this Monday seemed special. She wished like anything that she had gone on her weight-gaining program earlier. That was silly, of course. Her friends at Swan's Quarter never said a thing about how skinny she was; they were just happy to see her whenever she came for a visit. They were old people, lonely people. They didn't have many visitors. Consequently, they made Ginna feel like someone really special.

"Which I certainly am *not!*" she said, hurrying down Winchester's busy main street to the bus stop. "Not in *this* life anyway."

The red-and-silver bus pulled up, just as she reached the curb. The door swung open immediately.

"Cuttin' it close today, aren't you, Ginna? I looked for you on my earlier run." Sam, the driver, gave her a big grin and laughed. He was obviously a man who loved his work.

"I got held up, but at least I'm not *too* late, thank goodness." She fumbled in her purse for change.

"I'd of waited for you. I know it's Monday."

Good old Sam! He probably would have at that.

Ginna took a seat near the door, leaned her head back, and closed her eyes. As weary as she was after her eight-hour shift, she felt excitement bubbling in her blood. Again, she thought that for some reason this Monday seemed different—*special*. But why? She had no idea, but she knew she wouldn't have missed it for the world. Something was about to happen—her horoscope today had said so. "Something exciting, perhaps even life-altering," the paper had forecast, and she *believed* it.

Lost in thought, she didn't realize the bus had reached the highway rest stop, until Sam said, "Hey, Ginna! We're here. You gettin' off or going all the way to Front Royal with me today?"

She jumped to her feet and flashed Sam a warm smile. "See you later."

"You have a good one, now!"

Usually, she stood beside the highway to wave, as Sam pulled back into traffic. Today, however, she turned and rushed away. She was fairly quivering with excitement, as she hurried to the restroom to change clothes. Her friends at Swan's Quarter wouldn't know her without the old costume she had bought several years ago at a thrift shop.

The white ruffled gown and scarlet velvet opera cape were probably not authentic, but the gown looked as if it might have been made back before the Civil War. She could imagine some Swan family bride wearing it, as she descended the grand staircase at the old plantation on her wedding day. When Ginna put it on, she felt like a different person. She could almost forget that she lived alone, was still single at twenty-seven (twenty-eight in a few more days), and likely to remain so. She could even forget that she was a waitress with more bills to pay than money to pay them and more worries than joys in her life. On days like this—*special days*—she even let herself forget her doctor's stern lectures.

With the antique satin and lace caressing her skin, she became, miraculously, another person entirely—the lovely and mysterious "Miss Ginna" from out of the past, come to take tea with her friends at the beautiful old plantation. Although Ginna dreamed constantly about the glory days of Swan's Quarter, she knew she could never recreate the past. Still, she thought, somehow today *anything* seemed possible.

At times, especially when she wasn't feeling well, the walk from the rest stop through the woods to Swan's Quarter seemed to take forever. She would have to pause along the way to catch her breath. Today, though, clutching her cape against the autumn chill, it was as if she had wings on her feet. She felt breathless with her own speed and with the change she sensed coming over her. By the time she reached the edge of the smoky-gold woods, that other Ginna was completely gone, along with the Rebel Yell Cafe, her drab little apartment, and everything else in her life that was dull and ordinary. She might have been a time-traveler, happening upon the serene plantation with its lovely swan pond, manicured lawn, and giant tulip poplar.

She felt so different—almost childlike in her excitement. She imagined that a casual observer strolling through the forest might have taken her for little more than a wisp of autumn woodsmoke drifting among the trees. The brisk breeze blew her hair. Quickly, she tied it with a sky-blue ribbon, subduing her rampant waves that now looked the golden color of the turning leaves.

Ginna couldn't know what an uncanny resemblance she held to Miss Virginia Swan. Both women had the same smoky-gold hair, the same slight figure, and those startling eyes which were of no earthly color. Instead, they gleamed with shades of heaven. Once, long ago, while painting a portrait of Virginia, an artist from England had described their hue as "celestial hazel"—shifting tints of sky-blue, storm-gray, moon-silver, and sun-gold.

Now Ginna's eyes of that same heavenly hue focused on three figures in the distance. They were waiting for her, probably wondering why she was late for their weekly teatime visit.

She lingered beyond the swan pond, hidden by the gilded Virginia woods that smelled of sun-warmed holly and pine. A breeze stirred the branches of the huge tulip poplar, making them whisper secrets of long ago days and dreams gone awry. She felt herself drawn to the path that led to the house and to her friends. Something sharp and bittersweet beckoned to her soul, something not to be denied.

In some odd way, it seemed she remembered this feeling from the distant past, yet she could not interpret its meaning. Tears blurred her vision suddenly. Her heart raced. Was it the wind whispering, or did she hear a voice? It seemed to say, "He has come home. Home, at last!"

A shiver ran through her. A warm shiver, like the feel of spring rain on bare flesh. She stared again at the three women in the distance, nodding and whispering over the old silver teapot. She felt a tug at her heart.

Could it really be? Was he home, after all these years?

The strange thought puzzled her. *Who* had come home? And why would his return fill her with such keen anticipation and joy? Dismissing the questions, which obviously had no answers, she headed up the hill, almost running.

* * *

"Look!" Sister cried, pointing toward the woods.

The other two women turned to see the great tulip poplar shimmering ghostlike in the golden afternoon light. A moment later, they caught sight of a slight figure clad all in scarlet and white, gliding along the path past the pond. The pair of swans poised motionless on the mirror surface, their graceful necks bowed together to form a heart.

"It's Ginna," Pansy said, with a sigh of relief and satisfaction. "She's come. I knew she would."

"At last!" Sister added.

Elspeth said nothing. She got a queer feeling in the pit of her stomach at the first glimpse of Ginna, the same kind of flesh-creeping, hair-raising sensation she got when she looked out her window on moonlit nights and saw the shimmering blue and gray ghosts of soldiers moving silently about in the woods. There was a change in the air, as always, when their young friend appeared. But this time, something was different. She sensed sorrow ahead. It took all her willpower to keep from shouting, "Go back—back wherever you come from!" Only her eagerness to tell Ginna their news stayed the impulse.

"You're late, dear!" Sister scolded gently, as Ginna, glowing like fresh morning dew, took her seat at the table.

"Something kept me away." Ginna wasn't sure why she had hesitated so long at the edge of the woods. She still sensed a strangeness all about her.

"You young people lead such busy lives," Pansy said, brightly. "We're just thankful you can make time to visit us on Mondays."

Elspeth poured a fourth cup of tea and handed it to Ginna. Pansy and Sister remained silent. Now that their guest had finally arrived, they could savor the anticipation a moment longer. How sweet it was to have *real* news to tell for a change!

Usually, the minute that Ginna arrived, all three women began talking at once. Unnerved by their extended silence, she urged, "Tell me everything that's happened this week. I see you've all had your hair done. Have you had any visitors? Did the handsome young pastor from Front Royal come yesterday to preach and lead the singing?''

The three of them sat staring at her, smiling like cats that had just polished off the last of the cream.

"Well, *tell me!*" Ginna said, laughing at their pleased-as-punch expressions.

Pansy and Sister both turned to Elspeth, offering her the chance to be the first to break the news. After another pregnant pause, she said, "A young man's come to Swan's Quarter."

"A *mysterious* young man," Pansy put in.

"A *handsome* man," Sister added. "And he's *very* young."

The women's eyes danced with excitement, as they all stared at Ginna, eager to see her reaction to their news. It wasn't often that anyone under the age of sixty came to Swan's Quarter, and most of the sanatorium's inmates were closer to ninety. Ginna knew that her three friends fretted constantly, because she had no man in her life. The trio were eternally trying to make matches for her with the male doctors and nurses about the place. Once they had even tried to fix her up with old Marcellus Lynch, the institution's self-appointed Lothario in his mid-seventies. "Why, he's only a youngster," the ninety-two-year-old Sister had proclaimed, shocked when Ginna pointed out the difference in their ages.

"Did you hear that, Ginna? He's *young!*" Elspeth emphasized.

"*How* young?" Ginna asked suspiciously.

"His chart says thirty-two," Pansy whispered.

Ginna gave the woman a mock-stern look, then laughed. "You've been sneaking into Dr. Kirkwood's office again and rifling through his files?"

"I'd never!" Pansy blushed. She knew that everyone at Swan's Quarter called her a busybody and a snoop. "It wasn't *my* fault this time. The doctor had the chart on his desk when I went in for my last appointment. When he stepped out for a moment, I just thought I'd tidy up for him a bit. I couldn't help it if the chart fell open when I dropped it."

"And does this handsome thirty-two-year-old have a name?"

"Neal Frazier," they all chorused.

Then the chatter began in earnest, like hens clucking at feeding time.

"He's from Richmond, but lives in Washington."

"He's single."

"A widower, Sister," Pansy corrected.

"*Single* just the same."

"Very tall."

"Very sad."

"I'd say more angry than sad," Elspeth pointed out, with authority.

"Angry about what?" Ginna asked.

All three shook their heads. "We thought you might find out for us, Ginna," Pansy pleaded.

"What did his chart say?"

Pansy shrugged. "I didn't have time to read all of it, Ginna. The doctor came back in and took it away from me."

"You're losing your touch, Pansy," Elspeth said. "You've never been caught red-handed before. At least not by Dr. Kirkwood himself."

"My hearing's not what it used to be. He sneaked up on me," Pansy explained. "However, I did get a chance to read the diagnosis." She frowned and looked to heaven, trying to recall the exact words. "Survivor's Syndrome," she said emphatically. Then she glanced about the circle of faces all staring at her. "But what in heaven's name does that mean?"

"It means there was some kind of accident and someone was killed, but he survived, and now he's feeling guilty about it and needs help to get over it," Ginna explained.

"I wonder what happened," Sister said.

"There's no telling," Elspeth answered. "Not unless he'll talk to us. He's not real friendly."

"I bet he'll tell Ginna," Sister said.

"Oh, yes!" Pansy cried. "That's a fine idea."

All three women turned pleading gazes on their young guest. *He's come home!* The eerie voice spoke again to Ginna, and in that instant she knew that she would make it a point to do her friends' bidding. She had a feeling that Mr. Neal Frazier was the cause of her excitement today, even though she had yet to meet him. She meant to make his acquaintance the first chance she got. Finding out everything about him seemed a most intriguing way to spend her time.

"I'd like very much to meet your Mr. Frazier. It sounds like he needs a friend to talk to."

Elspeth, Pansy, and Sister beamed as one. They could almost hear the wedding bells ringing already.

Chapter Two

"It was not your fault, Neal."

Dr. Leonard Kirkwood's voice sounded amiable, but unconvincing to his patient. This was the same clinical tone he had used in his sessions for the four days that Neal Frazier had been at the Virginia sanatorium poetically named "Swan's Quarter." So far, the therapy had been less than successful. Neal still felt eaten alive with guilt.

"If you mean I didn't cause the wind shear that made flight 1862 fall out of the sky, you're right," Neal answered grimly. "Still, it was my fault some of those people died. Maybe all of them."

"You saved little Christine."

"Only because her mother was sitting next to me and shoved her into my arms. My only thought was getting out of there. I could have gone back for Christine's mother. I might have been able to save her too. I *should* have, dammit!"

"How do you figure?" the bearded, middle-aged psychiatrist asked.

"I was sitting by the emergency door. It was my responsibility to open it and help the others escape. Instead, the minute we crashed, I opened that door and got the hell out!'' Neal's voice rose angrily, his rage all self-directed. ''I should have gone back in there. Christine has two sisters and a brother. Now they're all motherless, and it's my fault. I never even tried to help that woman or any of the others.''

''But the plane was on fire, Neal. You might have lost your own life.''

''Yeah, well maybe that would have been all for the better. Maybe I could sleep nights, if I'd died with everybody else. Maybe I wouldn't have these dreams all the time.''

''Nightmares about the crash?''

''No. Crazy stuff! Has nothing to do with the crash—nothing to do with anything I can think of.''

''And these dreams began right after the accident?''

Neal's dark scowl turned to a thoughtful look, before he answered. ''No. As a matter of fact, they didn't start until I got here, to this place.'' He turned an accusing glare on Dr. Kirkwood. ''Are you guys giving me some kind of weird drug that causes hallucinations?''

The doctor shook his head. ''You're receiving only a very mild sedative at night. Something to help you sleep, not give you nightmares.''

''Well, they're not exactly what you'd call nightmares. Some of the stuff isn't so bad, actually.''

''Tell me about your dreams.''

''I'm not sure I can. I mean, you know how it is. You have these dreams and they seem so real and so vivid at the time, but then you wake up and they fade. About all I can remember is that I'm fighting in the Civil War. And the war's hell, of course, but that's not what's bugging me. I keep thinking all the time about this woman. And sometimes she'll be right there with me and seem so real that having her there kills all the pain. But then when I try to reach out and touch her, she just melts away into the smoke of the battle, and I wake up crying like a baby and calling to her.''

''Do you know this woman's name?''

Feeling sheepish, Neal looked down and shook his head.

"She's just part of the dream. If I knew her name, that faded too." Neal looked up suddenly and said, "She's Christine's mother, isn't she, Doc?"

Dr. Kirkwood thought for a moment. "I don't believe so. This doesn't sound like it's connected to the plane crash. More likely it's something else that you've been suppressing for a long time. But if we can work through your problems with the crash, I imagine the dreams will stop."

Neal slumped down in his chair and gripped the upholstered arms, the same way he had clung to the armrests, as flight 1862 had started its long, fatal spiral toward the earth, only minutes short of its final approach to Dulles airport in Washington.

After a moment of silence between the two men, Neal turned glaring dark eyes on the doctor. "Why *me?* I'm nothing special. What have I ever done with my life that I should be the only one left?"

Kirkwood smoothed one side of his narrow, blond mustache. "You might look at this philosophically. Maybe it's not what you've done, but what you've been saved to do. Or maybe little Christine is meant for greatness and your task was accomplished when you saved her life. Maybe your life is your reward."

"Don't get religious on me, Doc. You could be right about the kid, but I'm the same person now as I was before I boarded that flight to D.C. No near-death experience. No tunnel of light or angels singing to me. It was more hell than heaven—smoke, flames, people screaming and dying. But here I sit, same old me. Tell me, what great purpose could there be for a soldier without a war to fight? I'm a fish out of water, now that I'm out of uniform. I've just been bumming around for the past couple of years since the Army cut me loose, after Desert Storm. There's not a soul in the world who would feel the loss if I'd died in that crash. But it would have been different for the woman beside me—a wife, a mother, a teacher. The guy in the seat ahead of me was a heart surgeon. Think of all the people he'll never get a chance to save now." His head drooped and his angry voice dropped to a whisper. "And all those kids—the plane was full of them—college kids with their whole lives ahead of them, on their way back to school. Gone! All gone! And here I sit, not a scratch on me and no one to care, one way or the other." He glared at the doctor. "Where's the justice in that? Where's the sense in it? *Damn!*"

"I don't like sounding judgmental, but it seems to me you should be thanking your lucky stars, instead of feeling sorry for yourself, Neal. There are no guarantees that life will make sense all the time."

"You've got *that* right!" Neal growled. He wasn't thinking about the plane crash now; he was remembering his wife. It had been a lousy marriage from the start. They had been too young, too naive, too swept away with emotion to realize that they were not really in love—more "in lust"—when they dashed off to a justice of the peace to tie the knot. Still, Nancy had done her best to make it work. It might have, eventually.

Who knows? Neal thought. Who would ever know now?

Nancy hadn't deserved her fate. She had given the guy in the ski mask her money. Why had he also demanded her life? And even then, Neal hadn't been on the scene to ease her last hours. He had been off in the desert, fighting the good fight, living the soldier's life that he loved above all else.

Watching Neal's expression turn from distress to despair, Dr. Kirkwood asked quietly, "Do you want to tell me about it?"

"What?"

"Whatever you're thinking about right now. It might help to talk about it."

Neal uttered a pained laugh. "Not likely!"

Kirkwood shrugged. "Suit yourself. I don't want to rush you."

Neal glanced around the room, trying to get his mind off the past. He noted the antique furnishings, the tarnished trappings of a former age. Beyond the heavily draped windows, he spied a giant tulip poplar shimmering against the wooded backdrop. Funny, he hadn't noticed that big tree by the pond before.

"What kind of place is this anyway? I thought I was coming to a hospital. I thought there would be other vets here, guys I could relate to. So far, except for the staff, I haven't seen anyone younger than the pyramids.''

"Swan's Quarter is basically a retirement home.''

"You mean a *nursing home,* don't you, Doc? A place where families dump their old people when they don't want them around any longer?''

Leonard Kirkwood shook his head, patiently. "We don't like to think of Swan's Quarter that way. We do have a lot of elderly people here, but we do everything in our power to make their final years as full and happy as we can. That was the purpose that Mrs. Swan had in mind when she donated the house and the land. This was a fine plantation in the last century. The Swan family were early settlers here in Virginia. Five members of the family—the father and all four of his sons—rode off to the Civil War together. Only two of them returned. At the close of the war, the remaining family member, Mrs. Melora Swan, donated her home to be used as a retreat for aging Confederate veterans. And so it was, until the last one died at an advanced age. At that time, this became a private sanatorium, a rest home, if you will. A place for people like you to come and sort out their problems, or simply a home where those without places of their own could live and feel they belong. As for our golden-agers, we like to think they stay because they are happy here. Our younger patients tend to come, then leave to return to normal, productive lives, as I'm sure you will one of these days, Neal.''

Neal wasn't listening. Distracted by some movement out beyond the tulip poplar, he kept his gaze trained on a figure dressed in red and white, as she glided up the path toward the main house.

"Who's that?'' he asked, pointing toward the window.

Kirkwood swung his chair around to look. His solemn countenance broke into a wide smile. "Her name is Ginna,'' he said quietly.

"Is she a patient here?''

"No. She comes every week to visit.''

"Some of her folks here?''

The doctor shook his head. "No. As far as I know, she has no family. Several years ago, before I came here, she started coming to Swan's Quarter to visit an elderly patient. I believe she had been Ginna's foster mother, when she was young. After the woman passed on, Ginna continued her visits. I think of her almost as a member of my staff. She's made many friends here and does a lot for morale. Her visits give our people something to look forward to. They can count on Ginna. She never disappoints them."

"I guess she must live nearby? One of those do-gooders, compulsive volunteers?"

"I don't know where she lives. Actually, I don't know much of anything about her. But I do know that everyone here looks forward to Mondays because of Ginna. I wouldn't call her a *do-gooder,* though. That kind usually wants something in return for their good deeds. Ginna seems to come only for the enjoyment she derives from being with the people here at Swan's Quarter. She's certainly a ray of light to a lot of our older patients, especially the ones who don't have any other visitors. I'm glad she's arrived. I was getting worried."

"About what?" Ginna had disappeared from view. Neal turned his attention back to Dr. Kirkwood.

"She's late today. Several of the ladies came to me wanting to know why. Of course, I have no idea what delayed her. But I was afraid she might be ill. She's here now, though, so I won't worry about it. She's probably headed for the veranda to have tea with Elspeth, Pansy, and Sister."

"The 'terrible threesome,' " Neal said, with a laugh.

Kirkwood tried to hide a smile."Where'd you hear that?"

"From old Marcellus Lynch. I don't think he likes them much. He says they're stuck-up busybodies. He warned me to stay clear of them."

Now the doctor chuckled. "Don't mind Lynch. He's just jealous. They get to spend more time with Ginna than he does. He's fallen madly in love with her, you see."

"That old coot? *In love?*"

"Be kind, Neal. You'll be as old as Marcellus, someday."

"God forbid! Which brings us back to my main problem. How do I deal with living to a ripe old age? I don't think I can tolerate this guilt that long."

"For now, my advice to you is to mix with the others. Get to know them. Share your story and listen to theirs. I think you'll begin to feel better, once you realize that you aren't the only one here with problems."

"I know that, but it doesn't help much right now."

"Give it time, Neal. Take each day as it comes. Believe me, things will get better." Dr. Kirkwood rose, signaling an end to their session. "Why don't you go out on the veranda and join the ladies for tea? I have it on the best authority that the 'terrible threesome' are dying to meet you."

"Thanks, Doc, but I don't think tea is exactly my thing."

"You'd like to meet Ginna, wouldn't you?"

Neal felt torn. The solitude of his room seemed infinitely safer. "You're *sure* she's with the others on the veranda?"

Kirkwood nodded and smiled. "The same as every Monday."

"Then maybe I'll wander out there and just have a look around."

Bald, rotund Marcellus Lynch had joined the tea party by the time Neal Frazier ambled onto the front veranda. For the past few minutes, Lynch had been regaling the four women with tales of his exploits as a young diplomat in the foreign service, dropping names and royal connections as profusely as he dropped cookie crumbs down the front of his well-dated green polyester leisure suit. Every few minutes, Sister would hold up two fingers, her signal to their uninvited guest that she had heard that story before. Of course, Marcellus ignored her and blustered on, trying to impress Ginna with the sophistication and worldliness of his former years. Elspeth, Pansy, and Sister were not impressed. Pansy had sneaked a good look at his file and knew the truth—that he was a retired mail carrier from Hoboken, New Jersey, who had never traveled farther than his trip down to Virginia to be checked into Swan's Quarter. Seemed he'd had a drinking problem and his only daughter wanted her boozing father removed from the immediate vicinity of his young grandchildren. At least that was Sister's guess from the information Pansy gleaned from Lynch's file.

Neal stood by the door, pretending to scan the countryside for several minutes, before he could work up the nerve to make his move. This also gave him a chance for a better look at the group. The three old women were all very different. Elspeth was black with a tight cap of springy white hair, pulled tightly into a knot on the back of her head. She cradled a badly battered doll in one arm, as if it were a baby, from time to time speaking to it, calling it "Miss Precious." Elspeth was almost as skinny as the one named Sister—"the bossy one," old Lynch had told him earlier. Her hair was white, too, but she wore it down and chopped straight around at earlobe length, short and severe. Her face was a roadmap of lines, and he couldn't imagine her ever smiling. Pansy was as plump and pink as a baby. He noticed that even her fingers were dimpled. Her white hair fluffed out about her shoulders, like a girl's. She smiled almost constantly and seemed to defer to the other two at every turn. Pansy, he figured, had been a follower all her life, never a leader.

And then there was Ginna. The minute he looked at her, his interest was aroused and his blood ran a little hotter. She was lovely—as slender as a model, as pretty as one of those china figurines from France, as bright and pleasant as a sunny day in spring. It was clear that the other three women and old Lynch adored her, and just as clear why. She seemed to form the nucleus of an aura of warmth and love. But why on earth was she wearing that ratty old costume?

Neal didn't have long to ponder the question before the women spotted him.

Ginna felt Elspeth's sharp elbow nudge her ribs. "Look there! At the door. It's *him!*"

Marcellus tried to continue his rambling monologue, but now

all three of the old ladies were yammering at once. Only a deaf person would have called it whispering.

"I vow! He's never set foot on the veranda before," said Pansy. "Should we invite him to tea, Sister?"

"There's no tea left," she snapped, glaring up at Lynch. "This one drank it all."

"Surely there's a drop or two in the bottom of the pot," Elspeth put in.

"Oh, Mr. Frazier!" Pansy called, without waiting for an end to the discussion. "Do join us, won't you? We've all been dying to make your acquaintance. We have someone visiting who'd like to meet you, too, and she only comes once a week, and she's *single.*"

Ginna felt her cheeks warm with embarrassment. She did want to meet Neal Frazier, but she hadn't said one word about it. Now their introduction would be spoiled because he would think she was the pushy sort, always chasing after handsome men. And he certainly was handsome—dark and mysterious looking. Her friends had not exaggerated on that point.

"Pansy, *please!*" she whispered, trying to silence the over-eager matchmaker.

"You needn't beg, my dear. He's coming right over."

"You, Lynch!" Sister hissed. "You make the formal introductions. It wouldn't be proper for us ladies to have to introduce ourselves to a strange man."

Marcellus nodded his agreement and snatched the last sugar cookie from the plate before they could offer it to Neal.

"'Afternoon, ladies," Neal said, pantomiming a tip of his nonexisitent hat.

The older man hurrumphed loudly, then said, "Mr. Neal Frazier, I would like to present Mrs. Elspeth McAllister, Mrs. Sister Randolph, and Miss Pansy Pennycock." In a whispered aside, he added, "She's an old maid."

"Charmed, ladies," Neal said, with a smile, never taking his eyes off Ginna for an instant.

"And this fair young maid is *our* Ginna," Lynch said, alarmed by Neal's rapt attention to their guest.

She offered her hand. "Ginna Jones, Mr. Frazier. I hear you've just arrived."

"Please, call me Neal, all of you." Still smiling at Ginna, he added, "I hate to say it, but the four days I've been here seem like four years."

"You'll adjust," Sister said sharply. "We all do, in time. Set yourself a routine and stick to it. That's the way to get by."

"We understand you're single," Pansy piped up. "Just like Ginna."

Ginna clutched her throat, horrified, but Neal only chuckled. "So Dr. Kirkwood told me, Miss Pennycock. Personally, I don't know how she's managed it, as pretty as she is."

The three older women tittered over his reply. Ginna first blushed deeper, then chuckled. The private look Neal gave her, with his wine-dark eyes twinkling, let her know that he had said what he had simply to delight Pansy, Elspeth, and Sister.

"How long will you be here?" Ginna asked.

"I really don't know. I suppose that's up to Dr. Kirkwood."

"Well, Neal, you just consider yourself invited to tea every single afternoon," Pansy said. "We don't want you to get lonesome, staying all to yourself like you have been. Why, mercy's sake, we thought you'd never come out of your room!"

He bowed slightly and smiled. "Thank you, ma'am. It's always nice to be invited to a party."

"Some party!" Sister snapped, turning a vicious eye on Lynch. "We don't even have the crumb of a cookie to offer you."

"That's quite all right. Supper won't be long, now. I wouldn't want to spoil one of Swan's Quarter's gourmet meals."

They all laughed. The very thought of anything *gourmet* coming out of the kitchen at Swan's Quarter!

Ginna rose suddenly. "I didn't realize it was so late."

The ladies all begged Ginna to stay a little longer.

"Whose permission must I ask to take a walk with Ginna?" Neal glanced around the group.

"Who says she wants to walk with you?" Marcellus bellowed, feeling threatened by another fox in his henhouse.

As the others talked, Ginna kept staring at Neal. Where had she seen him before? He seemed so familiar. And it wasn't only that he looked like someone she knew: Seeing him also awoke feelings that she had experienced in the past. Mentally, she flipped through a file of all the men she had ever dated. Neal's face was not among them. He seemed a part of her distant past, yet a part of her immediate present, too.

"Miss Jones, since I'm new here, will you show me around the grounds?"

Ginna snapped herself back to the present. She smiled and took the arm Neal offered. "It's late and I really must be going now, anyway," she said, by way of apology, to her friends. "Neal can walk me down the hill. I'll see you all next Monday. Thank you for tea."

There was cheek kissing all around—except for old Lynch, who got a brief hug—then Ginna started down the stairs holding Neal's arm. An attendant in a starched white uniform appeared on the veranda to usher the ladies inside, out of the twilight chill.

"Ginna—I like that," Neal said thoughtfully, as they headed down the path toward the swan pond. "What's it short for?"

"Nothing that I know of."

"A family name, then?"

"I had no family to be named for. The stork simply dropped me on the steps of the hospital in Winchester. I had a silver locket around my neck with that name engraved on it. That's all I know." .

"So it really was your foster mother you first came to visit here?"

Ginna stared up at him through the gathering twilight. "Who told you that?"

"Dr. Kirkwood. I was in his office when you came up the path. Among my other many faults, I'm a nosey cuss. I hope you don't mind that he told me."

"Not really. And, yes. She was at least one of my foster

mothers. I never seemed to stay long in any home, and, of course, I was never adopted."

"Why not? From the looks of you now, I'd say you must have been a sweet, beautiful baby."

She rolled her eyes at him for laying it on so thick. "I had some medical problems when I was young. People want perfect babies when they adopt. But enough about me. What about you, Mr. Neal Frazier. What in the world are you doing at Swan's Quarter?"

"You mean the ladies didn't fill you in?"

"Well, sort of," she admitted. "I know you've been through some sort of trauma."

When his arm tightened under hers, she wanted to bite her tongue. She should never have brought up his problem. It was his place and his alone to do that.

He sensed her reaction. "It's all right. The doc says it will do me good to talk about the plane crash. That's what it was—the trauma."

Ginna shivered. "I've never liked flying."

"Flying never bothered me. It's when your plane stops flying that it gets scary as hell."

Wanting desperately to change the subject, Ginna said, "I've seen you somewhere before. Have we ever met?"

Neal chuckled. "That's a line as old as the hills. I used to use it on girls, when I was in the Army."

"It's not a line. You really do look familiar to me, Neal."

"If you read the newspapers, you probably saw my picture with 'HERO' plastered all over it, after the crash. I'm a long way from fitting that label, but I did bring a little girl out with me, thanks to her mother."

"Oh, yes! I remember reading all about that. I even saw you on television." She thought about it for a moment, then shook her head. "No, that's not why you look familiar. You had a beard then, if I remember correctly. Your hair was a lot longer, too."

"Yeah, I'd ridden my motorcycle out to Colorado and

camped in the Rockies for a couple of months. I still looked like a mountain man when I came back.''

"No, I'm sure that's not it. It'll come to me, though.''

"Hey, if I'd ever met you before, I'd remember. You can take that to the bank. I never forget a pretty face. When will you be back? Tomorrow?''

Ginna smiled at the eager tone in his voice. "Next Monday. I have to make a living, you know.''

"Shoot!'' He sounded truly disappointed. "You? Work? And here I thought you were a Southern belle, suspended in time, living in a phantom plantation house deep in these woods.''

"Don't I wish!'' She laughed. "No, just plain old flesh and blood Ginna Jones, who works hard for a living.''

They paused beside the swan pond. Neal slipped his hand into hers and noticed that her fingers were cold. He brought both her hands to his lips and blew hard to warm them.

"Swans are nice,'' he said out of nowhere. "Did you know they mate for life? It's the swan's way.''

"I never thought about it.''

"Well, you have it on the best authority now. They do. If one is lost, the other spends the rest of its life all alone— searching, never giving up hope that someday . . .''

"Stop!'' Ginna whispered. "You're going to make me cry. Poor swans!''

"They look happy enough to me,'' he said, "gliding around their pretty pond.''

"But now I'll worry all week, until I can get back and make sure that they're both still here.''

"People could learn from swans,'' Neal said. "When you find love, don't let it go.''

It was a good thing Ginna didn't question him about the strange remark. If she had, he couldn't have explained himself. He had no idea why he had said such a thing. He had never been the poetic type—far from it. He only knew that here in the dying sun that turned the swan pond as golden as Ginna's hair, he felt a little less lonely, a little more hopeful. Maybe the best part of his life wasn't behind him. Feeling the warmth of Ginna's body close to his, having her to talk to, knowing that she would come back—even if he had to wait a whole week—made him feel better, gave him something to look forward to, something to live for, after all.

"I really have to go now," Ginna said.

"So soon?"

"Yes, and you'll miss supper unless you hurry back up the hill."

"I'm not hungry anyway."

"We'll have more time to talk when I come back next week. I'll show you around. Have you seen the greenhouse yet?"

"No. I've been sticking pretty close to my room, nursing my own misery." He laughed, but there was no humor in it.

Ginna gave him a bright smile. "Well, we'll just fix that, won't we?"

"Will we?" He searched her face with his sad, dark eyes.

"I promise," she whispered, and then she was gone.

It was dark when Neal climbed back up the hill. He didn't notice that shortly after Ginna disappeared into the woods, the tall tulip poplar vanished as well.

Chapter Three

Ginna left Swan's Quarter on Monday evening feeling like a woman transformed. Meeting Neal Frazier had reawakened some part of her that had been dormant for a long, long time. For most of her life, she had felt like an outsider, merely an observer as things happened to other people, while she went about her own unvarying routine. Nothing ever seemed to touch her personally. *Don't get involved. Stay clear. Stay safe.* It had been the creed she'd lived by. Her early years, passing from one family to the next, had taught her that to love someone meant to be hurt, sooner or later.

Now, for the first time in her life, she was willing to allow herself to be vulnerable. It seemed that Neal possessed some magical key that might release her from her self-imposed prison of loneliness. Somehow she knew that their meeting today could make all the difference in her life, if she let it.

Getting off the bus, she walked the short distance to her apartment, just east of downtown Winchester. Nearby stood Stonewall Cemetery, where several thousand Confederate and Union soldiers lay buried. Her gaze was drawn to the memorial obelisk that marked the common grave of several hundred

Confederate unknowns. A shiver ran through her. How sad it must have been for these men's families to never have their loved ones accounted for.

Ginna turned away, unwilling to allow such grim thoughts to intrude on her good mood. Twilight's brisk breeze had turned to a blustery, cold wind with the coming of darkness. Bending into the gusts, she quickened her step, craving the warmth of home and bed. It had been a long day, an amazing day.

Her "apartment" had once been a small antebellum house. Some recent owner had installed a tiny modern bath and built another unit at one end, creating a duplex. Often, Ginna wished that she had chosen the newer quarters over the historical part. But she did enjoy the huge, flagstone fireplace, where she imagined meals had been cooked over a century ago, the rustic beamed ceiling, and the quaint atmosphere of a bygone era.

Before she pulled off her coat, she struck a long match and touched it to the kindling she had laid before leaving for work. Instantly, orange and blue flames leaped through the small stack of pine and oak logs. She hovered close, warming her hands. After several minutes, she felt comfortable. She yawned. She was tired. It was good to be home by her cozy hearth.

Ginna wasn't hungry in the least, but she had vowed to make herself eat. She heated a can of chicken noodle soup and toasted two slices of raisin bread. She thought about turning the television on, then decided she preferred the soothing crackle of the fire to the latest bad news from around the world. Quiet time was what she needed most—to think, to savor all that had happened to her today. Settled on the sofa in front of the fireplace, a red-and-green afghan tucked snuggly around her, she ate her supper slowly, watching the flames dance and thinking of Neal.

She wasn't ready to admit to herself that meeting him had been a case of love at first sight. Who would ever believe in such nonsense? She was certainly too level-headed to put that label on her feelings. Still, there was something about him. . . .

She closed her eyes in thought and, moments later, she was fast asleep.

An unfamiliar sound woke her. A girl was crying, not loudly, but as if her heart would break. Ginna tried to open her eyes, but it seemed an impossible task. Soon, she realized that the tears were her own, as were the soft wails of pain.

"Don't cry, Virginia. It will be all right," a boy said, in an uncertain, adolescent tone. "The male swan has probably only gone to look for food. He'll come back."

"But what if he doesn't, Chan? What if he's gone for good, and his poor mate has to spend the rest of her life alone?"

"That old cob would never stay away by choice."

"That's just it, Channing. What if some hunter shot him?" Now her sobs intensified.

She felt his hand settle gently on her trembling arm. "You shouldn't worry about that, Virginia. Everyone hereabouts knows the swans of Swan's Quarter. No one would dare harm that old cob. Your daddy'd have their hide."

The afternoon was fading. The woods beyond the swan pond were already in shadow. Virginia, beautiful even in tears, searched the skies, watching for Leda's mate.

"It's getting late, Virginia. I'll have to head home soon, or Mama will worry." Realizing that he sounded like a child, when he was trying very hard to be a man for the girl he adored, Channing added, "You know how she is."

The thought of his leaving, even to go home for supper, suddenly panicked Virginia. She leaned close and rested her head against his shoulder. "Don't leave me, Chan," she pleaded in a whisper. "Then I'll feel just like Leda. See how sad she looks?"

Made bold by his sweetheart's nearness, he slipped one arm around her waist. "You know I'd never leave you for good. We've always been together. We always will be, darlin'."

At fifteen, it seemed to Virginia Swan that she was on the very brink of everything wonderful and terrible that could happen in a girl's life. Channing's arm felt warm and right, holding her close. If she turned just so, he would probably kiss her. But the timing was all wrong. She was sad this afternoon, and she wanted their first kiss to be perfect. She wanted nothing to mar the happiness of that moment. She didn't turn. She simply let her head rest on Channing's shoulder and tried to fathom the eruption of emotions she felt deep down inside.

"You *will* leave me!" she said after a time. "When you and Rodney go off to the Military Academy together."

"That'll be different. You'll be sad, but you'll be proud too. And I'll keep reminding you in my letters that you have to be a cadet's sweetheart before you can be a soldier's wife. Besides, I won't be leaving for six long months, yet."

She smiled through her tears, thinking of all the years of togetherness stretching out before them. "And in your letters what else will you tell me, Chan?"

"That I miss you. That I remember every single thing about you." He brushed the tip of her nose with one finger. "The way your funny little nose tilts up." He traced the delicate line of her cheek. "They way you blush all rosy when I touch you." He rubbed his finger over her full bottom lip. "And I hope by then I'll be able to tell you how soft and sweet your lips are when we kiss."

Channing shifted until he could look down into her face. "One more thing," he said very quietly. "I'll tell you that I love you—over and over again."

Virginia was breathless. "In every letter?"

"In every single one."

The missing swan was forgotten suddenly. In fact, the rest of the world vanished in that moment. There were just the two of them, so close that only a breath hovered between them. Virginia was mesmerized by the dark intensity of Channing's eyes, by the touch of his hand, by the promise of their first kiss.

She closed her eyes, hardly daring to breathe. When she felt the soft pressure of his mouth on hers, she slipped her arms around his neck. The kiss was short and sweet, but the firestorm it kindled seemed to rage through Virginia from her head to her toes. And then it was over. They sat staring at each other in awe and wonder, as if they had just opened a secret passageway to a magical world beyond their wildest dreams.

Virginia was the first to speak, but only a whisper escaped. "It was not like I thought it would be."

"You're disappointed." A scowl darkened his handsome features.

Her own face lit with a brilliant smile. "No, Chan! I mean it was *perfect!* I'd thought it might be only half as good."

Now Channing's scowl was feigned. "Too bad, really. If we hadn't got it right, we would have to try again. Practice makes perfect, you know."

Virginia laughed and hugged him. "Well, maybe I was wrong. Maybe it wasn't *quite* perfect."

They sat beside the swan pond at the edge of the woods, practicing, until the sun had sunk nearly behind the trees. The sound of wings brought them out of their happy haze. They parted and looked up to see the old cob coming in for a landing. His mate welcomed him with a joyful flapping of wings. Moments later, Virginia and Channing watched, as the pair arched their elegant necks and leaned their heads close to form a heart, their mute tribute to their everlasting love for each other.

"There!" Channing said. "Now all's right with the world."

Ginna smiled in her sleep. But soon the pair of swans and the pair of lovers faded from her dreams to be replaced by the sound of rifle fire and the moans and screams of dying men. Ginna awoke with a jolt.

"Channing!" she cried. "Where are you?"

She looked around, feeling confused and utterly foolish. She must have slept a long time. The fire had burned low. A glance at her watch told her that in another hour, it would be time to get ready for work. She stretched out on the sofa, deciding it was too late to bother with bed.

As she drifted off again, her thoughts returned to Neal Frazier. He almost seemed a part of her dream. But how could that be? The two people in her subconscious had been total strangers— a pretty teenage girl and her handsome beau. Suddenly, she recalled what Neal had said about the swans, as he was walking with her. Maybe the dream had been spawned by his words.

Or maybe the dream came from some deeper, more distant memory. Whatever the source of her romantic illusion, it only made her more eager for Monday to come around again, so she could see Neal. She longed to get to know him better. Much better!

Before then, however, she had to get through six long days at the Rebel Yell Cafe and another six long, lonely nights, with only her dreams for company.

When Ginna arrived at work Tuesday morning, she wondered if—as distracted as she felt—she had come through the wrong door. Or maybe she was dreaming again. A dark-haired, middle-aged woman was wearing blond, bouncy Cindy's uniform and nametag.

"Ginna, meet Noreen." Lucille continued pounding dough for her famous biscuits with sausage gravy, as she introduced the two women.

Ginna greeted Noreen warmly, then sidled up to Lucille and whispered, "What about Cindy?"

"She was a no-show yesterday, never even called."

Guilt-ridden, Ginna said, "I should have stayed. I'm sorry, Lu."

"No, way! You were dead on your feet. Besides, those folks at the nursing home were counting on you. I know how important your Mondays are to you and to them. Noreen'll do fine. She's got plenty of experience, even comes with references. I may hire another waitress, too, to take some of the load off the rest of us."

Now Ginna really felt guilty. She knew she hadn't been pulling her share of the load lately. She tried, but ever since she had started losing weight, she was so tired all the time. Listless and lightheaded.

"There's no need to hire another girl, Lucille. I'll come earlier and stay later, if you need me."

Lucille stopped pounding her dough and turned to look Ginna right in the eye. "No, you won't!" she said adamantly.

"You've just about worked yourself sick these past few weeks since Marge left and I hired that shiftless Cindy. *Bad move!* You're the best waitress I've ever had, but you won't do me one speck of good if you wind up in the hospital. In fact, I'm thinking you need a whole day off, maybe Tuesdays. Then you'd have a day and a half to yourself. What do you think of that?"

"I don't know," Ginna answered lamely, not sure if she should be overjoyed at the thought of more time off or offended that Lucille was saying she could get along fine without her.

Changing the subject abruptly, Lucille asked, "How was your afternoon with the old folks?"

"It was different." Ginna went to work, filling the giant coffee urn as they talked.

"Oh? How so?"

"There's a new man at Swan's Quarter." She felt her face warm at the mere thought of Neal Frazier.

"Oh, yeah? What's he in for—just old and ornery, so his kids dumped him?"

"He doesn't have any kids. He's young."

"A *boy* in an old folks' home?"

"No, no. Not that young. In his thirties. Nice looking, too."

Wiping her hand across her cheek and leaving a smear of flour, Lucille grinned at Ginna. "So *that's* what's going on."

Ginna was immediately sorry she had mentioned Neal. "Nothing's *going on*," she answered, defensively. "He's just a nice man, a sad case."

"And you plan to bring a little light into his life?"

"Someone needs to." Ginna finished with the coffee and turned. "Lucille, have you ever met someone for the first time and felt like you've known them somewhere before?"

"Yeah, it's called déjà vu—just a trick the mind plays. It doesn't mean anything."

Ginna shook her head. "No," she whispered. "I mean, like you *really* knew them before. Like you were real close sometime, but you can't remember where or when."

"Hey, if we're talking carnal knowledge here, I promise

you, I'd remember. You *do* need some time off, hon. Or maybe you're just so taken with this guy that you *wish* you knew him that well. I've had that happen too." She laughed and her gray eyes twinkled. "When you fall in love, you feel real jealous of all the people who knew your fellow back before you met him, even as far back as when he was a kid. I know that feeling. That's the way it was when I met my Joe, God rest him."

Ginna thought about that for a moment. "No. That's not what I mean either. I don't know. It's real strange. It's like I've known him forever, but I can't quite place him." She paused and laughed. "I sound crazy as a bedbug. Don't mind me."

"What you sound like to me is somebody falling in love."

"Oh, sure, right! Like a few minutes one afternoon with Neal Frazier and suddenly—*boom!*—I'm a changed woman—not even Ginna Jones, any longer."

"Hey, don't laugh! Stranger things have happened. And it wouldn't hurt you a bit to have a little romance in your life, Ginna."

Six bikers sauntered in, the first of the breakfast crowd, and the women stopped talking to get to work. It was practically nonstop all day. By the time Ginna's shift was over at five, she was dead on her feet. The rest of the week wasn't much different. Maybe Lucille was right. Maybe they did need more help at the Rebel Yell.

By Sunday, Ginna was really dragging. She overslept, then hauled herself out of bed and managed to get to work only twenty minutes late. Lucille didn't say a word about her tardiness. She only looked at Ginna with concern, when she came through the door.

"You feeling all right, hon? You look kind of peaked."

"I'm fine. Just a restless night. Several, in fact. I've been having these weird dreams."

Lucille gave her a wink. "Dreaming about that Neal Frazier fellow, I'll bet."

"No." Ginna frowned. "I was dreaming about the Civil War again, but it was so real it didn't seem like a dream at all. I swear to you, Lucille, I think my house must have been built on a battle site or something. I believe the place is haunted. Why else would I dream about the war all the time?"

"Could be," Lucille answered. "There were plenty of battles fought around here. Why, according to the history books, Winchester changed hands seventy-two times during the war. Then, too, you're right there next to that old cemetery." Lucille gave an exaggerated shudder. "It would give me the willies to live that close to all those dead guys."

Things got busy, and the women had little time to chat. Ginna felt more tired and distracted as the day progressed. Her legs got weak and her arms ached. She mixed up a couple of orders, something she had never done before. About mid-morning, during a big rush, she dumped a full tray, then started crying hysterically as she tried to clean up the mess.

Lucille took her aside. "Listen, Ginna, I don't know what's wrong with you, but as of this minute you're off duty. Go home and get some rest."

"Oh, I couldn't!" She was still fighting tears.

"Oh, but you can and you will! Noreen and I can handle things. I don't want to see you back here until Wednesday morning. You take all of tomorrow off and Tuesday, like I mentioned earlier. I've got a new girl coming in."

Ginna's heart pounded, and another rush of tears scalded her eyes. "You mean I'm *fired?*"

Lucille put her arm around Ginna's thin shoulders and gave her a firm hug. "No way! You just need a couple of days off. Now, go on. Get out of here!"

Gratefully, Ginna did as Lucille ordered. She couldn't figure out what her problem was, but it certainly was messing her up. Try as she would, she couldn't get her mind off Neal and the feeling that she knew him from somewhere. That thought preyed on her mind night and day, except when she was having those exhausting dreams about the Civil War. In them, she always seemed to be searching for someone, but she could never find him. She would wake up with her mouth dry and her throat sore from calling his name in vain.

As she was walking home—dead-tired from her restless night and her legs aching from having been on the job since just after six that morning—she passed a flea market. Ginna had no vices to speak of, but the one thing she could never resist was the attraction of other people's old junk—"treasures from the past," as she thought of it. As weary as she felt, she still could not pass up the urge to browse.

For nearly an hour, she wandered among the bright umbrellas and canopies, gazing raptly at expensive Victorian glass, lovely old dolls, battered kitchenware, and mountains of patchwork quilts and chenille bedspreads. At the far back corner of the lot, she spied a display that drew her like a magnet.

A white-bearded gentleman, with a derby cocked at a rakish angle, beckoned to her with his twinkling blue eyes. Before him on the tables lay the most fascinating display of old daguerreotypes in gutta percha cases, ambrotypes, tintypes, *cartes de visite,* and the early cameras and equipment that had been used to produce the haunting images from out of the past.

"Afternoon, ma'am," the elderly vendor said. "If you're interested in photography or history—either one—you've come to the right place."

Almost immediately, Ginna's gaze fastened on an intriguing view of a Civil War battlefield, taken while the fight was in progress. The sepia-toned print made the figures in uniform seem alive. The smoke from rifles and cannon actually appeared to drift before her eyes. And she could make out the distinct figures of soldiers, both Union and Confederate. She knew she had to have this old photo.

"Ah, you have excellent taste," the man said. "That's a Mathew Brady photograph taken near Petersburg in 1864. One of his best. Of course, he didn't take it himself. See?" He pointed to a figure standing behind the line of fire with his hands plunged into the pockets of his canvas coat, obviously posing for the camera, as he observed the battle raging. "That's Brady right there in the shot. Probably Timothy O'Sullivan or

Alexander Gardner—one or the other of his top two assistants—was behind the camera. Most of the views marked 'Photo by Brady' were actually shot by some member of his staff. Brady had poor eyesight, you see.''

An image flashed through Ginna's mind of a dark-haired man wearing rectangular, blue-tinted spectacles in wire frames. Along with that came a fleeting whiff of a scent, which to her knowledge was totally unfamiliar. Somehow she knew, though, that it was Atwood's cologne.

''This is one of Brady's cameras,'' the man continued, not noticing the frown that had come over his customer's face.

Blue glasses? Atwood's cologne? Ginna mused, thoroughly puzzled. How could she know any of this? She knew who Mathew Brady was, of course, but not much about him. Only that he was a Civil War photographer and had posed President Lincoln and many other famous people. He had done ordinary citizens as well—working men and women. *Engagement portraits.*

As she glanced over the array of old photos, her gaze fixed on one of a couple, the woman standing behind the seated man. On a marble-topped table beside his Gothic Revival chair sat a clock, the hands frozen in time at ten minutes to twelve. She picked up the photo and turned it over, looking for a name or date.

''It's a shame, but the subjects in these old pictures are almost never identified. We can only guess at the date by the clothes they're wearing.''

Ginna pointed to the clock. ''At least we know what time it was.''

''Nope! 'Fraid not. That clock was just a prop. It was always set at eleven-fifty. I've seen dozens of photos with that same clock, showing the same time.''

Ginna continued studying the photo. The man and woman must have been husband and wife. They appeared to be in their forties, both with dark hair, both looking proper, serious, and stiff.

"Do try to relax, won't you? You look as if you're staring into a hangman's noose."

The voice out of nowhere made Ginna jump. She glanced about, but there was no one nearby other than the bearded vendor, and he was once more talking to her about Brady's large camera obscura.

She listened for a moment or two before her mind began to wander again. Suddenly, all manner of unexpected and seemingly unrelated bits of information flitted through her mind. *Broadway and Tenth streets. 859 Broadway, to be exact, over Thompson's Saloon. Chandeliers like stars. Gold-and-silver walls. Brady's Famous National Portrait Gallery.*

Just as that thought crossed her mind, the man holding the camera said, "Mathew Brady had a large studio in New York City, back before the Civil War. It was something of a tourist attraction in its day. People used to come in to see his collection of portraits of famous people, then, more often than not, they'd decide to have their own pictures taken. He set up a studio in Washington so he'd be closer to the action during the war. When he went bankrupt in 1873, most of his photographic equipment was sold to cover his debts. Would you believe that his glass negatives were even auctioned off as plain old plate glass? One glass negative of Ulysses S. Grant was found in a barn in Upstate New York a few years ago, wrapped in newspaper and forgotten for over a century."

Ginna eyed the man curiously. "Plate glass. You mean like windowpanes or the glass in greenhouses?"

The man chuckled and winked. "You know your history, sure enough, ma'am. Yep, the Victorians all went crazy building greenhouses. And though I've never seen one for myself, I've heard tell that some faces Mathew Brady captured over a hundred years ago on his glass plate negatives still shine down like silver ghosts from the walls of a few greenhouses hereabouts."

The greenhouse! Why hadn't she thought of it before? She had to get to Swan's Quarter right away.

"How much for this battle scene?" she asked quickly.

"Oh, let's see." The man stroked his beard and squinted his

eyes, as if trying to measure its worth. "I could probably get more from a collector, but seeing as how you're such a history buff and all, I reckon I could let you have it for six dollars."

Normally, Ginna would have haggled with the man, even though she knew his price was fair. Instead, she fished into her pocket, then counted out the money from her morning's tips. He handed over her picture with a broad smile.

"Thank you! Thank you very much!" Ginna said, excitedly. Then she whirled away and headed for the bus stop. She had her picture *and* her answer. The greenhouse behind Swan's Quarter. That was where she had seen Neal Frazier before—his face shining down from high up on the glass wall.

Neal strolled aimlessly about the grounds of Swan's Quarter. He had felt restless all week since Ginna's visit, but especially so today. He had opted not to attend the Sunday morning church service, even though Elspeth, Pansy, and Sister had begged him to come along. He could hear the singing now—a dozen or more age-cracked voices wrestling valiantly with "Rock of Ages." He thought how he used to love to sing in church when he was a kid. That seemed a lifetime ago—back before his parents split up. Then both died far too early, back before his older brother stepped on a land mine in Vietnam. Before Nancy. Before flight 1862.

"Before Ginna," he said, noticing for the first time the greenhouse behind Swan's Quarter.

He wandered over, curious suddenly. Hadn't Ginna mentioned the greenhouse? Yes. She had promised to show it to him on her next visit. Tomorrow she would come again. He was counting the hours.

A dark face popped around the doorframe and grinned at Neal. "Come right on in, sir. I'd be obliged for the company. You'd be Mr. Frazier, I reckon."

Neal stared at the grizzled old black man and nodded. "That's right. And who might you be?"

"Folks calls me Zee, 'cause that's the last of the alphabet

and I's the last of my line. I been gardener here at Swan's Quarter these past fifty-odd years and my pappy before me. Come right on in and meet my chillun, sir.''

Old Zee ushered Neal inside with a sweeping bow and a wide, gape-toothed grin. The glass greenhouse felt close and humid, warm even on this cool autumn morning. The place was a veritable jungle of exotic greenery, dominated by a gnarled wisteria vine as thick as a man's body. Amazingly, it was blooming out of season, its clusters of lavender and purple blossoms delicately scenting the air. Neal reached up and touched the silky green leaves.

''She a beauty, ain't she?'' Zee grinned and nodded. ''Been here longer than any of us at Swan's Quarter, longer than the greenhouse, even. Some say she was planted for love. If that be so, then I reckon love must last forever 'cause this old wisteria shore do.''

Neal wandered about, admiring Zee's ''chillun,'' as the old man called the plants. There were ferns of every sort, miniature palms, orchids, and even a banana tree.

''This is amazing,'' Neal said. ''How long has the greenhouse been here?''

Zee scratched his nappy head. ''My memory ain't what it used to be, but seems like Miz Melora Swan had it built some-time after the war. She wanted things always alive around her, a tribute to her poor boys that died in the war.''

''A fine tribute,'' Neal said, feeling the hair on the back of his neck rise. He felt suddenly as if someone were watching him, even though he and Zee were alone in the place. He gave a visible shudder.

Zee laughed. ''Don't let it bother you, sir. The greenhouse haints won't do you no harm.''

Neal stared at the man. ''*Haints?* You mean ghosts?''

''Yessir. But they's friendly enough. Keeps to theyselves, most often. They only shows up now and again. Sunny days, 'bout noon.''

Neal glanced at his watch. It was quarter to twelve and the sun was shining brightly. ''What kind of ghosts?''

Zee cackled, tickled by the question. "Why, dead ones, of course!"

The moment of the airplane crash flashed through Neal's mind—the impact, the flames, the screams. He rubbed a hand over his eyes, trying to block out the memory of that scene. "I don't believe in ghosts."

"Ghosts don't mind if you do or don't believe in 'em."

Unnerved by the crazy old man's tales, Neal decided to leave. When he turned to go, he couldn't believe his eyes. There, standing in the doorway was Ginna.

"Neal!" she cried. "Zee told you? I wanted it to be a surprise."

The gardener nodded to Ginna, then slipped outside, leaving the two of them alone in the "haunted" greenhouse.

"That crazy old coot!" Neal blustered. "All he told me was that a ghost would be showing up soon. I have to admit, I'm glad you came, instead." He went to her and took her hand. "I've missed you, Ginna."

Seeming to ignore his greeting, she tugged him back toward the wisteria vine. "Come see for yourself," she said.

"See what?"

"Zee's ghosts. They'll show themselves any minute now. Look up there, the third pane from the top, in the center over the door. What time do you have?"

"Eleven forty-eight."

"I got here just in time." She pointed up. "Look! You can see them coming."

"Hey, I don't want to see any ghosts!"

"Trust me," Ginna whispered, clutching Neal's arm. "You'll want to see these, and they aren't really ghosts."

As the sun inched higher, it flashed on the paned glass wall of the greenhouse, blinding Neal for an instant. He shaded his eyes with the back of his hand.

"There! Look!" Ginna whispered.

Neal gazed up in the direction she was pointing. He wanted to say something, but his throat closed against any sound. All he could do was stare in disbelief at the silvery images above.

Ginna had been right; they weren't ghosts. He could see, though, how the superstitious old gardener might have thought so. Within the coppery blaze of sunlight, two figures appeared— a man seated with a woman standing behind him, her hand resting gently on the shoulder of his uniform.

"You see," Ginna said. "I told you I'd seen you before. Neal, that's *you* in that old glass negative."

Neal wasn't looking at the man's image. His gaze was focused on the lovely woman, instead. How could Ginna not see it? If the man looked liked him, the woman was a mirror image of Ginna. The tilt of the nose, the light hair and eyes, the soft fullness of her lips.

"Who could they be?" Neal asked quietly, gripping Ginna's hand.

She shook her head. "I don't know. But whoever they were, they must have been in love. She's not looking directly into the camera. See how her eyes are focused downward? And that slight smile. It's clear she adores him."

"I wonder what became of them."

Drawing closer to Neal, Ginna whispered, "I guess, we'll never know."

Ginna was wrong about that. Before the words were well out of her mouth, a brilliant flash illuminated the greenhouse. The wisteria and all the other plants vanished, along with everything else that was of this time and place.

"Neal!" Ginna cried, clinging to him, blinded by the light.

For a long time, he refused to answer her. She could feel him close, so close that the heat of his body suffused hers. Yet she felt all alone, lost in the brilliance of the light.

"Neal, can you hear me? *Answer me!* You're scaring me. What's wrong? What's happening to us?"

At long last, she heard his voice. It sounded different somehow and seemed to come from far away.

"I'm here, Virginia," he answered, his voice softened by a deep southern drawl. "It's Channing, darling. Don't be afraid."

When she felt his lips on hers, the fear vanished. She remembered now—everything. Each moment they had shared, each

joyous laugh, each sweet caress, each bitter tear, each sad
farewell.

"You've come home," she whispered against his lips. "Oh,
Channing, you've come home at last, my dearest."

Chapter Four

The flash disappeared almost instantly. However, it left Ginna feeling stunned, her vision blurred. Out of the dense silence she heard a man's voice. "Thank you very much for coming. I will have your portrait ready by tomorrow afternoon."

"It was our pleasure, Mr. Brady." Ginna recognized this as Neal's voice, but then again it didn't quite sound like him. Suddenly, he had a Southern drawl as thick and smooth as buttered grits.

"I look forward to seeing the two of you become Mr. and Mrs. Channing McNeal." Brady smiled, and removed his blue-tinted spectacles. "June the first, you say. I'll write that date in my appointment book this minute."

Ginna shook her head, trying to clear it. *Mrs. and Mrs. Channing McNeal? June the first?* What could the man be talking about?

She was still mulling over these questions, when the taller and more handsome of the two men took her arm. "Are you ready to go, Virginia?"

She started to correct him, but thought better of it. All this was so strange. What could have happened? She recalled standing in the greenhouse at Swan's Quarter with Neal Frazier. She had meant to show him old Zee's ghosts and point out the resemblance between Neal and the uniformed stranger from the past.

Her vision and her mind clearing, again she glanced up at the man beside her. This time she did a double take. "Channing McNeal," the photographer had called him. Well, that must be his name because he certainly wasn't Neal Frazier any longer. This man—this *stranger*—was not quite as tall as Neal, yet they were remarkably alike in build and feature, although Channing's dark hair was a bit longer than Neal's. She noticed, too, that the expression of pain she always saw in Neal's eyes was replaced by a warm gleam in Channing's.

She glanced around the room, trying to get her bearings. A gasp escaped her when she caught a glimpse of herself—Ginna Jones—in one of the large reflectors set up to catch the light and brighten the studio. She found herself staring at the very image of the woman in the greenhouse wall. She wore an old-fashioned, silvery-blue gown over a bell-shaped hoop. The dress was trimmed at the neck and sleeves in white lace, accented with pink velvet ribbons. Her dark gold hair was dressed in an antiquated style that was really quite becoming, but like nothing Ginna would ever have dreamed of wearing.

I'm not myself any longer, she thought. *But who am I?* The gentleman named Channing had called her Virginia. Virginia *what?* she wondered.

What sort of place was this? Her gaze encompassed the studio, as she searched for some clue. There was a metal stand that reminded her of the racks used in hospitals to hang IV bottles. But she knew it had a very different purpose. Vaguely, she remembered that the arms at the top had held her head firmly stationary, while she posed for a portrait. A little scrap of distant memory told her that Channing had sat in the velvet-covered chair in front of her. And there on the marble-topped table sat an antique ormolu clock, its hands frozen on the twelve and the ten, 11:50. The magic hour. The time when Zee's ghosts appeared in the greenhouse wall.

Bits and pieces of two scenarios were coming back to her,

fitting together like a child's jigsaw puzzle. She had, indeed, come to this place—Mathew Brady's New York studio—a short time earlier to have her portrait made with Channing McNeal. That was not all she had done today, however. She had also been at work at the Rebel Yell Cafe this morning, and at a flea market, and on a bus. She had been excited, eager to show Neal his plate glass twin in the greenhouse. For years, she had been fascinated by the silvery images of the two nameless people, since the first time Zee showed her his secret, his "ghosts." But nothing like this had ever happened to her before. Not in the greenhouse. Not *anywhere!*

"It's time we were on our way now, darling," Channing said.

When he went into the adjacent dressing room to retrieve their cloaks, Ginna sidled over to the window and looked out. If this place was truly Mathew Brady's New York City studio and her hoop skirt wasn't some trick of her imagination and they had just posed for an ambrotype portrait, as she surmised, she should be able to see the street—Broadway—below as it had appeared over a century ago. Curiosity more than anything else drew her to the window. Heights had always made her lightheaded. But she had never been to New York before and, even if this was some sort of weird dream, she was eager to glimpse a world long vanished.

What Ginna saw instead all but took her breath away. She found herself looking down on the interior of the greenhouse. Empty now and silent. There was the wisteria vine in all its green-and-purple glory. The ferns and orchids looked the same. She could even make out her own footprints in the soft earth along with those of Neal and Zee.

She was still staring in amazement, when Channing took her arm and drew her gently to his side. "You had better not look down, darling. You know how heights make you dizzy."

"I might be dizzy, but it's not from the height. Take a look out the window. Tell me what you see," she demanded.

He chuckled as he placed her cape around her shoulders. "Is this some sort of parlor game, Virginia? 'I Spy,' perhaps?

What am I supposed to see? There's a ragged boy hawking newspapers on the corner of Broadway and Tenth, a slightly tipsy gentleman in a top hat coming out of Thompson's Saloon, a fancy cabriolet passing by. Have I guessed yet what you want me to see?''

Stunned speechless, Ginna took another look. Channing was right; she saw all that he had mentioned and more. But how could that be? Only a moment before . . .

"Come along now, Virginia. We have to see a man about a ring. Remember?''

Ginna nodded silently and took Channing's arm. They walked down the stairs to the gallery below and soon they were out on busy, bustling Broadway. Somewhere in the back of Ginna's mind, the thought registered that the first elevator would not be installed in New York City for several years. She wondered vaguely if the elevator had even been invented yet. Most of all, she wondered how she could have descended four flights of stairs without pausing to catch her breath. The old, weak-hearted Ginna Jones would have had to stop several times on the way down. Perhaps being in this new person's body had more advantages than she had realized.

Outside in the bright March sun, Ginna shaded her eyes to look up at the five-story building they had just exited. She saw Mathew Brady at the window of his studio. He waved and Channing returned his salute.

Channing had been talking all the while since they left the studio about the kind of ring she should have, her visit with her parents to West Point, and plans for after his upcoming graduation and their wedding. Ginna made no comment, afraid she might say the wrong thing. She listened closely to his every word, piecing together her life as Channing McNeal's betrothed.

"What's the matter, Virginia? You seem so distracted and nervous suddenly.''

"I don't know." She had to say something and this seemed the least likely to give her away. "All this is so new and strange to me.''

He laughed and squeezed her hand. "Don't tell me you're worrying about what your grandmother said."

Once again, Ginna had no idea what he was talking about. In fact, she had no idea who her grandmother was, or even that she had one.

"What do you mean, Channing?" she ventured.

"About photographers stealing your soul. That's just the older generation's mistrust of modern miracles. I've heard red Indians had the same reaction when they were first introduced to mirrors."

Ginna had a few minutes to think, while her companion talked on. She was tempted to confront him with the truth—tell him that he wasn't who he thought he was or maybe that she wasn't who he thought she was. At any rate, none of this was making any sense to her, and she needed to ask a lot of questions and get some answers. *Right now!* But then she thought better of taking that tack. Hadn't people been put into insane asylums in the nineteenth century for acting queer and asking odd questions? Worse yet, *women* who acted strange could be branded witches! No, she decided, that was in a different century. Still, she thought she had better play along and see what she could find out about Channing McNeal and this Virginia-person he was mistaking her for.

Without explanation, Channing turned north and began walking up Broadway.

"Where are we going?"

"To Mr. Charles Lewis Tiffany's jewelry establishment. It's only five blocks up, at Fifteenth Street. This is such a fine day, I thought we might walk." He looked at his companion questioningly. "If you don't mind, that is."

"I'd love to," Ginna said, flashing her handsome escort a bright smile. In truth, her worries about her current situation were being pushed aside by her curiosity and her interest in old New York. Horses dashed this way and that, with riders or hitched to all manner of conveyances, from honey wagons to fine traps. Street performers drew crowds to watch as they cut silhouettes, did card tricks, capered about in wild dances,

or played musical instruments. Channing and Ginna stopped
to listen to an old Italian man play his hurdy gurdy. A bright-
eyed monkey dressed in a feathered hat and a scarlet coat held
a tin cup, begging for coins.

"Oh, Channing, may I?" Ginna pleaded.

He laughed and gave her several large pennies, which she
dropped into the monkey's cup. In gratitude, he danced a little
jig on his master's shoulder.

Ginna was feeling better every minute. She all but forgot
that, by rights, she should be at Swan's Quarter, visiting with
Pansy, Elspeth, and Sister. This new old world around her was
both mysterious and fascinating. She glanced up at Channing.
He was most fascinating of all. Virginia, she mused, was a
very lucky lady. It was obvious that her fiancé adored her.
Ginna herself was not immune to the warmth of his nearness.

"Look there, just ahead," he said, after they had walked
some distance. "That's Union Square. You'll want to see the
new equestrian statue of President Washington sculpted by
Henry Kirke Brown. I believe it's quite a good likeness, an
imposing piece of statuary. It was dedicated only a few years
ago, on July the Fourth 1856, but already it's become quite an
attraction for visitors."

They had to wait while a detachment of U.S. Marines
marched past. Considerable excitement was aroused among the
bystanders on the street, seeing so many uniformed troops in
one place. Ginna heard one man nearby say to his companion,
"General Winfield Scott's getting ready, all right."

A glance up at Channing told Ginna that he had heard too.
"Ready for *what?*" she asked. "What are those men talking
about?"

Channing's hesitation made it clear that he didn't want to
give her a reply. It didn't matter. She got her answer from
the source of the question. The man with the bullhorn voice
bellowed, "They're off to reinforce Fort Sumter, down by
Charleston. When war breaks out, we'll need that outpost, deep
in rebel territory."

"War?" Ginna gasped, clutching Channing's arm tighter.

"Don't pay any attention to that, dearest. The man has no idea what he's talking about. I have it on good authority that those Marines are up from Washington and will be garrisoned at Bedloe's Island. The military is always on the move, shifting troops from one post to another. It means nothing, Virginia."

Ginna was not quite convinced.

Once the Marines had passed, Channing said, "Let's go see that statue now."

Braving the horse-drawn traffic, they crossed to the center of the intersection at Broadway and Fourth Avenue to get a closer look. The huge bronze of Washington towered above them on its stone base, surrounded by an iron spear fence and four elegant lampposts.

"It's magnificent!" Ginna said, duly impressed. She had seen pictures of this very statue in history books. She knew that in the twentieth century the monument would be moved from the busy intersection to nearby Union Square Park.

"This is supposed to be the very spot where the general was received by the citizens of New York after the British evacuated the city on November 25, 1783."

Ginna glanced up at Channing, her lovely eyes glittering. "I'm impressed! So many dates and details. You certainly know your history."

"Thanks to West Point," he answered. "It's my favorite subject, military history in particular."

A question popped into her head—one that seemed innocent enough. "What made a Southerner like you decide on West Point?"

His dark eyebrows drew down in a frown. "Virginia, what a question! You of all people know that. Why, haven't you and your brother and my father been after me all my life to go to the Academy? That's all I heard from the time I was old enough to pick up a toy saber. Father had me enrolled by the time I was ten, the same time Colonel Swan enrolled Rodney. And *you*, why, you always said you could hardly wait to be an officer's wife—*this* officer's wife."

Swan! Channing's mention of that name made some more

of the pieces of this exasperating puzzle fall into place. The "Colonel Swan" Channing mentioned must be Virginia's father, and Rodney her older brother. She had heard Elspeth telling the family history on more than one occasion. "Dear Miss Virginia, the prettiest belle in the Frederick County." Ginna tried very hard to recall what else she had heard from Elspeth and the others. She knew that Virginia had supposedly hit a Yankee over the head with the old silver teapot, scarring it forevermore. She had always assumed, though, that the tea-time tales of the Swan family were mere fabrications used by the three women to while away lonely hours.

"We had better move along now, darling. I promised your mother and father that we would meet them back at the hotel by two. They'll never trust me alone with you again if we're late."

Melora and Jedediah. The names of Virginia's parents suddenly surfaced in Ginna's memory. He had been a colonel in the Civil War. His wife had donated their plantation as an old soldiers' home when the rest of the family died off and Melora herself was quite elderly and all alone. *The rest of the family gone?* What could have happened to Virginia—to Channing?

"Watch your step, Virginia." Channing's warning, as she stumbled on an uneven cobble, snapped her thoughts back to the present—or the past, as it were.

"That horse nearly ran me down! We should have crossed with the light, Channing." The words were barely out of her mouth, before she realized her mistake. To cover her blunder, she changed the subject quickly, before Channing had time to ask questions.

"You said we're going to Tiffany's?"

"Yes. That's Mr. Tiffany's establishment, that fine looking building with the cast iron façade, there on the left."

"Won't a ring from Tiffany's cost a fortune, Channing?"

"Nothing is too good for the woman I love."

His words made her heart flutter. Or was she feeling Virginia's reaction to the man she loved? It didn't matter. She basked in this feeling of being cherished and adored. No one had ever treated plain old Ginna Jones this way. It felt good!

Channing opened the beautifully etched and gilded door for her. The moment she stepped inside, she was dazzled. Crystal chandeliers sparkled with gaslight, casting a brilliant aura on Mr. Tiffany's exquisite gems in their glass cases. Charles Lewis Tiffany, a distinguished looking man of about fifty, came toward them with a welcoming smile.

"Good afternoon, sir," Channing said.

"Mr. McNeal, how good to see you again. And this must be your lady fair." He reached for Ginna's hand and touched his lips lightly to her glove. "Welcome, Miss Swan. I have so looked forward to meeting you."

"Thank you, Mr. Tiffany." She smiled at having her present identity confirmed, once and for all. She was indeed Virginia Swan of Swan's Quarter, soon to become Mrs. Channing McNeal.

After a brief period of small talk, Tiffany brought out the first offering of rings, then tray after tray of others. Although Ginna would have been thrilled to wear any one of them, her fiancé was not so easily pleased. He was searching for something special, he said, something unique. "Something as lovely as my bride," he added, with a smile that all but melted her soul.

"Perhaps you might like to see some of my unset stones," Mr. Tiffany offered. "I returned only recently from a buying trip to Amsterdam and Paris. Some of the gems I brought back were actually worn by European royalty."

"By all means, sir." Channing sounded more than eager and cast an excited glance at Ginna.

Tiffany smiled at the two of them. "Come with me to my office in back," he invited.

Once in the lavishly appointed office, they settled into deep, plush chairs, while Tiffany excused himself to go to the safe. He returned with several velvet-lined trays of radiant diamonds, emeralds, opals, and rubies.

Ginna tugged Channing's sleeve and whispered when he

leaned close, "Chan, any one of these will cost more than a whole plantation. You shouldn't! I have you. I don't need an extravagant ring."

He chuckled and brushed her cheek with his lips. "That's a lovely sentiment, my darling, but I'm not exactly in the poor house, you know. I *want* to do this. Don't spoil it by worrying about the cost."

If there was one thing Ginna Jones *always* worried about, it was the cost of things. She was a coupon-clipper, a sale-shopper, a thriftshop patron. If anyone had ever told her that someday she would find herself in the private office at Tiffany's, choosing from among the jewels of royalty, she would have told Dr. Kirkwood back at Swan's Quarter to ready a padded cell for that crazy person. But here she was, big as life, with a fortune in jewels spread before her. She had only to choose her heart's desire.

Channing leaned forward, examining each stone closely. Finally, he shook his head. "I can't decide. Which one strikes your fancy, Virginia?"

Still nervous about the cost, in spite of what Channing had said, she pointed to a fiery opal, guessing that it must be the least expensive of the lot. And it was a lovely stone, all brilliant colors and deep gleaming fire.

Channing frowned. "Aren't opals supposed to bring bad luck?"

"Oh, Channing, you can't believe that? Why, it's a beautiful stone! Look how the colors shift and change in the light. I love it!"

He took a closer look, then gave Ginna one of his slow, lazy, bone-melting smiles. "You're right, darling. The opal matches your eyes—all glowing pastels and silver and gold."

"You've made a fine selection, Miss Swan," Tiffany said. "This stone has rare fire and warmth." He nodded solemnly. "And Mr. McNeal is right, it does match your lovely eyes. Now, what about the setting?"

Happy with his fiancée's choice, yet disappointed that she would never wear one of the flawless diamonds he had hoped to place on her finger, Channing insisted that the opal be set in platinum surrounded by a halo of diamonds.

"Perfect!" Tiffany agreed. "We will have it ready for you in a week's time."

Channing's face fell. "But Miss Swan will be gone by then. I wanted her to have something to wear, to show off to everyone when she gets home."

"It's all right, Channing. I don't mind waiting. You can give me the ring when I come back up for your graduation in May."

"Well, I promised you something and you *will* have something! That silver locket there, Mr. Tiffany. Could we take a closer look at it?"

The jeweler hesitated before he reached for the box on the shelf behind him. "I've only just fashioned this one. It's a new style I designed myself."

"Won't you let me buy it for Virginia, sir?"

Holding the tiny silver heart, Tiffany looked from Channing to Virginia. Her face—Ginna's face—was absolutely glowing. Neither of the men could know that she recognized the locket. She had been wearing one like it when she was found as a baby. What had become of it, she had no idea.

"I'll want her name engraved on its face," Channing said.

Tiffany frowned, measuring the miniscule space with a keen eye. "I'm sorry, Mr. McNeal, but I don't think we can do that. The surface inside the flower edging is quite small. Perhaps Miss Swan's initials would do?"

"Would there be room to write Ginna?" she asked softly.

"Five letters?" Tiffany was gazing at the heart, mentally engraving the piece. At last he nodded. "Yes! The letters will be small, but I'm sure I can do that. *Ginna* it shall be."

When they left the elegant store a short time later, Ginna was wearing the token of love Channing had chosen for her. She had no idea how or why it would happen, but over a century from now, when she was abandoned by her natural mother, she would again be wearing this heart, this token of unselfish and undying love.

"Thank you, Channing," she whispered, squeezing his arm. "I love my locket and my ring."

He didn't reply. Suddenly, Channing McNeal seemed a million miles away.

The minute Virginia suggested to Tiffany that he might engrave "Ginna" on the locket, some small door to Neal Frazier's memory opened to Channing McNeal. He knew that name, but how? No one had ever called Virginia by a nickname. Yet it seemed so familiar to him. As he tried to force himself to remember, bad feelings came over him. Feelings of guilt and hopelessness. Once the heart was engraved, he dismissed all this, attributing the sensations to the stuffiness of Mr. Tiffany's office and to the fact that they had yet to eat their noon meal.

Quickly, he paid cash for the locket—a mere trinket actually—then left instructions on where the ring should be sent. He promised to send a bank draught promptly to cover its cost. After thanking Mr. Tiffany and saying goodbye, he ushered Virginia out of the store. The flash of silver at her slender neck, as the sun struck her locket, brought a smile back to his face.

Seeing his reaction, Ginna touched the heart. "It's really lovely, Channing. I'll treasure it always."

"I'm glad you like it, darling, but it must be quite a disappointment, when you thought you would be wearing your engagement ring instead."

"Not at all! I have this, and I plan to put your picture inside. The tiny one you gave me when you went away to school. I'll still have my ring to look forward to."

She shivered suddenly, as a cold gust of wind whipped around the corner. Immediately, Channing hailed a carriage. "I don't want you to catch a chill," he explained. "Besides, it's nearly two. Your parents are probably tapping their toes with worry, already."

Traffic was unaccountably light and the drive up Broadway to Madison Square and the new Fifth Avenue Hotel took only minutes. As they drew up to a line of carriages, with their passengers waiting to alight at the classical portico of the swank establishment, Channing said, "You know, people called this place 'Eno's Folly' when it was built two years ago, because it was so far uptown. But just look at it now. This is the very center of the city and the hotel itself is the heart and soul of New York's social and political life."

Their first glimpse of Virginia's father, upon entering the hotel's lobby, corroborated Channing's words about it being a center of politics. Jedediah Swan was in a heated arguement with some stranger. They stood toe-to-toe, almost nose-to-nose, and, although the two men tried to keep their voices down in such a public place, Ginna heard the words "secession," "disunionist," and "damnyankee," the latter from Swan's own angrily pursed lips. His gray-blond mustache quivering, his face red with rage, Virginia's father was obviously "discussing" the possibility of a coming war with an equally outspoken and pugnacious Northerner.

A woman dressed in a fashionable gown of coppery colored bombazine hurried toward them, her exquisite face filled with torment and the red tinge of embarrassment. "Channing, do something!" she begged. "Colonel Swan has obviously lost his wits. The next we know, he'll be rolling on the Turkish carpet, exchanging blows with this total stranger. Why, I'm tempted to summon a policeman and have them both thrown into jail!"

"No, Mother!" Ginna exclaimed.

Mother? It was the first time in Ginna's life that she had ever addressed anyone in that manner. The word felt warm and sweet on her tongue. Once again, she realized that Virginia Swan had something Ginna had always longed for.

"Oh, I wouldn't really, dear," Melora said, "but don't think I'm not tempted. Lately it seems I can't take him anywhere. It's all this war talk. It gets him so riled up. When that fellow started handing out broadsides around the lobby, extolling the cause of abolition, Colonel Swan simply lost his head. They'll be duelling in the middle of Fifth Avenue, if you don't stop them, Channing."

Channing pressed his future mother-in-law's hand. "You ladies go into the tea room and wait, Mrs. Swan. I'll take care of this."

"Thank you, dear," she murmured, ushering Ginna toward a doorway across the lobby.

Ginna felt Melora Swan's hand trembling on her arm, as the men's angry whispers grew almost to shouts.

"It will be all right, Mother. Channing can handle Father."

"We really shouldn't have come North at this time. I'm worried to death about your father, Virginia. He has always been so quick of temper. With feelings for and against secession running so high all through the South, I should have known your father wouldn't be able to control himself up here. All that unrest at West Point didn't help any."

"Unrest?" Ginna asked. "What do you mean?"

Melora gave a short, humorless laugh and patted Ginna's hand. "Blind with love, that's what you are, my girl. How else could you have missed the undercurrents at the Academy? Goodness sake, your father was about to burst his buttons when that row broke out during the Washington's Birthday celebration."

"I never noticed."

"Of course, you didn't. How could you, with Channing McNeal filling your love-struck eyes? No one could blame you, though. He is a darling young man. He'll make you the best husband any woman ever had." Suddenly, she gripped Ginna's hands and squeezed tightly. Tears pooled in her lovely blue eyes.

"What's wrong, Mother?"

Melora brushed at her eyes with a lace-edged handkerchief. "Oh, don't mind me, dear. I'm just the sentimental sort, but I do wish the wedding were sooner."

"Channing can't marry until after graduation. It's not allowed."

"I know. I know." Melora shook her head and worried her damp handkerchief. "Everything will be fine. It's just that I had so hoped for my only daughter's life to be *perfect.*"

"And it will be, Mother. I love Channing. I couldn't be happier. There's nothing to worry about." Even as Ginna tried to reassure Virginia's mother, a niggling worm of doubt surfaced in her own heart. This was March of 1861. Her wedding to Channing was set for June first. She concentrated hard, trying to remember historical dates. It seemed that something very important would happen soon—something that would change all their lives.

Suddenly, from out of Ginna's past, a stern voice spoke to her, the voice of Miss Hemphill, her fifth grade teacher, the terror of Stonewall Elementary. "Ginna, you know the answer. Think, girl! Think! When was Fort Sumter surrendered to the Confederacy? When did the War of Northern Aggression begin?"

April 12, 1861. The answer came to Ginna so suddenly that she almost said it aloud. Relief at her not shouting it to Melora Swan vanished with the realization that accompanied that date. The country would be at war *before* Channing's graduation from West Point ... *before* he came home to her ... *before* they could be wed.

If Ginna knew little of Virginia Swan's past, she suddenly realized that she knew even less of her future—a future left hanging in uncertainty by the inevitable dates of history. Ginna's heart sank. She was only just beginning to accept her new life as Virginia Swan, and what a glorious life it had seemed. But thinking ahead to what the coming months and years would bring to the innocent Miss Swan, even Ginna Jones's drab life began to look enticing by comparison.

"Your locket is exquisite, dear." Melora's voice broke into her grim thoughts. "A gift from Channing?"

Ginna could only nod in response. She wanted desperately to warn this woman she had called "Mother" of the pain and sorrow ahead. But how could she? How would she explain her uncanny knowledge of events to come?

Just then, Channing and Colonel Swan came into the room. Swan seemed to have calmed down some, but his cravat was askew and his luxuriant hair mussed.

Obviously trying to reassure the two women, Channing offered them his warmest, most radiant smile. "I have asked the maître d'hotel to serve us tea, even though the dining room is closed. He'll bring it here to the parlor, if that suits you, Mrs. Swan."

"A fine idea, Channing." Melora nodded her gratitude to him. "A nice cup of tea and a bite to eat should be the very thing for all of us." She cast a withering look at her husband.

Ignoring her tacit rebuke, Jedediah caught the jacket sleeve of a passing waiter. His voice boomed through the quiet room. "Bring me a double bourbon, boy!"

Melora glared at him, but he refused to meet her gaze. He slouched down in his chair and looked at Ginna, instead. "Well, I reckon Channing here's spent his whole inheritance on you this morning, eh, baby-girl?"

Ginna felt Virginia blush heatedly. Somehow she knew that Swan's daughter hated being called by that epithet.

"I would have to spend my inheritance and borrow against my father's entire estate to come close to spending what she's worth, sir," Channing put in.

Jedediah slapped his future son-in-law on the back and bellowed a laugh. Then he winked at Virginia. "Good man you've got here, darlin'. He's gonna make one fine officer for the Confederacy. I'm proud he'll be riding with me."

Ginna saw Melora Swan's hand go to her throat in a gesture of horror.

Channing's smile turned to a frown.

Oblivious, Colonel Swan tossed down his bourbon and ordered another double.

Only Ginna knew the full truth of what the future held for these people, and for herself, if she remained in this time, in Virginia Swan's body. Another bit of information had dislodged itself from her subconscious. She could hear Elspeth's voice saying, "You'll recall Miss Virginia Swan was engaged to a fine young man before the start of the war. But she never married. You see, the man she loved had graduated from West Point, and he joined up with the Union forces when the war began. Her daddy, Colonel Swan, forbad them to wed. It nearly broke Miss Virginia's poor heart.''

Ginna went cold all over. In that moment, that flash of memory, she realized that she would never wear the opal and diamond ring that Channing had chosen for her today with its matching wedding band. They would never marry, never live together as man and wife. Ginna felt her own heart breaking. Tears spilled over her lashes and down her cheeks.

''Why, Virginia!'' her mother said. ''Whatever is the matter, dear?''

It was a good thing Channing spoke for her, because Ginna could never have found her voice. ''Our Virginia is over-wrought, Mrs. Swan, and I'm afraid it's all my fault. She must be exhausted after such a full day—sightseeing, having our portrait done, choosing a ring. I shouldn't have rushed things, but there's so much I want to show Virginia here in New York, and so much I want to share with her.'' Then he added in a solemn voice, ''But so little time.''

Virginia's mother demanded to know all about everything, especially the ring. She and Channing talked on and on, while Colonel Swan drank and Ginna sat numb, feeling stunned and hopeless.

Channing's words rang in her mind like a death knell: *So little time! So little time! So little time!*

If only he knew!

Chapter Five

Ginna needn't have bothered worrying that she should have remained at Swan's Quarter for a quiet visit with her friends, instead of popping through glass plate negatives and gadding about nineteenth century New York City with her handsome West Point cadet. No one except old Zee, the gardener, had seen Ginna arrive on the grounds and no one at all saw her leave. In fact, no one at Swan's Quarter saw anything for a brief space of time.

Around eleven-thirty, Pansy, Elspeth, and Sister had decided, as they were leaving the chapel service, that a few hands of bridge before Sunday dinner might be entertaining. They persuaded Marcellus Lynch to sit in as their fourth. Before Lynch joined them in the game room, the women cut the deck to see who would be forced to endure as his partner. Unlucky Elspeth drew the three of clubs and, with it, Lynch and his dubious talent at cards; he always overbid and could never keep track of trump.

At precisely eleven-fifty, Sister's right hand, holding the deuce of spades, was maliciously, gleefully poised to trump Lynch's singleton ace of hearts and so take the winning trick. A stay of execution was granted the defenseless ace, and Lynch's degradation was postponed at the moment Ginna and Neal accidentally stumbled back into the past. Their unorthodox action froze time in the present and stopped not only Sister's hand, but the hands of every clock at Swan's Quarter at exactly ten minutes before noon.

All through the big house and on the grounds of the sanatorium, time stood still. Dr. Kirkwood's pen scratched to an abrupt halt on a report he was signing, so that it read, "Leonard Kirkwoo—" Zee, working at his compost pile, was tossing a shovel of mulch into a wheelbarrow. Not only did his shovel stop cold, but the tossed loam froze in midair. On the back veranda, a calico cat, who had been chasing a pesky flea, stopped scratching. It made no difference. The flea stopped too. Even the Sunday fried chicken ceased its sizzling in the black iron skillet on the stove in the kitchen.

Silence fell. Swan's Quarter waited for the return of the pair of time-travelers.

So little time!

Ginna closed her eyes, trying to shut out the inevitability of Channing's words, but there was no way to escape that haunting echo. The war was coming and something was going to happen that would separate Virginia Swan from Channing McNeal forever. There would be no wedding, no future, no everlasting happiness for the two of them.

Soon Ginna felt the room, the Fifth Avenue Hotel, the entire city of New York swirling around her. She grew dizzy and disoriented. She had experienced these uncomfortable sensations before, whenever she overtaxed her imperfect heart. She was going to faint. There was absolutely nothing she could do to stop herself.

Bright pinpoints of light appeared against the red-black backdrop of her closed eyelids. Her whole body suddenly felt weightless. Next came a sensation of flying or falling through space. Then a fierce wind. Then nothing.

* * *

"Ginna? Ginna!"

Neal's urgent cries parted the black curtains that had closed over her consciousness. She opened her eyes slowly, dreading what she might see. To her surprise and vast relief, the two of them were back in the greenhouse. Overhead, she saw the gnarled wisteria vine, its delicate, purple cascades of blossoms trembling in a slight breeze. And Neal was there, his arms around her waist, supporting her full weight.

"God, you scared the life out of me!"

She rubbed a hand over her eyes, then glanced up at the pane of glass where the ghostly shades of Virginia and Channing had wavered in the bright sunlight, such a short time before. The sun had moved higher. Their images were no longer visible.

"What happened?" Neal asked.

She stared at him, trying to decide if he recalled any of the bizarre adventure they had shared. She couldn't tell for sure, although Neal's dark eyes still held the lovelight that had kindled each time Channing looked at Virginia. But now he was Neal again, and she was just plain Ginna.

She forced a faint smile. "Did you see the ghosts?"

Neal looked at her blankly for a moment. He frowned, then nodded. "I saw them. It was eerie—like they were right here with us."

She could tell by his hesitant answer and the puzzled look on his face that he remembered more than he was willing to tell. Had they merely shared a common vision, or had they really traveled back in time? Whichever it was, Ginna guessed that Neal knew what they had been through together, whether he wanted to admit it or not.

Ginna was right. Neal did remember most of what had happened, although he refused to admit the fact, even to himself. He chalked up the visions of New York to one more side effect of the trauma he had suffered at the time of the plane crash. *Just another one of my weird dreams,* he told himself. He decided not to think about it. Instead, he turned his attention back to Ginna.

"You fainted," he accused. "I'm taking you to Dr. Kirkwood right now."

"I did not faint!" she argued. "I'll be fine. Just give me a minute to catch my breath."

"No!" he stated bluntly. "You need a doctor, Ginna."

"Please, Neal." Her voice softened, and she begged him with her eyes. "This has happened to me before. It's a passing weakness. I'll be all right, really I will."

He gazed at her uncertainly, his dark eyes once more filled with the old pain she knew so well. "Humor me. Okay, Ginna? I never had a woman go all limp on me before. I'm worried about you. I'd feel better if the doc took your blood pressure or gave you one of his magic pills."

At the moment, Ginna would have done anything to wipe the concern from Neal's face. He had enough on his mind without having to worry about her. "I'll go," she said quietly, "but I promise you, there's nothing wrong."

"That's my girl!"

Neal made the remark casually, but something about the tone of his voice and the change in his eyes warmed Ginna through and through. He really *cared* what happened to her. Knowing that made her feel good.

Neal knocked at the door, and the doctor called for them to come in. When they entered Kirkwood's office, he was just adding the *d* to the end of his last name. A radio was playing classical music softly in the background. When Beethoven's Ninth Symphony ended, a sultry-voiced announcer came on and said, "The time is now exactly twelve o'clock noon."

Dr. Kirkwood checked his watch and frowned. "Do you believe this? I just bought this watch last week and already it's losing time." He reset his expensive timepiece, running it ahead seven minutes. Then he turned his full attention to Ginna and Neal. "What can I do for you two?"

"Somthing's wrong with Ginna, Doc." Neal blurted out what had happened, without giving Ginna a chance to say a word. "One minute she was standing next to me in the greenhouse, and the next minute it was like her bones turned to water. She just collapsed. Scared the hell out of me!"

Kirkwood rose from his desk and led Ginna to his leather couch. He took her pulse, then said, "Roll up your sleeve, please." When she complied, he fastened a blood pressure cuff around her arm.

"A maidenly swoon, eh?" The doctor tried to cut the tension in the room with a small joke. It didn't work. Neal only glared at him for taking Ginna's condition so lightly.

"Maybe she needs a *real* doctor," Neal snapped back at him.

"I apologize," Dr. Kirkwood said. "I didn't mean to minimize what happened. If you'll wait outside, Neal, I'll see what I can do to help."

Neal looked at Ginna questioningly. "It's all right," she said. "I'll be out in a few minutes."

Reluctantly, Neal left the room.

Leonard Kirkwood's manner turned professionally serious, once he was alone with Ginna. "So, it happened again, exactly like last month, when Zee found you unconscious in the woods. Are you ready to tell me what's going on, Ginna? The first time, you said you were running because it started raining and that you tripped and hit your head. I didn't believe that then, since there was no bump on your head, and I don't believe it now. But I *do* believe something is wrong with you. I also believe that you know exactly what it is. Am I right in my assumptions?"

Ginna didn't answer for a time. She wasn't sure how much she should tell him. Instead, she let her gaze roam the room. Somehow she knew that this had been the plantation office back when Swan's Quarter was a working tobacco farm. She could see a high plantation desk made of local pine as clearly as if it were here today, instead of Dr. Kirkwood's modern desk with its smooth design of sleek, polished oak. She remembered working at that old desk. Long hours of backbreaking, eye-straining labor, bending over ledgers and writing sums by candlelight into the wee hours of the night. But how could she remember such things? She had never even been in Dr. Kirkwood's office before today.

"Ginna? Am I right?" he prompted. "Are you ill?"

"It's nothing serious," she answered, watching him remove the blood pressure cuff. "I had a restless night and skipped breakfast."

"How about the *truth,* Ginna?"

Ginna sighed. She had tried to be so careful. She didn't want anyone at Swan's Quarter to know about her condition. Still, Leonard Kirkwood was a doctor; he would have to keep her secret. And one of these days, she might need his help. She might go for years with nothing more serious than an occasional fainting spell, but . . .

"It's nothing new," she began. "I was born with a slight heart defect. I've always figured that's why my mother left me on the steps of the hospital, right after I was born. She could probably tell from the start something was wrong with me. I doubt if she could afford to take care of a sickly infant. I know for certain that's why I was never adopted. I had interviews with plenty of prospective parents. When I was little, I used to wonder why I was always turned down. Then, when I was about eleven, I overheard one of the social workers discussing my case with a couple I had just been introduced to. They said they wanted a child desperately, but that I was not the one for two reasons. First, they were not financially able to provide the medical care I might need. Second, they said they could not bear the thought of taking me into their home and growing to love me, then possibly losing me at an early age. After they left, I asked the social worker what they meant. I was really torn up. I could tell I had made a good impression and they really wanted me. I was sure I was going to have a home and a family, as of that very day."

"What did the social worker tell you?" Dr. Kirkwood asked gently, passing her a box of tissues. "Take your time, Ginna."

"She said that I was born with a deformity of the heart. Then she told me that was the reason they tried to keep me quiet most of the time. While the other kids at the home were out playing and running, I spent most of my time reading, coloring, or just staring out the window, wishing I could go out and pitch softball or jump rope."

"Have you undergone any corrective surgery?"

Ginna shook her head. "There's nothing that can be done through surgery, short of a heart transplant."

"Well, then . . ." Dr. Kirkwood brightened, thinking that would be a solution to her problem.

"No," she whispered. "I don't want that, not even if I had a chance of ever finding a donor, and the odds are against that, since I don't know who or where my family is. Besides, I'm single, no ties, no kids. I'd feel like I was cheating someone else if I put my name on the list."

"But, Ginna . . ."

Once again she cut him off. "I don't want to talk about it, please. Waiting for a heart would be like going through waiting for parents when I was a kid. My life's fine. Maybe it won't be as long as I'd like. Then again, I could live to be a hundred. I just need to start taking better care of myself, eating better and taking my vitamins. Visiting here at Swan's Quarter helps, makes me realize how lucky I am." She smiled shyly at the doctor. "And now there's Neal . . ."

"Things are getting serious between you two? I'm glad. Neal needs someone. He's been through a lot."

"I know. But I feel like the needy one. And being around Neal makes me feel like a new person—a *real woman.*"

"Ginna, he's going to ask questions. What will you tell him?"

"We need to come up with a story, don't we, Dr. Kirkwood." This was not a question, but an emphatic plea.

He smiled reassuringly at her, wishing he could be of more help. "So this is to be a conspiracy between the two of us. What do you have in mind?"

She shrugged. "I don't know. You tell me. You're the doctor.

What could make me faint, just out of the blue like that? Something convincing, but nothing serious.''

"You could be coming down with the flu.''

"No good! I've got a couple of days off and I'm planning to come back tomorrow and the next day. If you tell Neal I have the flu, I'll have to stay home instead and pretend to be sick.''

"I see your point.'' He gave her a sardonic smile. "We certainly wouldn't want you infecting everyone at Swan's Quarter with imaginary influenza.''

"How about a mild case of food poisoning? Would that do it?''

Kirkwood chuckled. "That won't go over very well with the powers that be at the Rebel Yell Cafe, not if you ate your last meal there, anyway.''

Ginna felt her face drain of color. "How did you know where I work?'' she demanded in an angry tone. "Have you been checking up on me behind my back?''

"No, Ginna,'' he said. "Why would I do such a thing? But someone else ran a check on you. It was Dr. Felston, the man who filled in for a few months before I got here. He *warned* me about you as soon as I arrived. He was convinced that you were up to no good—that you were trying to endear yourself to Pansy, Elspeth, and Sister so that you could talk one or all of them into changing their wills and leaving you their money.''

"Of all the asinine ideas!''

"Easy, Ginna,'' the doctor warned. "Let me finish. Felston couldn't help himself. He was born paranoid. This sort of con game isn't uncommon. But Felson wasn't here long enough to receive the report on you. It came to me a few days after he left. By then I'd already met you. I knew immediately that you were visiting for only two reasons. To cheer up the people here at Swan's Quarter and because you're as lonely as they are. I've always wondered about that. You're so bright and young and pretty. I could never figure why you spent so much time here when you should have been out having a good time.''

He rose and offered his hand to help Ginna up from the couch.

"You won't tell Neal, will you?"

"Not until you want me to."

"That will be *never!*" She forced a laugh. "And I don't want him to know where I work. Understood?"

"Why on earth not?"

She smiled. "He thinks I'm *mysterious*. Dr. Kirkwood, no one has ever thought of me as mysterious before. It feels good. I'd like to keep a little mystery between us."

"I understand, Ginna. Hey, I have an idea! You said you have the next two days off. Why don't you stay here at Swan's Quarter with us? A short vacation for you, and everyone here would love to have you."

The thought of not having the long trip home when she was feeling so rocky and getting to spend more time with Neal brought a bright smile to her face. But reality set in fast.

"I don't have anything with me—not even a toothbrush. Besides, I'm not sure I can afford this place, not even for two nights."

Dr. Kirkwood patted her shoulder, affectionately. "You've more than earned your keep at Swan's Quarter, Ginna. And I'm sure the 'terrible threesome' can provide you with whatever you need. If there's anything else, just let me know."

"I don't know what to say." Ginna was positively beaming.

"Just say you'll stay. That's all I want to hear. Deal?" He stuck out his hand, and she shook it.

"Deal!"

When Dr. Kirkwood opened the door, Neal was pacing the hall outside, his face like a thundercloud.

"I'm fine, Neal." Ginna spoke quickly, since it looked like he was about to explode. "The doctor thinks I got a bad hamburger or something. Nothing to worry about."

"And just to make sure," Kirkwood added, "I've persuaded Ginna to stay here for a couple of days, so I can keep an eye on her. She told me she's on vacation right now, so I figured we'd take advantage and keep her right here with us."

Neal, grinning like a kid now, slipped his arm around Ginna's waist and gave her a squeeze. "That's great! Now you can really show me around." He paused and looked at her closely. "Are you sure you're all right now, Ginna?"

She hugged him back, while Dr. Greenwood looked on approvingly. "I'm just fine. Stop worrying about me. In fact, I think I'm completely back to normal. I'm starved! Is that fried chicken I smell cooking?"

"Yes. It's our regular Sunday dinner special," Leonard Kirkwood answered. "According to Elspeth, that's been the traditional Sunday fare here since back in plantation days, when her great-grandmother, Polly, was the Swan family's cook. Old Polly's 'secret recipe' is still used in the kitchen to this day. As soon as I arrived and started making a few changes around here, Elspeth took me aside and told me in no uncertain terms that this particular menu was not to be tampered with. She said she had been eating fried chicken every Sunday for her whole life, and she wasn't about to change now—cholesterol or no. She claimed that, at her age, her old joints needed a healthy dose of grease once a week to keep them working right. I added baked chicken to the menu for those who prefer to eat more cautiously."

"Bless Elspeth's heart!" Ginna exclaimed, ignoring the doctor's pointed remark about the baked chicken. "Fried chicken is my favorite food in the whole world. How about you, Neal?"

He was still holding onto her, almost as if he was afraid to let go, for fear she might have another fainting spell. "Actually, I'm a meat-and-potatoes kind of guy, but I'm not hard to please. A few years in the Army will teach you pretty quick to bite anything that doesn't bite you first. Why, when I think of the months I lived on hardtack and ground corn for coffee . . ."

Neal's words broke off when both Ginna and Kirkwood stared at him oddly. He couldn't think why he had said such a thing. He had heard of hardtack, of course, but he had no idea what it was. And ground corn for coffee? The very idea of such a thing turned his stomach.

Before any questions could be asked, Neal took Ginna's arm

and headed down the hall. "We'll see you later, Doc. Chow calls!"

When they were safely out of earshot, Ginna asked, "Neal? What made you say that? I thought the Army ate C rations."

"Only in the field. Army chow was pretty good, actually. It sure was a lot better than I ever learned to cook for myself."

Ginna stopped in an alcove and turned to face him. "You're avoiding my question. What would *you* know about eating hardtack?"

He shrugged. "Nothing. I don't even know what it is. I have no idea why I said that. Let's just drop it, Ginna."

"No, Neal! I don't want to drop it. Something funny is going on, and I'd like to know what. Hardtack was a sort of cracker of pressed meal that soldiers ate during the Civil War."

When Neal gently gripped her shoulders and stared down into her eyes, his face was solemn. "You're right about that, Ginna. Something's going on, and I'd like to know *what* as much as you would. Ever since I got to Swan's Quarter, I've been having these strange dreams. Time seems to go all lopsided. I'm still here, but I'm not here, either. I'll walk into my room sometimes and think *What happened to my library table?* or *Where's the painting that used to hang on that wall?* Then I catch myself and realize that I never had any library table—whatever the hell that is—and the only things hanging on the walls are a couple of prints of birds."

Ginna felt her arms prickle with goosebumps. This was exactly what had happened to her a short time ago in Dr. Kirkwood's office. She had no way of knowing what that room had looked like or what it had been used for before Swan's Quarter became a rest home. Yet every detail of that plantation desk—every mar and scratch on it—was etched in her mind.

"Does the name Channing McNeal mean anything to you?" she asked softly.

Neal frowned, thinking. She could tell he recognized it, but couldn't quite place it.

"No," he said finally. "Never heard of him."

"How about Virginia Swan?" she persisted.

That light kindled in his eyes again—the lovelight Channing had always showered on the woman he adored. "Ah, Virginia!" Neal sighed and drew Ginna close. "I thought you were gone forever. Can you imagine what it feels like to find you after all these years? I'm alive again, and I won't lose you this time, my love."

Before Ginna could react to Neal's inexplicable words— spoken in Channing's warm Southern drawl—she felt his mouth cover hers. It was a kiss sweet with hunger—a familiar kiss, one she had known before, one she had waited for a long, long time.

When Neal drew away, he looked startled by his own actions. "I'm sorry, Ginna. I don't know what made me do that."

She touched his cheek, smiling, her eyes brimming with happy tears. "I'd like to think you did it because you wanted to, and because you knew I wanted to be kissed."

"Who are those people you asked about—Channing and Virginia?"

Before Ginna could answer, Pansy Pennycock—gussied up in her Sunday best, all purple ruffles and lace—came swishing around the corner and all but ran into them. "So here you are! That dear Dr. Kirkwood just told us the good news, Ginna. We are simply thrilled beyond your wildest imagination."

Ginna doubted that! It seemed her imagination was exceptionally wild these days.

Pansy grasped Neal and Ginna each by a hand and herded them toward the dining room. "They sent *me* to find you," she said, importantly. "It's Elspeth's job to save our table— the big one by the windows that overlooks the greenhouse. Of course, it's a table for six, so we were forced to invite Marcellus to join us. But he'll behave himself, I promise. He's been put quite in his place already, today. Sister and I beat the pants off him and Elspeth at bridge." She giggled. "Oh, I wish you could have seen how red his face went when Sister trumped his ace! It was a sight to behold."

Poor Marcellus! Ginna thought. *He's no match for the "terrible threesome!"* However, it would never do to say such a thing aloud. That would only encourage Pansy and the others to taunt the misfortunate man further. Instead, Ginna asked, "And what is Sister's assignment?"

"Oh, she's on an important mission in the kitchen. It's a secret, but you'll find out after dinner, dear."

As they approached the dining room door, Pansy hurried ahead to announce their arrival. Neal leaned down and whispered to Ginna, "I'd hoped for an intimate table for two. Will it help if I tip the maître d'hotel?"

"Not a chance!" She glanced at him, oddly. Once more, he had used Channing's voice, Channing's words.

"Yoo-hoo!" Pansy called, waving frantically from their table. "We're over here. Do come sit! Hobson's fixing to start serving any minute."

Having been forced to endure Lynch as her bridge partner, Elspeth had chosen the seat farthest away from him at the dinner table. Two seats were vacant between them. Deciding to go with the boy-girl-boy-girl arrangement, Ginna sat next to Marcellus while Neal took his place between her and Elspeth. From the gleam of her gold front tooth, it was clear that Elspeth was pleased to have Neal beside her. In fact, dinner almost made up for her embarrassment at the bridge table earlier.

"Well, I swannee, it's a treat to have you two here with us." Elspeth spoke rather too loudly, wanting to make sure that everyone in the dining room heard and turned to gaze in envy. "It's always such a pleasure to have company for Sunday dinner."

"I understand we're going to have a treat today, Elspeth: a recipe handed down from your great-grandmother."

The old woman flashed her gold tooth at Ginna, beaming with pride. "Folks say my great-gran was the best cook in four counties, back before the war. As such, she was the most valuable servant on the place here at Swan's Quarter."

Marcellus Lynch, annoyed at being ignored and still smarting from his shame at the bridge table, gave a disgusted snort. "Elspeth, when are you going to learn to call a spade a spade? Your folks weren't *servants*. They were *slaves!* Colonel Swan

owned your people, same as he owned his mules for plowing
and his cows for giving milk.''

Ginna felt a twinge of pain for Elspeth when her smile faded,
and she ducked her chin to hide the tears gathering in her eyes.
Ginna reached across Neal and touched the old woman's arm.
''It's okay, Elspeth,'' she whispered.

Sister was not so discreet in her reaction to Lynch's affront.
She glared across the table at the man, her face betraying her
rage. ''You ungrateful, carpetbagging Yankee!'' she seethed.
''You've got some nerve, putting down Elspeth's people. Why
don't you tell us about your illustrious ancestors? What were
they—rumrunners, moonshiners, or just a bunch of worthless
sots like yourself?''

Lynch hurrumphed and glanced about nervously to see if
anyone at the nearby tables had heard. If they had, they at least
had the decency to ignore Sister's remarks. Gaining comfort
from this, he said loudly, ''I'll have you know, Sister Randolph,
that I come from a long line of diplomats and statesmen. Why,
a great uncle of mine even married into the royal house of
Hanover.''

''Hanover, my hind foot!'' Pansy cried, in such a high-pitched
squall that every head in the dining room turned. *''Tell me*
about diplomats and statesmen! The only state your ancestors
knew was the state of inebriation. You'd best stop trying to
put on airs around here, Marcellus Lynch. We know all about
you—where you come from, what you did there, and why your
daughter brought you way down here to Swan's Quarter from
New Jersey.''

''New Jersey?'' The shocked whisper moved through the
room like the wave at a baseball game.

''If there's one thing I cannot stand and will not abide, it's
a Yankee trying to pass himself off as a Southerner,'' Pansy
shrilled. ''That's something no one can fake. It's either passed
down in your genes from your ancestors or it isn't. And were
you a true Southerner, Mr. Marcellus *Yankee* Lynch, you would
have better manners than to speak to a lady the way you just
spoke to Elspeth. And now, sir, we are all waiting for your

apology. Even you Yankees know how to apologize, don't you?''

Tension crackled not only at their table but all through the dining room. Lynch's face had gone beet-red, then lost all its color. He looked ashen, ill. The minutes ticked by, silent and charged. Ginna shifted uncomfortably in her chair.

Finally, in a bare whisper, Lynch said, ''I beg your pardon, Elspeth. Forgive me, please.''

He shifted his gaze her way, pleading silently. The old woman refused to look at him. She sat motionless and silent, slumped in her chair.

''I really am sorry, Elspeth. I'll leave right now, if you want me to.'' He pushed back his chair as if he meant to get up from the table. ''I know how you were all looking forward to this meal with our company. I didn't mean to spoil it for everybody. But I guess I have. I just don't fit in here, do I?'' He paused and let out a heavy sigh. ''I should never have come to Swan's Quarter.''

''Then why did you?'' Sister snapped, still unforgiving.

Lynch shook his head and stared down at the pink napkin in his lap. ''I really don't know. It was like I was drawn here. My daughter brought home a batch of brochures and said I should look through them and choose where I wanted to go. When I saw the name ''Swan's Quarter,'' I knew this was the place. It seemed familiar somehow, as if I'd been here before.'' Bravely, he looked up, staring right at Sister. ''You're right, of course. I'd never been out of New Jersey before I came here. I'm not at all what or who I've claimed to be. I should have known you'd find me out for a fraud and a liar. The only connection I ever had with any royalty was an old bum who lived in a packing crate behind a store on my mail route. He wore a tin foil crown he'd made and called himself King Ozzie. He claimed his family had once been guests of the crown heads of Europe—diplomats, statesmen, and bon vivants. He told me wonderful stories every time I came by. Since my life's been so dull, I guess I thought you would like me better if I used those fantastic stories to make myself sound more interesting. Crazy old coots! King Ozzie *and* me!''

"What happened to him?'' Elspeth asked gently, her first words since Lynch's attack.

Marcellus looked very sad, suddenly. "I felt sorry for him, used to give him money for a meal now and again. I tried to help him, but I knew all along there was no use. He lived only for his next pint of whiskey. One day I came by and found him all stretched out, his crown on his head, and an empty fifth of rotgut whiskey clutched to his chest. He was dead, but he was smiling, like he'd seen an angel, or something. I saw he got a decent burial. He didn't have any family—none that claimed him, anyway. I figured it was the least I could do, since he'd entertained me for so long.''

Now the silence at the table had a different feel to it. The "terrible threesome" seemed to soften a bit toward Lynch.

"Didn't know a Yankee had it in him to be so sentimental,'' Sister said, with no malice in her voice. "I reckon you must have had a Southerner way back in your line somewhere.''

A slow smile crept over Lynch's face. "Could be. They say I had a grandpa who was a riverboat gambler, until he settled down and married a dance hall girl from New Orleans.''

Elspeth laughed out loud. "Well, you sure didn't inherit his card-sense.''

Pansy reached over and pressed Lynch's hand, smiling radiantly. "You've got a big heart, Marcellus. You'll get a star in your crown in heaven for what you did for poor old King Ozzie.''

"Or at least a cooler spot in hell, eh, ladies?'' He grinned back, obviously feeling much relieved now.

Just then, Hobson began serving dinner. The fried chicken smelled heavenly and was complemented by sweet potatoes swimming in butter, fresh creamed corn, sliced tomatoes, turnip greens, and golden squares of cornbread.

"The cornbread's my great-granny's recipe too,'' Elspeth said, proudly. "She always used buttermilk to make it.''

Ginna sank her teeth into hers and made a humming sound of pleasure. It tasted better than angel cake.

Conversation ceased, as the six people at the table dug in. By the time Ginna had cleaned her plate, she felt she must have put on at least five pounds of her lost weight.

Sister, Pansy, and Elspeth began whispering among themselves, while Hobson cleared the table. Elspeth tugged the waiter's sleeve, and he leaned down so she could have a word with him privately. Their secret moment over, he flashed her a grin and said, *"Yes, ma'am!* Coming right up!"

Once more, the trio were grinning like cats in the cream, or kids in a cookie jar.

"What?" Ginna demanded.

"It's a secret," Elspeth answered.

"You three have too many secrets. You had better tell us right now or I'll—"

Just then, Hobson came back through the door from the kitchen, wheeling a huge, five-tiered coconut cake with candles glowing.

"It's got great-granny's lemon-cheese filling," Elspeth announced to one and all. "It was her specialty for family birthdays."

"Whose birthday is it?"

"Yours, Ginna!" the three women chorused, amidst a gale of giggles.

And so it was, or the day she was found on the hospital steps, anyway. Ginna had completely forgotten. No one ever made any big deal over her birthday. She often let it slip by without even taking note. The only time she really noticed was when she had to renew her driver's license or fill out an insurance form.

"How did you know?"

Pansy grinned at Ginna and fluttered her eyelashes. "I'm not telling."

"Well, it doesn't matter. All that matters is that I've never been more surprised in my life. *You three!* Why, you're just the sweetest things!"

Ginna got up and went to kiss the cheeks of each of her friends, in turn.

"You should have told me," Neal said, when she sat down again. "I'd have gotten you something—a card at least."

He leaned over and kissed her cheek, now damp with tears, she was so touched.

"I really did forget," she said.

The whole dining room sang "Happy Birthday" to Ginna. She cut the gorgeous cake and Hobson served. Her friends all had gifts for her. Sister had embroidered a delicate doily with two swans in the center. Pansy had made her a drawstring purse of old lace. Even Marcellus was in on this secret. He gave her a sachet filled with dried rose petals from the garden. Elspeth had the most fascinating surprise of all. She had painted a small watercolor of a man and a woman standing beside the swan pond. The woman wore a pink gown belled by a hoop skirt. The man was tall and dark, and you could tell by the way he leaned toward the woman that he adored her.

"Oh, Elspeth, it's lovely!" Ginna exclaimed. "Who are they?"

The old woman frowned slightly. "I disremember right now. But I know them." She turned and stared Ginna right in the eye. "You know them, too, child. Maybe better than you know your own self."

Dr. Kirkwood interrupted just then. "Happy birthday, Ginna! We're so glad you could be here with us so we could help celebrate."

Ginna almost laughed. "Thank you, Dr. Kirkwood. Turning twenty-eight was not really something I'd looked forward to celebrating, but I've certainly enjoyed this. You all made it special for me."

"Your room is ready, if you'd like me to show you where it is."

"That would be nice." She glanced around the table, smiling at each person in turn. "If you all will excuse me?"

They all nodded, smiled back, and once more congratulated her. Neal whispered, "I'll see you later?"

"As soon as I've rested for a while."

"Yes. Rest, Ginna. Later this afternoon you can show me around."

"I will."

"Promise?"

"Promise."

"Well, quit stalling," Sister said impatiently. "Give her a birthday kiss, Neal."

He did—a sweet, soft, emotionally charged kiss. Ginna blushed when everyone in the dining room applauded.

"Later," Neal whispered. "Just you and me."

Ginna nodded, then followed the doctor out of the dining room. She felt as if her feet barely touched the floor.

"I think you'll like your room," Leonard Kirkwood said. "We usually don't open it up. But I have a feeling Melora Swan would approve of your staying there."

Ginna looked at him quizzically. Whatever could Melora Swan have to do with this? The mistress of Swan's Quarter had been dead for nearly a century.

Chapter Six

Leonard Kirkwood had read and studied the strange old deed, signed by Melora Swan, in her delicate, spidery hand. When she had turned over her home to one "General Mallory J. Fitzhugh, CSA," she had dictated a clause whereby one room at Swan's Quarter would be held in perpetuity by her family "for my own use as long as I live and thereafter, should any member of my family return desiring lodging and sanctuary."

Kirkwood had puzzled long over the odd clause. He knew from old records that Melora Swan had indeed stayed on at Swan's Quarter until her death. But, since she was the last surviving member of the Swan family, who could she have expected to return to the old homeplace? The records of the sanatorium showed that no one had used the room since Mrs. Swan's demise, in the early part of the twentieth century. In fact, that one bed chamber had been kept locked for decades.

Shortly after Kirkwood's arrival to take charge of Swan's Quarter, he had inspected the room and found it in perfect order, but clothed in the accumulated dust of years. He had sent one of the housekeepers there to give it a good cleaning. Every month since, he had had that chore repeated. Now, as it happened, Melora Swan's old chamber was the only vacant room at Swan's Quarter. Even if another had been available, he knew that he would have put Ginna in Melora's private sanctum. It just seemed right, somehow.

"This way, Ginna. Your room is at the end of the hall. I think you'll like it. There's a view of the front lawn and the swan pond."

Ginna felt winded after climbing the staircase to the second floor. Dr. Kirkwood had suggested they take the elevator, but her recent experience as the vigorous young Virginia Swan, tripping easily down several flights at Mathew Brady's studio in New York City, had convinced Ginna that stairs no longer presented a problem. Halfway up, she had realized her mistake. By the time she reached the upper landing, her heart was pounding and she felt weak all over.

"Let me catch my breath a minute." She leaned heavily on the hallway railing, waiting to regain her strength.

The doctor turned back to her, concern registering in his face. He took her hand, surreptitiously taking her pulse. "These stairs are pretty steep. I think you'd better use the elevator from now on, Ginna."

"You bet I will! Right now, I'd really like to lie down for a few minutes."

This had been an especially busy day. She felt as if it had been a week long already. Work, the flea market, the bus ride, then her trip back in time with Neal. Sunday dinner had been exhausting, too—all that tension at the table between Lynch and his three female tormentors. She had loved her surprise birthday party, but that, too, had taken its toll. She had been relieved when Dr. Kirkwood came in and rescued her, even though she hated to leave everyone, especially Neal.

"Rest is exactly what I was about to prescribe for you," Kirkwood answered. "You might even want to take a nap. That's what most everybody does around here on Sunday afternoons."

She smiled at him and nodded. "Wake me up tomorrow, if I'm still sleeping."

Kirkwood unlocked the door and handed her the key. "If you need anything, just phone down to my office. You rest now, Ginna."

He turned and walked quickly back toward the stairs before she entered, leaving Ginna feeling very much alone. However, the moment she stepped inside the room, she was glad the doctor was gone. She might have had trouble explaining her shock to him.

Once more, she felt as if she had stepped back in time. She remembered this room, with its tester bed, its marble-topped vanity, its faded pink-and-green, forget-me-not wallpaper. In a daze of memories, she walked about, touching the silver comb and brush set—a gift to Virginia from her parents on her sixteenth birthday—the antique china doll in its rough hewn cradle—its clothes made by old Polly, the cook—and on the bedside table, a miniature portrait done on ivory—a present from the subject himself, Channing McNeal. She picked up the framed picture and examined it closely. The artist had done a fine job; it was a perfect likeness. Miniscule dots of white paint made Channing's eyes seem alive with the light of love she knew so well. At the time the portrait was done, his hair had been cut shorter than she remembered it. In a moment of shock, she realized that this likeness was the image of Neal Frazier.

Still holding the miniature, Ginna sat down on the candle-wicked counterpane that covered the bed. She stretched out and pulled up the bright Sunday House quilt that was folded neatly at the foot.

"Common side weekdays. Bright side Sundays," she said, recalling the words, but not their origin.

Sometime, somewhere, someone had told her about the Sunday House quilt. She remembered that, unlike most quilts, this one had patterns on both sides, the more colorful and elaborate design to be turned up on weekends, when guests were most likely to be visiting. During the week, the less fancy side covered the bed, so that it received the dust and the sun's fading rays.

Again, familiar words came to mind. "Remember, dear. You

will have to gaze on your handiwork for the rest of your life. Make your stitches neat and small—ten to fourteen stitches per inch on the top. Very straight. Very even.''

Ginna stared down at the lovely pattern, with its green vine twining the border all the way around. "There's a reason for that," she murmured, trying to remember. This, too, came to her suddenly, out of nowhere. A quilt with a broken border brought bad luck—a broken marriage or a shortened life.

In a flash, the whole picture came back to Ginna. Virginia and Melora Swan had carefully pieced this quilt in the years before the war, using scraps from every gingham gown Virginia had worn as a child.

When Ginna closed her eyes, she could hear Virginia's mother saying, "This quilt will go into your hope chest, dear. Years from now, when you're an old married lady, you will be able to recall your whole life through these pieced scraps. See this yellow square sprigged in green? Mammy Fan made that dress for you to wear to your tenth birthday party. Remember?''

Ginna heard Virginia laugh in reply. "How could I forget, Mother? The twins climbed the tulip poplar and dared me to follow them. They said I was nothing but a sissy girl if I didn't.''

"*Your brothers!* Hollis and Hampton always have been a pair of scamps, always will be, I'm afraid." She uttered a mother's long-suffering sigh and turned mildly amused eyes on her only daughter. "You weren't much better, Virginia. A tomboy from the day you were born, always trying to keep up with Rodney, Jed, and the twins. As I recall, you climbed that tree, all the way to the top, and tore your pretty party dress to tatters, not to mention what you did to your stockings. *Imagine!* A young lady with skinned knees!''

Virginia covered a giggle with her hand. "And Channing had to climb up to get me down.''

"Such a sweet boy! Ah, well, what's left of that poor, ruined party dress will make lovely scraps for your quilt.''

Not long after their men rode off to war, the actual quilting

had begun—a joint effort by all their women friends from
neighboring plantations. A quilting bee at Swan's Quarter. Melora Swan had thought to distract her grieving daughter with
the social event. But those neighbors who failed to come had
only served to remind Virginia of what she had lost. The ladies
of Belle Grove, Channing's mother and sisters, were missing
from their circle. Channing was gone from his home, gone
from her life, gone to join his regiment. But he had not ridden
off to war with her father and brothers to fight for the Southern
Cause.

"Virginia?"

Ginna had drifted off to sleep. She sat bolt upright in bed
when she heard Melora Swan's voice close at hand. She rubbed
her eyes, trying to make herself believe that she was still only
dreaming of the past. She was not! Standing by the vanity was
Melora Swan, the same woman she had met in New York City
earlier in the day—long ago in time.

"I'm sorry to disturb you, dear. I know you must be
exhausted from the trip, but we do hàve guests coming tonight.
Remember? Channing's parents and sisters will be here before
long. They want to hear all about our adventures at West Point
and in New York City." She smiled brightly. "And, of course,
they will want a full description of the ring Channing chose
for you at Mr. Tiffany's."

When Ginna rose from the bed, she caught a glimpse of
herself in the vanity mirror. She paused, stunned for an instant.
Virginia was back!

"Shall I send Mammy Fan up to help you dress, dear?"

"No, thank you, Mother. I can manage." Ginna thought
suddenly of the tattered old gown she had worn to Swan's
Quarter. That would never do. In fact, glancing down at herself,
she saw that it was gone. She was dressed only in her camisole
and pantalettes. "What should I wear? Help me choose," she
begged of Melora Swan.

Virginia's mother went to the cedar-lined armoire and opened
the doors. "Let's see . . . what about your pale pink lawn with
the tiny violets? It always brings out the color in your cheeks."

"Yes, Mother. I've always loved that dress, and it's one of Channing's favorites. The next time I write to him, I'll tell him that I wore it for his family."

Melora Swan smiled. "That's a lovely thought, dear. I'll leave you now and see you downstairs within the hour."

Virginia's mother opened the door and exited to the hallway. Ginna heard the soft tap of her shoes fading in the distance. Her heart leaped suddenly, wondering what Dr. Kirkwood and the others would think when Melora Swan appeared downstairs. She rushed to the door to call the woman back. The hall was empty by the time she looked out. The whole house seemed inordinately quiet, but then it was Sunday afternoon naptime. *Wasn't it?*

Ginna turned back, expecting to see the room exactly as it had been when Dr. Kirkwood had shown her in. But it was not—not quite. The Sunday House quilt and her clothes were nowhere to be seen. Lying across the bed was the pink lawn gown she would wear to dinner with Channing's family. With a shrug of bewilderment, Ginna reached for the old-fashioned dress, which looked brand new, and began getting ready, feeling more confused, as each moment passed.

What could she expect to find downstairs? Would she still be Virginia once she left this room? Would she find the Swan and McNeal families gathering for dinner, or would the residents of the sanatorium be there to greet her?

With a sigh and a shrug, she fastened her gown, then smoothed her palms down the tight-fitting bodice. "It doesn't matter," she told herself. "If I'm still in the past when I get downstairs, I'll simply play along. If I find Neal and the others waiting for me, I'll tell them I found this old dress in the room and decided to try it on."

Confident that she was ready to handle either situation, Ginna opened the door and tiptoed along the empty hallway. At the head of the stairs, she paused. Such a mingling of sounds reached her from below that she had to stop and try to sort them out. She heard a piano playing softly over quiet conversation, the scrape of a chair, the neighing of horses, and finally Jedediah Swan's booming laugh.

"So that's it," she whispered to herself. "I'm still in the past. The McNeals must just be arriving."

Preparing herself to take up the role of Virginia, she started down the stairs. She had taken only two steps, when she heard Marcellus Lynch bellow, "What's trump, Elspeth? I can't remember."

Ginna stopped dead in her tracks. How could Lynch *and* the Swans be downstairs? How could she be hearing voices from the past *and* the present?

She was still too far up the staircase to see anything below on the main floor. Holding her breath, she listened carefully. The tinkle of glassware, the sound of footsteps, the quiet murmur of voices—nothing to give her any further clues.

Squaring her shoulders, she took a deep breath, then headed down. All she could do was take her chances and hope she could muddle through.

Neal was in the library on the main floor, looking for a book to read. With everyone napping, except for the one table of dedicated bridge players, the house was so quiet it was creepy. He half-expected one of old Zee's ghosts to come whooshing down the stairs any minute now. He had to do something to while away the time until Ginna came down. Without her around, he felt like he was about to jump out of his skin. His thoughts kept drifting back to the plane crash—not a good place to be.

He searched the spines of the old books on the shelves, hoping to find some escape fiction by Tom Clancy or Stephen King. No luck! The best he could do was Herman Melville or Joseph Conrad. He reached for a newer-looking book, without even checking the title. With the volume in his hands, he went to the door, his attention now tuned to soft voices that seemed to be coming from the hallway.

Neal peered out. The entrance way to Swan's Quarter looked

strange—all misty or smoky, as if someone had just passed
through, puffing vigorously on a cigar. But there was no smell
of smoke. He kept his eyes trained on the shifting cloud, as
goosebumps crawled along his arms.

Faint sounds issued from the mist. Neither whole sentences
nor even whole words, but definitely the murmur of voices. As
he continued to listen and watch, he imagined he could pick
out the faint outlines of several people gathered at the front
door. Mesmerized, he leaned against the door and continued
his vigil. He would almost see a face, only to have it disappear
before it came fully into focus. He would catch half a word,
but the rest would drift off before he could make out clearly
what it was.

"What the hell is this?" he swore softly.

Suddenly, a phrase came back to him—something he had
heard only once and thought he had forgotten years ago: *The
fourth dimension.*

He nodded slowly. "Yes," he breathed. "That must be it!"

As Ginna neared the bottom of the stairs, she realized that
she was indeed back in time with the Swan family.

"Virginia, dear, there you are." Melora Swan used the crystal-
bright tone that—somehow Ginna knew—her husband always
called her "company voice." "Do come join us. The McNeals
have only just arrived."

Ginna smiled at Melora and the others, as she descended the
last three steps. A tiny woman with Channing's warm eyes and
sweet smile came toward her, her arms outstretched.

"Oh, Virginia, you look a picture this evening," Letitia
McNeal cooed. "How I wish Channing could see you this very
minute."

The two women embraced, then Ginna said, "No more than
I wish I could see him, Miz Letitia."

"Was he well, dear? Are they feeding him properly? How
did he look?"

Ginna gave Mrs. McNeal an extra hug. "He looked marvelous! I believe he thrives on the military life."

"Oh, I do worry so about him!"

"Our Channing's a man now, Mother." Ginna turned toward the gentleman speaking: Mr. Thompson McNeal, obviously. From him, too, Channing had inherited some of his handsome features—his broad shoulders, straight nose, and dark hair, although the elder McNeal's was thinning on top.

"Mr. McNeal," Ginna said, offering her hand. He took it, but drew her into an embrace, just as his wife had done. It was clear that Channing's family approved wholeheartedly of their son's choice.

Holding Ginna at arm's length, McNeal said, "My dear, you grow more lovely every day. Why, you're simply glowing this evening!" He leaned close and whispered, "It must be love."

Ginna felt Virginia's cheeks flush warmly. She looked away from Channing's father, slightly embarrassed.

"Polly has made some of her special punch for us this evening," Melora Swan announced. "Won't you all come with me to the parlor to sample it?"

Ginna saw that the mistress of Swan's Quarter was leading her guests toward the room that would later be used as the reading and game room at the sanatorium. It was a large, airy place with French doors that opened onto the veranda. Ginna glanced out, as they entered the room. The sight that greeted her all but stopped her breath. There on the porch she saw the faint outline of the rockers moving slowly, as Elspeth, Sister, and Pansy sat together drinking lemonade in the glow of the setting sun.

"Dear, is anything wrong?" Melora Swan whispered, from beside her.

Still staring at the shadows of the three women on the veranda, Ginna shook her head. "No! Nothing, Mother." She turned and smiled, trying to shake off her uneasiness.

"I'm so sorry the girls couldn't come this evening, Letitia."

Channing's mother shook her head and took a sip of Polly's special punch from a silver cup. "Melora, I'm sure you under-

stand. These young people nowadays make their own plans.
Hester is off to spend the weekend at Oaklands and Janey is
visiting her cousins in Front Royal. They did ask me to send
their regards and regrets to all of you.''

Ginna knew, suddenly, that the next one in their group to
receive a proposal would be Channing's younger sister, Hester.
She would marry the son of the French planter who owned
Oaklands. But they would never live together in Virginia. Channing's whole family was destined to flee to Paris, once the war
started. As yet, this remained a secret to all the others.

Setting her punch cup down, Ginna made a conscious effort
to banish all thoughts of the future from her mind. If she was
to be Virginia Swan for the evening, she needed to stay in
Virginia's mind, as well as in her body. Otherwise, she might
blurt out something shocking in front of the Swans and the
McNeals.

"We will miss the girls tonight, Letitia, but I know exactly
what you mean about young people. Hardly had we returned
home before the twins and Jed were off on a hunting trip. I
invited Rodney's Agnes to come, but her mother isn't well,
you know.''

Mrs. McNeal clucked her tongue sympathetically. "That
poor woman! She has been sickly as long as I've known her.
I surely hope she lives long enough to see her only child wed
to your Rodney. Then she can die happy.''

Trying to lighten the subject, Jedediah Swan began a full
recounting of their trip. Nothing seemed required of Virginia
but to listen quietly. Trying to remain inconspicuous, Ginna
took a seat near the door, one that did not face toward the
veranda.

After a few moments, Melora Swan came over and whispered, "Dear, would you mind telling Juniper to hold dinner
for a time? It seems your father means to keep us here a bit
longer, and I don't dare interrupt him. You know how he enjoys
telling his tales.''

Ginna rose and slipped out of the room. For a moment, she
couldn't think who Juniper was. Then she remembered Pansy's

version of the silver teapot's story, wherein the Swans' butler, Juniper, supposedly dumped the pot down the well.

She started across the hallway toward the butler's pantry, when she saw a movement out of the corner of her eye. She glanced toward the library. At first, she saw only the shadow of a figure, much like those on the veranda. He seemed to be wrapped in a thick cloud of mist. But as she stared, he became more distinct. It was Neal, standing at the door, holding a book in his hands.

"Ginna? I thought you were still resting."

"Neal?"

"Well, I hope so!" He laughed. "You look like you've just seen a ghost."

Confused and stammering, Ginna allowed him to lead her into the library. He closed the door softly behind them, put his book on a nearby table, and drew her into his arms.

"I've been thinking all afternoon about that kiss earlier," he whispered. "Ginna, I don't know what's happening to me. I'm not the same man I was a few days ago. From the first time I set eyes on you, things have been changing."

"For the better, I hope."

In answer, he drew her closer and brought his mouth down to hers. Ginna tensed for an instant. After all, she was supposed to be on an errand for her mother—no, *Virginia's mother*. The taste of Neal and the feel of his body pressed to hers soon wiped all else from her mind. She relaxed in his arms and let herself experience this special pleasure to its fullest. No one had kissed her this way in a very long time. Not since Channing McNeal.

That thought made her pull away. She opened her eyes and looked up at Neal. Yes, this was Neal, all right.

"Would you think I was crazy if I told you I'm falling in love?" He stepped away and grinned. "No, that's a lie! I'm *already* in love with you, Ginna."

He caught her off guard. She could think of no reply.

Neal shook his head, warning her not to speak. "You don't have to say anything right now. Just think about it. Think about *me.* You know I've been married. But, Ginna, I've never really been in love before. I never thought this would happen to me. Now that it has, I'm not sure how to deal with it. I can't stand being away from you for a minute. I want to hold you, feel you close to me, all the time. When you're not with me, I fall back into that deep, black well where I was before I met you.''

"Neal . . .''

He cut off her words with another kiss. This time he held her closer, kissed her deeper. She slipped her arms around his neck and returned his embrace ardently. Her heart thundered in her breast and she felt herself trembling against him.

Yes! she thought. *This is right! This is what I've been waiting for all these years. Neal is the one!*

For a long time, they held each other, neither willing to break the perfect spell of the moment. Finally, it was Neal who drew away.

When she looked up into his face, he was frowning. "How did you do that, Ginna?''

She laughed. "It's very easy. I just put my lips on yours and my arms around your neck and . . .''

"No. I mean out there in the hall. You just appeared out of nowhere. One minute you weren't anywhere in sight. The next minute you were right there. Where did you come from?''

"What do you mean? I was upstairs napping, then I came down, and here you were.''

"You didn't come down those stairs," he accused. "I'd just been up there myself and the hall was empty.''

Thinking frantically, she said, "Well, I did step into the game room for a minute.''

Neal was still shaking his head. "It must be these pills the doc's giving me. They make me feel fuzzy around the edges. I keep imagining I'm seeing things. Would you believe I saw a whole group of people outside this door a little while ago? And earlier today I thought I was in New York City. But it wasn't the Big Apple—not the one I know, anyway.''

Just then, Ginna heard Melora Swan's voice. "Virginia? Virginia, where are you, dear?''

"There's something I have to do," Ginna said quickly, afraid that Virginia's mother might pop into the library and find her engaged daughter in the arms of a stranger. "Wait for me out on the veranda with Elspeth and the others. I'll be out there shortly."

At the exact moment she finished speaking, the library door opened. Ginna swallowed deeply, sure she was about to find herself in deep trouble.

"Virginia, what on earth are you doing hiding away in the empty library when we have guests?"

Empty library? Ginna glanced quickly about. Sure enough, Neal had vanished.

"I'm sorry, Mother. I didn't mean to stay away so long." *Think, Ginna, think! Why were you in the library?* She spied Neal's book—a slim volume of poetry—on the table. "I suddenly remembered a poem Channing suggested I read when I felt lonely for him. I thought I might find it."

"And did you, dear?"

Thinking quickly, Ginna answered with a smile, "Why, yes, Mother. That's what kept me. I was reading it."

"What poem was it?"

Trapped! Ginna hadn't bargained for this question. Reaching for Neal's book, she opened it and quickly thumbed through it.

"This is it," Ginna said, smiling confidently at Melora Swan. She read the first few lines of a poem to Virginia's mother.

"That's lovely, my dear, but I'm not familiar with the verse. Who is the poet?"

Ginna looked at the spine of the book and shuddered. Why couldn't Neal have been reading Shakespeare or Chaucer?

"Robert Frost," Ginna said hesitantly.

"I don't believe I've ever heard of him."

Of course, you've never heard of him, Ginna thought. *He won't be born until after the Civil War.* Aloud, she said, "He's rather obscure. A New Englander, I believe."

"Well, I have every confidence he will be famous someday,

if he continues to write so beautifully. Now, come, Virginia. We mustn't keep our guests waiting.''

Ginna put the book back where Neal had left it and followed Melora out of the library. She was trembling with relief, but still wondering how Neal had managed his miraculous escape.

Dinner proved long and nerve-wracking. Hours dragged by, while the men discussed crop prices, plantation management, and the coming hostilities. Ginna noted that both families were on the side of their state and the South. *Poor Channing!* she thought. But for most of the evening, her mind was on Neal. How long had she kept him waiting? There was no way of knowing how much time had passed in that other realm.

"We have decided on a double wedding," Ginna heard Melora say. "Virginia and Agnes agree that it will double their pleasure to share the ceremony. Of course, neither our Rodney nor your Channing seems in the least concerned with nuptial details. They simply want the weddings to take place, posthaste."

"Ah, how like men!" Letitia said, with a soft laugh. "Thompson was the same way. I think he would have settled for jumping a broomstick."

Jumping a broomstick? The phrase leaped out at Ginna. Where had she heard it before? Yes! She remembered, suddenly. During the war, Virginia and Channing had married in that odd slave fashion—the only wedding they would ever have. She was reminded of Mathew Brady and his promise to come to Swan's Quarter to make their wedding portrait. That picture would never be taken.

Ginna felt tears coming to her eyes at that thought. She couldn't cry! Not now! What would everyone think? How could she explain tears, when they were discussing her wedding?

Melora noticed her brimming eyes and whispered, "It won't be long, dear. I know how you miss Channing, but it won't be long before he's home."

The others politely ignored Virginia's red eyes and sniffles.

Dinner finally ended with old Polly's specialty: coconut cake with lemon-cheese filling. Then their guests took their leave.

"You had better run along to bed, now, Virginia," her mother told her. "I know you must be exhausted."

Without even worrying about the steep stairs, Ginna hurried up, trusting Virginia's good heart to carry her all the way. By the time she reached the top, however, she was short of breath and trembling. Ginna almost welcomed her weakness. She was back, back from the past, back with Neal.

Just to make certain, she walked down the hall to the elevator. Sure enough, there it was. She stepped inside and pressed the button to the first floor. When the doors opened, she peered out cautiously. There was no sign of any member of the Swan family. She hurried as quickly as she could to the veranda.

"Hey, that was fast!" Neal said, beaming at her. "I hardly had time to take a sip of lemonade."

Ginna went to Neal and slipped her arm through his. "I didn't want to keep you waiting. Let's take a walk."

The late afternoon air had turned cool. Already, everyone else had left the veranda and gone inside to escape the chill. Neal took off his jacket and slipped it around Ginna's bare shoulders. "Can't have my best girl catching cold."

"Is that what I am? Your *best girl?*"

He squeezed her arm and smiled down into her eyes. "You better believe it! The best I ever had. The best I ever want."

Ginna felt her heart commence its happy tap dance again. She felt giddy, like a kid with a new toy at Christmas. All of a sudden, with Neal here beside her, the sun looked brighter, the sky was bluer, and all seemed right with the world.

"Where do you want to go?" Neal asked, as they reached the lawn.

"Someplace where we can talk."

"Someplace private? Where I can hold you and kiss you again?"

"I know a place," she said softly.

"Then lead the way, darlin'."

Beyond the house and the main out-buildings, Ginna remembered a place where Virginia and Channing used to meet. It had been a playhouse for generations of little girls at Swan's

Quarter. A few years ago, a swimming pool had been added.
At that time, the old playhouse was converted into a cabana.
This time of year, the pool was closed. They would have the
privacy they both craved.

"Did you ever think we'd find each other again?" Neal's
question came out of nowhere, stunning Ginna to silence.

Realizing suddenly that his words sounded odd, Neal added,
"What I mean is, it seems as though we met somewhere before,
and I've been looking for you all my life. Maybe we knew
each other in a previous lifetime. I feel like we did, Ginna."

"You believe in reincarnation?"

Neal thought a minute, before he answered. "Makes sense
to me. Why should all the knowledge and talent and beauty of
each generation be wasted. Recycle! That's what I believe."

Neal's words gave Ginna pause. She had never really thought
about it, but it did make sense. Was a human soul any less
important than a plastic milk jug?

"You know, I heard a guy talking one time—a psychic—
about the fourth dimension."

Ginna looked up at him. "What's that?"

"He said it's this other layer of reality. Like a shell around
us. It's a place where past times and spirits dwell right alongside
all of us, here in the present."

"I'm not sure I understand, Neal."

He rubbed his jaw, trying to figure out a better way to explain.
"You know, sometimes you'll see a dog or a cat watching
something, but there's nothing there. Their heads will move as
if they see someone or something walking across a room."

Ginna nodded. "Yes. I've seen that. But animals have such
keen hearing, that's what accounts for their strange behavior
sometime, I think."

"It's more than that, Ginna. The way this guy explained it,
animals not only hear sounds we can't hear, but they can see
things we can't see. Things in this fourth dimension."

All of a sudden, a light dawned in Ginna's mind. The *fourth
dimension!* That could explain everything that had been happen-

ing to her. Two layers of time, co-existing at Swan's Quarter. The past and the present, side by side.

"But we can't see into this other dimension, can we, Neal?"

"Not usually. But this guy said that sometimes things happen that allow us to see. Like a crack in a wall that lets light in or a curtain that isn't quite closed. Then we can catch glimpses of what's happening in that other realm."

"Where did you meet this psychic? Why did he tell you about the fourth dimension?"

Neal glanced away, looking off in the distance toward the huge tulip poplar tree. He didn't want to talk about that. "It doesn't matter," he said quietly. He couldn't bring himself to tell Ginna about his wife, Nancy, and her tragic death, about the strange old man who had wandered up to him while he stood at her grave—dry-eyed, unable to shed the tears that were choking him, drowning him in grief and guilt. "All that matters is what he told me. I never believed it." He paused again, then muttered under his breath, "Not until now."

"What's happened, Neal? Can you tell me about it?"

He turned her toward him and looked deeply into her eyes. "*You* happened, Ginna. Since you've come, everything's changed. I see more, hear more, feel more."

Ginna was on the verge of asking him what he remembered about New York. It was time they discussed everything and compared notes. But just as she was about to question him, a heavy rain shower started. Holding onto each other, they raced for the pool house. Ginna felt for the key above the doorframe and unlocked the tiny cottage. A moment later, they were inside, in each other's arms, glorying in their nearness, their privacy.

After a long, deep kiss, Neal drew away and whispered, "I don't want to rush you into anything, Ginna."

Any other time with any other man, Ginna would have refused to be rushed. But this was Neal—the man she loved—and they didn't have much time, and she knew it.

Chapter Seven

The rain on the roof of the quaint little cottage had a silvery, music box sound. Off in the distance, thunder rumbled over the valley. Darkness was falling quickly, making Ginna and Neal's hideaway seem all the more private and magical.

For a long time, they stood together in the center of the room, their bodies locked in an embrace. Neal's kiss transported Ginna to another realm—somewhere beyond the fourth dimension. She lost track of where she was, even who she was. But she knew whose arms were holding her, whose mouth moved sensually over hers, whose warm, damp body was pressed close to her own.

Her heart raced so that she felt weak—not the weakness she experienced when she climbed stairs or when she ran to catch a bus. No, this was different. This was a sweet, languid weakness that flowed through her veins like a river of fire, kindling a longing so intense that she knew there could be no turning back. Not this time. Not with Neal.

"Oh, Ginna, Ginna," he whispered between kisses. "You don't know what this is doing to me. You've brought me back from the dead. I never knew I could feel this . . ." He paused, groping for the right word.

"This alive?" she supplied. "This free and crazy?"

He chuckled. *"Crazy?* Yes, that's it. This is a form of insanity. But what sweet madness! I'd like to stay this crazy forever."

"Forever and ever." Ginna's words came between sighs.

Still clinging to Ginna, Neal edged toward a daybed on the far side of the room. "Let me make love to you," he whispered. "Right here! Right now! It's been so long."

His urgent plea warmed her through. His final remark made her wonder. *"So long" since what?* Since he last felt this way? Since he last made love to a woman? Or did he mean, without knowing it, the *last time*—when he was Channing and she was Virginia?

All the questions drifted away like smoke when Neal eased her onto the bed and leaned over her. He kissed her lips, her eyelids, her cheeks. His mouth moved then to her neck, and from there to her bare shoulders. Soon she felt the warmth of his lips brush the tops of her breasts. She trembled and sighed, aching for him to come to her. It seemed that she remembered sometime long ago, when they had made love. That night, too, a kind of madness had swept them along on the crest of its wave. It had been a hot, still night filled with danger, uncertainty, and exquisite desire.

To clear the memory of that danger from her mind, she concentrated once more on the soothing sound of the rain on the roof.

"You're far away," Neal whispered. "Come back to me, darlin'. Come love me."

With gentle, knowing hands, he stripped away her gown. In turn, she unbuttoned his shirt, unzipped his jeans. Soon they were lying in each other's arms, feeling the sweet sting of flesh against flesh for the very first time.

Or was it?

Every move Neal made seemed familiar to Ginna. The way he cupped her breasts, the way he touched her thighs, the way he caressed her lazily, giving her longing all the time in the world to grow and expand, until her whole body quivered with need.

Then slowly, carefully, he poised himself over her, sure at last that she was ready. With his first thrust, Ginna shuddered beneath him. He was right; it had been a long, long time. She moved against him, urging him deeper, catching his rhythm and riding smoothly, with his every move. The heat and pleasure and madness intensified, growing and expanding, until Ginna thought she would burst into a million pinpricks of light, flying off into nothingness.

"Oh, Neal!" she gasped, wrapping him with her legs and clawing at his shoulders.

"Hold tight," he groaned. "Don't let go, darlin'. Not for a minute."

The next few moments seemed to Ginna as if she and her lover had been transformed. They were no longer two people reaching for the heights, but a single energy form—white-hot, boiling, writhing through space. Searching, searching, searching! Reaching out beyond their reach for that one perfect moment.

It came with a crashing, clashing, universe-shattering explosion of pure bliss. Ginna clung tightly to Neal, riding down with him from the heights. Their passions spent at last, they lay quietly together, breathing heavily, wet with love sweat.

"God, strike me dead now, and I'll die a happy man!"

Ginna giggled. She couldn't help herself. She felt as light as a feather and as happy as a lark. Her mind and heart were buzzing with happy cliches. She felt like Snow White, waking up from a long, deathlike sleep, because Neal had kissed her—Neal had loved her.

When she made no response to his remark, he demanded, "Well, what do you have to say for yourself, my fine lady?"

She giggled again.

"Come on," he urged. "Say *something!* You're making me nervous."

"This isn't real. It can't be. I'm home in bed fast asleep and dreaming the loveliest dream I've ever dreamed. There's no Neal Frazier. There couldn't be. I made him up. No *real* man could make me feel this way."

He pinched her nipple gently.

"Ouch!" she cried.

"There! See? You're not dreaming, Ginna. I'm right here. Want me to prove how real I am?"

Once more, he covered her, ready for another go.

"Neal!" she cried. "Give me a minute to catch my breath. I'm still coming down from the last flight."

Remembering the plane crash suddenly, she was sorry she had said that. But Neal paid no attention. For the time being, he seemed to have forgotten all his trauma and pain.

"You have to marry me, Ginna!" This wasn't a proposal, but a demand.

"Just like that?"

He nodded vigorously and brushed her lips with his. "Just like that! I don't see a reason in the world why we should wait. I know I love you, and I know I want to spend the rest of my life with you. I think I knew that the minute I saw you coming up the path from the swan pond a few days ago."

"But you don't know anything about me, Neal. And I hardly know anything about you, except that you and I . . . well, we seem to fit together like two pieces of a puzzle, and I like what you do . . . I mean, that was really something . . ." She trailed off with a stammer and another soft laugh.

"Okay!" He sat up beside her in all his naked glory. She let her gaze caress his muscular body, while he talked. "I was born Neal Mackey Frazier to Janice and Todd Frazier in Fairfax, Virginia, on June the tenth, thirty-two years ago. I had one older brother, killed in Vietnam. After an unspectacular career in public school, I went to the University of Virginia on a football scholarship, where I graduated without honors. Went in the army, loved every minute of it, got an honorable discharge after I was wounded in Desert Storm. Oh, I got married right before I went over. Her name was Nancy, and she was a nice lady, and she deserved better than I could give her. She died while I was away." He paused for a moment, regrouping his emotions. "I'm something of a slob around the house—never been really housebroken, I guess. I like to ride motorcycles,

play tennis and golf. I hate flying. And I *love* you, Ginna Jones!
So, now that you know my whole life story, *marry me!*'' He
leaned down and tongued her nipple, making her squirm. Then
he looked up and said, ''Marry me, or I'll drive you insane.''

She half-believed he meant it, when he leaned back down
and sucked the same nipple into his mouth, teasing it with his
tongue and teeth.

''Neal,'' she moaned, ''listen to me. We have to think about
this. You don't know anything about me.''

''Know enough! Love you! Don't care about the rest!'' He
spoke the words rapidly, then went back to his sweet taunting.

Ginna was torn. She wanted to marry Neal. She really, truly
loved him. But how could they rush into this? Didn't they both
need time? Yet, when she thought ahead to the empty years
stretching before her without Neal, she knew she loved and
needed him with all her heart and soul. She wanted to spend
the rest of her life with Neal. She *wanted* to marry him, wanted
it desperately.

''Well?'' he raised his head from his busy work and stared
at her. ''Do I get an answer or not?''

She reached up and touched his face, stroking his cheek with
her fingertips. The light in his eyes almost brought her to tears.
He wasn't joking around; he really did love her and want her.

''Can't I have a few minutes to think about it, Neal?''

''Every minute wasted in waiting is time lost,'' he said.
''But, yes, I'll even give you a few days. Not too long, though.''

''Not too long. I promise.'' She drew his face down to hers
and kissed him, softly and sweetly. ''And, Neal?''

''Yes?'' he answered, his voice choked with emotion and
longing.

''I love you, too. I think I always have. Maybe that's why
I kept coming back to Swan's Quarter all these years. Maybe
I've just been waiting for you to show up, so I could fall in
love.''

Her admission of her love for him turned him mellow and
tender. With ever so much care, he eased into her once more.
This time, unlike the previous explosion of emotions and sensa-

tions, Neal set a gentler pace. Quietly, with the languid flow
of an erotic ballet, they moved together slowly, feeling each
slight quiver of flesh against flesh, savoring each moment of
stillness, as they held each other. Their dreamlike lovemaking
went on and on, seeming to grow sweeter with each passing
moment.

Just as Ginna was about to reach the pinnacle again, Neal
whispered into her ear, "Marry me and it will always be this
way for us." He held very still suddenly, as if he knew that
Ginna was trembling on the brink. "If you love me as much
as I love you, there's no need to wait. There's no need to hold
back. We *need* to be together, darlin'."

Neal's stillness left Ginna almost gasping. She ached for him
to move inside her. The slightest twitch and she would be free
again to fly through the starry heavens. Blood pounded in her
ears. Her heart raced erratically. A hot mist of sweat encased
her whole body.

"Yes, Neal," she moaned. "Oh, yes, my darling!"

Her words seemed to send a shock wave through him. She
felt him expand deep inside her, then came the slow, hot slide
she loved so well. In that moment, the heavens opened up and
swallowed her, leaving her pulsing with pleasure, sighing with
emotion, gasping for breath.

Suddenly, her moans stopped. She went limp in Neal's arms.
Total blackness closed in.

The last thing she heard was Neal's frantic voice. "Ginna?
Ginna! My God, what's happened? Ginna, come back to me!"

When Ginna woke up, she couldn't get her bearings. A
flourescent light above the bed all but blinded her. She blinked
and looked around. A man was standing beside her, but she
couldn't see his face clearly.

"How are you feeling, Ginna?" She recognized Dr. Kirkwood's voice.

"Okay, I guess." When she tried to sit up, her head spun
crazily.

"No. Lie still." He pressed her shoulder gently. "You shouldn't try to move yet."

"What happened?" In a flash of returning memory, she knew, and that knowledge made her blush. She looked down at herself. She was wrapped in one of the terrycloth robes from the pool house, not a stitch underneath it.

"Neal brought you to my office a few minutes ago. He said you fainted again. You're in my examining room. I thought you would be more comfortable lying down."

She looked about the spartan room. "Where is Neal?"

"I asked him to wait outside. He's very upset, Ginna."

"I fainted." She repeated the doctor's words, as if trying to make herself understand.

"Neal told me what happened." Kirkwood's voice was level, unaccusing.

Ginna grimaced and put her hand over her eyes. "God, I feel like such a fool!"

"No need for that. You simply put too much stress on your heart. Ginna, you're going to have to be more careful. I've called an ambulance to take you to the hospital in Winchester."

"No!" Now she did sit up. "I won't go! I'm fine!"

"Obviously, you are *not* fine, Ginna. I think you should go in for an EKG. If there are no immediate problems, they'll release you. We're required here at Swan's Quarter to send any patient to the hospital when there's an emergency—even a slight one. I've bent the rules in the past, because you were only a visitor. This time, you're staying here, so it's different. Besides, I'm very concerned about you."

Ginna's mind was spinning. Everything that had happened during the past hours seemed to be crowding in on her. She couldn't think straight. When she did get it all sorted out, she wondered just how much Neal had told Dr. Kirkwood.

Gauging him with her eyes, she said, "Neal and I are planning to get married."

The doctor remained expressionless. He only nodded.

"That's all right? For me to get married, I mean?"

"As long as you don't overdo on your honeymoon, Ginna."

Was he making fun of her? She looked closely at him. No.
He meant that. That was his *medical opinion.*

"Am I being fair?" she asked.

"About what?"

"Marrying Neal—marrying anyone."

Dr. Kirkwood smiled. "Get married, have kids, be happy."

"I'm not rushing into this, honest. I know what I'm doing.
I think . . ." Tears of uncertainty brimmed in her eyes.

"Does Neal love you?"

She nodded, trying to get the lump out of her throat.

"Do you love him?"

Again she nodded.

"Then what's the problem? He'll be a good husband, Ginna.
And any man would be happy with you by his side. If you
love him, I say go for it!"

"There's no *if!*" she cried. "I love him more than anything,
and Neal *does* love me!"

"I'm not disputing that, Ginna. You asked for my opinion
and I'm giving it to you, that's all."

She darted another quick glance at the doctor. "We made
love. Did he tell you?"

"No, not exactly. Not in so many words. But I assumed as
much by the way you were dressed. I didn't think you'd been
swimming this time of year."

"I'm a grown woman! I can do what I want." She didn't
sound like a grown woman. She sounded more like a scared
littled girl. "And, besides, it's my birthday."

"You're absolutely right, Ginna. I'm not sitting in judgment
of your actions. I'm only hoping that what you and Neal did
in the pool house didn't bring on this attack."

"If it did, it was worth it," she muttered under her breath.

Dr. Kirkwood smiled. "Let's get you ready to go to the
hospital now."

"I don't want to go!" She raised her voice this time.

The door opened and Neal came in just in time to hear her
protest. "Oh, but you *will* go! The doc said I could borrow his

car. I'll drive following the ambulance to the hospital and bring you back here, once they've done their tests."

She turned to Dr. Kirkwood. "Do I have to?"

"I think it's best, Ginna. Just to be on the safe side."

Neal came over to the bed, leaned down, and kissed her. "You'll be fine, darlin'. And I'll be right there with you. We'll be back here before you know it." He looked into her eyes and said, in the sweetest voice she had ever heard, "I love you, Ginna. Let me take good care of you."

Just then, they heard the wail of the ambulance siren, as it came up the drive. Ginna finally gave in. How could she not when Neal pleaded so tenderly?

Things did not go *fine,* as Neal and Dr. Kirkwood had promised. After the electrocardiogram, Ginna was informed that she would have to spend the night in the hospital, while they ran some further tests and observed her.

"Don't worry," Neal told her. "I'll stay right here with you all night."

But Dr. Kirkwood needed his car back, and the head nurse told Neal that he couldn't stay in her room, anyway, because he was not immediate family. Reluctantly, Neal kissed Ginna goodbye and left.

Sometime after midnight, the hospital's pokers and prodders finally finished with Ginna. She was returned to her room and tucked into bed. The nurse gave her a sleeping pill and stood by, while Ginna placed it in her mouth and faked a swallow. Once the woman left, Ginna quickly spit out the nasty-tasting pill. As exhausted as she was, she didn't want to sleep. She wanted to think, to plan, to weave lovely dreams about her life with Neal. She had waited so many years to find the right man. Didn't she deserve a little happiness? Her childhood had been bleak and lonely. Her adult life until now hadn't been much better. Now, at last, she had her chance to grab the brass ring— only this ring would be made of gold. A wedding band!

Her thoughts turned suddenly to Virginia Swan. She, too,

had been in love, had planned to marry. But those plans had gone awry, because of the war. Ginna wondered what Virginia's life had been like after she lost Channing. The two of them had been so happy and so much in love during their time in New York.

When had the blow come? How had Virginia handled it? There was so much Ginna still wanted to know about Virginia Swan and Channing McNeal.

"Tomorrow," she whispered, her eyelids growing heavy. "Neal and I will go back to the greenhouse tomorrow. I have to find out more about Virginia—*everything.*"

Neal's drive back to Swan's Quarter seemed excrutiatingly long and painful. This was his fault. He shouldn't have put so much pressure on her. If he loved her as much as he claimed he did, he should have been willing to give her time to think things through. He should have just cooled it, popped the question, then let her take all the time she needed to think things through.

"Damn!" He banged the steering wheel with his clenched fist. "Just rush in like a bulldozer! When are you going to learn, Frazier?"

He made up his mind that the best thing to do was back off. Give Ginna some space. Maybe he wouldn't even go to the hospital to pick her up tomorrow. Let them bring her back in an ambulance. It was driving him nuts being away from her, but he would have to get used to it, for the time being, anyway. She would be going back to her home—wherever that was— after tomorrow. He wouldn't mention marriage again. No more pushing! No more pressing!

By the time he pulled into the drive at Swan's Quarter, he was grim with resolve. The old blackness was creeping back into his soul. For a time this afternoon, he had allowed himself to believe that he had been saved from the plane crash to find Ginna, to love her and make her happy. Now that seemed to Neal no more than a cruel joke. He hadn't been saved for anything. It was just an accident. One of Fate's pointless little twists.

Leonard Kirkwood met him at the door. "Where's Ginna?"

Stupid question! Neal thought. But he managed to keep a civil tone when he answered, "They kept her at the hospital for observation. She's supposed to be released in the morning."

"Did they tell you anything about her condition?"

"Not a damn word! Seems, since I am not *immediate family*—only the guy who's in love with her—I'm not entitled to any information."

"That's routine hospital policy, Neal."

"Routine or not, it sucks! I'm half out of my mind, and those jokers are treating me like I'm some bum off the streets who just happened in to ask nosey questions."

"Come on to my office, Neal. You look like you could use a drink."

"Don't mind if I do. It's been a long night, and it looks to get longer yet."

Once they were settled in the doctor's comfortable office, both sipping bourbon-and-branch, Kirkwood broke the silence. "Ginna told me you've asked her to marry you."

Neal nodded. "I did, and she said yes."

"You don't think the two of you are rushing this a bit?"

"What if we are?" he snapped, not wanting to hear it.

"Well, you *are* here for treatment, Neal. Do you think you're ready to deal with a new situation, when all your old doubts and guilt are still unresolved?"

Neal put down his glass and leaned forward toward Kirkwood, his eyes narrowed, his face grim. "Listen, Doc, you got two choices here—assign me to a loony bin or let me live my own life. Sure, I've got problems, probably some that will never get resolved. But I can deal with them as long as I have Ginna. I love that woman like I've never loved anybody in my life. I am going to marry her! *Understand?*"

"I only wanted to make sure you had thought this through."

"What's to think through? We're in love. We want to be together."

"And Ginna feels the same way?"

"I can guaran-damn-tee it! We've both been drifting around all our lives, trying to find each other. Now, at long last, we have. This is the real thing, Doc, no doubt about it." Neal wished he could be as certain as he sounded.

The doctor smiled. "It's nice, isn't it? Love, I mean."

"Best medicine in the world."

"I envy the two of you. I'm still looking for that special someone."

Neal brightened. "Then you won't stand in our way?"

Kirkwood offered his hand in congratulations. "Of course not, Neal. I couldn't, even if I thought you two were making a mistake. I don't think that. Ginna's a special lady. I've hoped for a long time that she could find happiness with someone. I'll admit that for a while, several years ago, I thought—or hoped—I might be the one. But she never felt anything for me. I gave up on that long ago. I wish you both a happy life together and all the luck in the world."

"Thanks, Doc." Neal grinned and pumped Kirkwood's hand.

"If you want to borrow my car again in the morning to go to the hospital and pick her up . . ."

Neal waved the offer away. "No. It'll be better if she comes back in the ambulance. I don't want to crowd her. My pushing may be what brought on her fainting spell. See? I think I have this thing figured out. It's like an escape mechanism for Ginna. When she doesn't want to face something or be rushed into something, she just tunes out. Faints. And, I admit, I was pushing her pretty hard for an answer. A woman needs time. I realize that now. I won't make the same mistake again."

"Well, if you're sure." Kirkwood wasn't so certain that Neal was making the right choice. Ginna was bound to be disappointed when he didn't show up to bring her back to Swan's Quarter.

"I know what's best for the woman I love. You can count on that."

"Very well." The doctor rose. "I'll see you in the morning, then."

After Neal left, Kirkwood sat back down at his desk. He had found out what he wanted to know. They *were* planning to get married. There was no doubt that Ginna would be good for Neal, snap him out of his depression and back into the normal world. He only hoped that Neal's love could heal Ginna as well.

"What do you mean, I have to go home in an ambulance?" Ginna was fit to be tied. She had had a terrible night, filled with worries and self-doubts. Her one ray of hope had been the thought of seeing Neal, first thing this morning. Now they were telling her he wasn't coming.

"I'm sorry, Miss Jones, but Dr. Kirkwood called and said Mr. Frazier wouldn't be coming this morning. He said to send you on back to Swan's Quarter the same way you came." The nurse, a kind-faced, chocolate mountain of a woman, gave Ginna a broad smile. "That's some fine looking young man you got yourself, if you don't mind my saying so, ma'am. And he is crazy about you! He pitched himself one royal fit last night when the doctor told him he couldn't stay in your room 'cause he wasn't family."

The nurse's chatty tone calmed Ginna. "We'll be family, soon enough. We're getting married."

"Oh, my, that's nice! When's the big day?"

"We haven't set a date yet, but it will be soon."

"Will you be getting married at Swan's Quarter? There hasn't been a wedding there that I know of, since Miss Agnes Willingham married Mr. Rodney Swan back before the war. My great-great-auntie worked for the Swans back then. Story passed down in my family says that was the grandest wedding ever held in Frederick County. I reckon it was a sad day, too, though."

"You know it was supposed to be a double wedding?"

The nurse, Rosene, nodded solemnly. "Everybody around

these parts has heard the tale of poor Miss Virginia and her grave disappointment. She must have been one sad lady on that day.''

Rosene's comments piqued Ginna's curiosity. "I don't know the whole story. What happened to Miss Virginia after that?''

"The story goes, she stayed on at Swan's Quarter with her mama and some of the other relatives, all through the war. I reckon she figured once the fighting was over, she and Mr. McNeal might get to marry after all, if he made it through the war alive.''

"And did he?'' Ginna asked breathlessly.

Rosene narrowed her eyes. "I don't rightly know, ma'am.''

"Then you don't know what happened to Virginia Swan, either?''

The nurse shook her head. She was about to say something, when the orderlies came for Ginna. Rosene waved goodbye and disappeared with a swish of white nylon, as they wheeled her patient away to the waiting ambulance.

All during the fast ride back to Swan's Quarter, Ginna pondered the fate of Virginia Swan. Again, she vowed to revisit the greenhouse and find out more about the couple, who seemed the mirror images of herself and Neal from out of the past.

Dr. Kirkwood was on the veranda when they arrived, along with Pansy, Elspeth, Sister, and Marcellus Lynch. Ginna looked all about, but there was no sign of Neal.

"Land sakes, we were worried about you, child,'' Elspeth said, stroking Ginna's hand.

"We didn't sleep a wink all night,'' Sister added.

Then Pansy, beaming and dabbing at happy tears, leaned over Ginna. "Is it true?'' she whispered. "Are you and that nice Mr. Neal Frazier really getting married?''

"Ladies!'' Dr. Kirkwood interrupted. "Please let these men get Ginna to her room. After she has rested from her ride, you can visit her.''

Ginna reached out and gripped the doctor's sleeve. "Where's Neal?''

The frown on Kirkwood's face told Ginna what the answer

would be. "I don't know. I haven't seen him around this morning."

"Tell him I have to talk to him," she begged.

"After you've rested."

"No! *Now!*" she insisted.

"Stay calm, Ginna. I'll find him and send him up to see you."

With a sigh of relief, she lay back on the stretcher and motioned that she was ready to go inside.

She had been in her bed, alone and restless, for nearly a half-hour before she heard a soft knock at her door.

"Who is it?"

"Neal. The doc said you wanted to talk to me."

"Oh, Neal!" she cried. "Come in!"

She was propped up on her pillows, her arms outstretched for a hug when Neal slipped in the door. But he made no move to embrace her. Instead, he stood across the room, looking solemn and a little uncomfortable.

"How are you feeling?" he asked at length.

"All right, I guess." She started to tell him that she would feel a lot better if he would come hold her and kiss her. Something about his expression stopped her from saying that, though.

"I was really worried about you last night, Ginna. They wouldn't tell me anything."

She forced a laugh. "I don't think there was much to tell, Neal. I fainted. You know that. As far as anyone told me, all the tests were normal." Now she chuckled out loud. "Tell me, when was the last time you had a woman swoon in your arms from sheer ecstasy?"

"Well, it won't happen again?"

She wasn't sure what he meant by that, but the words stabbed like a knife through her heart. Was he merely saying that he didn't want her to faint again? Or did he mean he had no intentions of making love with her a second time? Or, *worse yet*, had Neal decided that he didn't want to marry her, after all?

"Neal, come here." She patted the bed beside her. "Come sit with me, please."

He did as she asked, albeit hesitantly. When he was perched on the edge of the bed next to her, she reached out and took his hand. For a few moments, neither of them uttered a word.

"Tell me what's wrong, Neal. If you've decided that last night was all a big mistake, tell me now. Don't lead me on. It will only hurt more."

He turned and stared into her eyes, his face a mask of misery. "Is that what you think, Ginna? That we made a mistake?" He looked away. "I should have figured. A nice lady like you and a bum like me. You deserve better."

She brought his hand to her lips and kissed his knuckles. "You fool!" she said softly. "I told you I love you. I do! That's not a phrase I use lightly. Nothing's changed about the way I feel. If anything, I'm more sure than I was last night."

He leaned down and kissed her very softly.

"Don't, Ginna," he whispered. "Don't say another word right now. I was wrong to push you so hard last night. I caused your fainting spell. I don't ever want to hurt you again. God, if anything happened to you, I don't know what I'd do! So I want you to think about this some more. Think about last night and next week and next year. Think about what you *really* want to do with the rest of your life. See if I fit into the picture. I want you to be sure—as sure as I am."

He kissed her again, before she could answer. It was a long, lazy kiss that made her dizzy and set her on fire. She wanted him—right here, right now. But he drew away, stood, and turned toward the door.

"Neal, don't go," she begged.

"Doctor's orders. He said I could stay five minutes, no more."

"Listen to me, Neal. I want you to meet me in the greenhouse at eleven forty-five."

"Kirkwood said he wants you to stay in bed today."

"Never mind what he says. This is important. I want to

see Zee's ghosts again. I have to find out about something—
someone. And I need you with me. Will you come?''

Neal hesitated, then a slow smile lit his face. ''It'll be hell
to pay, if the doc finds out.''

''He won't find out. I'll slip down the back way, the old
servants' stairs. You will meet me, won't you?''

Neal nodded, still smiling. ''And where do you intend to
take me this time, *Miss Swan?* Back to New York or to some
secret destination?''

''You know!'' she exclaimed.

''Bits and pieces. A lot of what happened in the greenhouse
came back to me last night. I couldn't sleep, I was so worried
about you. Then I got to thinking what that old man told me
about the fourth dimension. You know how it is, once you start
thinking. Your mind wanders and things sort of start linking
up and filling in the whole picture. I'm still missing some
pieces, but I have an idea that you and I are sort of repeating
history. Am I close?''

''I don't know, Neal. I'm not sure what's happening, either.
But I do know we have to go back. I must find out what
happened to Virginia Swan.''

He touched his lips and tossed the kiss her way. ''The greenhouse, then, eleven forty-five.'' He opened the door as if to
leave, then turned back for a moment. ''By the way, darlin', I
almost forgot. I *love you!''*

After Neal left, Ginna hugged her pillow to her chest and
rocked back and forth. For no reason she could fathom, she
was crying suddenly, weeping rivers of melancholy, aching
tears.

''Oh, Neal, my darling,'' she whimpered, ''what's to become
of us? What does all this mean?''

She couldn't guess at the moment, but she vowed to do
everything in her power to find out.

Chapter Eight

Neal was waiting when Ginna arrived at the greenhouse. She felt a little shaky, but the sight of him reassured her and gave her strength.

"I sent old Zee on an errand, so we'd have the place all to ourselves," Neal said. Reaching out to take her hand, he drew her close and gave her a sound hug.

"Hm-m-m," she sighed. "I needed you to hold me earlier. Why didn't you?"

"Couldn't trust myself with you in bed, looking so cool and tempting. You don't know what you do to me. I wouldn't have been able to stop with a hug, darlin'."

"I wouldn't have wanted you to stop, either," she whispered, snuggling closer into his arms with a sigh.

"It's almost time," Neal said. "The ghosts should appear any minute now."

"Neal, how much do you remember of what happened yesterday? Tell me quickly, before the sun touches the glass."

"I guess I remember just about all of it. I tried to deny it at first—tell myself it was some kind of hallucination or daydream. But the more I think about it, the more real it seems.

You were Virginia Swan, weren't you, Ginna? And I was Channing McNeal. But I still don't understand. How did it happen? Why?''

''I'm not sure we're meant to know the answers to those questions, Neal. But maybe we'll understand, in time, if we explore further and learn more about Virginia and Channing and the world they lived in.''

Neal had set his watch alarm to go off at eleven minutes to noon. The small, repeating beeper sounded just then. They fell silent and turned toward the old glass plate negative of Virginia and Channing, waiting for the flash that would bring the pair of lovers back to life through them. The sun's rays found their mark and, for an instant, the ghosts of that long-ago couple shimmered before Ginna and Neal, seeming almost alive.

Ginna squeezed Neal's hand. ''I'll see you on the other side.''

''In the fourth dimension.''

Neal's words were the last sound in the greenhouse, before time stopped at Swan's Quarter.

Ginna soon found that she was mistaken about seeing Neal somewhere across time. When she found herself again in Virginia's body, neither Neal nor Channing was anywhere to be seen. She was alone with another young woman in the rose garden at Swan's Quarter. Both of them wore wide-brimmed straw bonnets that tied under their chins. They were dressed in pastel gingham gowns with yards-wide skirts. With gloved hands, they snipped colorful roses from the luxuriant bushes. A small black boy in knee pants and a ragged shirt followed along behind them, carrying a basket to hold their cut flowers.

''Now, don't you dawdle, Teebo,'' Virginia's companion scolded gently when she turned to see the little servant chasing a butterfly, instead of tending to his duties.

Virginia laughed—a happy, carefree sound. ''Let him play, Agnes. Goodness sakes, it won't be long before he's in the fields stripping tobacco.''

''He should learn to mind his business now, if he's to make a good field hand.''

Agnes was a petite young woman with ebony hair and sleepy gray-green eyes. She had a creamy complexion that had never felt the kiss of the sun. Rodney's fiancée had never climbed a tree, never ridden a horse, never done anything in her seventeen years that was less than perfectly ladylike. Often in the past, when Melora Swan had scolded her daughter for her tomboy ways, Agnes Willingham was the example Virginia's mother held up to her to be emulated. Even so, the two girls had always been close friends, and soon they would share their wedding day. Soon they would become sisters.

Nearly a month had passed since the Swans' return from New York. The days were rushing by, now. As Virginia and Agnes and their mothers prepared trousseaus and made wedding plans, each day seemed more exciting than the one before. To both girls, this time seemed the happiest of their lives, spinning away in a whirl of springtime parties and sunny, dream-filled days. The two young women ignored the men of the family, as they gathered in plantation libraries or in the meeting house in Winchester to talk heatedly of secession, or when they rode off to the fairgrounds to drill their companies, preparing them for war. War talk and wedding preparations didn't mix. Besides, who would want to spoil such a lovely spring with thoughts of the coming conflict?

"What do you hear from Channing?" Agnes asked, as she snipped a particularly beautiful blood-red rose.

"I received a letter only yesterday. Mr. Tiffany has sent my ring to Channing. He says it's quite lovely, and he can hardly wait to see it on my finger."

"Only *quite* lovely?" Agnes slipped off her gardening glove and held up her own engagement ring to catch the light. The diamond flashed a rainbow of brilliance. Rodney had given it to her on Christmas Day.

"Channing wanted me to have a diamond, like yours. He was not entirely pleased that I chose an opal instead. For him to say it is 'quite lovely' must mean that it is indeed magnificent."

"When will he be sending it to you?"

Virginia smiled. Agnes was at her most competitive this

morning. She knew the answer to that question well enough, but Virginia replied just the same. "He won't be sending it. He plans to give it to me when we go up to West Point for the commencement ceremonies next month."

"La, dear, how can you abide the wait?"

"The wait will make the moment all the sweeter when it comes."

"You mean *if* it comes."

Virginia whipped around to stare at Agnes. "Whatever do you mean?"

A small smile of triumph curved Agnes's thin lips. She always took pride in her ability to ruffle Virginia's feathers. "My daddy says we'll be at war before my Rodney and your Channing finish at the Academy. He says word could come any day—*any minute*—that the first shots have been fired. He is certain that's all Governor Letcher is waiting for, before he insists that Virginia secede from the Union. When that happens, our men will ride home to marry us quickly, before they go into battle. Rodney said as much in the letter I received from him this very morning."

Virginia kept cutting roses, her lips pursed tightly in annoyed silence. She refused to respond to Agnes's needling. And she refused to allow herself to think about war. Surely the cooler heads in Washington would prevail and figure out a way to bring the states back together peacefully. Thinking of the alternative turned her heart to ice. She knew all too well Channing's feelings on the subject and where his loyalties lay.

Both women were distracted from their roses and their thoughts, when a rider came charging up the lane past the swan pond at such a furious pace that the old cob and his mate flapped their wings in distress. The man was a total stranger— dirty, disheveled, and wild-eyed. His horse was lathered and muddy, stumbling with exhaustion.

"Who on earth could that be?" Agnes wondered, aloud.

"I have no idea."

"Just look at the beggar, Virginia. Why, he's riding right up to the front veranda! I'm surprised your mother would allow his sort at the company entrance. Surely, Miz Melora will have one of the servants tell him to go around to the back door.''

However, as the two young women watched, Colonel Swan himself burst out of the front door to greet the man, then ushered his filthy visitor right into the house.

''Well, my stars!'' Agnes exclaimed. ''Will you look at that?''

A dark cloud drifted over the bright sun just then, draining the riot of color from the rose garden and threatening a violent springtime storm.

''We had better go in, now,'' Virginia said. The calm quiet of her voice betrayed none of the cold fear raging through her. Fear for the man she loved was uppermost in her mind. Agnes's statement earlier about Governor John Letcher and his determination to join the Confederacy focused her thoughts on facts she had been trying desperately to ignore. She had an awful feeling that her whole world was about to come crashing down around her.

By the time Virginia and Agnes entered the front hallway, Jedediah Swan and his mysterious visitor were closeted together in the library, but the sounds of their excited voices boomed through the door.

''The Palmetto troops have fired on Fort Sumter, sir. A thirty-three hour seige. Three thousand shells fired from thirty guns and eighteen mortars. The officer in charge of the fort, Major Anderson, surrendered at two-thirty last Saturday afternoon. This is the start of it, sir. Governor Letcher is calling an emergency meeting in Richmond.''

''God's teeth and eyeballs, I knew it would come!'' the girls heard Colonel Swan shout, his voice quaking with excitement. ''Our state won't be long in joining the fray. I'll leave for Richmond this minute. And, if I know my son Rodney, he'll be on his way home from West Point, the minute he hears the news. My cavalry will be ready to ride when the first call comes.''

Virginia felt tears sting her eyes. The worst had come to pass. Now what? Would Channing come home with Rodney to join her father's cavalry unit? Or was this the end—the end of *everything?*

Neal panicked.

He had been holding Ginna's hand when the flash filled the greenhouse. He had expected to be with her when the light faded. But once the dust settled, he found himself all alone. For a few confused moments, he thought he was still at Swan's Quarter, still in the twentieth century. A quick check of himself, however, told him he was once more Channing McNeal, dressed in his trim cadet uniform, alone in his spartan room in the barracks at West Point. He was writing a letter to Virginia Swan.

For a time he sat very still, trying to get his bearings, trying to think where Ginna might be. He glanced down at the unfinished letter on his desk, at the pressed forsythia blossoms Channing had meant to send to his love.

                                                      20 April 1861

My dearest Virginia,

By the time you receive this, I am sure you will be aware of the dire news from South Carolina. My Southern classmates here are saying this is the beginning. I fear, instead, that it is the end, at least of the life that we have known in our beloved home state. But, believe me, my darling, nothing can possibly put an end to the depth of my love for you. Be assured, my dearest, that no cannon shot—not even one heard round the world—can alter my feelings for you, or my determination to make you my wife and spend the rest of my life with you. Without you, Virginia, I am no longer of this place and time. I have no place in this world without you. I would be only a gray, formless spirit, drifting alone and aimlessly in the fourth dimension, that realm of lost souls and half-lives. Be assured, my love, that this war, should it come, will never touch our affection for each other. No matter

what the future days and months might bring, I will be
at Swan's Quarter on our appointed date to see you
descend the grand staircase on your father's arm. I will
make you my wife, my mate for life, in the swans' way—
ever faithful, ever caring, ever yours.

Neal took up Channing's pen to finish his letter to Virginia,
but there was so much shouting and cheering from the quadrangle that he couldn't hear himself think. Before he could dip
the nib into the inkwell, Rodney Swan burst into the room,
without so much as a knock.

"Channing, old man, how goes it?" The big, blond, burly
Virginian was bursting with excitement, bristling with a hawk-
like verve.

"It goes less than well," Channing answered, grimly.

"Haven't you heard? The Virginia legislature has finally
recognized the Confederacy. They're sitting in Richmond right
now, drawing up a proclamation of secession. Since the surrender of Fort Sumter, all hell's broken loose. Superintendent
Bowman has announced that any cadet who wants to can leave
immediately for home. That's us, old buddy!"

"You mean classes have been suspended?" Channing was
not pleased with Rodney's news. He had worked too long and
hard for his degree and his commission in the United States
Army to have it all snatched away at the eleventh hour by the
rash act of a group of militiamen nearly a thousand miles to
the south.

"There'll still be classes, commencement, too, if there's
anyone left here to graduate. But, hell, who can study at a time
like this? As for our commissions, the rank we get will be
determined by the Confederacy now, not the U.S. Army. Rumor
has it that officers are resigning right and left to answer the
call of the South. Even Lieutenant Colonel Lee."

"Robert E. Lee?" Channing was sure Rodney must be making this up. Everyone knew President Lincoln had offered Lee
command of the Federal forces.

"That's right. He turned old Lincoln down flat and resigned

from the Army. There's a copy of the letter Lee wrote to Winfield Scott posted in the chapel. I don't remember all of it, but one line made his intentions quite clear.'' Rodney paused, frowning, trying to recall Lee's exact words. "He wrote, 'Save in defense of my native state, I never desire again to draw my sword.' So, he's with us, for sure."

"Colonel Lee?" Channing muttered, shaking his head, still trying to grasp this disturbing reality. He couldn't believe it. The man was his idol, a former superintendent of the Military Academy, a hero of the Mexican War.

"And Lee's not the only one joining up to fight for our Cause. Jubal Early, John Bell Hood, Joseph Wheeler, Benjamin Helm, Theophilus Holmes, John Magruder, Joseph E. Johnston—the list goes on and on. Even Samuel Jones, one of the instructors right here at the Point—but he's a loyal Virginian from Powhatan County, so that's no surprise. Of course, the West Pointers will get the choicest commands in the Confederate Army. Why, I'll bet Pa will jump us both to majors right at the get-go, since we're riding with him. Come on, McNeal! Quit mooning over that letter. You'll be bedding Virginia before the mail can reach her. I'm packing now and heading home on the first stage out of here. Get your gear together. We're going to war!''

Channing's heart went cold and colder, as his listened to his boyhood friend talk excitedly of the coming conflict. The moment of decision had arrived, the moment he had dreaded for months. *Virginia!* Both the woman and the state were uppermost in his mind and his heart. He loved them both, which made this all the harder.

"Come on, man!" Rodney boomed. "What are you waiting for? If we don't move fast, we'll miss our ride."

"I'm not going," Channing said quietly, his composure painfully enforced.

"What the hell are you talking about? Of course you are! What's gotten into you, Chan? This is what we've all been waiting for, training for, praying for."

Channing stood and stared at his friend, with dark, pleading eyes. "We've come too far, Rodney. Stay. Finish classes. There'll be plenty of time. There'll be plenty of war to go around."

"You damn idiot!" Rodney's face bloomed bright red, a mixture of excitement and frustration. "We'll whip the Yankees in a month. You think I'm going to sit up here *studying* the war tactics of Napoleon and Caesar, when I could be out there *using* them against the Yankees? Pa would skin me alive if I stayed. Besides, I don't want to miss a lick. I can't wait to shoot my first blue-belly!"

A grim scene formed in Channing's mind—through a screen of smoke and fire and chaos, he saw a face clenched in a grimace of hate, a face above a gun, a gun pointed at his own heart. He knew that face well. It was the face of his friend, his classmate, his brother. It was Rodney Swan's face.

Channing stared down at his unfinished letter to Virginia and shook his head slowly. "I can't leave now, Rodney. I just can't."

"Well, by damn, sit here, then! Let the world and the glory pass you by. Not me! I'm going home. I'm going to marry Agnes and leave her carrying my son, and then I'm going to mount one of Pa's blooded horses and ride off singing 'Dixie' and waving the Stars and Bars." He gripped an imaginary flagstaff and made great sweeping motions with his invisible banner. "Hail to Virginia!" he cried. "Hail to the South! Hail to our Cause!"

Channing knew there was no way he could dissuade Rodney from his plan to leave West Point. He rose, clasped the other man's hand in solemn farewell, and said in a grim tone, "Take care, my friend. When you get home, tell your sister that I will be there soon to make her my wife. Tell her I love her, won't you?"

The two men parted without Channing's having confided in his friend that he remained loyal to the Union. He couldn't yet bring himself to confess aloud what he had known all along in his heart of hearts—that as much as he loved his home state, he loved the Union more. He would wait until after graduation.

He would tell Virginia first and then confess his plans to all the others. Maybe Rodney's leaving was premature. Maybe there would be no war after all.

"And maybe hell will freeze over!" he said, in grim response to his own hopeless thoughts.

Channing went back to his letter, but the words wouldn't come. *How* would he tell Virginia? And what would his decision do to their lives?

Commencement ceremonies were held on a Monday, the sixth of May. Although Second Lieutenant Channing Russell McNeal had attained his goal at long last, the day was not what he had hoped for. Two hundred seventy-eight cadets had been at the Academy the previous November, eighty-six of them from the South. Sixty-five of his Southern brothers—many, like Rodney, who would have graduated with the Class of '61—had left West Point to fight for the Confederacy. Channing missed his comrades.

Since the current in the States was highly uncertain, neither the Swans nor the McNeals traveled North to witness and help celebrate the occasion. Channing missed not having his family with him. Most of all, he missed Virginia. He carried her ring with him everywhere. He had so hoped to be able to slip it on her finger on this glorious day in May. Now he would have to wait until right before their wedding, but that was less than a month away. He had waited this long; he could wait a little longer. All he thought about now was getting back home to her. He concentrated on his love and pushed all the troubling thoughts from his mind.

Channing received a congratulatory letter from his father, urging him to hurry home as soon as possible, after the ceremonies. Mr. McNeal said that Colonel Swan was waiting for Channing's return, so that his cavalry unit could be on its way. They hoped to see their first battle before the month was out. Channing's father also expressed his pride in his son's accomplishment in graduating from West Point, near the top of his

class, and his eagerness for Channing to return South to distin-
guish himself on the field of battle against the Northern
invaders.

In spite of his eagerness to see Virginia again, his father's
final statement was uppermost in Channing's mind, as he rode
under the arched entrance to Swan's Quarter. The moment he
had most looked forward to and most dreaded had come.

Virginia got up and stretched. She had put in a long morning,
working on her quilt cover. Now that it was finished, she felt
only disappointment, not the sense of accomplishment that she
had hoped for.

"It's not the quilt's fault," she sighed. "It's lovely." She
fingered her handiwork, but her thoughts were all of Channing.
Where could he be? Why hadn't she heard from him since that
last letter over a week ago—the one with the pressed forsythia
enclosed? She fingered the silver locket at her throat and smiled.
One of the golden-yellow flowers was now tucked inside, oppo-
site the miniature of Channing.

Suddenly, she heard a stir of excitement outside—dogs bark-
ing, geese honking, and the raucous chatter of slave children
on the front lawn. Before she could reach her window to look
out, she heard someone calling her name.

"Miss Virginia! Miss Virginia!" It was old Polly, the cook.
"He done come home. You best get on down here!"

A quick glance from her window told Virginia *who* had
come. *"Channing!"* she cried. "It's Channing! I can't believe
it!"

She tore out of her room and down the stairs. The front door
banged behind her so hard that it nearly came off its hinges.
She flew into his arms, sobbing his name.

He was dusty and sweaty, after his long ride from Washington, but Virginia didn't care. He was home! They were together
again! At last!

"Virginia, my darlin'," he whispered against her fragrant
hair. "It's been so long."

"Oh, Channing, I thought you'd never come! I've spent practically the whole last week on this veranda watching for you. I wanted to see you the minute you turned into the lane. I had it all planned. I was going to meet you by the swan pond. Then you go and sneak up on me, surprise me on the one day I decide to stay in and work on my quilt."

He laughed and hugged her tighter. "I'll ride back to Washington and give you another chance, if you want me to."

She leaned back in his arms and gave him a stern look. "Oh, no, you won't! I'm not letting you out of my sight until we're married."

"I think you'll have to talk to our mothers about that, darlin'. I'm pretty sure they'll want me cleaned up and shining for our wedding, and I don't think they'll approve of you sitting in on my bath."

She turned to cover her blush and tugged his hand. "Come inside. We have the house all to ourselves. Father and the boys are out drilling, and Mother is napping. I want to hear *everything.*"

Once they were in the parlor with the door almost closed, Virginia forgot about her need to hear what he had to say. When he took her into his arms this time, she was much more interested in being kissed—over and over and over again. By the time Channing finished with her, she felt flushed to her toes. She ached for him so that all sorts of lovely, wicked thoughts came to mind. She decided she wouldn't object at all if Channing placed her on the narrow gilt-trimmed couch and tossed her skirts right over her head.

"I know that look," he teased. "You're thinking naughty thoughts, Virginia Swan."

She laughed behind her hand. "It's all right, Channing darling. They're all about you."

He drew her close again. "Tell me," he whispered, letting his hand graze her tight, heaven-blue bodice.

She shivered against him. "Oh, I couldn't! Not now."

"Will you tell me on our wedding night?"

He pulled her closer against his hard, hot body. She almost

moaned aloud. She had waited so long to feel his nearness again.

"On our wedding night it won't matter. We'll have a big feather bed to share."

Without thinking, she glanced at the couch. Channing caught the look.

"Virginia! I'm surprised at you!" He kissed the blush on her cheeks, then whispered, "Besides, it would never work. That little old antique is far too fragile. We'd smash the poor thing to smithereens. We'd best wait for that feather bed on our wedding night."

"I know," she said in a serious tone. Then she looked up, drowning in the dark pools of his eyes. "But it's hard, Channing. We've waited so long. I love you. I *need* you."

Her words brought a lump to his throat and a bulge to his crotch. For a time, he couldn't answer. He simply held her, kissing her face, tracing the lace on her bodice with aching fingers.

Suddenly, he pulled back, his mind screaming a warning for him to stop before it was too late. Virginia seemed to share his reasoning, as well as his need. She stepped away, out of arm's reach.

"You must be thirsty after your long ride. I'm sure Father would offer you a drink if he were here."

Without waiting for Channing to answer, she went to the spirits chest and poured him a bourbon, then added water from a crystal pitcher. They settled on the fragile couch, but kept a safe distance between them.

"Now!" Viginia said. "Tell me everything, darlin'."

Channing quickly filled her in on all that had happened since Rodney's departure from West Point—the leave-taking of so many others, the quiet commencement ceremonies with so few graduates and even fewer guests, his long trip home.

"I wish I could have been there," she said, when he paused to take a sip of his drink. "Oh, Channing, I so wanted to see you graduate and receive your commission."

Only then did she notice that he wasn't in uniform. The

clothes he was wearing must be the ones he had worn when he left for the Academy over four years ago, she reasoned. The trousers were too short, the shirt and coat too tight.

"Channing, why are you in civilian clothes? You *are* a lieutenant now, aren't you?"

"*Second*," he emphasized. "A second lieutenant, darling. There's a difference."

A slow, knowing smile warmed her face. Of course! Channing would hardly wear the uniform of the United States Army, if he had come home to join her father's Confederate cavalry. And if that were the case, she could stop fretting. She would certainly worry, once he rode off to fight, but at least she wouldn't have to concern herself with a more immediate battle within her own family. She reached over and took his hand, then smiled into his eyes. She was about to tell him how relieved she was that he had changed his mind. He spoke first, however.

"Virginia, I have to talk to you, while we have some privacy. I had meant to give you your ring the moment I arrived, but I think you had better hear me out, first."

She nodded, all traces of her smile vanished. A thundering ache in her heart warned her that this was not going to be what she had hoped to hear.

"I think you know my feelings about this war, darlin'. I am against it with all my heart and soul. As much as I love you— that's how much I hate the thought of our country splitting apart. Because I feel this way, I have an obligation to do everything in my power to keep that from happening."

Virginia found her voice, as uncertain as it was. "Then you won't be riding with my father and brothers." It was not a question. She already knew the answer.

Channing looked away, out through the front windows, toward the swan pond. "I can't. This country, this very state, is the home of Washington, Madison, Jefferson."

"And the home of Robert E. Lee." She was sorry she had said that when she saw the wounded expression in Channing's eyes.

"Every man must answer to his own conscience. I would

never know another minute free from guilt if I took up arms against my own country. Can you understand, Virginia?''

She nodded, blinking back tears. ''May I have my ring now?''

''You still love me, after what I've just said?''

''With all my heart.'' She held her left hand toward him. ''My ring?''

Channing took her hand and showered it with kisses. Then he reached into his coat pocket and drew out a soft velvet bag. In the rays of the afternoon sun, the opal burned with lustrous fire and the diamonds shot sparks about the room. Slowly, lovingly, Channing placed it on her finger.

''It's even more beautiful than I remembered.''

Channing drew her into his arms. ''So are you, my dearest. So are you.''

When he kissed her this time, it was with a new depth of feeling. There was a bonding in their kiss. It seemed to make them one, from this moment on. Virginia realized she was weeping silent tears. Channing's eyes, too, were brimming. This was what life was all about—finding the one person who could complete the picture, and loving that person forevermore.

''Damn secession and hate and war!'' Channing said, in a low growl. Then his voice softened, as he looked at his fiancée and said, ''It will be all right, darlin'. You'll see. This war won't last three months. By Christmas, it will be only an unhappy memory. Maybe this is God's way of making us appreciate what we have. Who knows? But whatever happens, I'll always love you. Don't ever forget that.''

''How could I, Channing? How could I, when I love you so desperately?''

For a long time, they clung to each other in silence, both pondering troubled thoughts about the future.

Finally, Virginia spoke hesitantly. ''Channing? How will you tell the others? *When* will you tell them?''

He shook his head. ''I don't know. I just don't know. It's going to be hard, no matter how or when they hear the news.''

''Wait till after the wedding, after our first night together.''

When Virginia looked at Channing, she knew that wasn't

his plan. A new fear crept into her heart. Channing McNeal,
who had always been a part of her life and almost part of the
Swan family, was now the *enemy*. A damnyankee! A blue-
belly! And, worse than that, a turncoat Virginian. Her brothers,
who had always been his best friends, would now feel nothing
for him but contempt and scorn. Her father might even forbid
their marriage.

"Channing, you *mustn't* tell them before we're married!"
She clung to him, sobbing.

"We belong to each other, no matter what happens, Virginia." He spoke quietly, trying to soothe her, but she could
feel his heart thundering against hers. "Don't ever forget that,
darlin'. I love you, and that will *never* change."

Chapter Nine

Nothing was yet resolved when Channing left Virginia. He had imagined that the day he slipped the engagement ring on her finger would be one of the happiest of their lives. Instead, it had proved a sad event. His heart heavy, he rode the short distance to Belle Grove. Always before, his homecomings had been joyous occasions. His parents and sisters had been waiting a long time to see him. He had not been home since the Christmas holidays. Yet he dreaded this reunion.

As his horse plodded along, in no hurry, since neither was its rider, Channing thought back to those happy days of his last visit home—parties and balls and the traditional Christmas Eve bonfire. Then New Year's Day, when he had made the rounds to pay calls on all his friends. He had saved the best stop for last, eager to savor his time at Swan's Quarter with Virginia and her family.

Together, Channing and Virginia had decided that the first day of the New Year was the perfect time to declare their intentions to their families. Melora Swan had long suspected what was coming. Jedediah Swan had long hoped. Their announcement had been greeted with enthusiasm and joy. Mrs.

Swan had wept happily, as she embraced the man who would be her son-in-law. As for Colonel Swan, instead of the stern talk usually delivered by the fathers of young women, reserved for their young men, Jedediah had shown Channing into the library, closed the door, then bellowed delightedly, "By damn, son, I couldn't be more pleased. I've hoped from the moment my Virginia was born that someday the two of you would tie the knot. With you siring them, I can count on fine, strong grandsons—at least a dozen, I vow. Join me in a toast to that happy thought, won't you?"

Channing almost smiled at the memory of that glorious day, over five months ago. But even the ghost of a smile vanished when he thought about what lay ahead. He had grave doubts that Colonel Swan would offer him a drink when he heard this latest news. More likely, Virginia's father would dash a pony of bourbon into her fiancé's face. But surely Jedediah Swan would not demand that the wedding be canceled. Not that! It would be too extreme, even for these extreme circumstances.

The worry lingered, gnawing at his heart and his gut. Channing brightened a bit, as he turned into the wide, tree-lined lane that led to Belle Grove. The thought of coming home never failed to gladden his heart. The place held so many happy memories of his childhood. Every creek brought to mind long, lazy summer afternoons of dangling a worm at the end of his pole, while he lay in the tall, sweet grass drowsing under drifting puffs of cloud. Every tree recalled to mind a secret haunt, a hideout where he and the Swan brothers had planned mock battles to be fought in the peach orchard or among the tall rows of corn. How could he have known back then, in those sunny, carefree days of his youth, that eventually the battles would be all too real? There seemed no way to escape that pain.

Thoughts of the letter from his father brought a deeper concern to Channing. Thompson McNeal clearly expected his son to ride off to war with the men of Swan's Quarter. Before Channing told another soul of his plans, he owed it to his father to explain his decision. He was the one person Channing had always been able to confide in. Thompson McNeal was a level-headed, straight-talking Scotsman. He had given his only son good advice all his life. Now, as never before, Channing needed the opinion of someone older and wiser, someone he could trust.

Instead of dismounting and going into the house, where he guessed his mother and sisters would be waiting with open arms, happy tears, and a fresh-baked apple pie, Channing turned his horse toward the tobacco fields. This time of day, he knew that was where he would find his father.

Sure enough, Channing spied the battered old straw planter's hat bobbing mid-field in the distance. As he drew nearer, the erect form of his solid Scottish father came into clear view. Channing noted with pride that the old man still sat his mount as though he and the animal were one.

"Hallo!" Channing hailed, rising in the saddle to wave.

McNeal turned to see who was calling. When he spied his son, the Scotsman's leathery tanned face broke in a broad grin.

"So, you've come home at last, lad. Your mother's no doubt taken to her bed by now with a wine-soaked cloth over her eyes from all the excitement."

Channing and his father met at the edge of the field and dismounted. They first shook hands, then exchanged an awkward, rough embrace, as men will.

"I've seen neither Mother nor the girls yet, Father. I needed a word with you first."

Quick to note the somber tone in his son's voice, McNeal said, "There's a problem then, is there?"

Channing nodded. "I'm afraid so. One that may have no solution."

Thompson clucked his tongue. " 'He has a sliddery grip that has an eel by the tail.' "

An unbidden smile stole over Channing's face. His father had an old Scottish proverb to suit every occasion. And this situation, he had to admit, was a *sliddery* one, indeed.

"So? Out with it, lad. Why the *lang* face?"

Channing made a loose fist of his right hand and held up his

Academy ring for his father's inspection. "This band of gold and the four long years at the Point that it represents."

McNeal stared at his son's West Point ring and nodded. " 'Tis a fine symbol of your accomplishments, Channing my boy. 'Tis also, I'm guessing, a constant reminder of what the Military Academy stands for in your mind and heart. I can see your dilemma."

"Not the half of it, Poppa." In his emotional state, Channing reverted to his childhood name for his father. "I received your letter upon commencement day. I accepted your congratulations gladly, but some of your statements left me in a quandary. I have obeyed you as best I could all my life. For the first time, I may have to disappoint you."

McNeal rubbed at the bristle of whiskers on his chin. "I cannot think of a way in which you could do that, son. You'll have to tell me what's on your mind."

"This talk of war."

" 'Tis more than talk, I'm bound."

"Then I must tell you of my decision—difficult as it is— right now. You won't be pleased, Father, but a man must make his own choices."

A long, silence followed before McNeal said, " 'Twould seem a simple choice, son. North or South? Your country or your state?"

"You've guessed my problem." Channing stared at his father, wondering if he had been born with a caul to give him second sight.

"What else could you be deciding at such a time as this? You're not the only one hereabouts who finds himself faced with that choice. I can't say I'm surprised, son. Either way, I'll be proud that you bear my name."

"I thank you for your understanding, Father." Channing shook his head sadly. "But there's much more at stake here, I'm afraid, than with which side I'll cast my lot in the coming conflict."

"Then spit it out, lad. Nothing was ever decided by chasing the problem to Glasgow and back."

"It's Virginia, Father. I want to marry her more than I've ever wanted anything in my life. I *will* marry her!"

"Aye," McNeal nodded, agreeably. "He drives a good wagon load into his farm that gets a good wife, and there'd be none better for you than Miss Virginia Swan. You've no need to waste your time convincing me of that. Her folks feel the same toward you, I vow."

"They *felt* the same toward me. But now . . ."

Thompson McNeal's bushy eyebrows drew down like a snow-frosted hedgerow above his hawkish nose. "The Colonel's withdrawn his permission, then?"

"Not yet. He doesn't know of my plans."

"And what exactly are your plans, Channing? Are you bound and determined to cast your allegiance with the Union, even at the cost of losing the woman you love?"

Channing replied quietly, but firmly. "I won't lose her, but this country has been good to us, Father. Many's the time you've told me about your poor childhood back in Scotland."

McNeal sighed, a touch of moisture coming to his bright eyes at the mention of his Mother Country. *"'A guid tale's nane the waur o' bein' twice tauld.'"*

"I've heard that good tale more than twice, Father. The crowded, thatched-roof cottage, where you and all your brothers and sisters were raised, where most of them died from the fever or starvation before they were near-grown. Your dear, long-suffering mother, working from dark to dark. Your own father, drifting from town to town in search of honest work. And then you came here, working for your passage across the Atlantic, hiring yourself out to other landowners, until you could save enough to buy a few acres and a few more." Channing stood tall and spread his arms to encompass Belle Grove's wide expanse. "And finally, *all this, all yours!* What other country in the world could have offered a penniless lad from Scotland such good fortune?"

The elder McNeal pulled off his straw hat and wiped his balding head with his linen handkerchief. " 'Tis more than the strain of my back and the sweat of my brow that's brought us this good fortune, Chan. 'Tis the sweet, good earth of Virginia—our land, our home, our treasure. We'll not take kindly to invasion of our homeland, not we Virginians.''

Channing shied away from the staunch glitter of his father's eyes. "Then, you're saying my choice is wrong?"

"Dammit, lad!" McNeal exploded. "There is no right nor wrong to this! That's the hell of it all. When the final shot is fired and the final battle is done and the final man has breathed his last, then and only then will we know who was right and who was wrong. The victor will shout 'Huzzah!' while the vanquished falls to his knees. And after the shouting is over, we will all be the worse for what's happened. Mark my word, neither the state of Virginia nor the United States of America will ever be the same again. These are our final days of glory."

"You paint a grim picture, Father."

"Not near as grim as the war will be, son." McNeal clamped a hand on Channing's shoulder and bowed his head. "There's nothing so grim as that."

"Then there is no answer. Why fight for a lost cause?"

When Thompson McNeal looked up at his tall, fine son, his eyes were blazing. "Aye, you'll fight, lad. I've no doubt of that. But not till your back's to the wall. There's an old Scottish saying, *'The Scot will not fight till he sees his ain bluid.'* And I do believe that we'll be seeing our own blood flow over this comely land in the first hours of battle. We are too close to Washington City to go ignored. They will want Virginia worse than a seaman fresh off a three-year voyage craves a woman beneath him."

His father's mention of a woman brought the main focus of his problem back to mind. He met the older man's gaze, his own equally steely. "What if your own daughter—say, Hester—decided to marry a man who meant to fight for the North? What would you do?"

" 'Tis not a fair hypothesis, I fear."

"Of course it is, Father. Hester still plans to marry Auguste Fontaine, doesn't she?"

"Aye, son, that she does."

"All right, then. Should he decide to throw in his lot with the North, would you refuse to allow their marriage?"

"That will not happen."

Channing broke into a broad smile. "I'm glad I asked. And I'm glad you feel that way, Father. If you would allow Hester to wed under these circumstances, then I'm sure Colonel Swan won't stand in the way of my marrying Virginia."

"You mistake my answer, son." Thompson McNeal suddenly looked far older than his years. "That will not happen because they will be wed in France. Auguste has convinced our Hester to go to his homeland, until all this unpleasantness is over. Your mother won't hear of a wedding taking place without our being there. I was instructed by the women of Clan McNeal not to say a word of this to you until after our celebratory dinner this evening, but it seems best that I tell you now. You will protect me from their wrath with your silence, I presume."

Channing could only nod. His father's confession of their plans left him numb and speechless. The whole family, transplanted to France?

" 'Twould be a way out for you, as well, Channing. Come with us. Bring Virginia. No one could blame you for wishing her away from what is to come, least of all her own father."

The full impact of his family's plans hit Channing suddenly. He cast his gaze wildly about. "What about Belle Grove? Who will be here to look after our home?"

"Land needs little tending in time of war. Scorched earth yeilds finer crops after the fact. But there'll be no loss of life on my land, I vow. My family will be safely away. As for the slaves, I have been quietly manumitting our people over the past years. The few who remain in bondage, I'll free before I leave for France. They may stay or go, as pleases them. A few of the loyal ones will remain, I'm sure. They will see to safeguarding the place as best they can."

"France?" Channing muttered to himself, still unbelieving.

"Aye, Paris it is for Clan McNeal. We'll see a bit of the

world, buy your mother and sisters some fancy new gowns, and drink all the fine wines to be had.''

''While back here a nation is being torn assunder?''

Thompson McNeal looked sad for a moment, but then he smiled. '' 'Tis not my fight, lad, nor your mother's and sisters'. Should I force them to stay, only to prove some obscure point?'' He shook his head. ''Nay! I wish them safe and happy—far away from what's to come. You and your sweet Virginia would be a most welcome addition to our band of pilgrims.''

Channing felt cold, empty, and more alone suddenly than he ever had felt in his life. Slowly, he shook his head. ''I can't, Father,'' he whispered. ''My duty lies here.''

''So be it!'' McNeal said. ''I told your mother it would be so. She'll be sore disappointed, but as for me, I'm proud of you, son. No matter which side you choose.''

Sadly, but with solemn resolve in his voice, Channing answered, ''There's no doubt which side that must be, Father.''

Thompson McNeal put his arm around his son's shoulders and gave him a brusque, manly hug. ''We'd best not keep your mother and the girls waiting any longer. We'll talk of happy things at dinner and celebrate your return home and your coming wedding to Virginia. No *lang* face at the dinner table, lad. Understood?''

''Understood,'' Channing answered, but he couldn't imagine how he would be able to seem cheerful under the circumstances.

After Channing left Swan's Quarter to ride to Belle Grove, Virginia felt too nervous to be with anyone. Before her mother came downstairs or her father and brothers returned to the house, she hurried to her room. None of them knew that she had finished the quilt cover. She could hide out for hours with no one the wiser. They would think she was still working and leave her alone to think, to plan. She could not allow Channing to tell her parents his intentions until after they were married. What difference could a few days make?

She closed her bedroom door with a feeling of relief, as if

she had shut out all the problems in her life. As long as she was here, in the very room that had been her nursery as an infant and was now her sanctuary, she was safe. She could think straight, at last.

Her decision came as swift and as sure as thunder after a bolt of lightning. *Elopement!*

Hurrying to her armoire, Virginia pulled out a leather satchel that she often used when visiting friends for houseparties on weekends. She snatched clothes from drawers and stuffed them in, added two pair of slippers, and folded a reasonably elegant gown on the top of the rest. She was trying to close the case, when she heard a soft knock at her door.

"Virginia? Are you still working on your quilt? You'll ruin your eyes, dear."

Before she could say a word, the door opened and Melora Swan walked in. Surprise registered on her face at the sight of the bulging suitcase on the bed.

"What in the world?"

Caught in the act, Virginia didn't answer. She stood perfectly still, her head bowed to hide the trace of tears swimming in her eyes.

"Virginia?" Her mother's voice was soft but firm, demanding an answer.

The girl shrugged and sniffed. "Just some old things I thought I'd give to Polly for her daughters."

Melora moved to the side of the bed and touched the soft white fabric of the gown on top of the pile. "Why, you haven't even worn this yet. It's part of your trousseau—one of the gowns we bought in New York."

"It doesn't fit right."

"It most certainly does! I helped with the alterations myself. Come now, Virginia. Tell me what's going on."

At that moment, Virginia raised her left hand to her cheek to brush away a stray tear. Her mother's eyes missed nothing.

"Your ring!" Melora cried. "Channing's home!"

"Yes," Virginia choked out.

"You haven't had a misunderstanding, have you?" When

Virginia only shook her head, Melora gasped, "You aren't *with child?*"

"Oh, Mother, I wish I were!"

Virginia dissolved into a fit of sobs. She was in her mother's sheltering arms almost instantly, blurting out the whole sorry mess before she could stop herself.

Melora tried to stay calm, to reassure her daughter. But she knew as well as Virginia what effect Channing's decision would have on Jedediah. Hysteria was indeed appropriate, under the circumstances. Virginia's plan to elope seemed the only solution to her mother.

"Damn this war!" Melora cursed, in uncustomary fashion.

"What am I going to do, Mother?" Virginia begged.

"When and where are you supposed to meet Channing, dear?"

This question brought another wave of tears. Virginia could barely get her answer out. "He doesn't know anything about this. It's all my idea. I planned to ride to Belle Grove and insist that we go to the parsonage in Winchester to be married this very night."

Melora narrowed her eyes, thinking through Virginia's plan. "It just might work. Yes! Get that satchel closed, Virginia. I'll go down and tell Styx to hitch up the trap. He can drive you over. I'll write a note to Channing myself. Surely, he'll go along with this, if he knows you have my blessing."

Virginia felt such a sudden burst of elation that she could hardly contain herself. She almost swooned with joy. She kissed her mother's cheek and then her dainty hands.

"Oh, thank you! Thank you! I could never have managed this alone."

"That's why girls have mothers. Now, do hurry, Virginia! I'll go down and find Styx. Meet us out back as quickly as you can." At the door, she turned back and smiled. "No more tears now. It's your wedding day. Smile for me."

Suddenly, Virginia was so happy that the feeling almost frightened her. The plan seemed so easy—ride to Belle Grove, get Channing, go to Winchester, be married. No muss, no fuss, no waste of time. In only hours, she would be his wife. Still, a dark cloud of doubt loomed at the edge of her consciousness. Would Channing consent to tricking her father this way?

She refused to think such worrisome thoughts, as she hurried down the back stairs, suitcase in hand. Sure enough, she found old Styx, their driver, ready and waiting. Her mother was there, too. She pressed a folded sheet of vellum into her daughter's hand, kissed her, and said, "See that Channing gets this. Good luck, my darling."

A sudden feeling of loss swept over Virginia. "Oh, Mother, I wish you could be there when we're married."

"So do I, dear. But I'll have to stay here so I can make an excuse for your absence." She looked sternly at her daughter. "Do this quickly, Virginia. There's not much time. We're in luck that your father and the boys are late coming home from their drill this evening."

Styx touched up the horses and they were off. Melora Swan stood waving after her daughter. Now the tears were in *her* eyes. She had looked forward all Virginia's life to seeing her wed in a lovely ceremony at Swan's Quarter. A swift elopement into the night had never once crossed her mind as even the vaguest of possibilities.

"No matter," she whispered, through a teary smile. "A wedding lasts only briefly, but love lasts a lifetime and beyond."

Melora Swan had told Virginia that there wasn't much time. There was less than either of them could have guessed. Even as Styx drove Virginia toward Belle Grove, the news spread about the county that Channing McNeal had come home.

Young Ludlow, Polly's grandson, left Swan's Quarter at a full trot, headed for the parade ground. His orders from Colonel Swan had been very clear. "You tell me, Ludlow, the minute Mr. Channing McNeal shows up. You hear me, boy?"

Over a week ago, Ludlow's master had sent the overseer to pull him out of the field for a private chat. Ludlow had been trembling right down to the horn-hard soles of his big, bare feet. He had figured for sure that Massa Swan had got wind of his fooling around with Celie, the high-yeller housegal, who had been driving him crazy. He wanted her so bad. Colonel Swan had strict rules about his people. When they paired off, *he* did the pairing. At Swan's Quarter, there wasn't supposed to be any rolling in the hayloft or dropping down between the tobacco rows for a quick wick-dipping. Ludlow and Celie had broken that rule just a week ago in a back stall of the barn, late one stormy night. It had been good—mighty good—but Ludlow had to wonder, when he got Colonel Swan's summons, if it had been worth the punishment that was sure to come.

Looking sharply at the fifteen-year-old, who was as black as night but, amazingly to his master, as smart as any white boy, Swan had said, "Now, you listen good, Ludlow."

The boy had held his breath, waiting for the pronouncement of his punishment, sure of a whipping or worse.

But Colonel Swan had surprised him. "I have a special assignment for you, Ludlow. From now till Mister Channing rides home, you stay close to the house and watch for him. You let me know soon as he rides up. I'll tell Polly to give you chores to do for her around the kitchen, while you keep a sharp eye out."

For a minute or two, Ludlow had been so relieved that he went weak in the knees. That lasted only until Colonel Swan added, "I hear you got a powerful hankering for that gal, Celie." Hearing that, Ludlow's knees had gone even weaker for another reason. Maybe he was bound to get that whipping yet.

Seeing the wild look of fear in the boy's eyes, Colonel Swan had laughed and added, "You get me word soon as you see Mister Channing, and I'll see about getting you and Celie together. She's old enough now to start dropping suckers, and you look man enough to do the job."

Still trembling with the aftershock of terror, Ludlow had nodded solemnly and said, "Yessuh, Colonel Swan. I sure will let you know soon as Mister Channing McNeal rides onto the place.''

Sure enough, Ludlow had kept a sharp eye peeled. He had been the first one to spot Channing, as he rode past the swan pond that afternoon. With only a quick word to Polly, he had taken off, running as fast as he could toward the parade ground five miles away to deliver his message to the colonel.

When Jedediah Swan saw Ludlow loping toward him, waving his arms frantically over his head, the colonel shouted an order to put a halt to the drill.

''You've got news, Ludlow?''

The boy stumbled up to the colonel's horse, shuddering with fatigue from his long run. ''He come!'' Ludlow gasped, gulping for breath. ''He done come not a hour ago, Colonel Swan. He be with Miss Virginia right now.''

Swan turned to his men and yelled, ''McNeal's arrived! We're off to war, men!''

A great Rebel yell filled the still afternoon. Hats flew into the air. Horses reared. And someone broke into a spirited rendition of ''Dixie.''

Colonel Swan leaned down from his great, black stallion and winked at Ludlow. ''You go on back to the place now, boy. Tonight, after supper, you amble on over to Celie's ma's cabin. I reckon your girl'll be waiting for you, all primed and ready.''

Ludlow grinned real wide and danced from one bare foot to the other in his excitement. If he could get a youngun' on Celie, Colonel Swan would give them their own cabin with enough ground for a garden and a few chickens. What they didn't eat, he could sell and start putting away some cash. Maybe someday, he could buy Celie's freedom and then his own.

''Come on, boys!'' Swan shouted. ''Let's ride!''

Ludlow hot-footed it back to Swan's Quarter, arriving just in time to see Styx helping Miss Virginia with her suitcase, while Miz Swan looked on. He hung back in the shadows to find out what was going on. What he heard made his eyes go wide. This bit of information wasn't likely to please the colonel, but it had to be told, if he wanted his Celie.

Virginia instructed Styx to drive her around to the back of Belle Grove. She needed to speak to Channing privately. If she went in the front way, the whole family would surround them, wanting to talk about wedding plans and such. Her only hope was to send Styx to the back door to request of one of the McNeal servants that Channing step outside to meet a visitor.

The plan worked. Minutes later, Virginia was in Channing's arms, their embrace shielded by a large, sweet shrub bush.

"This is a quite a surprise," Channing whispered, between kisses. "I'd meant to ride over to see you later this evening."

She stared up at him, her face set in serious lines. "You weren't really planning to come see me, were you, Channing? You were planning to see my father. You meant to tell him about joining the Yankees, didn't you?"

He shifted her in his arms and looked away, out over the fields. "Virginia, I have to tell him sometime. The longer I wait, the worse it will be for both of us. Best to get it over with, then deal with the consequences."

"No!" Virginia cried. "There's another way."

"Then I wish you'd tell me. I've been going crazy trying to figure out a solution. I talked to my father. He even suggested we go to France with them."

"France?"

Channing nodded. "Hester and Auguste plan to be married in Paris. The rest of the family is going, too. They mean to stay in France for the duration of the war."

"But you didn't agree to go?"

"Virginia, darling, you know I couldn't. I'd never be able to live with myself, if I ran away."

This remark worried her. Would Channing see an elopement as another form of running away from his problems? She had to know. Their time was running out.

"Channing, listen to me. I understand why you can't go to

France, why you must stay and fight. But I can't get through the war, loving you as I do, yet having to wait for you to come back to marry me.''

"You know I love you, too, darling. But what can I say, Virginia? What can I do?''

"Marry me," she said firmly. "This very night. Styx can drive us to the parsonage in Winchester. By the time our families find out, it will be too late for them to do anything about it.''

"Tonight?''

"This very minute! We have Mother's blessing.'' She pressed Melora's note into his hand. "She sent you this.''

Channing squinted at the words in the half-light guttering from a lantern near the kitchen door. " 'Channing, my dear son,' " he read aloud, " 'I have sent my daughter into your arms and your safekeeping. I know you love her with all your heart. I also know that you will soon be going away. Please, do as Virginia and I both wish. Go to Winchester with my blessing. Give Virginia what little time you have left. War is but a passing condition. Love is forever.''

For a moment, he stood, still and quiet, staring at Melora Swan's note.

When Virginia could stand the silence no longer, she demanded, "Well? What do you think of my plan?''

She held her breath, until she saw a slow smile part his lips.

He crushed Virginia in his arms. "Yes!'' he breathed. "Oh, yes, my darling! It's a fine plan.''

Virginia uttered a cry of sheer joy. "I can't believe it! It's too good to be true!''

They hurried to the trap. "To Winchester, Styx!'' Channing ordered.

Virginia felt positively giddy. They rolled down the lane at a good clip. No one and nothing could stop them now. Soon Channing would be all hers, at last.

Channing laughed suddenly and squeezed her about the waist. "I feel like a kid, darlin', setting out on a marvelous adventure.''

"The grandest adventure of our lives,'' she whispered.

And then she was in his arms, feeling his insistent lips close over hers. Her heart pounded with joy and a touch of fear. Oh, how she burned for him!

"Darlin'? What about afterward?" Channing's tone had changed from one of jubilation to concern. "I won't exactly be your father's favorite, once he finds out what we've done."

She clung to him happily, still smiling, all her cares vanished. "You'll be real family by then, Chan. And family ties mean more than anything to my father. He won't cause trouble. Mother won't allow it."

They held each other close, as Styx set a true course for Winchester. At last, they spied the lights in the windows of the parsonage up ahead.

"We've made it," Virginia said, with a sigh of relief.

Minutes later, they were standing in the front parlor of Reverend and Mrs. Bulwer's cozy stone cottage with its huge fireplace. The parson at first hesitated to perform such a hasty marriage, until Channing produced Melora Swan's note. Festus Bulwer knew the lady well and knew better than to question her wishes, even if this whole situation did strike him as rather odd. Mrs. Swan had engaged him months ago to preside over the double ceremony at Swan's Quarter. The date was set for only a few days from now. Still, he had had an inordinate number of unannounced calls for nuptials these past weeks, due to the sudden war frenzy.

Mrs. Bulwer, a tiny slip of a lady in her sixties, went up on tiptoe to whisper to Virginia, "Dear, if you would like to freshen up, you may use my room."

Channing answered for his fiancée. "Thank you, ma'am, but there's no time. We need to get on with the vows. The short version, and hurry, please."

Hearing that, the reverend cleared his throat, opened his Bible, and began the proceedings.

Virginia's heart soared. At last, she could finally believe this was happening. She clung to Channing's arm, her hands cold

We have 4 FREE BOOKS for you as your introduction to KENSINGTON CHOICE! To get your FREE BOOKS, worth up to $24.96, mail the card below.

FREE BOOK CERTIFICATE

Yes! Please send me 4 Kensington Choice (the best of Zebra and Pinnacle Books) Historical Romances without cost or obligation (worth up to $24.96). As a Kensington Choice subscriber, I will then receive 4 brand-new romances to preview each month for 10 days FREE. I can return any books I decide not to keep and owe nothing. The publisher's prices for Kensington Choice romances range from $4.99-$6.99, but as a preferred subscriber I will get these books for only $4.20 per book or $16.80 for all four titles. There is no minimum number of books to buy and I may cancel my subscription at any time. A $1.50 postage and handling charge is added to each shipment. No matter what I decide to do, my first 4 books are mine to keep, absolutely FREE!

Name _____

Address _____ Apt._____

City _____ State_____ Zip_____

Telephone ( ) _____

Signature _____

(If under 18, parent or guardian must sign)

Subscription subject to acceptance. Terms and prices subject to change.

KC1197

AFFIX
STAMP
HERE

KENSINGTON CHOICE
Zebra Home Subscription Service, Inc.
120 Brighton Road
P.O. Box 5214
Clifton, NJ 07015-5214

and trembling. She stared up at him with adoring, dewy eyes. His look for her was loving enough to make her weak with longing.

When Reverend Bulwer reached the passage about anyone standing who knew just cause why Channing and Virginia should not be wed, he cleared his throat and, glancing about the otherwise unpopulated room, said, "I suppose we can dispense with that part and get right to the point."

At that very instant, they all turned, shocked to hear the furious pounding of horses' hooves outside. Without so much as a knock, the door flew open.

Virginia cried out and clung tightly to Channing when she saw her father's huge frame filling the doorway.

"Thank God, I'm in time!" he bellowed. Turning a steely glare on the cringing parson, the colonel said, "You can thank your lucky stars for that, Bulwer!"

"Father, no!" Virginia wailed. "We're already married."

"Maybe so, but not bedded." He strode into the room and pulled Virginia out of Channing's arms. "Jed, you and the twins take your sister home. Rodney and I have some business with Lieutenant McNeal."

Virginia's brothers all glared at Channing as they came in, forming a solid, blond wall of husky man-flesh.

Jed and the twins took hold of Virginia's arms. She struggled against them—screaming, clawing, and kicking. It was no use. They simply out-numbered and out-muscled her.

Channing tried his best to rescue her, but Colonel Swan and Rodney grabbed him, wrestling him to the floor.

"I won't go! I'm getting married!" Virginia shrieked. "I *love* him, Father!"

Staring at his daughter, his face filled with pain, Jedediah said, in a raspy voice, "If that's so, then your love will last beyond the war. But I'll not be meeting my own son-in-law on the field of battle. Now go quietly with your brothers, Virginia."

Her gaze locked with Channing's for a moment, before the boys led her away. With that one look he promised her love forevermore. His expression held all the pain of the ages, all the longing in his soul.

Her spirits badly battered, her heart broken, Virginia turned to the door and left, as her father ordered. That moment seemed the blackest hour of her life.

Chapter Ten

Virginia's mother was waiting on the dark veranda when her daughter arrived home with her brothers. Melora Swan's face was pale, her eyes red-rimmed from the scene between her and her husband that had taken place before he rode off to stop the elopement. Someone—some spy—had told the colonel that Channing was back and, even worse, that he intended to remain in the Army of the United States. Jedediah was a hot-tempered man, given to flying off the handle at the slightest provocation. Melora was used to his outbursts, but she had never before seen him in such a fit as he had flung when he realized his daughter was gone from Swan's Quarter. Even thinking about it now made Melora shudder, as she watched Virginia slide off young Jed's horse.

Virginia stumbled up the front steps and fell into her mother's arms, sobbing. "He wrecked everything. My life's over."

"Hush that, dear. Of course it's not. You and Channing will be married. Someday." Melora tried to soothe Virginia, though her heart was broken.

Pulling away, Virginia accused, "*You!* You must have told Father. Mother, how could you betray me?"

"It wasn't I, dear," Melora whispered, her voice quivering with sympathy for her heartbroken daughter. "Your father and the boys knew that Channing was back before they ever got here. He came charging into the house, demanding to talk to you about Channing's decision to remain loyal to the North— or, as your father put it, 'to turn his back on the South and all that we Virginians stand for.' When you weren't here, he surmised what had happened. He stormed out of the here like a hound on the scent. He and your brothers rode out again at a full gallop. Polly confessed to me that one of her grandsons has been doing some spying for your father. I saw the boy whispering to the colonel the minute he dismounted. Ludlow must have told him then that Channing planned to stay with the Union Army. I have no idea how Ludlow found out, but I don't think he will ever do anything like this again, after his granny gets through with him."

Still trying to comfort her weeping daughter, Melora watched her three youngest sons ride in silence around toward the barn. "Where are your father and Rodney, Virginia? Why didn't they come home with you?"

The question reduced the girl to pure hysteria. "They're with Channing. Dear God, Mother, what will they do to him? This wasn't even his idea. I'm the one they should blame."

"And I," Melora admitted, grimly. "They'll do nothing to him. You have my word on that." Then silently, she added, *Not if Jedediah Swan ever hopes to share my bed again.*

Back in Reverend Bulwer's parlor, an inquisition was in progress. Mrs. Bulwer had taken to her bedroom and bolted the door, moments after the angry men arrived. Her husband would have accompanied her panicked flight, had he not feared for his parlor furniture *and* for Channing McNeal's life. Murder gleamed in the eyes of the Swan men. Quaking with fear, Bulwer placed his thin body strategically, spreading himself as best he could to protect his wife's beloved rosewood piano from harm, should the men started throwing things—or each other.

"Here, now!" he shouted, in a voice as insubstantial as his frame. "I'll not have fisticuffs under my roof. Might I remind you, Colonel Swan, that God is watching you. He sees your every move."

"Then He will no doubt bless this act, since it is aimed at a traitor." With that, he took a swing at Channing, hitting a hard but glancing blow off his right cheekbone.

Channing staggered under the force of the punch. If any other man had attacked him, he would have beaten him to a bloody pulp. But he refused even to defend himself against Virginia's father.

"Let me at him, Pa!" Rodney clenched his fists, bouncing about on the balls of his feet, as he and Channing had been taught in boxing class at West Point. "I should have given the bastard what for when he refused to come home with me. I might have guessed then that he meant to go against us. And now he's disgraced my sister, besides." He glared at his old friend. "I want a piece of you, you sonuvabitch!"

Reverend Bulwer cleared his throat loudly, screwing up his courage at the same time. "You will pardon me for interrupting, gentlemen, but Mr. McNeal was marrying Miss Virginia when you barged in. I see nothing in the least disgraceful in a Christian wedding."

Rodney turned a snarl on the cringing preacher. "It damn sure is, if she's marrying a turncoat blue-belly!"

When Rodney moved in to take a punch at Channing, Jedediah Swan waved his son off. "Wait for me outside, Rod. You clear out, too, Bulwer. I have a few words to say to McNeal that aren't fit to be heard by one and all."

"But, Pa . . ." Rodney's argument was short-lived.

"You heard me, boy. *Outside!*"

"You'll not be breaking up the place?" Bulwer said, in as stern a voice as he could muster.

"Likely McNeal's neck, but nothing more. *Out!*" he yelled.

Rodney exited reluctantly by the front door. Bulwer went to the back of the house to be with his frightened wife.

For several moments, the two remaining men stood almost toe to toe, sizing each other up, both waiting for the other to make the first move.

Finally, it was Channing who spoke first. "I refuse to fight you, Colonel Swan. You're Virginia's father. I won't dishonor her."

"But you're willing to shoot me quick enough on the field of battle or force me to kill you. I see that as a great dishonor to my daughter. To my whole family. To the South! But we'd best not get into that now." He brushed a hand across his eyes, as if he were too weary to argue. "I sent Rodney and the reverend out, because it's talk I want, not a fight."

Channing relaxed a bit when he heard this. He had braced his whole body for the next blow, sure that Swan meant to beat him senseless.

"What's got into you, boy? Why are you doing this? You know I've always thought as highly of you as if you were one of my own sons. It's been my dream for you and Virginia to marry someday. You know that well."

Channing nodded. "Aye, sir, so I do." He went on to explain to Colonel Swan, as best he could, the reasons for his decision. He used much the same words he had used with his own father. But Swan remained unconvinced.

"This is madness, Channing."

"War is madness, sir! Neither side will come out the victor. The whole nation will suffer."

"It's Lincoln's fault, not ours. All we want is to form our own nation and live in peace."

"At the expense of our existing nation, sir. The president can't allow that to happen. We stand together, or we stand against each other. I stand with our President Lincoln and our country. For me, there can be no other choice."

Swan uttered a long, weary sigh. "If that's your last word on the subject, go now, Channing. Ride to Belle Grove and kiss your mother and sisters goodbye, then ride to Washington

City and join your troops. I pray to God we never meet face to face in battle.''

''As do I, Colonel Swan. But I still mean to marry your daughter.''

Swan nodded, but his face was grim. ''You still have my permission, but only *after* this war is over. I'll hold no grudge against you. But I refuse to run the risk of meeting my own son-in-law in battle. Be off at once, and God go with you. I'll tell Virginia that you've left.''

''And will you tell her, too, that I still love her and will return to marry her, after the fighting is over?''

Swan sighed deeply again. ''If any of us return,'' he added, in a grim tone.

Feeling cold through and through, Second Lieutenant Channing McNeal, of the United States Army, stood at attention and snapped a sharp salute to Colonel Jedediah Swan, Army of the Confederacy. Swan, looking far older than his years, returned the military courtesy.

After that, the two men left the parsonage together, to go their separate ways.

Saturday, the first day of June, dawned hazy and hot, with storm clouds gathering in the west. Virginia woke with a dull ache buzzing inside her head. It took a few moments for her to come wide awake enough to realize the import of this day.

''My wedding day,'' she murmured. ''The day Channing and I were to have been married.'' She turned her face into her pillow and shed the scant tears she had left.

The only man she would ever love had been gone for over a week. She had last seen him on that horrible night when her father and brothers had burst in and disrupted their marriage. Good to his word, her father had delivered Channing's final message to her. At least he had left her with some thin thread of hope. *If* this terrible war ended someday, and *if* Channing lived to see that end, they would be married. The uncertainty of their future together left a constant, sharp ache in her heart.

The sounds of bustling activity down below reminded Virginia again that she was expected to do her duty to her family and be on hand for the festivities today. How she would get through Rodney's wedding to Agnes, she had no idea. Her mother, ever sympathetic, had told her that she might remain in her room until the guests had come and gone and the ceremony was over. But she couldn't do that. It simply wasn't the way of the Swan family. Virginia knew that she must dress and go down to be a part of this special occasion, even though she would no longer play a major role.

The whole county knew what had happened. Even if the plantation families hadn't been prone to gossip, there would have been no silencing the slave grapevine. They all knew of her thwarted marriage to Channing and his abrupt leave-taking to join his unit in Washington. She wondered if Channing had taken part in the recent clash of troops at Alexandria. To date, she had received no messages from him. She worried constantly that Channing might be wounded, unable to write.

Virginia climbed out of bed and folded her newly finished Sunday House quilt. This very day she would put it away in her cedar hope chest. As beautiful as it was, the sight of the quilt brought hurtful memories. Neither Channing's mother nor his sisters had come to the quilting bee Melora Swan had hosted. How could they, under the circumstances? Nor would they be among the wedding guests today. They had sent their regrets, citing their preparations for the trip to Paris as their sole reason for not coming. But everyone knew that the cancellation of half of the double wedding was the true cause.

"Virginia?" A hesitant voice accompanied the soft knock at her door. "It's Agnes. May I come in?"

The bride! The *only* bride at Swan's Quarter this first day of June. The last person Virginia wanted to see at the moment.

She pulled on her robe. "Yes, do come in, Agnes."

To Virginia's amazement, the bride-to-be looked weary and worried, not at all like a woman about to marry the man she loved.

"Agnes? Whatever's wrong?" Virginia had half-expected

the young woman to lord it over her this morning, since she was to have the wedding all to herself. But her demeanor told a very different tale. The girl looked truly terrified.

"Oh, Virginia, I don't know if I can go through with this." Tears streamed down Agnes's pale cheeks.

"Why on earth not? You and Rodney have been counting on this day for years, making plans for months."

"But that's just it. We had planned it all so differently. I wanted us *all* to be married today. Will you think me a traitor if I go ahead with it?"

Virginia felt a sudden rush of warmth and affection for the weeping girl. She had misjudged her. She went to Agnes and gave her a hug.

"Of course I won't. I'm so happy for you and Rodney. Besides, he needs a wife to tame him and teach him some manners. And you're the very one who can do that, Agnes. You must keep a tight rein on my big brother. Don't let him bully you. He'll try, you know."

Virginia had hoped to tease Agnes out of her weepy state, but her words brought a new rush of tears.

"Do you know what Rodney means to do to me?"

Virginia blushed, knowing exactly what her brother—what *any* groom—intended for his bride after the ceremony.

She was relieved from having to answer when Agnes blurted out, "He is leaving, *tomorrow morning!* Colonel Swan plans to ride out before daybreak. Rodney told me only last night about this. It seems Federal forces are building up around Manassas. There's to be a big battle and they don't want to miss it."

Virginia's pulses raced at this news. No doubt that was where Channing was at this very moment. She was half-tempted to take a horse and ride straight to Manassas, straight to her lover.

"We'll have only tonight and then he'll be gone," Agnes wailed. "I don't think I can bear it, Virginia."

"We can all bear what we must, Agnes. At least you will have one night as Rodney's wife." Her tone was level, but barely controlled. "That's one night more than I had with Channing."

"Virginia, I'm so sorry," Agnes said. "And you're right. I *can* bear it, because I must. In wartime we must all make many sacrifices. But, oh, how I had hoped that he could leave me with child!"

"Agnes!" Virginia wasn't as shocked as she sounded. It was simply surprising to hear such a thing come out of the mouth of prim and proper Agnes Willingham.

"Well, it's true, so why shouldn't I admit it? Rodney might never come home again. I want a part of him to be with me always. I want to have his baby."

"Don't even think about his not coming back!" Virginia snapped. "You'll bring bad luck down on all of us. He *will* come home. And so will Channing, someday, to marry me."

"I wish I had your faith and strength," Agnes replied, weakly.

"You had better have. We must all muster every ounce we can. We're going to need that, and more."

Hearing her daughter's raised voice, Melora peeked into the room. "Oh, there you are, Agnes. I've been looking for you. Your mother is in the library, waiting to talk to you."

The young women exchanged glances. They both guessed the subject of Mrs. Willingham's mother-daughter talk. It would run the course of instructions on submitting to one's husband willingly, without showing the least interest or joy in the unpleasant business taking place in the marriage bed. No doubt, Mrs. Willingham would add that the Bible said we were meant to procreate, and therefore it was a necessary evil, in order to produce children and so insure the continuation of the line.

Oh, how Virginia longed to commit that *necessary evil!*

"What have you decided?" Melora asked her daughter, as soon as Agnes left.

Virginia stood a bit taller and squared her shoulders. "I'll be beside you in the receiving line today, Mother."

A gentle smile curved Mrs. Swan's lips. She touched her daughter's arm affectionately. "You don't have to, you know.

But I'm awfully proud that you will. Having you there will mean a lot to Rodney and Agnes."

Virginia tossed her long, golden hair over one shoulder. "Rodney and Agnes won't know whether I'm downstairs or not, Mother. They'll be too engrossed in each other. I'm not doing this for them. I'm doing it for myself . . . and for Channing. In a way, I suppose, it will be rather symbolic. My proof that this bride is waiting at the altar for her man." Her eyes flashed suddenly. "And I *will* wait, Mother! I plan to be right here—*still waiting*—when Channing comes riding home."

"You are a brave girl, Virginia Swan! The bravest of the brave."

Virginia didn't feel very brave a few hours later. She bit down hard on the inside of her lower lip to keep from bursting into tears. Standing in the parlor with the wedding guests, she turned her gaze toward the graceful staircase, when the music for the bride's entrance began.

For a moment she closed her eyes, imagining what might have been. Channing should have been standing beside her handsome brother, Rodney, at the bottom of those stairs. Virginia could almost see herself poised on the landing above, her satin and lace wedding gown glowing like candlelight.

Yet, when she opened her eyes, only Agnes was there. Petite, lovely Agnes, looking radiant and frightened at the same time. She stared down at Rodney, the ghost of a smile trembling on her lips. Little Agnes looked as if she might bolt back up the stairs at any moment. But halfway down, her demeanor changed. Had it not been for her father's restraining arm, she might have taken the steps two at a time, in her eagerness to reach her beloved. A wide smile broke across her face. Suddenly, she was beaming. Virginia could well imagine why. Her own heart gave a faint lurch when she put herself in Agnes's place. If Channing had been standing at the bottom waiting for her, she would have hiked up her skirts and slid down the banister to get to him the fastest way possible.

Conventions be hanged! she mused.

Time seemed to pass in fits and starts during the actual ceremony. The only way Virginia could get through it, without breaking down or actually fleeing the room, was to keep her mind on other things. She dared not listen to the minister's words or think of Channing again. She concentrated instead on the room itself. She tried to imagine what this room would look like a decade from now, a century from now.

Again, she closed her eyes. When she opened them this time, she had the strangest sensation. She felt quite faint for a moment. Glancing about, she realized that the wedding party, the minister, the guests all looked like mere shadows in the room. The parlor looked different—new wallpaper, new furniture. And an odd box with glass on one side occupied the corner where the Bible stand had been, moments before. Sitting about the room were a group of elderly people, all staring at the strange box.

One of the women, a slave, by the color of her skin, said, "That Peter Bergman is to-die-for gorgeous! He *is* Jack Abbot! If they ever kill him off of this show, I'm quittin' 'The Young and the Restless' for good."

The old woman sounded strangely familiar. She bore a striking resemblance to Polly, the cook, at Swan's Quarter. And that tattered doll she was holding in her arms. Why, that was Virginia's doll!

Virginia turned to look at the glass-faced box that seemed the center of attention. She gasped. Small people where trapped inside—walking, talking, looking perfectly normal, except for their strange clothing. How on earth did they get in there? Who could they be?

She was about to go over and speak to the woman with her doll, when all the strangers vanished from the room, as suddenly as they had appeared. The box went with them, as did Peter Bergman and Jack Abbot—whoever they were. Once more, the mahogany Bible stand occupied the corner. The ceremony was almost finished. Soon, Reverend Bulwer would open the huge family Bible to record Agnes and Rodney's marriage on the special page between the Old and New Testaments.

"I now pronounce you man and wife," the parson said.

Virginia felt tears of regret and envy choke her throat. She wondered where Channing was at this exact moment. Was he thinking about the wedding taking place at Swan's Quarter? Was he as sad as she?

Suddenly, the room began to spin around her. Strange sights and sounds mingled in her senses. The old black woman with the doll flew through the air, followed by the glass-faced box, whirling over the heads of the wedding guests. She heard Agnes's shrill, girlish laugh and her own mother's voice. But the old people from that other time were talking too. Virginia covered her ears, trying to block out the maddening babble. One voice cut sharply through the others.

"Ginna! Ginna, speak to me! Open your eyes. We're back."

Slowly, she did as the male voice instructed. She felt odd, disoriented. It seemed almost as though she were two people at the same time, groping for a single, stable personality.

"Channing?" she whispered.

"Ginna, it's me. Neal!"

"Neal?" The name sounded oddly familiar, but unfamiliar too.

"We got separated. I couldn't find you. When I got back, you weren't here in the greenhouse. God, I nearly went crazy! Then, all of a sudden, you reappeared. I'm not going back there, Ginna, not ever again."

She stared up at the face. One of his eyes was slightly puffy and the flesh below it showed the yellowish tinge of an aging bruise. Suddenly, she remembered the confrontation Channing had had with Jedediah and Rodney Swan at the parsonage.

"Your eye!" she gasped.

He touched the fading bruise. "It's nothing. I took a sucker punch a while back from an old man."

"My father hit you?"

No, Ginna! Not *your* father. It was Virginia's father, Colonel Swan. And it wasn't me he hit, it was Channing."

"Then why do you have a black eye, Neal?"

He touched the tender flesh gingerly and shook his head. "Damned if I know. I don't understand any of this, if you want the truth."

She lay back against the soft dirt floor of the greenhouse, her mind reeling once more. "What's happening to us, Neal?"

"I couldn't even venture a guess. But it's sure as hell not going to happen again." He leaned close and gathered her into his arms. "We're not of that place, you and I, and we shouldn't have gone there. We won't go again. Promise me that, Ginna."

She rubbed a hand over her eyes. "I don't know, Neal. I just don't know. I can't think straight, right now."

"Just lie still for a few minutes. You'll feel better. What happened to you? Where did you go when you left me at the parsonage?"

"My brothers, I mean, *Virginia's* brothers, took me home. Colonel Swan told me later that you had gone on to Washington to join your unit. I didn't know where you were. I was so worried when I heard of the fighting in Alexandria. You didn't send word. And then our wedding day came, but of course you weren't there." Tears streamed from her eyes when she spoke of the wedding. "Oh, Channing!" She reached up and clasped her arms around Neal's neck, pulling his bruised cheek close to hers. "I wanted everything to be so perfect for us. Why did they have to ruin it? Why did that terrible war have to tear us apart?"

"Sh-h-h, Ginna," Neal said softly. "Don't do this to yourself. It's over now. Channing and Virginia may be separated, but you and I are right here, together. Everything's going to be fine, darlin'."

She tried to smile through her tears to reassure him, but in her heart, she knew that nothing would ever be right between them as long as Channing and Virginia were so much in love, yet kept apart by the war. As her mind began to right itself, her first clear thought was that she and Neal somehow shared the fate and the destiny of Virginia and Channing.

"Ginna, I didn't want to press you before, but I have to ask again. Will you marry me? Soon?"

His mention of marriage brought a new flood of tears. She knew who and where she was now, but she still shared some of Virginia's deepest emotions. Although she didn't believe it was possible for her and Neal to be together as long as Virginia and Channing were apart, she nodded and whispered, "Yes, Neal. I'll marry you. Soon, my darling."

The kiss they shared to seal their commitment was interrupted when old Zee, the gardener, ambled into the greenhouse. He cleared his throat loudly to alert them to his presence. They pulled apart and both smiled sheepishly at him.

"Don't mind me," Zee said. "Just coming in to check if my ferns need watering."

Neal helped Ginna to her feet. He thought about trying to explain why the two of them were lying down on the greenhouse floor, but decided it would be a lot easier to let the old man figure it out for himself. With only quick nods toward Zee, Ginna and Neal left the greenhouse and headed back to the main building.

"What now?" Neal asked.

"I need to get back to town. I have to work tomorrow."

"But, Ginna . . ."

She brought his hand to her lips and kissed his fingers softly. "No buts, darling. I've stayed longer than I should have."

"I don't want you to go. I want to get married. *Now!*"

The eagerness in Neal's tone made her smile. "It's not that simple, darling. We'll have to get bloods tests, a license, arrange a ceremony. I'll check on everything when I get back to town. Then I'll call, and we'll set a time to take care of all the red tape."

As they walked up onto the veranda, hand in hand, Dr. Kirkwood came hurrying through the front door. "Oh, there you are, Neal. I've been looking all over for you. You have a phone call."

Neal frowned. "Who is it?" He couldn't think of a soul who would be calling him; no one even knew he was here.

"It's Christine's father, Mr. Henderson."

Still holding Neal's hand, Ginna felt him go tense. She looked up and saw a nervous twitch at the side of his jaw. His eyes had narrowed, and his lips were pulled taut in a grim line.

"It's all right, Neal," Ginna whispered. "He probably just wants to thank you for saving his daughter's life."

"I don't want his thanks," Neal snapped. "I don't deserve his gratitude. His wife saved their little girl's life. I should have saved *her.*"

"Do take his call, Neal," Kirkwood urged. "I think you need to talk to him."

"And I agree," Ginna said. "Go on, Neal. I won't leave until you get back."

"Promise?"

"I promise." She went up on tiptoe and kissed him gently, hoping to wipe the anguish from his eyes.

"You can take the call in my office," the doctor said.

After another moment's hesitation, Neal went to the door. He turned and looked back at Ginna. "Come with me?" he begged.

She gave him a reassuring smile, but shook her head. "No, Neal. You need privacy for this call. Go ahead now. You don't want to keep Mr. Henderson waiting any longer."

Once Neal disappeared inside the house, Kirkwood asked, "What happened to Neal's eye? Don't tell me he got fresh and you had to sock him."

Ginna forced a laugh. "Nothing like that. In fact, we've decided to get married as soon as possible," she stated bluntly, never quite answering his question, but diverting his attention satisfactorily.

Kirkwood frowned at her. "And what are you doing out of bed? I told you to rest today."

She shifted her gaze away, unable to look the doctor straight in the eye. "I needed to be with Neal more than I needed a nap."

"You're impossible, Ginna Jones!"

A warm smile lit her face. "Not impossible, just in love. I've never felt so absolutely marvelous in my whole life."

It was on the tip of Dr. Kirkwood's tongue to give her a good scolding for not following doctor's orders. But why spoil her happy mood? What good would it do anyway? Ginna did as Ginna pleased!

"How soon are you planning to get married?"

"As soon as we can make arrangements. Neal will have to come to Winchester. Will you allow that?"

"Of course. He's considerably better now. I doubt he'll be staying at Swan's Quarter much longer."

Ginna smiled brightly. "That's wonderful news. I had wondered how we would manage, where we would live after we got married. We can't very well stay here, and my place is so tiny."

"Neal has a home in the Washington area. I know that from his records. I don't believe he's lived there since his wife died."

This information brought a frown to Ginna's face. "Maybe he'll sell it and we'll buy a place of our own. I don't like the thought of sharing him with a ghost."

Elspeth had been sitting at the far end of the veranda, rocking Miss Precious. She could be deaf as a post, when she conveniently wished not to hear, but, in truth, her senses were all intact and as keen as a young person's. When she heard Ginna mention ghosts, she rose and came to her. Standing directly behind Ginna, the old woman said, in a sharp whisper, "You've been sharing Swan's Quarter with more than one ghost."

Ginna nearly jumped out of her skin. She had had no idea anyone else was around.

Just then, someone called Dr. Kirkwood inside. The two women were left alone.

"Elspeth, you scared me," Ginna said.

"Didn't mean to. Just thought I ought to let you know you and young Mr. Frazier aren't the only two that knows about Miss Virginia and her Channing."

Ginna took Elspeth by the arm and led her back to the rockers. "Tell me what you mean."

"Zee's ghosts in the greenhouse. I know you and Neal've been visiting them. I went there once my own self. Got to visit with my great-granny. Those were painful times. You shouldn't go back, unless you mean to set things right, good and proper. This ain't something to play with."

Once Ginna got over her shock, she was fascinated that Elspeth shared their secret. "Neal doesn't want to go again, but I feel like we must. I have to find out what happened to Virginia and Channing."

"Their heartache ain't yours, Ginna. Leave it be. Let go of the past. You ain't got the strength Virginia had."

"I can't leave it be." Ginna was suddenly convinced that she would go back, that she had no other choice. "Tell me what happened to them."

"Only if you promise to marry your young man and stay right here where you belong—in the here and now."

Staring into the old woman's eagle-sharp eyes, Ginna knew she could not lie to her or fool her. "I can't promise, Elspeth. I'm sorry."

"Then it's woe be to you and to your young man." Having said her piece, Elspeth rose from the rocker and went inside, leaving Ginna alone on the veranda to ponder her warning.

For a long time, she sat in silence, thinking over all that had happened, all that had been said. Suddenly, she realized it was getting dark. If she didn't hurry, she would miss the last bus. But she couldn't go without saying goodbye to Neal. She went inside to find him.

Leonard Kirkwood spotted her coming down the hallway toward his office. "If you're looking for Neal, he's not here."

"Where is he?"

The doctor looked solemn, worried. "I don't know, Ginna. I came in just as he finished talking to Mr. Henderson. He slammed the phone down, rushed right past me, and took off. I thought he was going to find you."

"He didn't come back to the veranda." Her heart was thundering. What could Christine's father have said to Neal to upset

him so? "I have to leave or I'll miss my bus. Don't you have
any idea where Neal might have gone?"

"I'm afraid not. I checked his room. He isn't there. I think
he just took off to the woods to clear his head. Whatever Mr.
Henderson said got to him, that's for sure."

"I'll check his room again, but then I really have to go. Will
you explain to him why I had to leave? Tell him I'll call him."

"Of course I will."

Ginna was feeling weak and dizzy. She took the elevator to
the floor above. As Dr. Kirkwood had said, Neal's room was
empty. She found a sheet of stationery and wrote him a short
note, telling him she was sorry she had to leave and that she
loved him.

She waited a few more minutes, hoping Neal would return.
She paced his room, scanning the grounds from his window.
There was no sign of him. Finally, with a sigh, she headed
back downstairs.

Her heart was heavy, as she walked past the pond and saw
that only one lone swan swam on the mirrorlike surface.

"Neal?" she called. "Neal, where are you?"

But the rising wind took her words and threw them back at
her. As she hurried into the darkening woods, fear clutched her
heart. Not fear of being alone with darkness gathering, but fear
that something in that call from Christine's father had driven
a wedge between her and Neal.

"Please, Neal," she whispered, "please don't let anything
come between us, this time."

Chapter Eleven

Neal left Ginna and Dr. Kirkwood on the veranda, when he went inside to take his call. He dreaded picking up the receiver. Some warning tone seemed to sound in his brain, as if he anticipated bad news. What could Christine Henderson's father possibly have to say to him? And why did he have to call? If all he wanted to say was "thank you for saving my daughter," a note would have served.

"But that would have been too easy on me," Neal murmured.

He reached for the phone, his fingers tingling with dread. "Yes?" he said.

"Hello. Neal Frazier?"

"Yes," he repeated.

"Mr. Frazier, this is Donald Henderson, Christine's father."

"I know. How is she?" Neal realized in that moment that he really did care how the little girl was, even if he had tried not to think about her for the past weeks.

"She's fine, thanks to you." Henderson's voice faltered and he paused for a moment. "Our family has so much to be grateful for, and we owe it all to you, Mr. Frazier."

"Thanks, but your wife deserves all the credit. *She* saved

Christine. I just happened to be in the right place at the right time.''

"Christine told me that her mother all but threw her into your arms. Still, you're the one who brought her out safely. I owe you her life. I wish there were some way I could pay you back for your bravery.''

This was getting entirely too maudlin for Neal. One more word of gratitude, and he was going to yell at the guy to shut up. He felt hot, dizzy, the same way he had felt when he was charging out of that crashed, flaming plane. If Henderson didn't hang up, he was either going to pass out or start screaming obscenities at the man. He couldn't think, couldn't breathe.

Donald Henderson was talking again, but his words weren't connecting. Neal heard himself saying, "Yeah, sure, anytime,'' but he had no idea what he was agreeing to. Finally, only blessed silence came from the receiver. Neal hung up the phone and sank into Dr. Kirkwood's chair.

"Dammit!'' he muttered. "Why'd he have to call me? Why can't everybody just leave me alone?''

For a few moments, he rested his forehead on the palm of his hand. Henderson's words kept swimming around in his head, mingling with the sounds of people screaming and fire crackling all around. Then the echo of Donald Henderson's voice came to him very distinctly. He said, "Christine and I would like to come to see you at Swan's Quarter. Would that be all right?'' Neal heard his own voice reply, "Yeah, sure, anytime.''

When Neal realized what he had just agreed to, he shot up out of the chair and banged out of the door, a silent scream caught in his closed throat. He didn't want to see them. He *couldn't* see them! Looking into that little girl's big blue eyes would bring it all back again. And there was certainly no way he could face the husband of the woman he had allowed to die.

In his haste, Neal brushed by someone in the hallway, someone who called his name. But he barely saw Dr. Kirkwood and didn't speak to him. Only one thought drove him—he had to

get out of this place, get away from everyone, get some fresh
air.

Before Neal knew where he was going, he found himself
outside, in back of the house. He never slowed, but kept running
until he was in the woods beyond the greenhouse. He felt like
a trapped animal. He had to keep going, before the hunter
caught up with him. It was like in the desert, when the very
sand around you could explode and send you flying in bits up
to the oily, smoke-blackened sky. Panic made his heart beat
rapidly, erratically. He stumbled and fell several times, but
dragged himself on.

"Gotta get away. Can't let them find me. Ginna? Ginna,
where are you?" His words became more incoherent and jum-
bled, as the moments passed. He was living it all again—the
fiery plane crash, Desert Storm, and another battle where he
faced a ragtag army in dirty gray uniforms. He had to shoot
them before they shot him.

He crouched down behind a large bush and peered around.
A thick haze of smoke hung just below the tree branches in
the forest. Holding his breath, he listened with full attention.
The stillness all around him was suddenly filled with sounds:
The crack of a twig beneath a horse's hoof. The rustle of leaves.
The click of metal against metal.

They're coming, he thought. *Closing in. And I'm cut off from
my squad.*

Trying not to make a sound, he slumped lower behind the
bush. It was getting dark. Maybe they wouldn't see him. Maybe
they'd pass on without ever knowing he was there.

"Fall out!" came a muffled command. "We'll camp here
for the night."

Neal froze, hardly daring to breath. He knew that voice. He
knew these men.

For what seemed like hours, he held perfectly still—watching, listening, hoping that the racket his heart was making
wouldn't give him away to the Rebels.

The soldiers dismounted and began pitching their tents. The
air had turned cold. A fine mist of rain fell steadily. Neal

shivered. He wondered where he had lost his oilskin cloak. His rifle was missing, as well. If they spied him and it came to a fight, his only defense would be his bare fists.

"Are we going up to the house tonight, Pa?" Again, Neal recognized the voice. It was Virginia's brother, Rodney Swan.

"Not tonight. We wouldn't want to startle the ladies. Why, your mother might shoot us for Yankees. And she's a dead shot, you know. I taught her myself."

"I could sure go for one of Polly's homecooked meals."

"You'll have to wait awhile on that," Colonel Swan replied.

The men began to settle down for the night. Neal knew who he was and where he was. What he couldn't figure was how Swan's Cavalry had ridden out of the past and into this twentieth century Virginia night. He tried to tell himself that this was all his imagination, that he could simply stand up and walk back to the house without drawing their notice. But he wasn't quite convinced this was so.

He stayed put for a long time, until silence—except for isolated snoring—fell over the camp. Sure that the men—or ghosts?—were all asleep, he rose to his feet, ready to make a run for it. When his shoe caught on a root and he crashed to the ground, a sentry called, "Halt! Who goes there?"

Neal didn't answer. He froze as he saw the Confederate soldier advancing toward him, rifle at the ready. Whirling toward the house, Neal took off at full speed. He glanced back only once. The Reb was in hot pursuit. A single shot rang out through the quiet woods. Neal saw the man's face in a burst of flame. He threw up his arm to cover his eyes. Then pain burned through his right arm.

Neal sank to the ground, rolled into a ball, and groaned.

It was long after dark before they found Neal. Ginna had been gone for over three hours. The cold mist of rain that had begun at twilight hadn't let up. By the time Leonard Kirkwood and old Zee spotted Neal's huddled form deep in the woods, he was shivering with cold and shock.

"Step on it, Zee!" Kirkwood ordered. "Get back to the house and send help. Tell Big George and Hubert to bring a stretcher and blankets."

Without wasting time on words, the gardener loped through the dark woods like a fox after a hare. Minutes later, he returned with a pair of hulking male nurses. The two men lifted Neal onto the stretcher and covered him with a blanket.

"Get him back to the house, fast," Kirkwood said, "but go gently. He's bleeding and in shock."

Neal was vaguely aware of what was going on, as he drifted in and out of consciousness. His right arm throbbed and burned. He could feel the stickiness of his own blood soaking his shirt sleeve.

"Who was it, Neal?" Dr. Kirkwood asked. "Who shot you?"

"The Rebs," Neal moaned. "Camped in the woods."

Kirkwood and Zee exchanged puzzled glances.

"He's out of his head, Doc," Big George said. "Unless he means those gray ghosts that old Elspeth talks about all the time."

That thought had crossed Leonard Kirkwood's mind, too. But ghosts didn't shoot real bullets—*did they?* "Just get him into the house. Easy on the stairs, boys."

The next thing Neal became aware of was a bright light shining into his eyes. And again, he felt the throb of his wounded arm.

"Neal, it's Dr. Kirkwood. I'm going to give you something for the pain. The bullet's lodged in the fleshy part of your forearm. I've got to get it out."

"Gimme whiskey, Doc, and a stick to bite on." Neal's voice sounded slurred and weak.

"He thinks he's really back there, during the war," Hubert said.

"He's suffering from loss of blood. But he's going to be all right, as soon as I get this bullet out."

The shot put Neal under. Silence reigned in the room, while the doctor probed his flesh for the bullet. "There! Got it!"

Kirkwood said, triumphantly. He held the piece of metal up to the light for a closer look.

"Jesus-H-Christ!" Big George exclaimed. "It's a goddamn Civil War Minie ball!"

"It can't be."

"If you'd dug as many war relics in the fields around here as I have, Doc, you'd know as sure as I do. They don't make 'em like that anymore. It *was* them Rebel ghosts that shot him!"

Dr. Kirkwood refused to discuss such an outrageous notion. "Sew him up and bandage the wound," he ordered. "I'll be in my office when you finish."

Leaving Neal in the capable hands of Big George, Kirkwood left, taking the bullet with him. He meant to disprove this ghost theory immediately by checking a reference book in his office. He thumbed through several pages, before he found what he was looking for. He compared the bullet to the picture. Once he did, he poured himself a stiff Scotch, while still staring at the page of illustrations. A sound at the door made him look up.

"How's he doing, Big George?"

"Resting. Hubert stayed with him."

"He'll be fine. Weak and sore for a few days, but the wound isn't life threatening."

Big George moved over to the desk and looked at the open book. He tapped the picture of the Minie ball with one thick finger. "I told you, Doc. That's what it is, all right. But I never knew anybody shot by one before. I didn't even know ghosts could fire a rifle."

Kirkwood narrowed his eyes as he looked up at the other man. "There's a perfectly logical explanation for this."

"Yeah? What, Doc?"

"I don't know, but I'm going to find out. Come on. We're going back out to those woods and have a look around."

Big George raised his beefy hands in front of him. "Sorry, boss, not me. There ain't no man I'm scared of, but I don't mess with no ghosts."

"All right. You sit with Mr. Frazier. I'll go alone."

And he did, only to find exactly what he had expected—
nothing. Just a rainsoaked forest and trampled ground, where
he and the others had been. Wet and cold, desperately wanting
another Scotch, Kirkwood headed back to the house, shaking
his head.

He looked in on Neal. His patient was sleeping soundly.
Only the twitch of his eyelids hinted that he was dreaming.

"You can go on to bed," Kirkwood told Big George.

"I'll sit a spell with him. He's been muttering off and on,
kind of restless like."

"Suit yourself. I'm turning in. Call me if there's any
change."

Neal was restless, for sure. He kept seeing the sentry's familiar face at the instant the trigger had been pulled. Neal could
still feel the pain of the bullet's impact. He knew someone had
come to his aid—the Rebels themselves, he assumed. So now
he must be their prisoner.

"Virginia," he moaned. "Where are you, Virginia?"

Big George rose and went over to check the bandage. It
looked secure and clean. The bleeding must have stopped. A
good sign. He settled back down, dozing off and on, waking
each time his patient called out for Virginia.

Ginna got home, just as the misty rain turned heavy. All the
way to Winchester on the bus, she had experienced the same
nagging dread that had come to her in the woods. Something
was wrong. Very wrong! *But what?*

She unlocked the door and hurried in. The place felt damp
and chilly. She decided to build a fire before she called Neal.
The minute she switched on the light in the front room, a feeling
of déjà vu overwhelmed her. She glanced about, holding her
breath, willing the odd sensation away. But there was no deny-
ing it; the reason was all too clear.

Her old house suddenly looked more than familiar. It wasn't
just home; it was a place she knew from Virginia's life. The

parsonage, with its big fireplace and mantel, its rough-hewn beams, its plank floors. Why, of all the places she could have chosen to rent, had she picked this one? The obvious answer sent a shiver threw her. Virginia had willed it so. She had been drawn back to the very setting of the lovers' near-marriage and Virginia's parting from her lover.

Suddenly, Ginna felt an overwhelming urge to talk to Neal. She hurried to the phone and dialed the number at Swan's Quarter. It rang and rang, until finally Leonard Kirkwood answered.

"Doctor, it's Ginna. I need to talk to Neal right now."

"He's sleeping, Ginna."

"Wake him up. This is really important."

Kirkwood hesitated before he answered her urgent plea. "I'm afraid I can't do that, Ginna. I had to give him a sedative."

"Why?"

"Well—" Again he seemed to be stalling, groping for an answer that would satisfy Ginna. "It was that call from Mr. Henderson. It disturbed him. Apparently, it was too soon for him to be reminded of the crash."

"That couldn't be the problem. We've talked about the plane crash plenty of times. He seems to have gotten over the shock of it. He's never gotten upset talking about it."

"This time he did," Dr. Kirkwood answered firmly. "I told you before you left that he ran past me out of my office. He just took off out into the woods."

"So, you sedated him after he came back?"

Another long pause. "He didn't come back, Ginna. We had to go out and find him. When we did, he was in shock."

"My God! What could have happened?"

"I'm not sure. But he's sleeping now and seems to be fine."

Ginna realized, by the hesitation in his voice, that Dr. Kirkwood wasn't telling her everything. "Has he had a total relapse?"

"Now, don't jump to conclusions, Ginna. There's nothing to worry about. He should be on the mend by tomorrow."

"On the mend?" Ginna's voice went up an octave. "You mean, he's hurt?"

With a sigh of resignation, Kirkwood realized he couldn't keep this from her. The woman was too sharp for her own good. "Listen, Ginna, I'm going to tell you what happened. But I want you to promise me you will not get overwrought. I assure you, Neal will be fine in a day or two."

"For heaven's sake, just *tell me!*"

"Neal's been shot, but it isn't serious. The bullet lodged in his right forearm. I removed it, and now he's resting quietly. He'll have a scar, nothing else to remind him of the episode."

"Shot? By whom?"

"We don't know."

"Wasn't Neal able to tell you anything?"

"Only what he imagined happened."

"What did he say?"

"That he came upon a Confederate cavalry unit. He claims one of the soldiers fired at him."

"You don't believe that?"

Kirkwood gave a grim chuckle. "Of course, I don't believe that."

Ginna's mind was in chaos, but one thought stood out from the others. "You said you removed the bullet. What kind was it?"

Another deep sigh on the other end of the line. "A Minie ball," he said, quickly and quietly.

"Then that proves Neal is telling the truth."

"It doesn't prove anything. How could such a fantastic story be true? There has to be another explanation."

"I believe him."

"Ginna, just let it go for now. Don't worry about him. You get some rest. By the time next Monday rolls around, Neal will be as good as new."

"I'm not waiting till next Monday. Tell Neal for me that I'll see him tomorrow."

Dr. Kirkwood was still pleading when Ginna hung up the phone.

She leaned back in her chair and took a deep breath. She was trembling all over.

"Neal, shot," she repeated, trying to make herself believe it. There was no doubt in her mind *which* cavalry unit he had stumbled upon. "Colonel Jedediah Swan's men," she assured herself. "Virginia's father and brothers."

In that instant, she vowed to herself that she would go back in the past again. She had no choice. Tonight was proof that, if she didn't go back and set things right, the ghosts of that other time would give them no peace. Not even in this time.

She closed her eyes, trying to relax, trying to tell herself that everything would be all right—eventually. All she had to do was correct the mistakes in that earlier time. Then, and only then, could she and Neal marry and have a happy life together.

Even as Neal lay dreaming of the war, Ginna joined him, slipping into sleep and back to the past without even realizing she had dozed off.

"Hell, yeah, I shot him!" Virginia's brother Hollis proclaimed proudly. "I reckon I didn't kill him, but I sure put a good hurtin' on that damnyankee spy."

"I heard the shot," Melora Swan said calmly. "I got my pistol out of the blanket chest and kept it next to me in bed all night."

"I'm sorry we distressed you, my dear," said Colonel Swan, contritely.

His wife patted his arm and smiled up at him.

Melora, Virginia, and Agnes, who was now great with child, had been delighted when their men rode in unexpectedly, only moments before. Now the women stood close, touching, patting, hugging their soldiers, trying to reassure themselves that they were not only alive, but well and uninjured.

"You're all soaked to the skin. Why on earth did you camp out all night in the rain?" Melora demanded of her husband.

He chuckled and kissed her hand. "I figured, as dirty as we

were after our long ride from Richmond, you'd be happier to see us if we spent a night getting washed down.''

"Besides, Ma," Rodney added, beaming at his heavily pregnant wife, "we knew that blue-belly was out there sneaking around. We had to take care of him first, to protect you ladies.''

"I don't see how one lone man could have been much of a threat to us," Virginia argued. "We could have handled him without you all lifting a finger.''

All eyes turned to Virginia. They had hardly noticed her, in the excitement of their reunion. Rodney looked his sister up and down with more than a hint of disapproval in his gaze.

"How come you're dressed like that, girl?''

Virginia hadn't meant to let her father and brothers catch her this way. However, they had given the ladies at Swan's Quarter no hint of their approach. She hadn't had time to change.

"I decided it would be a good idea to let anyone passing by think that there's a man on the premises.''

"Those *my* britches?'' Rodney demanded.

Virginia blushed. "No. Yours were too big for me. These belong to Hampton.''

"Here now!'' Her younger brother, one of the twins, stepped forward, looking both angry and embarrassed. "I don't let no women wear my pants.''

"It was my idea, son,'' Melora Swan interjected. "Your sister is dressed this way as much for her own protection as for ours. She is young, beautiful, and unmarried. A temptation to any soldier who happens by—Union or Confederate.''

Colonel Swan frowned down at his delicate-looking wife. "You've had many come this way?''

She nodded, primly, recalling the terror she had felt on some of those occasions, but successfully hiding it from her husband. "More than I can count. But you needn't worry. Most of them are quite gentlemanly, no matter which side they're fighting for. Still, there is always a chance of deserters accosting us. I won't have Virginia put in such danger. She will dress as a man until this war is over.''

"Well, she makes a mighty handsome fellow," Colonel Swan said, with a wink at his only daughter.

Rodney tightened his arms around Agnes's slender shoulders. "Just so long as you don't go putting my wife in trousers."

Agnes giggled, embarrassed, as all eyes turned on her enormous belly. "Don't be silly, Rod darlin'. *No* man would find me attractive, the way I look now."

Rodney leaned down and whispered for her ears alone, "I do. *Mighty* attractive, honey bunch."

Agnes giggled again and blushed all over. The others tried to ignore the sexual tension between Rodney and his bride. Virginia, however, found it impossible to suppress her envy. But for her father and brothers, she would be married to Channing now, perhaps carrying his child. The thought hurt down to her very soul.

Colonel Swan had brought a larder of confiscated victuals with him. Polly's eyes grew big as melons to see so much food, after their meager rations of the past few months. Other troops from both sides had confiscated the contents of their smokehouse and decimated their chicken yard and pig stye.

"It's been mighty lean pickings around here, of late. But, Colonel, sir, we gone eat tonight, shore enough," the cook crowed, with glee.

And they did. They ate for hours, as Polly brought out dish after delicious dish of steaming food. Fried chicken, plump smoked ham, crisp cracklings, sweet potatoes bubbling in buttery caramel sauce, feather-light biscuits, and real coffee. Apple pie with a flaky crust topped off the feast.

As delicious as the meal was, Virginia could only pick at her food. Something was gnawing at her mind, something she desperately needed to talk about. A dream early that morning, just before she awoke, had convinced her that the time for action had come. It was late that night before Virginia had a chance to approach her father with her urgent request. Her mother had gone to their bedroom to prepare for her husband. Virginia found the colonel alone in the library, enjoying a brandy before bedtime.

"May I come in?" she asked from the door.

"By all means, my dear. And I must say, I like you better in that lovely gown than in Hampton's britches. You truly are a beauty, Virginia."

"Thank you, Father, but I didn't come to coax compliments from you. There's something else that I want, much more."

"Name it, Virginia. If it is within my power, it will be yours."

She sat primly on the very edge of the chair nearest her father's, her back ramrod straight, her eyes locked on his face.

"I need a pass."

The colonel frowned, not taking her meaning.

"A pass to get through the Confederate lines," she explained.

He started to speak, but she held up her hand for his silence.

"Please, Father, hear me out."

He nodded, but the pleasure in his countenance had changed to something quite different, much darker.

"I have waited and waited, but there has been no word from Channing all these months. I know that his troop has been involved in several major battles. I *must* reassure myself that he is well. My plan is to ride to Washington City. I've heard his company is encamped there. A Union officer, who passed this way last week, told me. I have to go to him, Father."

"The hell, you say!" Jedediah Swan came half out of his chair and, in the process, tipped over his brandy. "I'll have no daughter of mine riding about the countryside like a common camp follower."

Virginia held her anger in check. How could he refuse her? Didn't he understand about love and need and the pain of separation? Silently, she counted to ten before she allowed herself to reply.

"I have a feeling something has happened to Channing. I had a dream. I think he's been shot."

"*A dream.* You women!" Colonel Swan scoffed. "If I had a Yankee greenback for every dream your mother has ever had, I'd be as rich as Midas. Dreams mean nothing!"

"This one was different, Father. It was strange. I saw Channing in the woods outside the house, but somehow he wasn't the Channing I know. He was dressed differently. He wasn't in uniform, but was wearing the oddest clothes I've ever seen. Suddenly, he came upon a group of soldiers. I heard a shot, saw a flash, then Channing called out to me. He was in pain, Father. He needs me. I know it! I *must* go to him.''

"Daughter, you're just overwrought. Do you think Channing would want you putting yourself in such danger for his sake? I don't believe so. Not if he truly loves you.''

"Do you think Mother would stay here, only to be safe, if she knew that you needed her?''

The colonel sighed deeply. His gaze focused on the dark brandy stain shining damply on the Turkish carpet at his feet. "Your mother, God bless her, is the bravest, most stubborn woman to ever walk the face of the earth.''

"And I am her daughter,'' Virginia reminded him.

"Nevertheless, I won't permit this.'' He paused and shifted his gaze to Virginia's face, staring deeply into her beautiful, innocent eyes. "This war is not the glorious adventure your brothers had imagined it would be. It's mean and ugly and terrible, Virginia. The things I've seen . . .'' His voice trailed off, as his mind seemed to wander back to distant battlefields. "I may never sleep nights again. I can't let you see all that, daughter. Even if you got through to Washington and found Channing and returned home without incident, you would come back a changed person.''

"I'm willing to take that chance,'' she said, quietly.

Just as softly, he answered, "But, you see, I am not. No, Virginia! I will *not* give you a pass, and I *forbid* you to leave Swan's Quarter!''

The discussion was clearly at an end. Virginia rose, went dutifully to kiss her father's cheek, then left the library, without speaking another word. She didn't trust her voice. If she said so much as "good night'' to her father, he would surely hear the defiance in her tone. A pass signed by Colonel Jedediah Swan would have eased her journey. But she could manage without it, and she would if she had to.

Virginia went straight to her room from the library, her mission clear in her mind. She couldn't make her move as long as her father and brothers remained at Swan's Quarter. But the minute they left, she would be ready to go, too.

Alone in her room, she devised a knapsack from a large bandanna, and stuffed it with the bare essentials. She would have to travel light, on horseback, and there was no telling how long she would be gone. Long after midnight, Virginia finally went to bed. She was trembling with fatigue, aching with anxiety. She only hoped she wouldn't be too late. As much as she loved her father and brothers, she prayed that duty would call, and they would have to leave Swan's Quarter shortly.

Her last waking thought was of Channing. With her eyes closed, she could see him lying somewhere far away, a bandage wrapped about his right arm.

"I'm coming, darling," she whispered. "I won't let you down. I love you with all my heart, Channing."

One floor below and over a century into the future, Neal Frazier heard his beloved's words. He moved on his bed and strained, trying to reach out to her. "Virginia, my dearest," he moaned.

Big George, roused from sleep by Neal's mumbled words, got up and tucked the covers around him. He stared down at Neal's frowning face and twitching eyelids.

"You keep this up, buddy, and I'm gonna have to ask the doc to shoot you again with another sedative. You lay easy now, you hear?"

Far off, Channing McNeal heard a snatch of Big George's words—spoken to him by a Rebel guard, he assumed. The phrase "shoot you again" came through, loud and clear. Channing forced himself to lie very still. He concentrated all his thoughts on Virginia—visualizing her lovely face, recalling the sweet softness of her lips, telling her silently, over and over again, how much he loved her and missed her and needed her.

Channing McNeal's words reached Ginna Jones, who was drowsing on the sofa at the old parsonage and dreaming of him. She knew that he was wounded and that she must go to him. But, even in sleep, she realized she dared not make her move until Virginia Swan's father and brothers rode back to the war.

"Channing," she murmured in her dreamlike state, "I'm coming. Don't worry, Neal, I love you and I always will. I'll find you. We'll be married. Everything will be all right. You'll see. This war can't last forever."

Ginna woke up, just as she spoke the final sentence aloud. She knew immediately where she was—the parsonage. But it wasn't the parsonage any longer. *Was it?* And she knew who she was—Virginia Swan. But she wasn't Virginia any longer. *Was she?* Well, one thing at least was clear in her mind: She loved Neal Frazier as never before!

"But the Rebel soldier shot him," she said, sitting up and blinking her eyes in wonder.

Chapter Twelve

The news of Neal's encounter with the Rebel soliders spread through Swan's Quarter like wildfire. Big George couldn't resist telling one of his relic-hunting buddies, who worked in the kitchen, about the Minie ball. He, in turn, confided in Marcellus Lynch, who whispered the secret to Pansy Pennycock, who simply could not keep anything from Sister Randolph. The two women and Lynch were on the veranda after breakfast, discussing the matter and trying to figure out how such a thing could have happened to a nice fellow like Neal. None of them noticed Elspeth's approach. After a restless night, she had slept through the morning meal. She had just come from the kitchen, where she partook of tea and milk toast alone.

No one had yet told Elspeth about the events of the previous night. No one needed to. In tune with all otherworldly happenings in and around Swan's Quarter, she had felt the approach of the Rebels in her bones, the same way she could always feel the approach of a thunderstorm by the sharp ache in her joints. Expecting the gray ghosts to put in an appearance, she had lingered at her window most of the night, her eagle-eyes trained on the woods. She had seen Neal run from the house.

Only moments later, she had spied the dark mist that always materialized into the phantom troupe. She knew them well. Swan's Cavalry.

Most often, when she saw these pale ghosts on their fiery-eyed steeds, their appearance brought great joy to her heart. The men of the family were home again! But last night had been different. She had felt a menacing presence the very moment she saw the first wisps of gray-black fog. She knew in that instant what was about to happen. Somehow the past was about to clash with the present. The moment the silent ghosts materialized— menacing and dangerous—she knew that someone at Swan's Quarter was in grave peril.

"Yankee spy!" The words had drifted up to her from the haunted woods, like a whisper on the sharp night wind.

In the blink of an eye, she had realized at whom their accusations and threats were aimed. She had tried to call out to Neal Frazier, but her old voice was too weak, and he was too far away. Moments later, she had seen the flash, then heard the shot.

"Poor boy!" she had murmured. "He's not set on spying, just seeing Miss Virginia, after all this time."

She had kept watch at her window for a good while, after that, until she was sure that Neal had been found and would be taken care of. Since no one called an ambulance, she guessed that his wound was not serious. She gave it more than an hour, before she sneaked downstairs to make sure he was all right. When she had peeked into the examing room, Neal was calling for Virginia, while Big George snored on, oblivious.

"Lordy me!" she had murmured, on the way back up to her room. "What's to become of us, now that the past and the present done met?"

When she reached the veranda that morning and saw Pansy and Sister with their heads bowed close to old Lynch, hanging on his every word, she knew that they knew. She smiled with self-satisfaction.

"Well, I guess you all won't be pooh-poohing my sightings of Confederate ghosts, from now on."

All three at the table jerked around as if they had just been
caught in the commission of a crime.

"Why, Elspeth!" Pansy said, with a flutter in her voice.
"We thought you were still sleeping. You missed breakfast,
dear."

"Milk toast, your favorite," Lynch added, with a pleased
smirk.

"Had my own in the kitchen. Cook made it special."

"With sugar?" Sister asked.

"*And* nutmeg! But never mind that. You all are just trying
to change the subject."

"We were talking about breakfast," Pansy said.

"Not before I walked up, you weren't. So, out with it! What
are you three up to that doesn't include me?"

Lynch opened his mouth to tell all, before the women could
steal his thunder. But he got no more than two words out before
Elspeth held up her hand to silence him.

"If it's about Neal Frazier getting shot last night, you needn't
bother. I saw the whole thing. Even slipped in to make sure
he was all right after Dr. Kirkwood finished patching him up.
He seemed fine. Just sort of restless."

"Then he *really* was *shot?*"

"Indeed he was, Sister. The Rebel ghost was at close range.
Could have done real damage. But I figure the ball must of
veered off course, traveling through time as it did. Lucky, for
Neal too. His right arm might have just as easy been his heart,
if that bullet had been fired off in the here and now."

Lynch hurrumphed loudly. "Seems to me the cook must
have put something more than a dash of nutmeg in your milk
toast, Elspeth. You're talking out of your head."

Neither Pansy nor Sister made any comment. It was clear
from the skeptical looks on their faces, however, that they fully
agreed with Lynch.

"I been telling you and telling you about those Confederate
ghosts in the woods." She leaned close and leered at each of
the three, in turn. *"Well, haven't I?"*

They nodded.

"And last night's my proof."

"See here, Elspeth, you can't expect us to believe that some Rebel soldier fired off his gun back in the past and shot Neal Frazier in the present." Lynch sounded outraged at the very thought.

"Oh, can't I? What are you saying, that I'm *senile?* If you don't believe what happened, you must take me for being not only old, but blind and deaf, as well. I *saw* the flash from that gun barrel. I *heard* that shot."

"Here, now! Nobody's accusing anybody of being senile," Lynch said, by way of a blustering apology. Secretly, though, he wondered if Elspeth might not be wrestling with the early stages of Alzheimer's. *Rebel ghosts, indeed!*

"You have to admit, dear, that your account of what happened is a touch farfetched." Pansy smiled warmly at Elspeth, not wishing to hurt her feelings.

"We can settle this right now. Come on with me!" Elspeth ordered. "We'll just go see what Neal has to say about what happened."

"Dr. Kirkwood won't let us in to see him," Sister reasoned. "Not if he's really been shot."

"Well, he damn-sure won't let us see Neal, if we don't try. You all coming or not?" Elspeth challenged.

They all rose and followed her eagerly into the hallway. There, they slowed their pace, creeping toward the examining room and ducking into doorways at the slightest sound, like thieves about to burgle the place.

If they had stayed a moment longer on the veranda, they would have witnessed the miracle of the tulip poplar. Out of the clear morning air, it materialized, just as Ginna came hurrying out of the woods near the swan pond. When Sam had driven up to the bus stop, she had been waiting to catch the very first bus on the Front Royal to Winchester run.

Her heart pounded furiously, as she hurried up the hill to Swan's Quarter. What a night it had been! Her sleep had been interrupted by the most curious and disturbing dreams. It had seemed she heard someone calling to her out of the distant past. Could Channing McNeal be trying to contact her? Was he begging her to come back? Or had it been Neal she had heard calling her name?

As Ginna reached the tulip poplar, she saw Marcellus, Pansy, Sister, and Elspeth all hurrying through the front door, as if there were some great emergency. If the house were on fire and they were inside, she imagined that they would have moved at about the same pace and with the same degree of urgency.

"Now what?" she wondered aloud, speeding her own step to find out as soon as possible.

Dr. Kirkwood, who had spotted Ginna through his office window, was waiting for her on the veranda, when she came up the stairs.

"You shouldn't take that hill so fast, Ginna. You'll be fainting on me again, next thing I know."

"I will be just fine once I see Neal. Where is he?"

Kirkwood held the door for her. "Come with me. He should be awake by now."

"How is he?"

"Doing well. I told you, the wound wasn't serious. There's no need for you to worry so, Ginna."

She stopped and stared at him. "The man I'm going to marry has been *shot,* and you're telling me not to worry?"

Kirkwood saw her point. Besides, women *always* worried. "At least don't let him know how upset you are. I'd like to get him through this with a minimum amount of trauma."

Ginna nodded and forced a composure she didn't feel.

If "minimum trauma" was what the doctor prescribed, he hadn't bargained for a visit to his patient from Neal's elderly friends. When Kirkwood and Ginna entered the room, Lynch, Elspeth, Pansy, and Sister were all firing questions at Neal.

"Who was it shot you?" Elspeth demanded. "I'll bet it was Colonel Swan hisself."

Pansy bustled about, tucking covers and fluffing pillows. "Does it pain you much, dear boy?"

Sister was offering to run to the kitchen and brew some of

her special sassafrass tea for Neal. "It'll cure whatever ails you."

Lynch was regaling the whole group about the time he was shot, fighting in Korea. He was being duly ignored by the lot of them.

Neal was lying in bed, struggling to accept Pansy's unwanted ministrations with grace, while he attempted to answer all of their questions. Finally, in a brief period of silence, he got a word in. "Ginna? Have any of you seen Ginna?"

"I'm here Neal," she said from the doorway.

"Out!" Dr. Kirkwood commanded. "All of you! What are you doing in here pestering my patient?"

"I saw it all, but *they* didn't believe me." Elspeth stood firm, even though the others were headed for the door.

"You, too, Elspeth—*out!*"

She brushed past the doctor and Ginna, with her head held high. "Well, just in case you need a witness," she said, "that's *me*. I'll be in my room till the sheriff comes."

Once Elspeth closed the door, Dr. Kirkwood let out a huge sigh of relief, then muttered something under his breath about busybodies and nuisances, and old people in general.

Ginna wasn't listening. She hurried to Neal and bent down to kiss him, lingering over his lips for a long time.

"Hey, that was worth getting shot for," he said, smiling up into her troubled eyes. "It's okay, honey. The doc says I'm going to be fine. Look, I can even raise my arm."

"Don't!" Kirkwood said. "You'll start the bleeding again."

"Hey, Doc, could Ginna and I have a few minutes alone?"

Kirkwood hesitated, but finally decided that Ginna was probably the best medicine for his patient, at the moment.

"Don't excite him," Kirkwood said, just before he left them.

Neal chuckled at that. "I guess I'd better not tell him that you got me excited, the minute you walked into the room."

Ginna smoothed her hand over his forehead. "Neal, are you sure you're all right?"

"I am, now that you're here."

"Don't make jokes. I really want to know, Neal. How are you?"

"I'm not joking. The minute you walked through that door, the last twinges of pain just vanished. My arm feels like it did this time yesterday—before the incident last night."

"Do you remember what happened?"

"Some of it." He frowned. "Other parts are kind of fuzzy in my brain. I'm still not sure who shot me. The doc won't talk about it. Has he told you anything?"

Ginna wondered if she should tell Neal all she knew. After all, Dr. Kirkwood had warned her not to upset him. She decided against telling him everything.

"I don't know a lot of details either. Dr. Kirkwood said that you rushed out after that phone call, but you didn't come back in. It started raining, and they went out to look for you. I think there was probably a hunter in the woods and he must have fired off a stray round. You just happened to be at the wrong place at the right time."

Several seconds of silence stretched between them, before Neal said, "So, you don't buy the line about my being shot by a Confederate soldier?"

Ginna avoided his gaze. "I don't know what to believe," she admitted. "But I do know this." Again she leaned down and kissed him. "If anything had happened to you, I wouldn't have wanted to live any longer. I love you, Neal. I want to get married just as soon as we can."

Neal let out a whoop. "You sure know how to get a guy well in a hurry!"

He reached up and gathered Ginna close with his good arm. She was practically lying next to him on the bed. Slowly, gently, with ever so much tenderness, he kissed her, tangling his hand in her hair to hold her near.

Finally, she drew slightly away. Her heart was thundering; she had to catch her breath.

"Not too much excitement," she whispered, smiling into his eyes. "Doctor's orders."

"To hell with doctor's orders. Come here to me, Virginia."

In a love daze, she didn't realize he hadn't called her by her own name. She was only aware of his nearness when he drew her close again, kissing her face all over—eyelids, cheeks, nose, chin. Finally, he captured her lips once more. Ginna was trembling against him—wanting him, needing him, loving him as she had never known she could love him before. All the loneliness and hurt of her childhood vanished, when Neal held her this way. The rest of the world ceased to exist. Only the two of them were here, loving each other, as if nothing else mattered.

"Where do you want to live after we're married, Ginna?"

The question came out of the blue, but gave her a warm feeling. She thought about it, before she answered. "Anywhere that you are."

"That's my girl! You know all the right answers." Neal chuckled and brushed her forehead with his lips. "Do you like Washington or Alexandria, or would you rather stay in Winchester?"

"I think Alexandria is lovely. I've been there only a couple of times, but it seems such a cozy place—away from the bustle of Washington."

"Then Alexandria it will be! I've been planning to sell my house. We'll find a place together that's all ours. No ghosts from the past."

His mention of ghosts drew a cloud over Ginna's happiness. "Neal, will you do me one favor, before we're married?"

"*Anything,* darling—before or after we're married. Just name it."

"I have a feeling we need to go back one more time. I know you don't want to, but I had this dream last night. I have to find out what happened to Channing and Virginia. I'll never know any peace until I find out. Go back with me, darling, just once," she begged. "Then we'll get on with our own life together and forget about the past."

Ginna held her breath, waiting for Neal's answer. She knew she was asking a lot. She would understand if he refused.

Neal smoothed the hair back from her face. "Ginna, look at me."

She did as he asked, damning herself for the tears gathering in her eyes.

"This really means a lot to you, doesn't it?"

She nodded, afraid to trust her voice.

"Well, I guess, if you think we must, then we must. I don't understand any of this. I wish we'd never gotten involved with Channing and Virginia."

"But don't you see, Neal, they brought us together. Without them, we might never have found each other."

"And, supposing you're right, why would they do that?"

"Because they need us. Because nothing will ever be right between them unless we help make it right."

"But things are right between *us,* Ginna. Isn't that all that matters?"

"I'm not sure, Neal. I can't explain it. It's just a feeling I have. You have to trust me. That's all I can tell you."

He hugged her and wiped away her tears. "Okay, darlin'. Once the doc lets me up out of this bed, we'll do whatever you want. But we need to do it right away. I don't want to have to wait long to get married."

"Neither do I, Neal." She smiled with a brilliance that lit the room. "You couldn't be more eager than I am. I've been waiting all my life to marry you."

Just then, Dr. Kirkwood knocked and called from the door, "Neal, you have visitors."

He rolled his eyes. "Not the interrogation committee again, I hope."

Ginna laughed. "I imagine they've been banned from this room, for good."

"Who is it?" Neal called.

Dr. Kirkwood opened the door a crack. "Mr. Henderson and little Christine. Do you feel up to seeing them, Neal? They've driven a long way, but I can tell them to come back another time, if that would be better."

Neal grimaced. "No time would be good. I guess I might as well get this over with."

"Are you sure, Neal?" Ginna was worried.

He gripped her hand. "It'll be all right, honey, if you'll stay here with me."

"Of course," she answered, unsmiling.

"Tell them to come on in, Doc."

The man who entered looked more like three-year-old Christine's grandfather than her father. His hair was as gray, as was his face. His dark eyes seemed sunken deep into his head. The smile creases around his mouth showed that once he had been full of life and fun. But those lines were not in use today. He held his little daughter's hand and walked slowly toward the bed, staring at Neal.

"Thank you for seeing us, Mr. Frazier." His voice quivered with emotion. "I know this is an imposition, especially since you aren't feeling well."

Neal sat up straighter in the bed. He was squeezing Ginna's hand so tightly that it almost hurt. Neal looked every bit as somber as Donald Henderson. It took a bright smile from Christine to cut the tension in the room—a smile she showered on the man who had saved her life.

Without a word, she ran over to the low bed, climbed up, and wrapped her arms around Neal's neck. "Thank you, Mr. Frazier," she said softly. "Daddy said to tell you that."

Ginna watched Neal's eyes redden when he looked at the pretty blond child. Someday, she mused happily, he would make a wonderful father to their children.

"That's a pretty dress for a pretty girl," Neal answered, in a choked voice. "Blue's my favorite color."

She laughed brightly. "It's mine too! And my mommy loved blue."

Dr. Kirkwood had been standing by the door, observing. He knew that Donald Henderson wanted to talk to Neal alone, without the child in the room.

"Christine?" he said. "Would you like to walk down to the pond and see the swans? I have a lady here who will take you.

And she has sugar cookies from the kitchen and a glass of lemonade.''

Christine turned pleading eyes on her father.

For the first time, Mr. Henderson smiled. ''You run along, honey. Have a good time.''

Silence fell over the room, as Christine climbed down from the bed and ran to the door, where one of the nurses was waiting just outside with the promised cookies and lemonade. After she left, Kirkwood closed the door.

''I hope you don't mind if I stay,'' he said to Christine's father. ''Neal had an accident last night, and I don't want him to get upset.''

Henderson nodded to the doctor, then turned back to Neal and said, ''I'm sorry. I hope it was nothing serious.''

Neal half-raised his arm to show the bandage. ''No more than a scratch. The doc's just overcautious.''

''Is this your wife?'' Henderson asked, nodding toward Ginna.

Neal smiled up at her. ''Not yet, but soon. Once I'm back on my feet, we plan to be married right away.''

No one noticed the frown that those words brought to Leonard Kirkwood's face. No one but Ginna, that is.

''Ma'am,'' Henderson said, with a slight bow, ''I wish you a long life and all the happiness in the world. There's nothing like being married and sharing your life with the one person in the world who can make it complete.''

Henderson's voice broke on the last few words. It was clear to all of them that he was thinking of his wife and her tragic death. Again, tension filled the room.

''I'm sorry,'' Neal murmured.

''At least I still have Christine, thanks to you, Mr. Frazier. That's more than I could have hoped for. That's what her mother would have wanted. She worshiped our baby. And Christine is the image of her mother. I'll have that. All our other children look like my side of the family. I'm not going to take up much of your time. I just had to see you and thank you in person. Because of you, I'll get to see my little girl start school, graduate, get married, and give me grandchildren, I hope. Your actions were totally unselfish, risking your own life to save my baby. I know there's no way I can ever thank you adequately, Mr. Frazier, but I wanted to tell you that if there's anything—*anything*—I can ever do for you, you have only to ask. And I want you to know, too, that my wife, Sally, is up in heaven right now, smiling down on you, watching over you. She'll always be there."

Ginna noticed that Neal was shifting uncomfortably on the bed. She exchanged glances with Dr. Kirkwood. It was clear that Neal hoped Mr. Henderson would finish and leave soon. He couldn't take much more of this. Both Ginna and Kirkwood knew how guilty Neal felt about not being able to save Sally Henderson. Her husband's words were only rubbing salt into Neal's emotional wounds. This couldn't be good for him, no matter that Donald Henderson meant his words to the very depth of his scarred soul.

"I think my patient needs to rest now," Dr. Kirkwood said, in his most authoritative voice.

"Yes, well, I'll be going, then. But I had to see you," Henderson said. "Sally would have wanted me to thank you for our child's life."

Neal lurched up in bed suddenly. "Don't thank me! I'm the sorry sonuvabitch who let your wife die. If I'd had the guts, I would have gone back into that plane and brought her out, too. I don't want your thanks, Henderson. I don't *deserve* any thanks! You shouldn't be thanking me. You should be blaming me. *I* let your wife die! I'm the no-good bastard who made you a widower and left all your kids motherless."

He was actually yelling at the man. Henderson's complexion went from gray to pasty-white.

Dr. Kirkwood took Mr. Henderson by the arm and led him into the hall.

"I'm sorry," Henderson said. "I didn't mean to get him upset."

"I know. It's not your fault. He just wasn't ready to see

you, yet. I should have known that. I'd better get back in there now and see what I can do to calm him down.''

Donald Henderson was still muttering about how sorry he was, as he ambled off down the hallway.

Inside the room, Ginna had her hands full. For a few seconds after Dr. Kirkwood ushered Neal's visitor out, he continued yelling and thrashing about in the bed. Ginna tried to hold him still, so that his arm wouldn't start bleeding. It was no use. He was much too strong for her and too distraught. Then, suddenly, Neal went limp. He fell back against the pillows and didn't move. He hardly seemed to be breathing.

"Neal? Neal, can you hear me?" Ginna was hovering close, trying to get some response from him, when Dr. Kirkwood came back in.

"What's happened?" he demanded.

She stared up at him, frantic. "I don't know. He was raging on and on about the crash, and then he suddenly just fell back and went still. I can't get him to speak to me or even open his eyes. It's like he's not here in this room any longer.''

"Neal!" Dr. Kirkwood said, sternly. "Open your eyes!"

"Neal, can you hear me? Speak to me," Ginna begged.

Neal did not open his eyes, but he did speak. In a voice harsh with anxiety he said, "It's going to be all right, Mrs. Henderson. Just an air pocket. We'll be on the ground soon. You're not scared, are you, Christine?"

Ginna and Dr. Kirkwood looked at each other. It was all too clear what was happening to Neal. He was back in that airplane, flight 1862. And the plane was about to crash . . . *again.*

Chapter Thirteen

"What's happening, Dr. Kirkwood?" Ginna was frantic. "What can we do?"

Neal was still talking in a strange monotone, still back on board that ill-fated plane. He was trying to soothe Sally Henderson's tears, trying to make Christine laugh.

"I could sedate him, but I'd rather try to talk him through this without medication."

"But wouldn't a shot be faster?" Ginna gripped Neal's hand, as if by hanging on tightly, she might draw him back to the present.

"That might be faster, but not entirely safe. If I put him to sleep, what he's reliving might simply continue in the form of a dream. That could do him great harm."

Dr. Kirkwood came to the side of the bed and stared down into Neal's face. *"Neal!"* he called loudly. "Neal Frazier, you can hear me. I know you can. I want you to listen very carefully to what I'm saying. You are *not* on an airplane. You are at Swan's Quarter. Ginna is here, and she's very worried about you. We both want you to wake up right now. Neal? Are you listening to me?"

Kirkwood paused to see if his words had any affect. Neal continued mumbling, talking to Sally and Christine. His voice had lost its calm. He was becoming more and more agitated.

"Neal, listen to me! Forget Sally and Christine. They don't need you any longer. Ginna needs you now. She wants you to wake up. She needs to talk to you."

"Don't panic! Stop screaming!" Neal himself screamed. "We'll be okay. Just hang on. Put your face down in this pillow. *Everybody, stop screaming!"* Then in a whisper, like a prayer, he said, "God, help us! We're going to crash."

"No, Neal!" Ginna yelled. She grabbed his shoulders and shook him as hard as she could, tears streaming down her face. "No, you are *not* going to crash! You're coming back to me. I need you! Virginia needs you! You can't leave us like this. I won't have it!"

Dr. Kirkwood grabbed Ginna's arm to try to pull her away from Neal, but her grip was like a steel vise. She refused to let go of Neal.

"Ginna, don't. It's not helping."

Ignoring Kirkwood's pleas, Ginna repeated, "We need you, Neal. Both Virginia and I do."

Suddenly, Neal's eyes opened. He was staring right into Ginna's face. His own face looked ashen. Perspiration beaded his brow. "Ginna?" he whispered.

"Oh, Neal!" She leaned close, hugging him, kissing him. "I was so afraid you were gone for good. You scared me so! Don't *ever* leave me like that again!"

"I could have saved her. I should have."

"It's all over, Neal. What's done is done and was meant to be." Dr. Kirkwood kept his voice level and calm. "Let it go."

Neal didn't reply. He held Ginna close and took a deep, shaky breath. "I know it's over, Doc. Whether or not I can let it go remains to be seen."

"It will take time, but, believe me, you *will* get over this."

Suddenly Neal frowned and glanced about the room. "Where's Virginia?"

Ginna leaned down and whispered, "Sh-h-h. I'll tell you

later." Then she rolled her eyes significantly toward the doctor. "When we're alone, Neal."

But Kirkwood had heard. "Who are you talking about? Who's Virginia?"

Neal said nothing. Ginna passed off the doctor's question with a shrug. "Probably someone else he met on the plane."

"That's not true!" Kirkwood snapped. "If so, Neal would have mentioned her to me during our sessions. This has nothing to do with the crash. *Ginna?*" he said, in a warning tone.

Neal seemed oblivious to their conversation. He was still wide awake, but he seemed to be thinking of something or someone else. Ginna knew. He was thinking of Virginia.

"It's nothing, Dr. Kirkwood. Believe me. Neal's talking about Virginia Swan, a woman who used to live here." Thinking quickly, she fabricated, "Neal and I have been researching some of the Swan family's history. Virginia was Melora Swan's daughter. We've been trying to find out what happened to her. There don't seem to be any records. She's become something of an obsession with us." In a quieter voice, she added, "I think it's a good sign that Neal's thinking about her, instead of the crash. We were talking about Virginia, just before he slipped away."

"*That Elspeth!*" He sounded disgusted. "You've been listening to her tall tales, haven't you? It may be true that one of her ancestors was a slave at Swan's Quarter, but I think she's made up half her stories just to entertain Pansy and Sister and anyone else who'll listen to her. If she knows so much, she would have told you that Virginia Swan had a child out of wedlock, a child who was raised here at Swan's Quarter by her grandmother, Melora Swan, after the rest of the family was gone."

Ginna's heart raced. "How do you know that?"

"The Swan family Bible. All the births, marriages, and deaths are recorded there."

"You never told me this Bible existed."

"You never asked."

"Is Virginia's date of death listed?"

He paused for a moment, thinking. "No. I don't believe so. Nor her marriage. Only the birth of her daughter. That's the only time the child is listed, either, except for a notiation of her baptism and the fact that her grandmother was the only relative present on that day."

"Virginia's daughter—what was her name?" Ginna was so excited she could hardly speak.

Kirkwood thought for a long time. "Something unusual. Oh, what was it?" Then he brightened. "I know! It was Channelle."

"Named for Channing," Ginna murmured aloud, but speaking only to herself.

"I didn't know you were interested in the history of this place and the Swan family. Neal either, for that matter. When did all this come about?"

"After we met, and I realized that Neal bore a striking resemblance to Channing McNeal, the man Virginia Swan was supposed to marry." She started to mention the glass plate in the greenhouse, but decided against it. Instead, she said, "There's a miniature of McNeal in my bedroom. The likeness is uncanny. It could be Neal himself."

"Seems like it must have been a mighty tragic family situation. Unwed mothers weren't looked upon highly, back in those days. I'm not sure Neal should be delving into all this."

"But isn't it better for him to think about the Swan history than to dwell on the crash?"

"Not if he's getting so caught up in that history that he believes he's been shot by a Confederate ghost."

Neal had closed his eyes again. However, now he seemed to be napping peacefully. The other two talked in low whispers, so as not to disturb him.

"Neal didn't say he'd been shot by a ghost. That was what *you* told him, wasn't it?"

Dr. Kirkwood was visibly agitated now. "I never told him any such thing, because I don't believe that's what happened. It was Big George who put this fool notion into his head. And Elspeth has done her best to make everyone believe it. She's been seeing Confederate ghosts in those woods for years. I've always just passed it off as one more of her fantasies. Now she's got everyone on the place believing that the woods are haunted. As if I didn't have enough problems around here!"

"Then why didn't you call an ambulance for Neal last night?"

"He obviously didn't need one. I got the bullet out with no complications."

"But you told me that any patient at Swan's Quarter who had any kind of accident had to be sent to the hospital. You made *me* go, and all I did was have a little fainting spell."

"I wouldn't exactly call what you had a 'little fainting spell.' Neal's different. He's strong and healthy."

"But rules are rules, Doctor. That's what you told me. Besides, I thought all gunshot wounds had to be reported to the police, by law."

He nodded, frowning. "You're right about that. The thing is . . . how do I fill out this report? I'll be the laughing stock of the county, if I put down that he was shot by the ghost of a Confederate soldier."

"You don't believe that, so why put that in the report? It could have been an accident, a hunter shooting at what he took to be wild game."

"We don't have any hunters around here that use Minie balls, and I'll have to turn over the bullet with my report. But, you're right, Ginna, I do have to call the police, so they can investigate. I'll just put down 'shooter unknown.' " But just the same, this place will be in an uproar for days, with them investigating and asking everybody questions. Elspeth's sure to volunteer her 'eye witness' report. I dread thinking about it. I guess I'd better go make the call right now—get it over with. Call me when Neal wakes up."

Ginna nodded. "I will."

She was glad to be alone with Neal, after Dr. Kirkwood left. If he meant to call the police now, then there wasn't much time. And now that she knew Virginia had given birth to Channing's daughter, she was more anxious than ever to go back in time and find out the rest of the story.

"Neal," she whispered. "Neal, wake up. We're going to find Virginia. She needs us."

Neal roused slowly, smiling. "Virginia, my darlin'," he said, in Channing's deep Southern accent.

"We have to hurry." Ginna helped him up from the bed and handed him his trousers. It wouldn't do for Neal to be seen, up and about, wearing only his hospital gown, nor, once they got back to the previous century, would Channing be pleased to find himself dressed in such a shocking fashion.

"Where are we going?" Neal still seemed drowsy and confused.

"To the greenhouse. It's almost time."

"Time? Time for what?"

She let that question go unanswered and quickly led Neal out of the room.

Luckily, they met no one, as they tiptoed through the hallway and out the back. It was almost lunchtime, and most of the residents were waiting in the game room to be called for their noon meal. Elspeth had clued Ginna in on the senior citizens' obsession with being on time, or early, for the opening of the dining room doors. "You get to be as old as us and any meal could be your last. 'Wouldn't want to miss one, you know."

Neal was leaning heavily on Ginna. He still seemed very weak.

"It's not much farther," she encouraged. "Can you make it?"

"I'm fine," he said, just as they reached the greenhouse door. "But this is the last time, Ginna. Remember? You said you'd marry me as soon as we get back from checking on Virginia and Channing."

She smiled brightly and went up on tiptoe to kiss his cheek. He really was fine. He remembered now what they had been talking about, before Mr. Henderson and Christine came. And, yes, she would marry him after this one last visit back in time.

* * *

One person had spied Ginna leading Neal out the back way. Elspeth was leaving her room, headed for the dining room, when she heard Ginna's voice. The old woman watched from the shadows, as the pair disappeared out the back way. She nodded and smiled, approving of their actions. She alone knew exactly where they were going and why; she knew the rest of Virginia and Channing's story and the fact that it had yet to end.

"High time!" she muttered. "High time, indeed, that those two got together, once and for all."

As tempted as Elspeth was to follow Ginna and Neal, so that she could make the trip with them, she decided against such action. Her presence might disturb the flow and cause them to wind up in the wrong place or time.

"Best leave those young folks be, for the now," she whispered. "Time's running out and shouldn't nothing go wrong, this late in the game."

When she reached the game room, she found all the others still waiting there, anxious and fretting, most of them, because the dinner bell had yet to ring.

"Oh, Elspeth, here you are at last," Pansy whined. She patted the couch beside her, inviting the other woman to sit down.

"Dinner's late today!" Marcellus Lynch grouched.

" 'Tis not!" Elspeth countered. "Why, it's only quarter to twelve. It just seems late to all you early birds who got up with the crack of dawn to eat breakfast."

Suspecting that Elspeth was having a bad day, and not wanting to be around the grouchy old woman, Lynch got up and walked to the far side of the room to join another group.

"Where's Sister, Pansy?"

"Gone to powder her nose. You just missed her."

"Good! That'll give me and you a chance to talk, private."

"About what?" Pansy's eyes went wide. No one ever wanted to share secrets with her, least of all Elspeth. She felt a measure of excitement flow through her.

"About Ginna and Neal. And keep your voice down. I don't

want everybody hearing what we have to say.'' She leaned close and whispered, ''They're in the *greenhouse!*''

Pansy made a large, silent *O* with her mouth, and her eyes grew even wider.

''They're fixing to go back, I just know it, even though I warned Ginna that it might not be safe.'' Elspeth grinned. ''I figured that would do the trick, get them to go back again. So, Pansy, things might work out, yet.''

''Even after the ghosts shot him? I'd think he'd be scared.''

''Neal's a brave boy. Besides, I'm sure this is Ginna's idea. She knows the secrets—almost all of them.''

''But she doesn't know about *me,* does she?'' Pansy wiped perspiration from her face with her lace hanky.

''Not yet, I don't think. But she's bound to find out.''

Pansy whimpered softly.

''Now don't you start that.''

''She'll think bad of me, once she knows. I'd hate that. I love Ginna like my own daughter.''

''Then you ought to have enough faith in her to believe she'll understand. You weren't to blame, any more than poor Virginia was at fault for what happened to her. But, don't you see? Once they go back in time, they can put things to rights.''

''You really believe they can change what happened to Virginia and Channing and their baby, so long ago.''

Elspeth gave a stern nod. ''Not only that—I think that by changing the past, it'll change all that's happened since. I don't want to get your hopes up, but, mark my words, stranger things have happened.''

''We can't tell Sister.''

''Certainly not! She'd laugh in our faces. She doesn't know about the fourth dimension. She wouldn't know it if she stepped in it.''

Silence fell between the two women. Elspeth seemed deep in thought, while Pansy worried the embroidered violets on her lace handkerchief.

All of a sudden, Pansy sniffed and dabbed at her nose.

Elspeth gave her a sharp look. ''Now don't you start that!''

"I can't help it. I always figured it was my fault, what happened to my daughter. If I'd only known I was carrying her, I'd have married her daddy, before he went off to fight in the Pacific."

"If you'd had a brain under all that fluff, you'd have told him to keep his damn pants zipped! *That* was your one and only mistake, old girl."

Pansy turned teary, pleading eyes on Elspeth. "But we were *so* in love. How could I refuse him, when he was going off to war? He begged so sweetlike—said he might never come back, that we might never have another chance." Her voice broke. "And he didn't, and we didn't."

"I know, I know." Elspeth patted Pansy's trembling hand, in rough compassion. "A lot of nice girls fell for that line and wound up just like you did, Pansy. But what your daughter did wasn't your fault. You can't go on blaming yourself forever. What did happen to her man anyway? You never told me."

"I never knew, exactly. She said he died."

"And you believed that?"

Pansy shook her head and dabbed at her eyes again. "I never knew what to believe. Then she went away. I haven't heard from her since."

Elspeth knew she had to change the subject fast. Pansy was on the verge of all-out hysterics. "Well, you found Ginna. That's something to be thankful for. And right now, she and Neal are in the greenhouse, about to go back and make everything all right."

"Oh, I pray so!"

The dinner bell put an end to their conversation. Patients who normally shuffled about Swan's Quarter, seeming to have difficulty putting one foot in front of the next, were up and hustling to get the choicest seats in the dining room. Elspeth and Pansy joined them.

The sun touched the glass plate negative in the greenhouse wall, just as Elspeth was taking her first bite of juicy country

ham. The salty, smoky flavor tingled her taste buds for only
an instant, before time stopped at Swan's Quarter.

No one was there to see the flash in the greenhouse or the
sudden disappearance of Ginna and Neal. Their transformation
was swift and silent.

When Ginna woke up, back in time, she wasn't surprised to
find that she and Neal had once more been separated. She found
herself—or rather Virginia—in her bedroom at Swan's Quarter,
her bandanna knapsack stuffed and ready. All she had to do
now was wait for dawn and the departure of her father and
brothers. She felt restless, too nervous to sleep. Where could
Channing be? How long would it take her to find him?

Her thoughts turned suddenly to her brother's words about
shooting a Yankee, out back in the woods. He had gotten away,
Hollis said, but he was definitely wounded. Virginia wondered
if the poor man had a sweetheart somewhere waiting for him.
Her heart twisted at the thought. If Channing were shot, would
some Rebel woman take pity on an enemy soldier and tend his
wound?

"Please, God, I pray so."

At that moment, she decided what she had to do. Quickly,
she pulled on her brother's trousers and shirt. It was dark outside
and raining. That poor soldier could die of exposure, if he were
badly hurt. She had to find him and do what she could to help.

Neal woke up moaning, after the flash in the greenhouse.
His right arm was burning like hell. He was cold and wet and
shivering. He had been through this before. He remembered it,
all too well.

"Come on, Big George," he groaned. "Come get me. Bring
some blankets."

He drifted off briefly into unconsciousness. When he roused
again, the pain and the cold were still there, but he was no
longer Neal Frazier. Channing McNeal remembered sneaking
through the woods behind Swan's Quarter. He had to make
sure it was safe, that there were no Rebs about, before he

approached the house. But he had gotten careless in his eagerness to see Virginia. He had let a Confederate patrol sneak up on him. The man who had shot him hadn't recognized Channing in the darkness. He knew these soldiers, though. He knew their voices before he saw them. It was Hollis's face he had seen in the flash from his pistol, a moment before the Minie ball tore into his arm.

Ironic, he thought. Colonel Swan had been afraid they might meet on the field of battle. Instead, the confrontation had taken place right here at Swan's Quarter, when all of them had been seeking a brief respite from the war.

Channing heard the bushes rustling near him. Gritting his teeth against the pain, he struggled to drag himself farther back, under a bush. If they found him, he would surely be sent to one of the notorious prison camps farther south, where he would spend the rest of the war rotting and starving.

"Hello?" came the soft call. "Are you here? I know you're hurt."

He was drifting off again, losing consciousness. In his present state, Channing could almost imagine that the voice calling out to him was Virginia's.

"Please, I want to help you. Where are you?"

"Virginia." Her name from his lips was more a moan than a word, but she hurried quickly toward the sound.

As she neared his hiding place, she spied the shine of rain-slick boots sticking out from under a large bush. She dropped to the ground beside him.

"Don't be afraid," she whispered. "My brother shot you, but I'm here to help. Come out from under there. Give me your hand. We have to get you to shelter right now."

"Virginia!" This time his voice was stronger, and he distinctively spoke *her* name.

"Channing?" she cried. "Dear God! It *is* you! Oh, my darling, what has Hollis done?"

"Just a flesh wound," he murmured. "Nothing to worry about. Kiss me, so I'll know I'm not dreaming—that it's really you."

Virginia leaned down, shielding his face, as she covered his cold lips with hers. Tears mingled with the raindrops— Virginia's tears, Channing's tears. But to be in each other's arms again washed away all their pain and loneliness.

"I was coming to see you. Couldn't stand it any longer. Had to hold you, to tell you I still love you . . ." Channing's words drifted off.

"Don't try to talk, my love. Let me help you to the barn. Father and the boys are still at the house. I'll hide you, until they leave in the morning."

Struggling through the darkness and the heavy rain, they finally made it to the barn—a warm, dry place that smelled of horses and clean hay. Ginna wondered if she had made the right decision. All the Swan men's mounts were stabled here for the night. They might find Channing, when they came for their horses in a few hours. If they did, they would have to shoot her to get at him, she decided. Besides, one of the stable boys would saddle the horses. She hoped so, anyway.

In the very back of the barn, where broken harnesses and tools were stored for repair, she made a bed of straw for Channing and put a blanket over it, then found another blanket to cover him. He sank gratefully onto the soft, warm pile and offered her a weak smile.

"Come lie with me, darlin'. Warm me. I'm so cold."

"I need to see to your wound first. Let me have a look at that arm."

She was relieved to find that it wasn't too bad. Painful, certainly, but not life-threatening, unless it wasn't tended and went septic. She found a crockery jug of corn whiskey, where one of the stablehands kept it hidden. Strong drink was strictly forbidden among the Swan slaves, but she knew they kept a bit on hand for special occasions—births and deaths. First, she gave Channing a few good swigs, then, when he was looking happily glassy-eyed, she poured some of the whiskey over his arm. He winced.

"I'm sorry, darling," she said, "but it will clean out the wound."

He gave her a goofy grin. "Pain from the woman I love is better than a kiss from any other woman."

"Oh?" she said archly. "And just what other women have you been kissing that you can make such a comparison?"

He chuckled. "Only my mother and sisters. Rest easy, girl. You're the only one I want to kiss. The only one I want to love."

The whiskey had not only eased his pain, but stripped away his inhibitions and made him amorous. He grabbed Virginia with his good arm and drew her close, kissing her so deeply that the whiskey-taste of his mouth made her feel quite lightheaded.

"Come lie with me," he begged. "Make me warm, Virginia."

She hesitated. What if someone found them together this way? But it was still a good two hours until dawn. No one in the house would be up yet. Any slave who might happen in could either be bribed or threatened into silence.

Virginia lifted the blanket and slipped underneath, next to Channing. She closed her eyes, savoring this long-awaited feeling of his nearness. But when his hand slipped beneath her shirt, she stiffened. That reaction lasted only for a moment. He was doing wonderful things to her breasts—teasing, stroking, kneading. If Channing wanted heat, he was certainly getting it. His touch was burning her alive.

"Are you still going to marry me, Virginia?" he asked, between fevered kisses.

"Except for the final promises of the ceremony, I'm your wife already. I have been, since the night you rode away, darling." Her voice was breathless, her words trembling with emotion.

"Then why don't we finish what was so rudely interrupted that night at the parsonage? Right here, right now, just the two of us? Do you, Virginia, take me to be your lawful wedded husband?"

"Oh, yes, *I do!*"

"Now, you ask me." As he spoke, his hand was easing down toward the belt of her brother's trousers.

"Do you, Channing, take me for you lawful wedded wife?"

"Yes, darlin', I most certainly do! To have and to hold from this day forward. So, I now pronounce us man and wife. And I mean to kiss my bride."

He drew her close, so close that their bodies were touching, from their lips down. Her breasts quivered against his hard chest. Through her brother's pants, she could feel Channing's heat and hardness.

"We're married now, Virginia," he said, pointedly.

"Yes," she breathed, "forever and ever."

He waited a moment more, before he finished his thought. "I want to make love to my wife."

A thrill of excitement and fear rippled through her. "But you're injured."

"*That* part of me isn't. It's alive and well and throbbing for you, darlin'."

Virginia said nothing; she couldn't speak. She held perfectly still, as Channing eased her shirt up, until she felt the chill of the night air and the scratch of the rough blanket against her bare breasts. But most of all, she felt Channing's touch on her flesh, a thousand times over, like tiny, licking flames of pleasure. He shifted a bit. A moment later, she moaned, as his lips touched her nipple. When he dragged his tongue over her tender flesh, she squirmed in his arms.

"This isn't much of a honeymoon," he said with a nervous laugh, "but it's wartime, after all."

His mention of the war broke down her final barrier. Channing was right. He would soon go back into the thick of the battle. Could she let him go without having known his love? *No!*

"Any honeymoon with you is more than I could ever have hoped for, Channing. I love you. I've grieved for you, since the night you left. I've been so worried. I have a bag packed up in my room this very minute. I had planned to leave here in the morning to find you. Now—wonder of wonders—I have you. I know you must go away again, but not before this."

She undid his shirt and began kissing his chest. Light little feather-kisses that made him arch his back and moan with pleasure.

"God, Virginia, what are you doing to me?"

"Making you *mine!*" she said, without hesitation or any second thoughts. "I want you, Channing! I want you to be my husband and the father of my children."

It took a bit of doing for the both of them to get out of their trousers under the blanket. The work, however, proved worth the effort.

In Virginia's mind, the pile of hay and scratchy blankets seemed as wonderfully soft and inviting as lavender-scented sheets against her bare skin. Actually, she felt nothing other than the slide of Channing's flesh over hers. Forever, it seemed, he kissed her, caressed her, told her all that was in his heart, and that his heart belonged only to her.

"Remember how you cried that day the old swan disappeared?"

She nodded and smiled. "That was the first time you ever kissed me, darling. How could I forget?"

He nibbled at her shoulder, and she could feel a smile curve his lips. "How, indeed? You were so sweet and innocent, so very precious to me. Almost as precious as you are now. But my point is that I want you always to remember that the old cob came home to his mate. That's the swans' way, and that's my way. I'll always come back to you, darlin', no matter what separates us, or for how long. We both know that I'll have to leave soon. But, Virginia, while I'm gone, I want you to think about me everytime you look at the swans. I want you to recall, not that I'm gone, but that I'm coming back to you."

A wayward tear slipped down her cheek. "Please don't talk of leaving, Channing. Hold me. Love me!"

When finally the loving thrust came that made them one for all time, Virginia could no longer hold back her tears. She cried silently, joyfully, knowing that at last the dream of a lifetime had come true. No matter how far away the war might take Channing, a part of him would always be with her.

The perfect moment they shared, a short time later, was her

proof that the two of them were meant to be husband and wife. She prayed silently, as her exquisite passion ebbed, that Channing had given her a child.

Spent and exhausted, her lover rested his head on her shoulder and drifted off, still smiling, still whispering her name, even in his dreams.

Until the first gray-pearl light of dawn crept in through the cracks in the barn, Virginia lay with Channing, watching his dear face in sleep. Her heart was so filled with love for him that she thought it might burst inside her breast.

"Damn this war!" she murmured. It means *nothing!* Love means *everything!*"

With a deep sigh of regret, Virginia kissed Channing's lips softly, then eased his head from her shoulder. She tucked the blanket snugly around him. "I love you," she whispered, just before she slipped out of the barn.

It would never do to have her father and brothers catch her sneaking back into the house at this hour. She must go to her room, compose herself, and appear at breakfast looking like the same innocent sister and daughter she had been the night before.

If only they knew how much I have changed, she thought, as she hurried up the stairs and into her room.

She was too excited to sleep, too filled with love and hope and yearning for the future—her future with Channing. For a long time, she stood in front of her mirror, staring at her own image by the first rays of the rising sun. Had making love with Channing changed her? She looked the same, but there was something about her eyes. They glittered a bit more brightly. And wasn't the curve of her lips slightly fuller? Virginia suddenly realized what the change was. She was looking at herself as a woman, now, instead of as a child. And she was observing everything through a woman's lovestruck gaze.

A soft knock at her door made her jump. Who would be up and about at this hour?

Quickly she pulled on her long nightgown over her brother's

clothes. "Yes?" she called, trying to sound as if the knock had roused her from sleep. "Who is it?"

"Your father, baby girl. We'll be leaving soon. I'd like a word with you, if I may."

Virginia was about to open the door, when she spied the knapsack on her bed. She grabbed it and stuffed it in the armoire.

"Come in, Father."

He found her perched on the side of her bed, looking as if she had just come out of a lovely dream—a little girl's dream of candy and fairies and pretty party dresses. The thought brought a smile to his rugged, tanned face.

"I'm sorry I woke you, Virginia, but our discussion last night has been troubling me."

Virginia had to think for a moment to recall what he was talking about. Her plea for a pass and her disappointment at her father's rejection of the notion now seemed insignificant, after what had happened to her since.

"I want your solemn promise, Virginia, that you won't do anything foolish and bullheaded, like running off to find Channing. It's not safe out there. And I can't leave with an easy mind until I am assured that you will stay right here at Swan's Quarter with your mother, where you belong."

Virginia nodded. "I promise, Father."

Colonel Swan narrowed his eyes. He had prepared a whole battery of arguments to convince her. This was too easy. The daughter he knew never gave up without a fight.

"You'll stay put?"

"I will. You have my solemn promise on it. In return—"

Aha! Swan mused. He had been sure there must be a catch to her submissiveness. "In return, *what?*"

"I want you to promise me that the minute this war is over *nothing and no one* will stand in the way of my being with Channing. There'll be bitterness and hard feelings. Yankees aren't likely to be accepted with good grace around here. Channing and I might even have to move away to have any peace. If that's the way things are, so be it. I will go *anywhere* to be with him!"

Jedediah Swan caressed his daughter's cheek with one big
hand, clumsy in his attempt at tenderness. "You're your mother's daughter, that you are. I swear, Melora would fight the
whole Union army to be with me. She as much as told me so
last night. You have my promise, Virginia. Once the war's
over, it's over. Channing McNeal will be one more son in the
Swan family. There'll be no hard feelings, no grudges at Swan's
Quarter."

"Thank you, Father." Virginia whispered the words, her
voice choked with emotion.

"Well, now that all that's settled, why don't you pull on
your brother's britches and come to the barn with me to saddle
my horse?"

"The barn?" Virginia gasped.

He nodded. "I've become quite attached to that beast over
the past months. Can't abide anyone else handling him. I mean
to saddle him this morning, just like I do every day in the
field."

He turned, ready to leave so Virginia could get dressed.

"Father, wait!"

He paused at the door and looked back at her.

"Let me do that for you. Please! It will send you off with
luck on your side to let me perform the task for you."

Had any other woman proposed such a thing, Colonel Swan
would have laughed in her face. A woman saddling his mount,
indeed! But Virginia had been riding almost before she could
walk. She was a better horseman than most of the soldiers in
his cavalry unit.

"Very well!" He gave her a crisp nod. "Then see to it
immediately, daughter. We ride out soon."

When Colonel Swan closed the door behind him, Virginia
sank down to her bed, trembling all over. That had been a close
one. Her father might have promised to hold no grudges *after*
the war, but, if he found Channing in the barn now, there was
no telling what he might do to him.

Hastily, she tossed off her nightgown, pulled on her boots,
and headed for the barn. She would have that horse saddled

and out of there before a ghost could say "Boo!" For good measure, she would see to her brothers' horses, as well. As much as she loved the men of her family, she wouldn't draw an easy breath until she saw them ride away from Swan's Quarter.

"Channing, *please be all right!*" she murmured, as she ran for the barn.

She froze when she spied Hollis coming out of the barn. Her heart all but stopped when their eyes met. It seemed her worst fears had been realized.

Chapter Fourteen

"Hollis! What are you doing out here so early?"

He gave Virginia a lopsided grin. "I might ask you the same thing, sister-gal. I figured you'd still be in bed, working at getting your beauty sleep."

Virginia's skin felt too tight for her body, suddenly. She went hot and cold, in disconcerting flashes. Her breath seemed to seize in her throat. Of all her brothers, Hollis was the only one she could never read. He managed to look cool and casual, even when he was mad enough to chew nails. When the twins were kids, it was always Hampton who got into trouble for Hollis's transgressions. Hollis always looked too innocent to be guilty of anything. For this very reason, the cherubic expression on his face at the moment chilled Virginia's blood.

What had he been doing in the barn? In the barn with Channing!

"Are you fixing to leave already?" Virginia's voice quivered dangerously, but she hoped Hollis would translate the tremor in her words as emotion at the thought of the men of the family going back to the war.

Hollis laughed. "Not before breakfast. Hell, if the Yankees

surrendered this morning, I'd skip the ceremony for a stack of Polly's pancakes and a side of bacon.''

Virginia asked no more questions, but the puzzlement on her face begged for an explanation.

"It's like this, Sis, I got to thinking soon as I woke up about that Yankee I shot. *Where'd he crawl off to?* I kept wondering. Then it hit me right between the eye. *The barn!* Had to be. It's close enough to the woods, so he could drag himself, if need be. All those nice dry stalls. All that fresh hay. Perfect place for one of those bad boys in blue to hide and lick his wounds.''

Hollis paused and smiled. It was a smile that shriveled Virginia's heart. What if she were too late? What if Hollis had already found Channing and tied him up to take with them as his prisoner? Worse yet, what if Hollis had finished the job he'd started last night? Virginia swallowed a sob in a feigned cough.

"You coming down with something, Sis? You don't look so pert.''

She shook her head and gasped, "I'm fine.'' Her glance toward the partially open barn door served to ask the question she could not put into words.

"He was in there all right.''

Going weak all over, when she heard this from Hollis, Virginia gripped a fence post to keep herself erect. She clamped her jaw tightly to hold in a scream of pure anguish.

"Yep, he was right there where I figured he'd be. I followed his trail in the bloody straw right to where he lay down. Come look.''

Virginia wanted to turn and flee back to the house, screaming for help, screaming for Channing—her husband, her love. But Hollis clamped a hand on her arm and all but dragged her into the gloomy barn, where she had known such joy only a short while before. Now it seemed a place of horror and pain.

Hollis, with Virginia in tow, went straight to the back of the barn, to the very stall where she and Channing had shared their love and sealed their future together. She closed her eyes, afraid of what she would see when she reached the spot.

"See there!'' Hollis said. "Right there's the big old bloody spot where he was lying in the hay. Damn, I wish I'd come out here sooner."

Virginia opened her eyes when she heard Hollis's statement. Her heart sang with relief and joy. Channing's blood might have stained the place, but Channing himself was gone. At that moment, she could have hugged Hollis, she was that happy.

But the question remained: *Where was Channing?*

"Damned if I know where he could have got off to," Hollis muttered, in angry frustration. "I looked all around, but there's not a clue."

Virginia was trying to think of some reply to that, when she suddenly remembered her mission in the barn. "Father sent me out to saddle his horse. I'd better get to it. Do you want me to do yours, too, Hollis?"

He grinned at her, his prey forgotten for the moment. "That'd be nice, Sis. I figure Polly must be setting out our breakfast right about now."

"You go ahead. I'll take care of the horses and see you inside, shortly."

Hollis left the barn, still shaking his head and muttering to himself over the strange disappearance of the "Yankee spy."

As soon as her brother left, Virginia searched the barn from top to bottom. She found nothing. Channing had simply vanished, without a trace. She had to find him, but she couldn't begin her real search until after her father and brothers left. Skillfully and quickly, she saddled their mounts, then headed back to the house. She didn't want them waiting breakfast for her and delaying their departure.

The minute she entered the house, she heard laughing and talking from the dining room. They hadn't waited breakfast, after all. That was good.

"All fed, watered, saddled, and ready to ride," she announced, as she entered the dining room.

"Good girl!" her father said, around a mouthful of pancakes.

"You didn't see anything of that Yankee while you were out there?" This was Hollis, of course.

Virginia only shook her head. All the men rose, as Hampton

jumped up to hold his sister's chair for her. Then they all fell upon their food once more.

The talk at the table was mostly of the war—none of the gory details, which would have been unfit at table, or anywhere else, in the presence of ladies. Instead, their tales ran to humorous episodes, such as the Yankee who had shot himself in the foot to keep from facing Rebel forces in battle. There was the old woman and her young grandson who had held off a whole Yankee troupe with a couple of squirrel guns, threatening to blow daylight through their blue bellies, if they were to set foot in her yard. Then there was another wily plantation owner's wife down in South Carolina, who had kept the Yankees off her land by purposely eating fruit she knew she was allergic to. She broke out in hives immediately and was a grotesque sight, when she met the Union soldiers at her front gate. She told them that they thought they had smallpox on the place, but they were welcome to use her house, just the same.

"One look at her put those Yanks in full retreat," Rodney said, with a loud guffaw.

He hadn't talked much at breakfast. It was clear to Virginia that he and his bride had spent their one night together making love. Agnes wore a blush during the entire meal, and she kept her eyes on her plate, when she wasn't staring up adoringly at her husband. Virginia felt a strong kinship with Agnes this morning. Now they both knew the magic secret of love.

The third woman at the table, Melora Swan, had a glow about her, as well. Her night with the colonel had eased some of the worry lines from her face. She looked mellow and restored, this morning. From time to time, Virginia caught her mother gazing at her father with a tenderness that surprised the younger woman. It was difficult to imagine her parents indulging in the same emotions and passions that she and Channing had shared a short while ago.

Virginia noticed that the only other woman in the room seemed to be giving her significant glances, from time to time. Old Polly was serving this morning, something odd in itself. Usually, Polly's work was done, once she cooked a meal.

Juniper took over in the dining room, passing the silver platters around, like an efficient, silent ghost. Maybe Polly had chosen to serve breakfast because she wanted to spend more time with the Swan men before they rode off again. She had always been partial to the twins. They had been raised with her own boys. Still, Virginia herself was obviously the main focus of Polly's attention this morning. It almost seemed that they shared some secret. What it might be, Virginia had no earthly idea, but she would certainly make a point of speaking with Polly privately, after the meal.

"I've packed each of you three new shirts," Melora told her husband and sons. "And I had all your clothes washed and pressed, while you slept. Mercy, I've seen white trash dressed in cleaner clothes than you boys wore home!"

"This is war!" the colonel said. "Keeping tidy is not our main concern, my dear."

"Well, I won't have my sons' health ruined by poor hygiene, and I hold you responsible, Jedediah."

Virginia's brothers exchanged amused glances and a few chuckles, but their mother silenced them with a stern look.

"That's quite enough!" She spoke to the lot of them. "You boys, when you find a stream, bathe in it, wash your clothes. I want your solemn vow on that."

They all nodded and murmured their promises, but Virginia heard Hollis whisper to Hampton, "If we can ever find a stream that ain't running red with blood."

Melora didn't hear the remark, and Virginia was glad of that. The very thought made her feel ill.

Colonel Swan crossed his silver fork and knife at the top of his china plate, signaling that the meal was at an end. It was a simple move, an ordinary gesture that everyone at the table had witnessed a thousand times. But this morning was different. All eyes focused on that crossed cutlery for a moment. Then Virginia saw Agnes look up at Rodney with tears brimming. Her whole face looked as though it were about to crumble. Melora, too, turned to gaze at her husband. Her features remained placid, but there was a wild look of panic in her eyes.

"So soon?" she whispered to the colonel.

In a rare public show of affection, he covered his wife's hand with his own. "It's time, my dear. We've a long ride ahead of us today." He glanced around the table and nodded. "You are excused."

Everyone rose and left the room to prepare for their departure—everyone except Jedediah and Melora. They lingered, alone together, over the dregs of their coffee, sharing a few last words of private farewell.

Virginia left them to their privacy. In the hallway, she saw Rodney and Agnes huddled together. Her pregnant sister-in-law was weeping openly, while her husband tried to soothe her.

"I'll be back soon, darlin'," he assured her.

"When the baby comes?" she whimpered.

"Well now, I can't promise that. But you'll do fine. I know you will, sweetheart. And you'll have Mama and Virginia here to help you. And old Maum Sugar, the midwife."

"But I want *you* here, Rodney! How will I bear it without you?"

He cradled her gently and kissed her cheek. The sight of her big, gruff brother's tenderness toward his wife almost brought tears to Virginia's eyes. This was a side of Rodney she had never seen before.

"You're stronger than you think, honey. I know you are. And just keep focusing on our future together. Once this war is over, we'll be a real family. We'll get our own place and raise a dozen children. We'll be so happy, you and me. You love me, don't you?"

"Oh, Rodney!" Agnes melted into his arms, weeping all the harder. "You know I do."

Virginia moved on, not wanting to intrude on their tender farewell. She was heading out back when she ran into Polly. The woman motioned her into the pantry. Virginia followed without question.

Polly's words were brief and to the point. "Brother Zebulon

got something at his place that belongs to you. Soon as the master leaves, you come right out to the quarters, you hear?''

Virginia nodded. "I'll be there." She squeezed the woman's hand, affectionately. "Thank you, Polly."

The cook swished out of the pantry and on her way, as though nothing had passed between them. Virginia remained where she was for a few moments, allowing relief to wash over her, until she felt she could face the others without anyone realizing that something had changed since breakfast.

Virginia went out and led the horses around front, instead of waiting for one of the grooms to perform the task. The sooner the men mounted up and rode out, the sooner she could go to Channing. She prayed that her mother and Agnes would not prolong their goodbyes, once the men left the house. Her prayers were answered. The women had said all they had to say in private. Now, both Melora and Agnes kept a stiff upper lip, as their husbands mounted their horses, waved their hats in one last farewell, and rode down the lane toward the swan pond.

The minute they were out of sight, Agnes fell into Melora's arms, sobbing her heart out.

"I'll not have this!" Melora said sternly. "Get hold of yourself, Agnes."

"But he's *gone!*" the girl wailed. "How can you be so calm?"

She held her daughter-in-law at arm's length. "Because I know that the sooner they leave, the sooner they'll come home to us again. You should hold that thought, Agnes. All this weeping and carrying on won't bring Rodney back a minute sooner, and it's liable to harm the baby. You need to concentrate all your efforts now on giving your husband a strong, healthy son."

Virginia bristled when she heard those words. How could her own mother say such a thing? "Or a strong, healthy, beautiful *daughter!*" Virginia added, defiantly.

Her mother ignored her words, but Agnes turned on her. "It

is going to be a son!'' she exclaimed. ''That's what Rodney wants, and that's what I'm giving him.''

Virginia turned and left the veranda. It was on the tip of her tongue to say to Agnes, ''Did you ever think that *your* father might have wanted a son, too?'' Discretion won out, over annoyance. She hurried away, toward the swan pond. She smiled when she saw that the old cob was still there with his mate. Virginia tarried there long enough to see her mother and Agnes go into the house. Then she ran back up the path and headed toward the slave quarters, toward Zebulon's cabin— toward Channing.

She knocked softly at the rough board door. No one answered, but it opened immediately with a squeaking of rusty hinges.

''Got to put some goose grease on those pesky things.'' Brother Zebulon glared at the hinges, then smiled at Virginia. ''Come in, child. And wipe that worry offen your pretty face. He be fine.''

Channing didn't look fine when Virginia saw him. He was stretched out on Zebulon's cornshuck mattress, seemingly unconscious, looking pale and sickly.

''What happened?''

''He been shot.''

''I know that. But he seemed much better than this earlier.''

''He wouldn't of been for long. That ball in his arm was fixing to fester, sure as thunder. I had to get it out. Polly, she fixed him up a right strong dose of roots and such to cut the pain. He didn't suffer none while I was working on him, but could be old Polly poisoned him.''

''Did no such a thing!'' Polly hissed from the doorway. ''He be right as rain when he wakes up. He just getting the rest he needs that he didn't get none of during the night.''

Virginia blushed. Did Polly know? To cover her embarrassment at that thought, and because she really meant it, she said, ''Thank you both. I was so afraid he'd been found.''

''He was,'' Polly said, ''by me. I saw you coming out of the barn way too early for white folks to be up to anything ordinary. I was out by the woodpile fetching kindling, since that no-account Ludlow didn't haul none in last night to fire up the cookstove for breakfast. After you went back to the big house, I figured I better go to the barn and have me a look-see. And there was Mister Channing, fast asleep, looking real feverish. I called Zebulon, and we got him moved right quick.''

"Thank the Lord!" Virginia breathed, thinking again what might have happened if Hollis had found him instead. She no longer cared that Polly knew she and Channing had been together. All that mattered was that Channing was safe and would recover under the ministering hands of the two slaves.

"You gonna marry him now, Miss Virginia?"

"I already have, Polly, at least in my heart and soul."

"Well, it's high time you did it in the sight of God too. First thing, when he's strong enough, Brother Zebulon's gonna take care of that. Might not be much more than a broomstick jumpin', but I reckon if that's good enough for us folks, it's good enough for you."

Virginia smiled at the thought of her polished and sophisticated Channing jumping a broomstick in the common slave manner of marriage. "I'm sure it will be good enough for us. Thank you both again."

Channing was vaguely aware of voices nearby. From time to time, he could make out a word or two, but nothing seemed to fit together. He felt that Virginia was there, somewhere near. Repeatedly, he tried to speak her name. Repeatedly, he failed. Something had made his tongue thick and foul tasting. His head seemed to be three times its normal size, with his brain rattling around inside, useless. All he could do was lie still and keep breathing. He told himself that the sooner he recovered from whatever was ailing him, the sooner he could be with Virginia again. He put all his effort into focusing on that one thought.

But soon the dreams began. Terrible, horrifying nightmares

about smoke and flames. He was falling, out of control. He heard people screaming and begging for God's help. He tossed on the bed, until strong hands clamped his arms to hold him still.

"Got to save her," he muttered. "Can't let her die. Her husband . . . her kids! It'll be all right, ma'am. Let me get Christine out, then I'll come back for you."

Channing's words were plain now, all too plain. *Who was Christine?* Virginia wondered. *What could Channing be raving about?*

"It's the potion I give him," Polly explained. "It oft times makes a body crazy in the head for a spell. He be fine soon."

Suddenly, Channing yelled, "The airplane's on fire!"

"What?" All three of them said the word at once. None of them understood.

Polly nodded, knowingly. "It be them roots, all right. They just got him off his head for a time. Don't you worry none, Miss Virginia."

That was easy for Polly to say. Virginia was half out of her mind with worry. Channing's whole face was twisted with anguish. He opened his eyes once and glanced wildly about, seeing nothing, only adding to Virginia's fears. Maybe Polly had blinded him with her strong potion.

Virginia determined not to leave Channing's side, until the crisis passed. But just then the plantation bell started ringing raucously. Used only for emergencies—fire, accident, or to announce a death—the sound of the bell went through the stuffy room like a shock wave.

"You best get up to the big house right now, Miss Virginia," Polly urged. "We keep watch over Mister Channing. But it sound like your ma needs you."

Virginia leaned down and kissed Channing's burning brow before she hurried out. "Call me if there's any change," she told Polly and Zebulon.

Up at the house, chaos reigned. Virginia found her mother

wringing her hands in the library, while Agnes writhed on the couch.

"It's the baby!" Melora exclaimed. "Go fetch Maum Sugar, quickly!"

"But she's not due yet."

"Babies come in their own time. And it seems this one is demanding to be born, here and now. Move, Virginia! Get Sugar!"

"Rodney-y-y! Come back!" Agnes's anguished wails followed Virginia down the hall.

Virginia went flying out the back door, screaming for Sugar. Her cries roused all the slaves who weren't in the fields. Soon, she was followed by a ragtag army of children, a pack of hounds, and most of the house and yard servants. She found the midwife in one of the cabins, cleaning up after the delivery of a small caramel-colored boy who looked amazingly like Virginia's brother, Jed. But this was no time for speculation.

"We need you up at the house, Maum Sugar. Miss Agnes is in labor. You have to come right now!"

"Lord, lord!" Sugar groaned, hefting her ungainly weight up from the birthing stool. "It don't rain but it pours. First, the old cat has kittens, then Xena drops her first sucker, now Miss Agnes. Must be the phase of the moon. Tell your ma, I be there directly, Miss Virginia."

"But Miss Agnes need you *now!*"

"When'd her pains commence?"

Virginia thought quickly. She hadn't asked, but she knew how long she had been at Zebulon's cabin. "Less than an hour ago."

Sugar cackled. "Miss Agnes, she got a *long* time to go yet. Ain't no hurry. I be finished here right shortly."

"But what do we do until you get there? She's screaming, Maum Sugar. She sounds like she's going to die."

"She ain't gone die, don't you worry none. Tell Miz Melora to give her a sip of your daddy's brandy. That'll calm her some, till I get to the house."

Virginia glanced one last time at the new little slave. Yes, he most definitely looked like Jed. Then she turned and fled the cabin. Her entourage was waiting outside, calling out questions concerning both births. Virginia brushed past them and hurried on her way.

Agnes was alternately screaming and moaning, by the time Virginia returned to the library. Several of the house servants hovered about, bringing sheets to put under Agnes on the library couch, hauling in steaming kettles of water, plumping pillows.

"Give her brandy!" Virginia gasped, as she raced through the door. "Maum Sugar says brandy will help."

"Where *is* Sugar?" Melora Swan demanded.

"Coming! Coming soon." Virginia was still trying to catch her breath. "She just delivered a baby down in the quarters."

"Whose baby?" Melora asked, calculating that it had been almost nine months to the day since she caught young Jed behind the smokehouse with pretty, light-skinned Xena.

Virginia tried to think. She had been concentrating on the baby, not the mother. "I don't know. One of Polly's grand-daughters, I think. She lives in the cabin next to Sugar's, on the far side."

Melora nodded. So, it was Xena. A bizarre twist of fate that two of her sons should father children born on the same day. But Agnes was screaming again, louder than ever. She put aside thoughts of her son Jed's transgressions and went to the spirits chest for the brandy. She looked at the bottle. There wasn't much left, and the only other bottle on the place was one she was saving to celebrate her husband's return from the war.

"Hurry, Mother!" Virginia urged. "She's in terrible pain."

Melora held a small glass to Agnes's lips. The girl coughed and sputtered when the first drops hit her throat.

"A little more," Melora urged. "I know it tastes nasty, but it will ease your pain, dear."

Grimacing, Agnes managed to swallow a bit more of the fiery liquid. The patient grew less agitated, but she was still experiencing regular contractions.

Just then, they heard Maum Sugar yell at the slave children

loitering around the back door, "Get on outta here now! This ain't no barbecue, it's a birthin'."

Moments later, old Sugar bustled into the library. "Well now, what have we here?" she said, with a jovial laugh. "A mite early, ain't we?"

"Not *too* early, I pray," Melora whispered to the midwife.

"Mister Rodney coming home most likely hurried things along."

Both Virginia and her mother blushed, taking the old slave's meaning.

"But she'll be all right, won't she?" Melora asked. "And the baby, too?"

Sugar stood back and stroked some wiry hairs that grew out of a mole on her chin. "She be a good eight months gone. The baby girl be big enough, I vow."

"Girl?" yelled Agnes. "It better not be! This is Rodney's *son!*"

Sugar chuckled. "Not if I know the birthin' business. How come you rich folks aways wanting sons, anyways? A sweet, little ole girl-child is a heap nicer than some ole nasty boy. You get a son, you got to always worry about him be messing around down in the quarters, where he don't belong."

The comment was made very pointedly, and Sugar looked straight at Melora when she said it. So that settled that! Xena's son was definitely fathered by Jedediah Swan, Jr.

Alas, Melora thought, *it happens in the best of families.*

Sugar hunkered down at the foot of the couch and began talking soothingly, as she examined Agnes. "You gone be jest fine, ma'am, now don't you worry none. Old Maum Sugar see to that! You do like I say, and this little girl youngun' pop right out as easy as that litter outten their mama cat this morning, about sunup."

"Kittens?" Agnes's voice was weak, but she was clearly interested, and distracted by the topic.

"That's right! Four of 'em. One black-and-white, one tiger, one yellow tom—I know 'cause yellow kittens is always toms—and the prettiest little long-furred calico you ever did see. She purely looks like a rainbow, dressed in all them bright colors. She gone be a fine mouser, that one.''

"Where are they? Can I see them?'' For the moment, Agnes forgot she was in labor.

"They be down to my cabin. Their ma be that trampy tiger, name of Jezabel. She plain don't care—lift her tail for any old tom that come sniffin' 'round, she will. But I reckon, with cats it don't matter. It's just when it comes to folks that it makes any difference.''

Virginia wondered if Maum Sugar was talking about Jed and Xena or her and Channing. She dared not ask. It was clear from the look of anguish on Melora Swan's face that she realized Sugar knew that Jed had fathered Xena's son.

Just then, the tale of the cats was forgotten, as Agnes let out another blood-curdling scream. On and on through, the day her contractions continued. Everyone in the house was on edge by evening, but still Agnes labored.

"Go on to the kitchen and get something to eat,'' Melora told Virginia, sometime after sunset. "Get some fresh air, too. You're looking almost as pale as Agnes, dear.''

Virginia gratefully accepted her mother's offer. She didn't feel hungry in the least, but she desperately wanted to check on Channing.

"I won't be long,'' she promised.

"Take your time, Virginia. I'll be here with Agnes, until it's over.'' Turning to Sugar, she asked, "It won't take much longer, will it?''

The old midwife shook her head and rolled her eyes. "They comes when they comes, Miz Melora.''

"Run along, dear,'' Melora urged Virginia.

Agnes's screams were weak with exhaustion now, but they still followed Virginia down the hallway, out of the house, and all the way to the slave quarters.

When she reached Brother Zebulon's cabin, she was almost afraid to go in. What if Channing was worse? What if he still didn't know her? How could she bear that?

Polly poked her head out of the door, her dark face a mask of concern. "Thank the Lord you here, Miss Virginia. You better come quick!"

Virginia's heart sank, and her feet felt frozen to the spot.

Chapter Fifteen

After only a moment's hesitation, Virginia hurried inside. Channing must have taken a turn for the worse, for Polly to look so distressed. Well, if that was the case, her mother and Maum Sugar would just have to deal with Agnes and the baby. Virginia herself didn't mean to leave Channing's side until he was over this crisis and back on his feet. She absolutely *refused* to let him die!

"You gots to do something with this man!" Polly exclaimed, the minute Virginia came in. "He got the brains of a billy goat, if you ask me."

"Channing!" Virginia's cry was half-delight, half-fear. "What are you doing up and dressed?"

"Tha's 'xactly what I say!" hurrumphed Polly, but no one paid any attention.

"I've got to get back, darlin'. My unit is waiting just the other side of Winchester. They'll think I've deserted. I had a pass for a few hours to ride out to see you, but that's long since expired."

Virginia hurried over to him and pressed her palm to his

forehead. "Why, you still have a fever! You can't go anywhere in your condition."

He smiled. The warm look of love in his eyes touched her heart. "I don't want to go, Virginia. You know I'd rather be here with you than anywhere else on earth. But you needn't worry about me. I really am feeling much better now. I'll take things easy in camp for a few days, once I get back." He reached for her hand and kissed her fingers, his eyes never leaving hers. "I *must* go, darlin'. You understand that, don't you?"

Channing drew her closer, wanting to hold her, to savor their last few minutes together.

Neither Channing nor Virginia noticed when Polly and old Zebulon slipped out of the cabin to give them some privacy. Virginia sank down to the bed, beside her lover.

"Channing," she whispered, "I don't think I can bear to say goodbye again so soon."

"How's Agnes?" he asked, trying to change the subject and stay the tears he saw glittering in Virginia's eyes.

"She's suffering terribly. But Maum Sugar says she'll be fine. Both Mother and Sugar say that labor is always bad the first time. I'm afraid Agnes isn't reassured by that. Poor girl, she's been struggling for hours now. Surely, though, the baby will come soon."

Virginia noticed a change in Channing's features. He looked pained and uncomfortable. At first, she thought he felt a twinge from his wound. She remembered, though, that the men of her family often wore that same expression whenever they happened to overhear talk of "woman-things," as her father called it.

Virginia forced a bright smile and even managed a little laugh. "Sugar swears it's going to be a girl. Agnes is fit to be tied because, as Rodney told *everyone,* he had his heart set on a son."

Looking far less distressed, Channing chuckled. "Yes, I can just imagine that he would."

"Would you want a son, Channing?"

"Someday." He brushed Virginia's cheek with his lips. "I think a daughter would please me more, though. A pretty little girl who looked just like her mother."

"Channing?" Virginia paused and looked away. "Do you think it could happen?"

"What, darlin'? That you could give me a daughter and then a son? Of course it can. And it will!"

She shook her head. "That's not what I mean. Do you think that I might be . . . *now?* After last night?"

Channing hugged her close and kissed her lips tenderly. "One can only hope, darlin'," he whispered.

When Virginia uttered a half-supressed sob, Channing asked, "You aren't afraid, are you? I mean, because of what Agnes is going through."

Virginia clung to him fiercely. "No. Not in the least. I would gladly go through her pain ten times over to have your child to hold and cherish. Think of it, Channing! A part of you, a part of me, a little miracle created from our love."

He smiled, then kissed her again, deeply, lingering over her lips for a long time.

When they parted at last, he said, "It won't be much longer until we can be together. I promise you that, Virginia. Every last man who was so eager to get into this *glorious war* has discovered already that there's little glory involved. I truly believe that the powers that be will find a way to put an end to hostilities at their first opportunity. There is nothing to be gained by all the bloodshed and devastation."

"Oh, Channing!" She hugged him, being careful not to press his injured arm. "I love you so! I wish I could believe you. But men are so stubborn. I've seen it when Father bargains over a horse he wants or a new piece of land he'd like to add to Swan's Quarter. And this isn't a stallion or a few acres being fought over. There's a whole country at stake—a whole way of life."

He had hoped Virginia would take his words at face value. He should have known better. She was too smart for that. Besides, she knew him too well. He didn't believe the war would come to a quick conclusion any more than she did. For the South, winning meant preserving the institution of slavery and retaining their land against "invaders." For the North, victory meant saving the nation and now, after all the battles that had been fought, paying the South back for their rebellious actions—actions which were taking such a tremendous toll in human lives.

As grim as he felt, Channing tried to make light of the moment. "If you love me so much, I assume you'd rather not see me hang for desertion, my darling. So I think I'd better get going, if the coast is clear."

She nodded, trying desperately to be brave. "Father and the boys left some time ago."

"Then I'd better take my leave while I have the chance, before more unannounced visitors arrive." Still holding her, unwilling to let the moment end, Channing said, "By the way, I ran into a chap from Tennessee a few weeks ago, who was at the Academy with me, an upper classman. He's now in the Confederate army. Captain Jacob Royal. I told him all about you and Swan's Quarter. He promised if he was ever in this area, he would stop by to pay his respects."

"You were actually consorting with the enemy?"

Channing laughed. "He's no enemy of mine. Actually, he did me several good turns at the Point. And we have a lot in common. You see, he left his sweetheart back home too. Her name's Amanda Kelly. Like us, they grew up together. Jake said he would never even consider marrying any other woman." He paused long enough for another brief kiss and then a smile. "The same as me. You were always the one, Virginia, the *only* one. And you always will be."

"Massa Channing, you best git, now," Polly called from just outside the door. "They's a scoutin' party of Rebs coming up the lane."

Virginia and Channing's leisurely farewell took a more frantic turn.

"I'll write to you, darlin'," Channing promised.

"And I to you, my love."

"And I'll be back at my first opportunity." To Polly he said, "You and Brother Zebulon have that broomstick ready."

Polly chuckled and nodded. "Yessir, Massa Channing."

A final kiss from his love, then Channing strode hurriedly out of the cabin and disappeared into the deep woods.

Virginia fell back on the sagging bed and let her tears erupt. She lay there for a long time, waiting for her anguish to subside. Once she had cried herself out, she too left the cabin. She must think now of Agnes and the baby. Thinking of Channing was much too painful.

Virginia heard the squall of the newborn the minute she entered the house. She hurried to the library to see for herself. Sure enough, she had a niece—all tiny and wrinkled and red. But already, the mother and grandmother were exclaiming over what a beauty she would be. How they could tell was beyond Virginia's comprehension.

Still, when Agnes said, "Isn't she beautiful, sister?" Virginia smiled and nodded, then reached down to stroke the infant's beet-red cheek.

"Rodney will adore her, Agnes."

"As will her grandfather and all her uncles," Melora added. "You've done well, my dear. I told you your struggle would be rewarded."

"That one, she probably gonna be a writer, being borned in the library like she was." Maum Sugar nodded sagely, as she gathered up her things. "She be bright as a button, you mark my words, Miss Agnes."

"Thank you, Sugar," the new mother said, beaming at the old woman. "For everything."

"Ppshaw! Ain't nothing, Miss Agnes. I brung so many youn-guns into this world, I could do it blindfolded, with one hand tied behind me. You take good care of her, now. And iffen you needs a wet nurse, Xena's got more than enough milk for two."

"No!" Melora said, before Agnes could answer! Somehow the idea of Rodney's child suckling at the dark breast of his own nephew's mother seemed almost incestuous to her.

Virginia noticed the pained expression that crossed Agnes's face at the thought of having to handle all the nursing duties herself, but it would have been unseemly for her to argue with her mother-in-law under her own roof.

Just then, they heard the sound of horses on the drive. Agnes sat up and broke into a huge grin. "It's Rodney! He's come back!"

"No," Virginia said. "I don't think so. I forgot to mention that Polly spotted some soldiers riding up toward the house."

"Blue or gray?" Melora asked, sharply.

"Polly said 'Rebs.' "

Melora let out a sigh of relief. "Well, thank the Lord. I don't think I'm up to entertaining the enemy at the moment. I suppose we'll have to feed them. It's a good thing your father brought fresh supplies. Go out and greet them, Virginia, while I finish tidying up here. Tell them they're welcome to stay the night in the barn, but that we have a new mother and her baby in the house, so I can't offer them beds inside."

Virginia nodded and turned to go. She knew that Agnes's new baby had little or nothing to do with her mother's desire to keep the soldiers out of the house. They had learned from past experience that even the officers were infested with "gray-backs," as the men called the filthy lice.

When Virginia walked out onto the veranda, she counted two officers and about a dozen men.

"Good day, gentlemen," she called.

One of the officers, a tall, dark-haired captain with a boy's sweet face, dismounted and swept off his hat in a gentlemanly salute.

"And to you, ma'am," he replied. "Captain Jacob Royal at your service."

Virginia's heart gave a flutter. This was the very man Channing had spoken of only a short while ago—his friend from West Point.

"We met Colonel Swan and his sons down the road. He told us there had been some trouble here last night with a Yankee spy. I promised to stop by and make sure that everything was in order hereabouts.''

"We're all fine, Captain Royal. In fact, better than fine. My sister-in-law just gave birth to my brother's firstborn. Should you happen to see my father and brothers again, please inform Rodney that he has a beautiful little girl, and that mother and daughter are both doing well.''

Royal beamed at her, and all the men waved their hats in a salute and gave a quiet Rebel yell, so as not to disturb mother and child.

"Our congratulations to all the family, Miss Swan.''

"Miss *Virginia* Swan.'' She wondered if Channing had told Captain Royal her name. She found out immediately.

"Oh, so *you* are Miss Virginia!'' His smile warmed all the more. "I can't tell you how pleased I am to meet you.''

"And I you, sir. Perhaps after all this unpleasantness is behind us, after you and Miss Amanda are married, and my fiancé and I, as well, we can all get together somewhere for a celebration.''

"A fine idea, Miss Virginia. Might I offer my mountain house in Tennessee as the site for our reunion? Amanda would like that.''

Virginia glanced over her shoulder and saw Melora peering out of the library window. She remembered her mission at that moment. "My mother said to tell you you're welcome to stay the night, if the barn will suit. There's supper that we can share with you, as well.''

"Thank you kindly, Miss Virginia, and please thank your mother for us, but we must be on our way immediately. You've seen no sign of this Yankee spy?''

Virginia shook her head, not willing to put her lie into words. "It's quite peaceful here, for the time being.''

"Well, we'll be off then. But might we take advantage of your hospitality at some later date, if we happen to ride this way again?''

"Most certainly, Captain Royal. We will look forward to your return.''

"Our best to the new mother."

"Thank you, sir."

He mounted his horse. Then they turned and rode away. Virginia stood on the veranda, watching them. She thought about Amanda Kelly and how much she would have loved to see her sweetheart, even for these few brief moments. She decided to give Jacob Royal a gift for Amanda, if he ever returned to Swan's Quarter.

For now, it was time she got back to the routine of her everyday life—a wartime life that held few joys and many fears. But there were bright spots to dwell on today—Agnes's baby and Channing's love. Both, Virginia knew, would grow and flourish with time.

That long winter of 1861 passed uneventfully. There were no further visits from either Swan's Cavalry or Channing McNeal, although almost every week, soldiers arrived, begging food, shelter, or simply a moment's respite from the horrors of the war.

"We've been lucky," said Melora, as she stood on the veranda one day in May, watching a troupe of Rebs ride down the lane, leaving Swan's Quarter in peace once again. "So many of the houses hereabouts have been torched. Only the good Lord knows what would become of us if we lost the roof over our heads."

Virginia, dressed in her brother's clothes, stood next to her mother. She wasn't watching the Yankees; she was staring at the swan pond and frowning. The old cob was nowhere to be seen this morning. His mate seemed restless and anxious, flapping her wings and bobbing her long neck. Virginia knew it was foolish, but she always worried more about Channing when the male swan was missing.

"Well, I'd best go in and see how Agnes and little Roslyn are this morning. The baby has been so restless these past few nights that Agnes hasn't been sleeping."

"Has Agnes thought of giving Roslyn a dose of Polly's

spring tonic? You always used to make us take it this time of year, Mother.''

Melora Swan smiled brightly at her daughter. "What a good idea! I'm sure Polly can mix a light dose that will make Roslyn feel much better. Thank you, dear, for reminding me. You're going to make a wonderful mother someday.''

Melora hurried off to find Polly, leaving Virginia alone with her thoughts.

"A wonderful mother,'' Virginia repeated, with a sigh. How she had hoped! But there could be no doubt. She was *not* carrying Channing's child. "Will I ever have that opportunity?'' she wondered aloud.

Her attention was soon diverted. She heard shots ring out in the distance. She shaded her eyes against the sun's glare to get a better view of the road beyond the tulip poplar. Sure enough, a cloud of dust rose in the distance.

"Horses, heading this way.''

She backed toward the door, her gaze still fixed far down the lane. "Mother!'' she called. "Someone's coming. They're almost at the pond already.''

"Blue or gray?'' Melora called out the question she always asked.

"I can't tell, but I'd guess blue, since I heard them exchange fire with our departing guests.''

Melora came rushing onto the veranda. Except for that one day when Agnes had just given birth, she never allowed Virginia to greet arriving Yankees. As the war dragged on, she grew more nervous each time enemy forces approached.

She came through the front door just in time to hear Virginia cry, "Oh, no! The apple orchard's on fire!''

"Get in the house, Virginia!'' her mother ordered. "Quickly! And stay out of sight.''

But it was too late. The rough-looking Yankees were already dismounting at the foot of the steps. Both women scanned the dusty uniforms, searching for the officer in charge. To their fear and dismay, there was no one of rank with this ragtag group of men.

"Looks like you just had company." A big man with a dusty black beard and a gap-toothed grin addressed Melora Swan. "Well, they won't be coming back no more, not all of them anyway. We shot two of the bastards right out their saddles— *damn Rebel scum!*"

Melora clutched her throat, trying not to cry out. Standing in the shadows near the door, Virginia felt her blood run cold. She had yet to see the real war. But even talk of shooting and killing turned her weak with fear—for her father and brothers and, of course, for Channing.

"We're parched as dry as tinder, lady. How about sending your boy there for something to wet our whistles? Whiskey'd be good."

"We have no spirits on the premises." Virginia winced at the arch tone in her mother's voice, afraid she might anger the man. "Our water here is sweet and cool, better to quench the thirst than whiskey."

All the men grumbled and cursed. The man who had been doing the talking started up the stairs, all the while scowling at Melora.

"You got quite a mouth on you, lady." He waved one thick, dirty arm toward the orchard. "All water's good for is putting out fires. But I think it's too late to save your apple trees. You be nice and polite to us soldier-boys and we *might not* torch your house."

When Melora's face blanched, the men behind him guffawed. One, who could have been no more than in his teens, yelled out, "But then again, we might anyway, eh, boys?"

Melora turned and nodded to Virginia. "Fetch some water for them. Quickly!"

Before their previous guests had departed, the Confederate officers had taken tea on the veranda with Melora. Without thinking, Virginia grabbed the beautiful English silver teapot from the table and ran through the house to the well out back. Along the way, she warned the household that their new arrivals were less than friendly.

When she returned only minutes later, the teapot filled with

water, the six men were on the veranda with her mother. They
were circling her, taunting her, making frightening threats.

Virginia slammed the door behind her and all eyes turned
her way.

"Here's your water." She tried to make her voice sound
deep and manly. It was no use.

The leader of the group, the one who had been doing the
talking, snatched the silver teapot from Virginia. They passed
it around, tipping the spout to drink directly from the elegant
vessel.

When it was empty, the rough soldier shoved it back at
Virginia and ordered, "More!"

She heard a soft gasp from her mother. Virginia hesitated,
the teapot in her hand, wondering what was wrong. She didn't
realize that, in her haste to fetch the water and warn Agnes to
stay hidden, her father's cap had slipped, allowing one long,
blond curl to fall to her shoulder.

"Well, will you lookee here, boys? This ain't no lad, after
all."

As the big man moved in on Virginia, Melora stepped
between them. "I want you to go this minute! You may camp
down beyond the gate, but you are to leave my property."

The rude fellow only laughed at Melora. He reached over
and snatched the cap off Virginia's head. "Damned if you ain't
a beauty! Come here, gal."

He reached out and grabbed Virginia about the waist, pulling
her toward him.

"You leave her be!" Melora shrilled. "My daughter is
untouched and promised to a brave officer in your own army.
Leave now! I'm warning you."

The men all laughed and gathered in closer, shoving the
distraught Melora aside to move in on Virginia.

Virginia felt her face flaming. This was a different sort of
heat from the sweet warmth she felt when Channing touched
her. The bearded man's hand on her waist burned her, hurt her,
revolted her. She could smell his unwashed body and the foul
odor of his breath.

"Ain't she a nice piece, boys? And, hell, if she's engaged to one of our own, well, it's all in the same army. Share and share alike, I say."

The other men whooped their approval, yelling obscenities and encouragement. The boy in his teens called, "Just leave some of that for me, boss. I ain't had me a good piece of tail in I don't know when."

Now the rude soldier was toying with her, teasing her—fingering the rough shirt she wore, pulling the shirttail out of her belt, tugging at the waist of her brother's trousers. Each time he touched her, Virginia felt her cringing fear turn more toward dangerous rage.

"How 'bout a little kiss, girlie?"

When he leaned down, pulling her hard against him, something in Virginia snapped. She swung her arm with all her force, striking the brute in the head with the heavy silver teapot. He stumbled backward, lost his balance, and went crashing, head over heels, down the veranda steps. He lay there, moaning, blood oozing from the gash in his head.

Waving the dented teapot triumphantly over her head, Virginia let out a cheer—her own Rebel yell.

Melora came to her and quickly closed her arms around her daughter. She was weeping, but without tears or sobs.

The click of metal made both women look up. They found themselves staring into the barrels of five rifles and five mean faces, ugly with rage.

"We ought not to shoot 'em yet, boys," the second-in-command said, with deadly calm. "I say we haul the both of them inside, have at 'em, then tie 'em up and burn the goddamn house down around 'em."

Melora prayed silently for a bullet. Virginia was too numb to pray. These men were about to kill her mother, probably Agnes and little Roslyn, too, and it was all her fault. She should have held her temper.

"*Please leave now,*" Melora begged. "We've done nothing to you."

"Oh, yeah?" the Yankee snarled. "I happen to know your

man's off fighting for Jeff Davis right now. And I hear tell you spawned a passel of stinking Rebs that are riding with their old man. You call that *nothing,* woman? Well, I call you a traitor, and traitor's fair game."

"I'll go with you!" Virginia cried. "But leave my mother alone."

The men exchanged glances, all the while keeping their guns trained on the two women.

"That ain't no kind of deal," said one of the other men. "Hell, I bet we could stay here for a week and never have the same woman twice. I seen them slave cabins back of the house. I bet they got wenches back there that ain't even been busted yet. I say, we take these two, then help ourself to every last bitch on the place. *Then* burn the house down!"

"No!" Melora cried. "Are you *animals?* Think of your own mothers, your daughters, your sweethearts. Think how you would feel if . . ." Her voice broke in a sob.

Virginia watched the men closely. One or two of them looked away as if Melora's words had struck a nerve. The moment passed, however.

"Hell, ain't no Rebs going to threaten my ma or sisters!" the youngest soldiers exclaimed. "I'm from Pennsylvania, and there ain't a Rebel alive who'll ever set foot that far north and live to tell it. I say, this place is ours, along with everything on it."

A tense silence followed. The men were thinking over their next move. The women were thinking over their next breath, wondering if they would live to draw it.

Suddenly, the thunder of hooves sounded on the drive. A loud shout split the silence. "You men there! *Halt!* Put your weapons down. Whoever harms a hair on the heads of these ladies will answer to me!"

Virginia couldn't believe it. "Channing," she breathed.

"God bless him," her mother added.

The men lowered their rifles and backed off.

Captain Channing McNeal dismounted and growled, "Who's in charge here?"

All the soldiers on the veranda pointed mutely to the inert figure with his face in the dirt and blood clotting in his tangled hair.

"This Rebel slut about kilt him, sir," the youngest soldier said.

Virginia watched Channing's eyes narrow. For a moment, she thought he meant to shoot the fellow or beat him senseless. When he spoke, his voice was as cold as the pond in the dead of winter. "I want you off this property, immediately." Channing poked their leader with the toe of his boot. "And take this trash with you. General Nathaniel Banks's troops are now in full retreat from Winchester. You will find and report to your unit commander at once. Now, get out of here, before I shoot the lot of you!"

"Yessir," they all mumbled, offering him half-hearted salutes.

Channing and the two women stood in frozen silence, until the men had loaded Virginia's victim back on his horse and headed at a good trot down the lane.

Melora was the first to move. She threw her arms around Channing's neck, sobbing, "Oh, thank God! Thank God! Channing, I couldn't have been happier to see my own dear husband ride up. You saved us."

Not until Channing could extract himself from Virginia's clinging mother, could he take his love into his arms.

"Darlin'," he whispered, "I've missed you."

She realized, when she went into Channing's arms, that he was trembling as much as she was. They both understood what a close call it had been.

Their first kiss, after so long, was a wonder.

"I want to marry you," Channing whispered. "I can't wait until after the war."

Overhearing his words, Melora said, "You should have been married before all this foolishness, the same day as Rodney and Agnes. I've had my fill and more of bad times. We're going to celebrate."

Virginia glanced at her mother. Melora's face had gone from abject misery and fear to a brilliant smile.

"Both of you, clean up," she told them. "Then we're going to have a party. One to beat all!"

With that, Melora Swan swished her skirts like a girl and swept into the house, leaving Virginia and Channing to wonder exactly what she had in mind.

Chapter Sixteen

From the moment Channing banished their tormentors and took Virginia into his arms, she felt as if this were all a dream. Everything around her took on a look of unreality. The swan pond mirrored perfect silvery clouds on its surface, distorted only by the heart shape formed when the old cob affectionately bowed his neck toward his pen. The tall tulip poplar shimmered in its leaf frock of dazzling spring-green. Even the air seemed cleaner, purer, softer, perfumed with wood violets and the first budding clover. The gentle breeze that caressed Virginia, as she stood encircled by Channing's arms, swept away the last of her fears, leaving behind only the richness and fullness of her love for this man.

"Channing," she whispered, "I can't believe you're really here."

He kissed her ever so tenderly. *"Believe it,* my love!" he answered.

Holding each other—touching, kissing—they savored each moment of the dying afternoon, lost in their own feelings and emotions. Locked away in their own enchanted world, they remained oblivious to the stir of excitement inside the big house.

The sun had slid far down the sky, by the time Melora Swan opened the front door and called them back to reality. "Channing, you'll want to wash up before dinner. You may use the guest bedroom. Virginia, you come with me."

"Must I?" Virginia protested mildly, still staring up into her lover's dark eyes.

"At once! There's much to do."

Channing smiled down at Virginia. "Go with your mother. She's right. I'm all dusty after my ride from Winchester. I'll see you directly, darlin'."

"You won't leave?" Panic edged Virginia's words.

"Channing isn't going anywhere," Melora answered for him. "Polly's in the cook house, preparing a special supper. And after we've eaten, I've a surprise in store for the two of you. Now, do come along, Virginia."

The besotted young woman stole one last kiss from her lover, before she followed her mother inside.

"Why did you make me leave him, Mother? He won't be here long, and I want to spend every single moment with him."

"Take a look at yourself in the hall mirror, dear, and you will understand why I drew you away."

Virginia glanced toward the tall glass over the petticoat table. She uttered a small cry of dismay. She was dressed in her brother's clothing, her shirttail untucked, her face smeared with dirt, and her hair looking much like a crow's nest.

Melora laughed at her daughter's expression. "I'll say this much for Channing, dear: If he can love you in your present state, he must, indeed, have given you his heart—totally and without reservation. Go up to the attic and fetch the gown we hid under the floor."

"My *wedding gown?*"

"It's the only decent thing you have left to wear. I'll have Mammy Fan press it, while you bathe. This is one night you will not wear britches. I mean for my lovely daughter to look like the true lady she is. After this dreadful war is over, we'll get you a new gown—one from Paris—for your wedding."

Virginia hugged her mother, then hurried to do her bidding.

Her heart fairly sang as she climbed the stairs. She took no note of the gleeful gleam in Melora's eyes.

Melora felt a great weight lift from her heart, as she watched her daughter go. She was about to undo a great wrong. She had felt guilty, since the night of the botched elopement. Surely, she could have thought of some way to keep Jedediah from ruining Virginia and Channing's wedding. Coupled with that heart-wrenching pain, Virginia had been forced to endure the happy scene on the day that Rodney and Agnes had married. This should have been Virginia's own wedding day. Nor had Melora missed the look of envy on Virginia's face the day her niece was born. She knew that her daughter was wishing that she were giving birth to Channing's child.

"Well, that's all in the past," Melora mused aloud. "Damn this war!"

She had had quite enough fighting. To her way of thinking, it was high time Virginia and Channing got the happiness they both longed for and deserved. The Colonel might pitch one of his roaring, storming fits when he heard, but his wife had ways to deal with his towering rages—effective ways, loving ways.

When Channing stepped through the doorway, Melora motioned him to her. "Please come with me to the library. I'd like a word with you."

Melora smiled at Channing, but she could tell from the puzzled expression on his face that he had no idea what she was about to propose. No doubt he thought that she meant to reinforce her husband's edict that these two young people stay at a distance until the war was over. Well, she certainly had a surprise for him—for both of them.

Channing strode into the room quietly. Every muscle in his body seemed tense when Melora turned and looked at him.

"Do relax, Channing. There's no need to be nervous with me. I may not be on the same side as you in this War of Northern Aggression, but we do share identical views, where it really counts."

"I'm sorry, ma'am. I don't understand."

Without asking if he wanted a drink—he obviously needed

one—she poured a tumbler of bourbon and handed it to him. "I want to talk to you about Virginia."

This statement drained the color from his face.

"For heaven's sake, Channing, you act as if you're facing your executioner! I'm on your side, I tell you. But I need to ask you an important question, before I go ahead with my plans."

He took a swig of his drink, some of his color returning. Then he nodded. "Ma'am?"

"You love my daughter, don't you?"

The question obviously came as a pleasant surprise. He fumbled for words, before he finally stammered, "Why, of course! More than anything—more than life itself. I'd do anything, *anything* to make her happy."

Melora smiled and nodded. This was the answer she wanted to hear. "Do you love her enough to marry her?"

Now it was Channing's turn to smile—a boyish grin that transformed his entire countenance. In reply, he set his glass down and went to hug Melora.

"Are you offering your daughter to me?"

Embarrassed suddenly by Channing's embrace, Melora stepped away and flashed her eyes at him in a way that reminded him of Virginia, when she was in a flirtatious mood.

"I don't believe I need to make that offer. It seems to me that she has made her intentions perfectly clear for some years now. What I'm asking is, are you willing to marry her this very night?"

Channing was struck dumb by the question. His charming smile grew wider and wider. Then he threw back his head and laughed—a full-throated, deeply male sound that made Melora think of nights when her own husband was close and especially amorous, with the onset of spring.

"I would marry Virginia anytime, anyplace. I've thought of little else these past years. All the time I was at West Point, my classmates counted the days until graduation. I counted the days until Virginia and I could wed. Since then, I've been counting the hours until this war comes to an end, so that I can rush back to Swan's Quarter and make her my own. When I rode up here today, I never dreamed . . ."

"You aren't dreaming, my boy. I mean what I say. The two of you will be husband and wife before this evening is over. I'm sick to death of all her mooning about. Watching her makes my own heart ache with her pain. And for what reason must you wait? Because her father is a stubborn mule of a man who can't see what's perfectly obvious to all of us."

"Ma'am?" Channing once more missed her meaning.

"Men!" she said with a sigh. "The *obvious* fact is that this war could go on for years. Years in which Virginia could be raising your child, instead of acting and feeling like an old maid auntie."

Melora could hardly believe her eyes. Her words actually brought a blush to Channing's face. He pulled at his collar, as though it had suddenly shrunk, choking him. This big, handsome, battle-toughened officer looked like a boy caught necking with his girl. Then the truth dawned on Melora. Somehow, somewhere, Virginia and Channing must have found a way. Channing must believe, from what Melora was saying, that Virginia was already in a family way, which she was certainly not. Melora thought through her next words carefully.

"I've seen it happen to girls more than once—they retain their virginity too long and they begin to think and act like shriveled old maids. I refuse to allow that to happen to my own daughter. I *demand* that she be properly wed immediately, *if you are willing,* Channing McNeal."

"Oh, Miz Melora! I'm more than willing!" He grinned and nodded, until his hair fell over his suntanned forehead.

"Fine, then! After supper. We'll surprise Virginia. Not a word. Understand?"

"Yes, Ma'am!" Again he bobbed his head.

"Go make yourself presentable, then, son. Supper will be ready shortly."

Channing caught Melora in his arms again and gave her a wet smack on the cheek.

"Go on with you!" she cried, laughing at his exuberance.

He went, as she ordered. At the door, he turned. "Miz Melora? Thank you. Thank you for trusting me with your daughter. You'll never be sorry, I promise you."

"No," she said solemnly, "I don't believe I ever will be, Channing. Not if you love her as much as she loves you."

"More, I'd venture." His voice was husky, choked with emotion.

"Then you have my blessing."

Up in her room, Virginia had bathed and was already donning the fragile gown of satin and lace that she had always expected to wear on her wedding day. She felt slight regret, thinking that when the time finally came for her and Channing to be wed, she would not be dressed in the same gown her mother and grandmother had worn before her. Still, tonight was special. And her mother was right; she had little else to wear. Most of her clothes—those that hadn't been pilfered by passing troops—were threadbare or far too tight. Such luxuries as needles, thread, and fabric had gone from scarce to unobtainable, these past months. She might have made new dresses from old, had she not cut up so many frocks to use for her Sunday House quilt. Yet who could have guessed that a labor of love for her hope chest would seem like an extravagant waste, such a short while later?

Mammy Fan scurried in just then to help Virginia finish dressing and to do her hair.

"Sorry I's late, Miss Virginia. But I brung news. Whoppin' big news!"

Virginia smiled at the thin, ebony-colored woman who had taken care of her from the moment of her birth. As the self-appointed head of the slave grapevine, Fan *always* had news.

"If you're going to tell me that Mother is planning a party for tonight, I know that already."

Mammy Fan pinched her face up in a frown and shook her chignoned head. " 'T'ain't that, Miss Virginia. This ain't got nothing to do with no party. See? I was down to the edge of the woods, digging roots from Polly's spring tonic, when them sorry-lookin' Yankees come ridin' right up the lane. They ain't seein' me, so they just keep a-talkin', big as you please. Braggin' to beat all, like Yankees does.''

The servant paused dramatically, as she always did, before imparting the really important details of any story.

"And?" Virginia prodded.

"And I heard 'em talking about Colonel Swan, your own daddy. 'Cording to them, Swan's Cavalry was at the big fight t'other side of Winchester yesterday. Them bad boys in blue come here, special, to do damage 'cause the Colonel shot some of their men. They claimed they was bent on burning this place down and killin' ever'thing that moved, hereabouts.''

Ice ran through Virginia's veins when she heard this. Channing had indeed arrived in the nick of time.

Then another thought crossed her mind. She turned and gave Mammy Fan a level gaze. "Have you told my mother about this?"

Her mouth full of ivory hairpins, Fan nodded. "Um-huhm."

"And what did she say? With my father and brothers as near as Winchester, surely she wants to ride in to see them, now that the fighting is over."

Mammy Fan eased the last pin into Virginia's hair, before she answered. "Miz Melora say that she got *special plans* for this night. She say, tomorrow be plenty soon to take the wagon to Winchester—safer too, she say."

This all seemed quite odd to Virginia. She could think of no reason why her mother would delay a reunion with her husband and sons. However, safety could be a factor. The Yankees were still in retreat, probably on all the roads for miles around. As long as the women stayed at Swan's Quarter, they were fairly secure. But unescorted, traveling through the countryside, they could encounter all sorts of danger.

"Mister Channing be lucky iffen the Colonel don't ride out here and catch him on the place. Look at what happened last time he come for a visit."

"You know about that?"

"Ain't nobody on the place don't know, Miss Virginia. Nobody 'cepting Miz Melora and Miz Agnes and little Miss Roslyn, I reckon. *Yankee spy!*" She chuckled and winked. "Mister Channing ain't no spy, no more'n I's a lily-white plantation mistress."

Now Virginia was truly worried. What if her father did come? He would certainly make every effort to see his family. And if Channing's friend, Captain Jacob Royal, had told Rodney about his daughter's birth, there would be no keeping her brother away.

"Mammy Fan, you must do me a favor. But no one can know—no one here at the big house."

The servant gave a quick nod. "Ain't no need to ask. I done done it, Miss Virginia. I got all six of my boys out to the woods. Iffen the Colonel and your brothers turn in at the lane, we gone know before they reaches the swan pond. I don't want nobody shootin' Mister Channing again." She winked at Virginia once more. " 'Specially not *this night!*"

Before Virginia could ask Mammy Fan what she meant, the wiry servant flitted out of the room, headed for the back stairs.

Virginia sighed. How she wished she could blink her eyes and make the war go away. Life at Swan's Quarter had been so good, so sweet before April of 1861. Even her separation from Channing, while he was at West Point, had had its bright moments, when his love letters arrived, when she and her mother worked on plans for their wedding, and especially when Channing had come home for holidays. Then their love for each other had seemed all the more precious for the time they had been apart.

But separation during wartime was entirely different. Not knowing where Channing was or when she would hear from him, not even knowing if he were alive or dead, from one day to the next, was a special kind of torture.

She swept a hand over her eyes, as if she could brush away all worrisome thoughts. Channing was here now. She would enjoy having him with her for now. Tomorrow—who knew?

She left her room quickly, eager to be with her lover again.

* * *

The evening was grand. Virginia's mother had ordered Polly and the other house servants to bring out the damask, the silver, the crystal. Their feast might be meager, but it would be served in high style. "In style befitting this happy occasion," Melora Swam had whispered to Polly, her chief co-conspirator.

All through supper—fried chicken, beans flavored with the last of the bacon, and yams—Virginia kept gazing at Channing, wanting to pinch herself to believe that she wasn't simply having another of her lovely dreams.

Melora had seated the two of them side by side. She pretended not to notice when Channing slipped his hand under the table, time after time, to touch Virginia's. She recalled Jedediah taking the same liberties, when they were young and so much in love that their longing seemed likely to consume them both with its heat and fervor. She simply smiled and daintily ate her chicken.

Agnes joined them at table, once she had nursed little Roslyn and turned her over to Mammy Fan. Rodney's wife looked paler than usual and far too thin. She was suffering, Melora knew, from a malady that afflicted all the women at Swan's Quarter—indeed, all the wives and sweethearts throughout Virginia and the South: too little to eat, too much to worry about, and, most devastating of all, little or no physical love.

"Have you seen Rodney at all, Channing?" Agnes's tone begged for his answer to be in the affirmative.

He shook his head slightly. "I'm sorry, Agnes, but no. Actually, it's probably for the best that I haven't, given the current unpleasantness."

"Yes, of course," she murmured, staring down at her plate, only picking at her food.

"I did hear, though, that Swan's Calvary is in Winchester. Perhaps Rodney and the others will stop by for a visit."

Agnes looked up, her eyes glittering with hope. Melora Swan's expression changed. Fear suddenly darkened her features.

The mistress of the house motioned to Polly. They had a

whispered conversation, which none of the others could hear. However, Polly was smiling and nodding, and Virginia did hear her mention Mammy Fan's name. After that, Melora relaxed visibly. Virginia realized in that moment that her mother was giving up time she might have spent with her husband and sons, so that Virginia and Channing could be together. She had never loved her mother more.

"Have you heard from your family, Channing?" Melora was a master at polite, dinner table conversation. All through the meal, she had refused to allow grim talk of the war to intrude and dampen their spirits.

"As a matter of fact, I had a letter from my father only last week. The whole family is ensconced in a spacious chateau on the outskirts of Paris. They seem to be adjusting to and enjoying their new way of life. Can you imagine my father turning his hand to the culture of vines? He swears that once he returns to Virginia, he will have the finest vineyards on this side of the Atlantic."

"A marvelous idea!" Melora exclaimed. "I've heard that Thomas Jefferson did quite well with his vineyard at Monticello. If he could make his own wine, why can't we?"

"Have Hester and Auguste married?" Agnes asked.

"Indeed! A lovely ceremony, Father said, in the old cathedral of Nôtre Dame. He suspects that Hester is already in a family way, although she and Auguste have yet to make the announcement."

"And your dear mother?" Melora asked, wistfully, missing her girlhood friend.

"She is well, I'm happy to report. In a postscript to Father's letter, she sent her love to you, one and all. It seems she, too, has taken to French country life. She's learning to paint with oils. She has met a young artist named Claude Monet, who says the only way to catch the true light of nature is to paint in the open air. They often roam the fields and lanes together, setting up their canvases out-of-doors to create their *masterpieces.*" Channing finished with a chuckle, obviously less than

convinced of his mother's talents and amused at the thought
of her becoming friends with some bizarre young Frenchman.

"Laugh, if you will," Melora scolded gently, "but Letitia
has talent. I have seen it in her delicate needlework. Anyone
who can handle a needle with such authority can certainly
match that dexterity with a brush." Now it was Melora's turn
to chuckle. "As for her young protégé, perhaps your father is
spending too much time with his vines."

"Mother Swan!" Agnes gasped.

"Don't get yourself in a state, Agnes, dear. I'm only jesting.
Letitia is far too much in love with her husband to have her
head turned by some callow young swain." She couldn't keep
herself from teasing her daughter-in-law just a bit more, as she
added, "Still, they do say that the French air does something
to a woman."

Channing laughed. "Not *my* mother! I've heard her say time
and time again that it took her too long to tame the wild
Scotsman she married to ever want to go through that process
again with any other man. No, Miz Melora, my parents are
lovingly *comfortable* with each other." He squeezed Virginia's
hand under the table. "That's the way I hope my wife and I
will be someday."

Melora noted Virginia's deep blush. "I have a feeling you'll
get your wish, Channing, my boy."

"I only hope we get to wed *before* we reach that age of
loving comfort." Virginia had said almost nothing throughout
the meal, but she longed so to be Channing's wife. All this
talk of weddings and babies made her ache clear to her soul.

She met Channing's eyes and felt something deep and strong
simmer between them. It seemed almost as if a bond, a silver
cord of belonging, bound them already. She was everything
but his legal wife.

He squeezed her hand again. At that moment, she felt tears
spring to her eyes.

Dear God, don't let me weep now! Virginia prayed silently.
In answer, God sent her mother to save the day.

"I'm sorry we haven't any dessert tonight," Melora said,

as she crossed her knife and fork to signal the end of their meal. "Shall we all adjourn to the parlor. I have decided to open the Colonel's last bottle of French brandy for the occasion. I trust you'll all join me in a toast to a swift conclusion to the war and a safe homecoming for all our family and friends."

Virginia, Channing, and Agnes all murmured their approval, even though they knew that Melora Swan's toast was an impossible wish. Already, several of their neighbors had been reported dead or missing—heroes on the battlefields of Bull Run, Manassas Junction, Shiloh. And one unfortunate member of Swan's Calvary had been killed in a duel with a fellow officer, as graphically recounted in a letter from Rodney to Agnes some months earlier.

As the others filed out of the dining room, Melora remained a moment for another whispered conference with Polly.

"Yessum! Right now! By the time you all's had your brandy, we be ready."

"Thank you, Polly." Melora smiled and hurried to join the others in the parlor.

When she entered, Agnes was seated by the front windows, gazing longingly down the lane, no doubt hoping to catch a glimpse of Rodney riding home. Channing and Virginia were at the Bible stand, perusing the entries that recorded family records of births, deaths, and marriages going back almost two hundred years.

"Interesting reading, isn't it?" Melora said. "Think of all those lives and the secrets that went with our ancestors to their graves. Sometimes I like to make up stories about them and imagine what they must have been like in life."

"I think the empty lines are far more fascinating," Virginia said. "When I read these pages, I try to imagine which lines will be mine, and my children's."

Channing squeezed her hand and whispered, "We'll take up a lot of those lines, by and by, darlin'. I promise you that."

Juniper, the butler, passed a silver tray with tiny crystal snifters of brandy, each filled with no more than a thimbleful of the Colonel's precious liquor. Virginia noticed, as she took her glass, that Juniper's white gloves were spotless, but mended many times over. Was there nothing at Swan's Quarter that had gone untouched by this war?

Melora raised her glass. "Shall we have our toast now?"

The others turned toward her, ready to hear her plea for the brevity of the war and the safe return of loved ones. She surprised them.

"On this very special occasion, I would like to propose a toast to two very special people." She smiled at Channing and Virginia. "To my only daughter and her only love. From this night forward, may you live together happily for many years, with deep understanding, true affection, and comfortable love."

Channing smiled and bowed to his hostess. Agnes and Virginia on the other hand looked totally befuddled. But they all raised their glasses to their lips and drank to Melora's toast.

"And now, my dears," the mistress of Swan's Quarter said, "I have a surprise for you."

Even as she spoke, they heard sounds of a fiddle coming from beyond the closed door.

"Why, it's Fiddlin' Joe!" Channing exclaimed. "I thought he must be with the angels by now."

Melora laughed. "One hundred and two, but still going strong. He says his fiddle keeps him young. And the way he still chases the women down in the quarters, I have to believe it's true. Come, all of you!"

When Melora opened the doors, they spied old Joe with his crippled legs and flying fingers, seated beside the stairway, coaxing magic from his strings. Gathered around him were all the house servants and many of the plantation children. The women were dressed in their best frocks and all wore bits of bright ribbon or strings of berry-beads. Virginia knew, from years of observation, that they dressed this way only on Christmas Day or for weddings.

She turned and stared at her mother. "What's this?"

Polly answered for her mistress. "Me and Zebulon, we done brung the broomstick, Miss Virginia, lak we promised you and Mister Channing. And we all come to witness the jumpin'."

Virginia looked at Channing. He was grinning from ear to ear. *"You!"* she cried, happy tears welling in her eyes. "You knew about this all along, didn't you?"

He nodded. "Your mother had to tell me. She wasn't sure I still wanted to marry you, now that you've reached such an advanced age. It's not every man who'll take an old maid for a wife."

They all laughed—all but Virginia. She went into Channing's arms, letting her tears of joy and relief flow freely.

When they parted, Polly thrust a bouquet of fragrant purple wisteria into Virginia's trembling hands. "Fan done found this blooming in the woods. I reckon it'll do for your bridal bouquet."

Virginia hugged Polly. "Thank you! You know how I love wisteria."

"We best get on with it now, Miz Melora."

"Indeed, Polly! Virginia, Channing, please come and stand before Brother Zebulon."

Still holding hands, the happy couple did as Melora instructed. Virginia had to smile at Brother Zeb. He was wrapped in a clerical robe of patched homespun. Someone— Polly, no doubt—had twined bright ribbons through his hair and beard. He held a huge Bible in his hands, which Virginia knew he could not read. Yet his voice boomed, as he led the group in reciting the Lord's Prayer and asked for the safety of all the family members who could not be present for this happy occasion.

Afterward, the entire group hushed in silent anticipation. Brother Zebulon cleared his throat, then spoke directly to Heaven. "Lord, me and You been on the same side all dese years, since I was a little biddy scrap of black flesh suckling at my ma's breast. You done heared my prayers ever' morning, noon, and night, these eighty-odd years. Some You's answered, some wasn't worth listening to. But this evening I got serious business that need Your attention, Lord. These here two white folks is hankering to be man and wife, real proper-like, with Your blessing. Mister Channing, he be a fine man—good to his ma and pa, understanding with his people, and in league with You, Lord. And he do honest-to-goodness want to make Miss Virginia his wife until death do they part."

Brother Zebulon paused, drew his gaze down from above, and stared full at Channing. "Ain't that right, sir?"

Channing nodded solemnly. "I *do* wish with all my heart to make Miss Virginia my wife."

Zeb's eyes shot back to Heaven. "See, Lord? Mister Channing, he done tole You so hisself. And now we comes to Miss Virginia. There ain't another lady in Frederick County—maybe all of this here state—as fine and well-bred as this dear lady, 'cepting her own mama, of course. Miss Virginia, she teach me Your words from Your own Book from the time she was knee-high. She believe Your words, too, and she tell me to mind them always. Now Miss Virginia got a favor to ask. She want to be Mister Channing's wife, and she want Your blessing on the union."

Again, Brother Zebulon's gaze shifted from on high to the subject of his conversation with the Lord. "Tha's right, ain't it, Miss Virginia?"

She bit her lip to stay her tears. "Oh, yes, Brother Zebulon! I *do* want to be Channing's wife, the best wife he could ever wish for. Tell the Lord I'll do my very best, always."

Brother Zeb smiled and nodded. "I reckon He done heard that. You been knowing Him longer than me, Miss Virginia."

They all assumed that the service was at an end, but Brother Zeb wasn't finished talking to the Lord yet. "I reckon they's got Your blessing, since You ain't sent no sign to the otherwise. Now, there be just one more thing, Lord. We needs to talk about fruitfulness. You done made them husband and wife, now You needs to see that this here union doth provide. They wants younguns to raise up, fine and good. Again, we ask Your blessing and ask that You send them down some sweet baby-lambs to tend."

Virginia felt her eyes sting with tears and her face burn with a blush. She glanced around to find all the servants beaming at her. It seemed Brother Zebulon meant to take longer on his fruitfullness speech than he had taken on the wedding service. Granted, Virginia wanted children, but if Zeb kept on in this vein, she'd have three dozen before it was done.

Finally, Polly put an end to his monologue. "Time for the broomstick jumpin', Brother Zebulon."

He said a quick, "Amen!" and beamed at the couple he had successfully married.

"Don't I get to kiss my bride?" Channing begged.

"Iffen you do it quick," Zeb answered. "Polly's got that broomstick ready and she ain't a patient women."

Virginia flowed into Channing's arms and forgot the rest of the world existed, as he covered her lips with his. Even in the euphoria of that moment of first-wedded bliss, her thoughts went to the old Bible in the parlor. One more line could be filled in tonight. A line that would link her soul and Channing's for all time.

Fiddlin' Joe struck up his music again. All the servants clapped and sang and cheered. When Virginia looked around, she saw two of the fancifully dressed children parading about the hall with an old broomstick, beribboned and decked with flowers.

"Shall we?" Channing said, laughing, beaming.

"Take dem shoes off first," Polly warned. "It don't take, lessen you's barefoot."

Channing tried hopping on one foot and pulling his boots off, without luck. Finally, Polly brought a chair. When he sat down, she showed Virginia the proper way to put her backside to her man and tug off his boots. Laughing and blushing, Virginia almost fell flat on her face when the second one finally came loose.

"Now you sit, Miss Virginia. Mister Channing got to take off your slippers."

Virginia tried to protest. After all, it might not be unseemly for her to bare her feet before her new husband. But in front of her mother, her sister-in-law, and all these servants?

"You got to do it, Miss Virginia," Polly urged.

She looked toward Melora, who smiled and nodded. Only then did Virginia sit down.

Channing might have made quick work of the process, but he chose not to. Instead, he drew up her skirts slowly, until her satin slippers and bare ankles were exposed for all to see. Caressing her ankle gently, sending fire up her legs, he drew off the first shoe inch-by-inch, then repeated the process. When both her feet were naked, Channing rubbed his palms over her soles. She felt hot and cold and trembling with longing, by the time he released her and rose. For long moments, she sat staring up at him, afraid to trust her legs to hold her.

He offered his hand. "Come, darlin', everyone's waiting."

The children with the broomstick danced about, teasing the bride and groom. "Catch us, iffen you can! Dis ole broomstick, she like to dance."

Fiddlin' Joe played faster and faster. Having no luck at catching the dancing broomstick, Channing caught Virginia in his arms and whirled her around the room—faster and faster, until it seemed they would take wing. All the while, he kept his eyes on the naughty scamps who held the stick. When they became mesmerized by Channing and Virginia's dance, he swept her toward them, pretending not to notice they were there.

"Now!" he whispered into Virginia's ear. "Jump, my love. Jump the broomstick!"

They left the floor together, clearing the final obstacle to their marriage by several inches. When they landed on the other side, everyone cheered. The children marched up and down the stairs, holding the broomstick on high. Fiddlin' Joe played on and on. Everyone danced. Polly disappeared into the pantry and returned with punch for the wedding guests.

"I make you all a cake, soon as I get me some sugar," she promised the bride and groom.

A short time later, Melora gave the signal that it was time for the party to end. Each servant came to the newlyweds to wish them well. Then they all filed out of the house, leaving only Virginia, Channing, Agnes, and Melora in the wide entranceway that had been the site of the spirited ceremony.

"Agnes," Melora said, "you look weary, dear. Why don't you go on up to bed?"

Realizing that this was more order than suggestion, Rodney's wife said her goodnights and left them.

Melora turned to the happy couple. "I want you to know that both the Lord and I bless this marriage. Channing, Virginia, you are one now. Hold each other dear for all your lives. I'm going to leave you now. You must be gone by sunrise, Channing. It would be dangerous for you to stay longer, with my husband and sons so near. But you have this night. Cherish it, and each other."

Virginia was beyond words when her mother came to kiss her cheek and give her an affectionate hug. Next, Melora turned to Channing. "Welcome to the family, son," she said. Then in a whisper for Channing's ears alone, "Take your bride to her room. The two of you should be *lovingly comfortable* there for the night."

"Thank you, Mother Swan," he said. "For *everything!*"

A short time later, with the house all quiet at last, Virginia felt her heart sing. Lifting her into his arms, Channing carried his bride up the wide staircase, down the hall, and into her room. Polly and Melora had been there since Virginia left to go to supper. Wisteria set in vases perfumed the cool night air, and on the bed was the Sunday House quilt from Virginia's hope chest.

The couple wasted little time on preliminaries. Before Virginia knew it, she was as naked as her handsome husband, lying in the bed where, until tonight, an old maid had slept. But it was no maiden who fell into Channing McNeal's arms that night, who slept not a wink, but gave her man all she had to give and accepted his loving tribute in return. They made love that night, as though every moment might be their last on earth. They pledged with their bodies what their hearts and souls had long since vowed. They would be together *always*— in spirit, when not in the flesh.

As the first pearly-pink rays of dawn crept into the room, Channing kissed his well-loved wife, then rose from the bed to dress.

"How long before I'll see you again, Channing?"

"I don't know, darlin'. There's no way I can give you an answer. But you'll be in my heart and in my mind every minute I'm away."

"I love you so, Channing!" She reached out and caught his hand, brought it to her lips, and kissed it.

Channing leaned down over her, caressing her breast and staring into her wide, brilliant eyes that were all the colors of heaven.

"I love you more than you'll ever know, Virginia McNeal. And, if the good Lord was listening to Brother Zeb tonight, I'll be home when you give birth to our first child. Early spring, when everything comes to life—the trees, the flowers, and our baby."

He kissed her one last time—a long, sweet, tender kiss. Virginia felt her heart breaking when he strode out of the room.

"Come back to me, Channing. "Oh, please, my darling!"

Only a short time after Channing left, Virginia rose from her bed, recalling something they had forgotten to do. With her wisteria wedding bouquet in hand, she tiptoed from the room. Outside, in a plot behind the house, she planted the vines by dawn's rose-gold light.

"There," she whispered. "Let our love last as long as this sweet wisteria grows and blooms."

Chapter Seventeen

Just after sunrise, on a dusty day in early August that was already hot enough to curl a pig's tail, the unannounced visitor rode up the drive past the swan pond.

"Virginia! Agnes!" Melora Swan's call of alarm echoed down the upstairs hallway. "Someone's coming. Be ready!"

Be ready! had become their watchword over the past weeks, as more and more strangers came to their door, begging or demanding food. In spite of the young mother's protests, Virginia had taught Agnes to shoot one of the Colonel's old squirrel guns. At the signal from Melora, Virginia and Agnes, both armed, would station themselves at upstairs windows that commanded a clear view of the veranda steps below. They all knew their positions and their duties. With the two young women covering him from above, Juniper would greet the visitors outside, while Melora, a loaded derringer clasped at the ready inside her apron pocket, stood watch from the shadows of the entranceway. After their near-disastrous run-in with those Yankees back in May, they weren't about to take any chances.

Virginia watched from her window, as the lone rider came to a halt at the foot of the stairs and dismounted. She felt ill this morning, as she had for several days past. But she gritted her teeth and swore that the chamber pot could and would wait. She had her duty to perform. The man might be alone and seemingly harmless. Until he made his business clear to Juniper, however, the stranger would remain squarely in the sights of Virginia's rifle.

She heard the man mumble something to Juniper.

"Captain Royal, you say, sir?" Juniper's deep, clear voice drifted up from down below. "You's a friend of Mister Channing?"

Virginia eased her trembling finger off the trigger and lowered the gun. Could it really be? Was she about to get some news of her husband, finally, after all this time? She had had one brief note from him that he wrote a week after their broomstick wedding. He had said they were on the march, headed West. She had received his short message, vowing his love anew, over a month after Channing wrote it. Since then, not a word.

"Captain Royal, how good that you've returned." Melora stepped outside to greet their visitor warmly. "My daughter told me of your last visit. I apologize for not coming out to speak to you then, but you arrived at a rather awkward moment. Do come in, won't you?"

"Thank you, ma'am."

Jacob Royal looked like a gray ghost, covered from head to toe as he was with the powdery dust of August. When he disappeared from view, following Melora Swan into the house, Virginia leaped to action. She had to talk to him immediately. There was no time to dress. She grabbed an old red velvet evening cloak out of her armoir and draped it around her shoulders. In moments, she was headed downstairs, her earlier queasiness forgotten in her excitement at seeing Channing's friend once more. Maybe he would bring news of her husband.

By the time Virginia reached the main floor, her mother and the captain were in the library. She hurried to join them without waiting for an invitation.

Melora turned, shock registering on her face at her daughter's unorthodox attire. "Virginia! You might have dressed!"

"I'm sorry, Mother, but I had to speak to Captain Royal at once." She turned to him, glowing with expectation. "What news from Channing?"

He shook his head and averted his gaze. "I'm sorry, but I haven't seen him in months, although our paths probably came near to crossing last month, during the Seven Days' Battle, as it's being called."

"Seven days of fighting?" Virginia said, imagining all sorts of horrible scenes.

"Actually, it lasted much longer—nearly a month. McClellan's forces under General Fitz-John Porter made a push toward Richmond. We clashed at every little crossroads along the way—Gaines' Mill, Fair Oaks, Seven Pines, Glendale, Frayser's Farm, White Oak Swamp, and Malvern Hill, which was a clear victory for the North. We were totally out-gunned and out-manned. Even General Lee couldn't believe it, when McClellan called a retreat. But "Ole Marse Bob," as the soldiers call our commander, took immediate advantage of the situation. We forged ahead, pushing over one hundred thousand Federals back twenty miles, from the Pamunkey River clear to the James."

Virginia's heart sank. With so many battles fought, involving so many men, the casualties had to be enormous. She prayed silently that Channing wasn't merely a statistic, by now. And what of her father and brothers?

As if reading her mind, Jake Royal said, "I do have news from Colonel Swan and the boys, though."

"Are they well, Captain?" Melora's voice was as rigid as her spine. She steeled herself for the worst.

"Alive, ma'am. I suppose, after such a campaign, that's the same as well."

Virginia watched her mother relax visibly.

"Tell me, Captain Royal. Please! Don't spare any details."

He glanced around, first to make sure that he was alone with the two women. He knew that Rodney Swan's wife, the mother of his child, was also somewhere in the house. Luckily, Agnes had yet to join them. The news of her husband would be easier, coming from her mother-in-law than from a total stranger, and a man at that. Women seemed to have a knack for softening cruel blows.

"Your sons, Rodney and Jed, have been wounded, ma'am." He voice was quiet with sympathy.

Both Virginia and Melora gasped. Virginia went to her mother and slipped an arm around her shoulders.

"How badly?" Melora asked.

From his discomfited expression, Virginia could tell that Jake Royal wished he were not the bearer of such news. He took a deep breath before he answered.

"Young Jed took a shot through the shoulder, ma'am. He was taken away in a hospital wagon, so I can't report on his current condition, but I doubt it's serious."

"And Rodney?"

Royal hesitated for long moments and focused his gaze out the window at some distant point. "A head wound," he said at length. "His father was with him when I last saw them. The Colonel believes that Rodney will recover, in time."

In time. The words hung in the air like a pall.

Melora looked directly at Virginia. "Not a word of this to Agnes, do you understand? She is not a strong woman. There's nothing she can do, so there is no need for her to know."

Virginia and Jake Royal exchanged solemn looks, then both nodded.

"My husband is uninjured?"

"Fine, ma'am. The Colonel thrives."

Still holding her mother's shoulders, Virginia felt Melora release a pent-up sigh of relief. Then, shrugging her daughter's protective arm away, she said archly, "Just like a man, to thrive on war! I believe it's past time we offered you some breakfast, Captain Royal. And, Virginia, you go and dress. This minute!"

Just then, one of the ever-present kittens on the place came bounding into the room, chasing a moth. The sight of the ball of calico fur bounding and leaping eased the tension in the room. Jake reached down and caught the little cat in mid-pounce.

"Hello, there, you pretty little girl." He snuggled the kitten under his whiskered chin and laughed when she batted his cheeks.

"How did you know that Rainbow's a girl?" Virginia asked. The men in her family cared little or nothing for cats.

He chuckled and scratched the kitten's ears. "I never saw a calico that wasn't a female. Good mousers they are, too. And this one—Rainbow—is a mighty pretty thing. My Amanda would love her."

A thought dawned on Virginia, at that moment. "Then your Amanda shall have her, Captain Royal. A gift from the Swan family."

Rainbow stared up at him with her wide, gold-green eyes and meowed, as if she agreed with the plan.

"That's a sweet gesture, Miss Virginia, but I don't know when I'll get home again to take Rainbow to Amanda."

"She can wait here, until you find yourself headed for Tennessee. Channing told me that you and Miss Kelly plan to be married over the holidays. Perhaps you can take Rainbow then."

A warm smile spread over his handsome face. Virginia could tell he was thinking of his love and their coming wedding.

"Did you know that Channing and I are married now?"

He stared at her. "No. When?"

"Virginia, don't you think you had better go up and get dressed now?" Melora asked. She did *not* want her husband finding out that his only daughter had been wed.

However, before Melora could stop Virginia, she had told Captain Royal the whole story about the Yankee soldiers and the silver teapot and Channing's arrival in the nick of time and their broomstick wedding.

When she finished, Jake Royal was chuckling. "Well, as we say down home in Tennessee, that sure takes the rag offen the bush, Miz McNeal!"

"It was *supposed* to remain our secret," Melora warned. "Please, Captain Royal, don't tell anyone. My husband absolutely forbad them to marry, until after the war."

Jake put the kitten down and turned to Melora. "You needn't worry, Miz Swan. Your secret is safe with me. I'm sure glad Amanda's daddy doesn't feel that way. I can hardly wait to get home and marry that girl."

Suddenly, Virginia was sorry she hadn't heeded her mother's instructions to go upstairs and dress. She went from feeling fine to feeling faint and ill, in the span of a moment. She felt her mother's hand touch her arm. She couldn't see her, because of the strange, bright spots floating in front of her eyes.

"Please excuse us, Captain Royal. It seems my daughter's taken ill."

"I'm so sorry. I hope it isn't the grippe."

"I'm sure not," Virginia heard her mother answer. "It's something far more natural for a woman in her state."

Virginia's mother helped her to a chair. "Something far more natural?" What did that mean?

"Don't worry, dear. I'll have Polly mix you a morning sickness potion. The first three months are always the worst. You'll be over this soon, I vow."

Virginia still felt dazed. Then realization came. "Do you mean I'm *pregnant?*"

"I wouldn't be at all surprised, dear. Hadn't you guessed? Why, Polly and I have been speculating on that possibility for weeks."

All sorts of bright, happy thoughts danced in Virginia's head. Still, her gaze was fuzzy, and she felt lightheaded and strange. The room suddenly seemed to be filled with people. Only they weren't real people, but mere shadows laughing and talking all around her.

"A wedding!" she heard someone say. "Won't it be fine?"

"The best time we've had at Swan's Quarter since that young preacher from Front Royal first came to lead the Sunday singing."

Virginia seemed to recognize the two female voices, but, then again, she didn't.

She moaned softly, disoriented and feeling as though she

were drifting through space. The room appeared to be turning upside down.

"A baby," she sighed. "Channing's baby."

The next moment, everything around her went black.

"Ginna? Ginna, wake up!"

"A baby—mine and Channing's . . ."

"Here, darlin', let me help you sit up. Remember me? Neal?"

Ginna felt only half herself. Part of her was still Virginia, the woman carrying Channing McNeal's child. She almost hated to give up that part of the past.

When her head cleared and she looked up, she spied the heavy wisteria that hung like a green and purple curtain overhead. This was the very vine she had planted the morning Channing rode off, after their marriage and their long, sweet night of love-making. Her bridal bouquet had now grown and matured, like her love for her husband.

"Ginna? You're still a million miles away." Neal was right. She was.

"We're back so soon?" she whispered. "But it wasn't finished. I still don't know what happened."

"You know that Virginia and Channing were married, that they had a baby. That's what you wanted, wasn't it?"

"There's still so much I don't know. Did Channing come home from the war? And what about Colonel Swan? How about Rodney and Jed and the others. Poor Agnes! What if she had to raise little Roslyn all alone?"

"There are other ways to find out," Neal insisted. "You said Kirkwood mentioned an old Bible containing the family records. We'll take a look. But I *really* don't think we'd better go back to the past, Ginna, ever again. We belong here— together."

She turned to look at him. Why had he said that? He, above all people, should understand that Virginia belonged with her husband, Channing.

"I intend to find out what happened to all the Swans, one way or another."

"And *then* you'll marry me? I mean, I'm really beginning to feel cheated. You married Channing, now marry *me*. Hey, I'll even jump a broomstick, if that's the way you want it. Anytime, anyplace, you name it!"

Ginna couldn't help but laugh. And she couldn't help but love Neal for the way he put up with her whims and excuses.

She leaned forward and kissed his mouth ever so softly. "How does the day after tomorrow sound for our wedding?"

Neal threw his arms around her and hugged her close. "Do you really mean it? *Day after tomorrow?*"

"If that's too soon . . ."

He cut off her sentence with his lips, holding her gently, kissing her deeply.

Old Zee strolled in, interrupting their intimate moment. "You folks gonna miss dinner. They's already in the dining room, you know. I done had mine in the kitchen."

"Goodness! How did it get so late?" Ginna said, slightly flustered. "Come on, Neal. We'd better go."

Hand in hand, they hurried to the dining room. Sure enough, everyone was seated. Elspeth motioned for them to come sit at her table.

"We just got started," the old woman called. "Come on over, and we'll send to the kitchen for two more plates."

Ginna thought quickly, trying to come up with some excuse for their tardiness. She needn't have bothered. Neither Elspeth nor any of the others asked where they had been. Instead, all the attention focused on Neal.

"Well, I declare!" Elspeth said. "I thought you were laid up in bed, Neal. The doctor let you up so soon?"

Suddenly remembering that he had been shot, Neal glanced down at his arm. There was no bandage, no wound, no scar. Also, no explanation. He laughed and raised his arm for all of them to see.

"Looks like you were right, Elspeth. That must have been a ghost who shot me. And I guess it was a phantom bullet, too."

Elspeth gave him a knowing smile and leaned close to whisper, "Time cures a lot, don't it? The greenhouse got powerful magic in it, sure enough."

Ginna stared, amazed, at Neal's uninjured arm. "How could this happen?"

Again, Elspeth spoke in a whisper. "I know where you two been. And you needed to go one last time. Did you see my great-gran, Polly?"

Ginna nodded. "She saved Channing's life."

"Well, I reckon her potions must of helped Neal heal up too. She was a wise woman, that Polly."

Sister and Marcellus Lynch were across the table, deep in some private conversation, ignoring the others. Only Pansy seemed left out by everyone. Ginna smiled at her, trying to draw her into their group.

"What's wrong, Miss Pansy? You're so quiet today."

Pansy glanced toward Elspeth, as if asking her permission to speak. Elspeth answered for her.

"She needs to talk to you private, after we finish dinner, Ginna. Isn't that right, Pansy?"

She nodded, but still looked ill at ease. "If you say so, Elspeth."

"About what?" Ginna asked.

Elspeth was quick to cut her off. "It'll keep for now."

Dr. Kirkwood burst into the dining room just then, looking like a thunderstorm about to rain on all of them. He glanced about, then came directly toward Neal and Ginna.

"What are you doing out of bed?" he demanded.

In answer, Neal raised his arm to show the doctor. "All healed," he said with a smile.

"And the Mini ball? Did you take that from my office?"

"Haven't seen it," Neal answered.

"Well, it's gone. Somebody took it. What am I supposed to tell the police?"

Elspeth spoke up. "Seems to me, Dr. Kirkwood, that if Neal's all well and the bullet's gone, then the whole thing must have been them ghosts fooling around, like I said all along. You reckon the police are going to take kindly to you calling them out here to report on some Confederate phantoms?" She paused and laughed. "Why, they be locking *you* up in some padded cell!"

"I really should report this incident," Kirkwood mused aloud, his face one massive frown of puzzlement.

"No need now, doc," Neal said. "I'm fine. Seems almost like I dreamed the whole thing."

Kirkwood let out a sigh and shook his head, muttering under his breath.

"Doctor, Neal and I would like to have a look at that old Bible you mentioned to me. The one with the Swan records in it," Ginna requested.

"I'm not sure where it is. Somewhere in the store room, I suspect."

"This really is important," Ginna urged. "Could you find it for us? Please?"

"All right. I'll go upstairs and see if I can locate it. Maybe that will take my mind off all this ghost mess."

Ginna smiled and squeezed Neal's hand under the table.

"But I must talk to you first," Pansy begged. *"Before* you look at the Bible."

"All right, Pansy. As soon as we finish."

"Oh, thank you, Ginna. I have the courage now, but I might lose it, if I have to wait."

Ginna eyed Pansy suspiciously. *What now?* she wondered.

She didn't have to wait long to find out. As soon as the plates were cleared, even before dessert was served, Pansy rose and motioned for Ginna to come with her.

"I want to go, too," Neal said.

Pansy hesitated, but, seeing a slight nod from Elspeth, she motioned for Neal to join them.

The three had the parlor all to themselves. Pansy closed the door and locked it, something Ginna had never seen her do before.

"I don't want that busybody, Lynch, bursting in and interrupting us," Pansy explained. "Sit down, both of you. I have a tale to tell."

Ginna and Neal sat close, both of them on edge, not knowing what to expect.

"I have something of yours, Ginna." Pansy fished into her pocket and brought out something small and shiny. She handed it to the younger woman.

Ginna gasped. "My locket! Where did you get it, Pansy? It's been lost for years."

The old woman looked down, embarrassed to face the locket's owner. "I stole it," she confessed.

"Pansy, no! I can't believe that."

"It's true. The very first time you came here to visit your foster mother, you were wearing it. I knew at the moment who you were."

"I don't understand."

"Let me begin at the beginning, dear. I'll try to explain, although I know you'll never be able to forgive me." She paused and sniffed, then blew her nose daintily into her lace hanky.

"I come of fine old Virginia stock. Never was there a blemish on my family name—not until I put one there. You see, back before the second world war, when I was young and pretty and foolish, I fell in love. He was such a handsome boy—so sweet and adoring. He, too, came of old Virginia folks. Had times been different, he would have wooed me, courted me, then finally asked my papa for my hand in marriage. We would have had a long, lovely life together, I'm sure. But that was not to be. To make a long story short, the night before he left to go fight in the Pacific, I allowed the unthinkable."

Ginna might have smiled, had Pansy not been so miserable. The "unthinkable" was obviously the act of love, something women gave hardly a second thought to, nowadays. But back when Pansy had been young, a girl's virginity was something to be closely guarded until after she wed.

Pansy was crying now, silently. "After we—*you know*—he gave me that silver heart locket. He said it had been in his family for a long time and that his grandmother had passed it on to him to give it to his wife."

"But I don't understand, Pansy. If the locket was yours, how did I get it?"

"I'm coming to that, dear."

Transfixed by Pansy's story, Ginna was hardly aware when Neal reached over and took her hand.

"My poor, dear Billy, the only man I ever loved, was sent to Pearl Harbor. He never knew when our daughter was born. I did my best to raise her alone, but it was never easy. I suppose Billy Jean was my cross to bear for the sin I had committed with her father."

"It wasn't a sin," Ginna said, gently. "It was love, Pansy."

"Well, maybe now it would be considered so, but not back then. At any rate, I gave Billy Jean your silver locket on her sixteenth birthday. Two days later, she ran away from home. I never saw her again. I tried to find her, but young people were roaming all over, back then, living in communes, practicing free love. I didn't understand any of it. I just wanted my baby back. She called me a few months after she left. She said she was fine and that I shouldn't worry. She said she was in love. I begged her to come home, but she said she couldn't leave her man. I never even found out his name. She did sound happy. That gave me some peace of mind. But a few months later, she called again. She was crying, hysterical. She said she was all alone, that her fellow had left her. I remember her words exactly, 'Mom, I've had a baby and something's wrong with her. I'm real scared. I can't take care of her.'"

Pansy broke down, at this point. She had to stop for several minutes to regain her composure. Virginia went to her, trying to soothe her tears.

"It's all right, Pansy. It wasn't your fault."

"Oh, but it was! I should have married Billy before . . . I should have been a better mother to my daughter."

"What happened to your granddaughter, Pansy? Did you ever find her?"

Pansy raised her eyes to Ginna's. Tears flowed down the old woman's cheeks. "Yes," she whispered. "Yes, Ginna, I found her."

Pansy reached out and touched the silver locket that Ginna had fastened around her neck.

"The last thing Billy Jean told me was that she had named her baby Ginna, because that was the name on the locket. When you came here and I saw that silver heart—the same one Billy gave me so long ago—and you told us the story of how you were found on the hospital steps, I knew that you were Billy Jean's daughter, my own granddaughter, Ginna."

Neal rose and came to put his arms around Ginna. She stood in stunned silence for a moment, before she wrapped her arms around her grandmother.

"What happened to my mother?" she whispered.

"I never found out. Like so many other young people in that lost generation, she simply vanished. I had no one, until you came into my life, Ginna. And, oh, I have grown to love you so!"

"Why didn't you tell me all this sooner?"

"I was ashamed. Not because of what Billy and I did, but because I stole the locket from you. When you first came here, I didn't make the connection. I only knew that the locket belonged to me and that it was all I had left of Billy and Billie Jean. I wanted it back. Then when I realized who you really were and that you *should* have the locket, that it was rightfully yours, I was too embarrassed to admit that I'd taken it. Can you forgive me—for everything?"

Virginia's emotions were churning inside her. She wanted to weep for her grandfather and her mother. At the same time, she wanted to cry out with joy at finally finding out who she was and where she came from—at finally having a family. She had loved Pansy long before today. Now that love was multiplied a thousandfold.

"You look like her, you know," Pansy said, gently stroking Ginna's cheek. "And you look even more like Billy Jean's great-great-grandmother, my dear Billy's grandmother."

"Who was she?" Ginna asked, holding her breath in wonder.

"Virginia Swan."

Silence fell in the room, and the name seemed to echo off the walls.

"*The* Virginia Swan?" Neal asked at length.

Pansy nodded. "That's why I came here when I could no longer live alone. Somehow, being at Swan's Quarter made me feel closer to my Billy. Sometimes I think I see him down by the pond, or sitting out under the tulip poplar. It's only my imaginiation, I know, but it makes me feel closer to him."

"Oh, Pansy, I don't know what to say."

"You needn't say anything for now, Ginna. But I knew I didn't have much more time, and I did want you to know. You've made my last years the happiest of my life, dear. I love you, Ginna."

"I love you, too, Grandmother Pansy."

Pansy stepped out of their embrace and looked sternly at Ginna. "There's been too long a history of love gone wrong in this family. I want you and Neal to get married, Ginna, just as soon as you can."

"Is day after tomorrow soon enough?" Neal smiled gently at the old woman.

"Glory be!" Pansy cried. "I never thought I'd live to see the day!"

She hugged them both, crying tears of happiness now.

Noise from out in the hall told them that the dinner hour was over. Soon, someone would be pounding on the door. But it was done, the story told. Pansy looked happy, but weary.

"I think I'll go up to my room for a nap now, children. It's been a long day . . . a long life. But, my goodness, it's been worth it, now that I've found you, Ginna."

Pansy kissed her granddaughter, then unlocked the door and left Ginna and Neal alone.

For a long time, Neal held Ginna, letting her cry it all out. Tomorrow would be soon enough to search the old Bible for the secrets it held. For now, they needed time alone together, time for Ginna to rethink and reshape the entire picture of her life.

Chapter Eighteen

"I need to go into Winchester," Ginna said. "It's important."

She and Neal had been strolling about the grounds, watching the two swans glide over the pond, talking quietly of this and that. Her statement came out of the blue.

"What about the Bible? I thought you wanted to look at that, before we do anything else."

"Yes, I do want to see the Bible. But we have other business to take care of first. We need to get blood tests and a marriage license. Also, there's someone I want you to meet. A good friend of mine."

"Ah!" Neal laughed, but he sounded nervous. "I have to pass inspection, eh?"

"Don't be silly." Ginna went up on tiptoe and kissed his cheek. "You've passed *my* inspection, and that's all that matters. I just think you should know more about me, darling."

Neal already knew a good deal of her life story, from hearing Pansy's confessions. Still, there was one more segment of her life that she had kept secret from him. Besides, Lucille had been a good friend for many years. She wanted Neal to meet her and see the Rebel Yell Cafe. She wanted the man she loved to know *everything* about her.

"Maybe Dr. Kirkwood will let us borrow his car. We'll only be gone a couple of hours."

"Whatever you say, Ginna. Let's go ask him."

They headed back up the hill in silence. There was too much to discuss today, so not talking at all seemed the best course of action.

When they reached Kirkwood's office, he was bending over the Swan family Bible, a massive tome bound in rusty-black leather. He looked up and grinned at them.

"I found it!" he said. "There's some interesting stuff here. You can use my office to look it over, if you'd like. I hear you have a family connection, Ginna."

"News really travels fast in this place, Doc."

Kirkwood chuckled. "There's little else these people have to do but gossip. And to find out, Ginna, that you are actually one of them, through Pansy, is the best news they could hear. There's also word that we're having a wedding here day after tomorrow. Am I right?"

Ginna gave Kirkwood a huge smile, glad that he approved. "That's what we've come for. May we borrow your car for a couple of hours? We need to drive into Winchester to get a license."

"Sure. But I thought you were so eager to get at this Bible."

Ginna glanced longingly at the old book. She would have loved to dive right into her research this very minute. "That will have to wait until we get back."

Dr. Kirkwood handed Neal his car keys. "Drive carefully," he said.

They slipped out the back way to avoid getting held up, if they ran into Elspeth or any of the others, who'd be bound to want to talk a blue streak about Pansy's revelation.

They climbed into Dr. Kirkwood's car, and Neal took off with a squeal of tires. Safely off Swan's Quarter property, they both visibly relaxed.

"Ah, alone at last!" Neal said, with a sigh and a wink.

Ginna laughed. "You keep your eyes on the road. We'll have plenty of time alone later."

"Promise?"

"Promise!"

"Are you going to show me where you live?" Neal asked.

"If you'd like." Ginna smiled and pressed his hand. "You'll be surprised when you see it. Amazed, in fact."

"Why's that? You live in an old mansion or something?"

"Better still. I live in the old parsonage, where Virginia and Channing went when they eloped."

Taking his eyes off the road for a moment, Neal turned to stare at her. "You're kidding me! You knew all along?"

"Not when I rented the place. Not until after we went back in time and actually experienced the elopement. I think the spirit of Virginia Swan drew me there, even before all this started."

They passed a car headed toward Swan's Quarter about a mile up the road. Neal grimaced.

"Looks like we left in the nick of time. Did you see who that was?"

"No. Did you?"

"Mr. Henderson and all his kids. I sure don't want another session with that man."

Once again, Ginna gripped his free hand. "Neal, don't. We're on our way to get our marriage license. Don't even think about anything else. It's all in the past. It wasn't your fault. You have to get over it."

Neal made no reply, but pressed harder on the gas, as if his only wish were to put more distance between himself and the Hendersons. Ginna made it sound so easy—forgetting. It wasn't!

They rode the rest of the way to Winchester in strained silence, Ginna thinking of the future, while Neal's mind remained on the past.

"Turn left here," Ginna directed, when they reached the heart of town.

"Where are we going?"

"Just up there in the middle of the block. The Rebel Yell Cafe."

"I can't eat a bite. I'm still stuffed from dinner—all that ham and potato salad."

Ginna smiled at him, excited about getting her friend and her lover together for the first time, but nervous too. She was about to destroy her illusion of mystery. "We missed dessert. You can at least have a piece of Lucille's apple pie."

"Lucille? That's your girlfriend?"

"Yes, Neal. Lu's both my friend and my employer. She's helped me through some rough times, in the six years I've worked for her as a waitress at the Rebel Yell."

"You? A waitress in a greasy spoon?"

"Don't let Lucille hear you call it that. Does it bother you that I work there—that I'm not the mistress of some grand old plantation?"

Neal didn't hesitate before he said, "Not at all. I'm just surprised. I figured you for some computer expert, or maybe a model. It's hard for me to picture you slinging hash."

Ginna laughed gaily. "It's the best hash in town, my love."

Neal pulled up to the curb and got out to open the door for Ginna. Lucille spotted them and came to the front door, waving frantically.

"Well, if it isn't the prodigal daughter! Where on earth have you been, Ginna? I must of phoned your place two dozen times."

"Any problems? Don't tell me Noreen quit!"

"No. I was just concerned about you. I knew you weren't feeling well. I even called the hospital to see if you'd checked in again."

She grinned at Lucille. "I'm fit as a fiddle, etc. And, Lu, I'd like you to meet Neal Frazier, the man I'm going to marry."

Neal stuck out his hand to shake, but Lucille grabbed him in a bear hug. "Well, if this don't beat all! I knew it was serious the first time she told me about you, Neal. When's the big day?"

"Day after tomorrow," Ginna said. "Out at Swan's Quarter."

"Well, glory! I couldn't be happier for you, Ginna. You all come on in here and have something to eat. I just took a fresh apple pie out of the oven."

Over pie à la mode and steaming black coffee, Ginna and Neal caught Lucille up on some of the curious happenings of the past few days.

"So, you found your family, at last." Lucille leaned over and gave Ginna a peck on the cheek. "I'm real happy for you, honey. I knew you'd find your people someday."

"I can't wait for you to meet my grandmother. I know you'll just love Pansy. She's so sweet and dear."

All the while Ginna was talking, Lucille was giving Neal the once over. She leaned down and whispered to Ginna, "You got you a good one, girl!"

Ginna giggled. "I think so."

Neal looked up. "What are you two whispering about?"

"*You!*" they both said together. Then Lucille added, "But you needn't worry, Neal. It's all good stuff we're saying about you. I reckon Ginna is just plum head over heels in love for the first time in her life. It's brought out the bloom in her cheeks."

"That goes both ways," Neal said, seriously. "Meeting Ginna is the best thing that's ever happened to me. You could say she brought me back from the dead. Now I'm looking forward to living again—with Ginna, for a long, long time."

Lucille gave a sudden cry. "Speaking of long times, I've got something for you, Ginna. I almost forgot. Old Huckabee down at the post office brought it over here and said I should give it to you."

"What is it?" Ginna couldn't imagine who would be writing to her at the Rebel Yell.

"A letter. Wait a minute. I'll get it. It's in my purse."

Lucille returned a minute later and handed Ginna a dirty, ragged envelope. It was addressed to "Mrs. Virginia Swan McNeal, Swan's Quarter, Virginia."

"Huckabee figured you could take it out to Swan's Quarter next time you visit. It's been lying in the dead-letter file gathering dust all these years. They just found it when the post office was being remodeled."

Ginna took the fragile envelope with trembling hands. She could just make out the return address. "Why, it's from Tennessee! From Captain Royal's sweetheart, Amanda."

"Well, open it!" Lucille prompted. "Let's see what she has to say."

"Should I? It's not addressed to me."

"But according to what Miss Pansy told you, you're her closest living relative," Lucille remined her. "Maybe the only one."

"Open it, Ginna," Neal urged.

Ginna slit the brittle paper carefully with a knife. The ink on the folded piece of vellum was still sharp and dark. "It's dated April the twentieth, 1863." Ginna first scanned the letter silently, then read it aloud to Lu and Neal.

Dear Virginia,

Please pardon me for using your Christian name when we have never met. My Jake told me so much about you in his letters that I feel I know you personally.

I must share some sad news. Captain Jacob Royal was killed on December 31 of last year, while camped with his men of the Rappahannock. He had been wounded at Fredericksburg earlier in the month and was soon to return home for our wedding. I cannot tell you how I grieve for my lost love.

But this is meant to be a letter of gratitude to you. On his final visit to Swan's Quarter, you gave my Jake a lovely gift for me. Although he was unable to deliver the kitten in person, a friend brought her to me. Rainbow has been the light of my life these past months, my last, sweet offering of love from dear Jake. Thank you for your kindness to him and for this wonderful gift. Even now,

*my darling Rainbow is curled up in my lap, purring as
she sleeps.*

*I like to think that someday you and I shall meet, dear
Virginia. My warmest regards to you always and my best
wishes on your marriage to Captain McNeal.*

> Ever affectionately
> Amanda Kelly

Tears were streaming down Ginna's cheeks, by the time she
finished reading Amanda's letter.

"Don't cry, darlin'," Neal said gently. "Think how happy
Virginia would have been to know that Amanda got that kitten.
And this letter fits one piece into the puzzle. We know that
Captain Royal returned to Swan's Quarter at least once more."

"But it's so sad that he was killed before they could be
married. Poor Amanda! Poor Jake!"

"Well, I just think it's amazing," Lucille said. "Imagine
that old letter being lost all these years, then finding its way
to you, Ginna." She looked over at her friend and saw that her
face had gone deathly pale suddenly. "Ginna? Are you all
right? You aren't about to have another attack, are you? Lord,
I'm going to call an ambulance!"

Ginna caught her hand. *"No, Lucille!* I'll be fine in a minute.
It's just . . . Amanda's letter came as a shock."

"What are you talking about, Lucille?" Neal demanded.
"What kind of attack?"

"You mean she hasn't told you, and the two of you fixing
to get married?"

"Told me *what?"*

"Lucille!" Ginna warned in a stern voice.

"It ain't right, Ginna, you not telling him."

"What is going on? *Somebody tell me!"*

"It's nothing, Neal," Ginna fibbed, putting a reassuring hand
over his.

"Nothing, my eye!" Lucille exclaimed. "If you don't tell
him, Ginna, I'm going to."

"Tell me, Lucille, please," Neal begged.

Before Ginna could say a word, her friend blurted out, "She's got a bum ticker, that's what!"

Ginna sobbed and Neal slipped his arm around her shoulders. "Ginna?" he whispered. "Why didn't you want me to know? That explains so much. Your fainting spells."

"She's been fainting again?" Lucille said. "Well, I should of guessed, the way she was dragging around here. Girl, you better get yourself over to that hospital right now."

"No!" Ginna cried. "I'm fine! Now both of you just leave it be. Yes, Neal, I have a heart condition. I didn't want to tell you because I was afraid you wouldn't want to marry me. Not after you'd lost one wife already."

Neal cradled her in his arms. "Ginna, Ginna, of course I still want to marry you. I want to take care of you, darlin'."

"I don't want to be taken care of. I want to be loved. Now you'll be scared to touch me."

He chuckled, a low, sexy sound. "Wanna bet? It's your call now, darlin'. Do you need to see a doctor, or are you okay?"

"I'm fine," she murmured, her heart racing erratically.

"Then why don't we go on and take care of our business, then get on back to Swan's Quarter. You can rest a while, and then we'll tackle that Bible."

Ginna brightened. "The Bible! It totally slipped my mind. After reading this letter, I'm more eager than ever to read those old entries."

"You take good care of her, Neal," Lu said.

"Don't you worry. I'm not going to let anything happen to the woman I love."

They stopped only briefly at Ginna's place. She didn't want to say anything to Neal, but she was feeling weak and drained. It would be good to get back to Swan's Quarter. The sooner the better.

Neal grew quiet the minute they walked through her door. He seemed caught between times in this place. The memories the parsonage brought back were anything but pleasant for him.

"I hate to rush you, Ginna, but could we get out of here?

It's like Jedediah Swan and Virginia's brothers are still here, at least in spirit. Gives me the creeps.''

''I'm ready,'' she said. ''Just needed to pick up a few things. Let's go get that license.''

''Good idea, love!''

The lurking presence of the Swan men didn't stop Neal from taking Ginna into his arms and giving her a deep, thorough kiss.

''I thought you were in a hurry to leave,'' she teased. ''Keep that up, and we'll be here all afternoon—all night.''

''Hm-m-m! Sounds nice, but . . .''

''Let's go!''

The blood test made Ginna's head swim, but she felt better, once they were in the car and headed back to Swan's Quarter. Her excitement rose to a fever pitch, as the big house came into view. She could hardly wait to get her hands on that Bible.

''We're in luck,'' Neal said, as they drove up the lane. ''There's no one on the veranda. Must be suppertime. We can sneak in and go straight to Kirkwood's office.''

''Oh, dear!'' Ginna gave a distressed cry.

''What's wrong?''

''The female swan—she's gone!''

Neal chuckled, trying to make light of the fear he heard in Ginna's voice. ''She's probably just getting even with that old cob for wandering off all the time. She'll be back before dark.''

Ginna tried to take heart from Neal's explanation. Still, the absence of the pen seemed to her an ill omen.

The swans were forgotten, once they reached Dr. Kirkwood's office.

''*The Bible!*'' Ginna's words were like a benediction.

She hurried around the doctor's desk and sat down. Slowly, carefully, she opened the great book to the place marked by a faded purple satin ribbon. Before her eyes were pages and pages, line after line of spidery script, recounting the entire history of the Swan family of Virginia in marriage, birth, and death notations.

''Oh, Neal,'' she breathed. ''Come look. It's *all* right here.''

He moved to her side and placed a hand on her shoulder. Leaning down, he squinted at the flouished writing. "I hope the doc has a magnifying glass. I can't make out a word of that."

Ginna wasn't really listening. Instead, she was scanning the lines, searching for the entry that announced the birth of Agnes and Rodney Swan's daughter, little Roslyn.

"Here it is!" She spoke, as much to herself as to Neal. "I remember that day so well. I even recall watching Mother—I mean, Melora Swan—write in the name and date."

She checked the next line, sure that she would see Virginia and Channing's names and the date of their broomstick wedding. There was no mention of any such a happy occasion.

"It's not here!" she cried.

"What, darlin'? What are you looking for?"

She rubbed a hand over her eyes. "Surely I didn't imagine it. I *know* it happened. Afterward, we made love until dawn. I became pregnant that very night."

Neal crouched down beside her chair and took her hand. His face filled with concern, he gazed up at her. "Take it easy, Ginna. You're getting too caught up in all this. Are you talking about Virginia? You said '*I,*' honey. What is it that's missing?"

She leaned her head down on her arm. "Oh, Neal, I'm so tired, so confused. Of course, I meant Virginia. Why wouldn't their marriage be recorded here in the Bible?"

Thinking the matter through logically, he answered, "Maybe Melora Swan was too busy with all that was going on, and she just forgot. Or maybe she still planned on a big wedding, after the war was over, and she didn't want to confuse things by listing two weddings in the Bible."

Ginna sat up straight and wiped her eyes. "More likely, Virginia's mother never considered that broomstick jumping a legal marriage. There was no real minister, just old Brother Zebulon. And I doubt any other bride in the Swan family ever married in the slave fashion. No, Melora only allowed Virginia and Channing to believe they were married. It was all a sham, Neal. It might as well not have happened."

Gently, he gripped Ginna's shoulders and turned her to look at him. "If ever there were two people who were married in their hearts and souls—where it really counts, darlin'—those two were Channing and Virginia. The fact that Melora Swan failed to write it down means nothing. You are the living proof that Virginia Swan married Channing McNeal and gave birth to his child."

"Yes," Ginna said. You're right, Neal. I *am* the proof of their love, if not their marriage."

Trying to distract her, Neal asked, "What's on the next line?"

Ginna leaned close, trying to decipher the tear-stained scrawl. "Oh, no!" she cried.

"What?" Neal was beginning to be alarmed. All these revelations from the past could not be good for Ginna's weak heart. He found himself worrying over her, even after he had promised her he would not.

"Jed died. Captain Royal told us the last time I saw him that Jed had been wounded, but he said it wasn't serious. What could have happened?"

Neal thought about the primitive medical practices back during the war, the lack of drugs, especially among the Confederate ranks. Disease had been rampant throughout both armies. He decided against expressing such thoughts to Ginna. That might only upset her more.

"What could have happened?" he said. "In wartime, Ginna? Anything. Does it say where he was killed?"

She read from the tear-blurred page. " 'Jedediah Swan, Junior, killed at the Battle of Antietam in Maryland on the seventeenth of September, 1862, fighting for our Cause.' "

"He had probably recovered from his first wound," Neal said, "then got hit at Antietam. If I remember my history, that was one of the bloodiest battles of the war." He recalled seeing an old Alexander Gardner photograph of Confederate corpses lined up by a fence bordering Farmer Miller's cornfield.

"Yes. That's probably what happened," Ginna answered quietly, her eyes focused on the next entry.

"Can't you read that next one?" Neal asked, when she studied it for so long.

"This one's different," she said. "It's just a note Melora jotted in between the lines."

"What does it say?"

Ginna's voice quivered as she began reading. " 'As of the first day of July, 1863, my husband, Colonel Jedediah Swan, was still alive and well. I have saved his dear letter written on that date, the first to arrive in months, for I felt in my heart that it will be his last. On the third day of July, I felt a strange emptiness, a loss, a slipping away of cherished bonds. My husband is dead. I know not how I know. God, please grant him safe passage into Heaven, and bring my two remaining sons home safely.' "

"Only *two* sons?"

Ginna ignored Neal's question. She was too busy turning the pages, hoping to find Colonel Swan's last letter to his wife. She found many things—pressed flowers, fancy calling cards, a few faded Confederate bills, and, finally, the Colonel's precious last words to his wife. She unfolded the ragged square of brown paper and scanned the lines.

1 July 1863
Pennsylvania

My darling Wife,

It is time to send our Rodney home to you. He still breathes and his heart still beats, but he is otherwise dead to us. Poor, brave boy! The surgeons here say there is naught else to be done for him, save seeing to his bodily needs and providing him a comfortable place to rest. Please soothe his little wife as best you can. This will not be an easy blow for her to take. At least Agnes has baby Roslyn to cherish for years to come. Perhaps, with God's mercy, and your tender care, our son will return to himself, once he reaches Swan's Quarter. I pray so, my dearest.

Hopes run high in camp these days. We have crossed

*into the North, the very homeland of the enemy. They
shall soon get a taste of the suffering they have caused
us. Rumor has it that both armies will meet near here at
a town called Gettysburg. I scouted the area yesterday
and found it to be a quiet hamlet, nestled among green,
rolling hills, one dominated by a seminary for young
men. Battle in such a quiet place seems unthinkable, but
so it must be. This is to be the turning point, according
to General Lee, our chance to end this long and bloody
conflict. Another prayer to God, if He is still listening,
to put a swift and merciful conclusion to all this madness.*

*Melora, my dearest, I have always been a man of
action, but few words. On the eve of this battle, I feel
the need to tell you how adored you are, how cherished
and loved by your husband. I hope that when you look
past the swan pond to the tulip poplar we planted on the
day we were wed, you think of me as I am thinking of
you always.*

My love and affection to Virginia, Agnes, and Roslyn.

> *Ever faithfully,*
> *Your adoring Husband*
> *Col. Jedediah Swan*

Ginna's eyes were swimming with tears by the time she
finished reading the Colonel's letter silently. She handed it to
Neal, too choked up to say a word. She used the few minutes,
which Neal took deciphering Jedediah Swan's old-fashioned
handwriting, to compose herself. All she could think of was
Melora, hundreds of miles away, feeling a physical loss at the
moment her beloved husband was killed on the battlefield at
Gettysburg. Had Virginia felt that same loss? she wondered.
Had Channing returned to her after the war, or had he, too,
fallen in some farmer's corpse-strewn pasture?

"This explains why Melora turned Swan's Quarter into a
home for Confederate soliders," Neal said, reading through
the letter a second time. "I wonder how long Rodney lived
and if he ever recovered."

Ginna thumbed back through the pages and traced the lines with one finger. "He lived through the end of the war," she said. " 'He died quietly in his sleep'—Melora wrote—'on the very day that General Lee surrendered to Grant at Appomattox, the ninth of April, 1865.' "

Both of them remained silent for a time, experiencing the weight and sorrow of that terrible war, as if it were a personal tragedy. It was, in fact. They were not simply reading about strangers who had lived and died over a century ago. They knew these people; they had lived among them for brief periods and had come to know and love them.

Dr. Kirkwood came in. "Have you found what you were looking for?"

"Not everything," Ginna answered. "Not yet."

Neal filled the doctor in on the facts they had leaned so far. Meanwhile, Ginna had gone on to the next entry.

"Here's another of Melora's notes," she said. "After Rodney's death, Agnes took Roslyn and moved away. Her mother needed to go the a healthier climate, so Agnes accompanied her."

"What about Virginia?" Neal asked. "And Channing?"

Ginna shook her head. "Not a word. It's as if both of them dropped completely out of the picture." Still reading, she cried, "Oh, wait! Here's something. It's out of sequence, as if Melora jotted it down as an afterthought. No, it's simply a sad update."

"Well, read it," Neal urged.

"It's dated the tenth of May, 1865. 'The twins arrived home today, both in good health, but thin and downcast. They are making plans even now to head West and seek their fortunes. I had hoped they might bring news of Virginia. When she received word nearly a year ago that Channing had been wounded at Petersburg, she insisted on going to find him and bring him home. Since that time, I have taken care of her darling baby, Channelle, who was born nine months to the day after Channing McNeal's last visit to Swan's Quarter, the occasion of the broomstick ceremony. After all this time, I have about given up hope. Surely tragedy has befallen both my daughter and the man she loved. Will I ever see their dear faces again? Will Channelle ever know her parents?' '' Ginna finished reading with a shudder and a sob.

Neal closed his arms around her, trying to comfort her. ''This isn't the end of it, darlin'. We can go to Washington, to the Library of Congress. They have records there. Maybe we'll find Channing listed.''

''Ginna?'' Dr. Kirkwood said, in a tone of alarm. ''What's wrong?''

She had sagged in Neal's arms, her eyes closed, her breathing labored.

Neal looked up at the doctor, stricken, pleading. ''Do something, Doc!''

Kirkwood reached for the phone to call an ambulance, but Ginna, rousing, caught his sleeve to stop him.

''No,'' she gasped. ''I won't leave Neal.''

''I'll go with you, Ginna. I'll stay with you. I promise.''

''Too late,'' she whispered. ''Time's run out. Take me to the greenhouse. Take me back, Neal. Back to Virginia.''

''What's she talking about?'' Kirkwood asked. ''She's delirious.''

''No, she's not. There's no time to explain now, but she knows exactly what she wants, and it makes sense.''

He lifted Ginna gently in his arms and started out of the room. They would go to the greenhouse, go back to the past, and live long and happily as Virginia and Channing. Neal felt a new confidence, a new excitement. Then he stopped.

''It's dark out,'' he said.

''Of course it is. It's nearly nine o'clock, and I'm not waiting another minute. Ginna needs to be in a hospital.''

Elspeth suddenly appeared at the door to Dr. Kirkwood's office. She was smiling, even though she could see Ginna's limp form in Neal's arms.

''You come with me,'' she said to Neal. ''Don't need no noontime sun. I know the secret. Come quick, now!''

All the way to the greenhouse, Neal was aware of Elspeth

muttering to herself. Every now and again, he would catch a
word or two.

"Love don't die ... we gone have us a weddin' ... full
moon tonight ... ghosts come out sure enough ... you hurry
along now ... come one, come all ..."

Neal never noticed that, as they moved through the hall,
the others fell in behind them—Pansy, Sister, Marcellus, Big
George—they all came. Elspeth drew the inmates of Swan's
Quarter like the Pied Piper. Only when they reached the greenhouse and people came pouring in, did Neal realize that everyone was there.

"Elspeth, what's going on? It's too crowded in here. Ginna
can't breath."

The old woman smiled at him, still unperturbed. "But Miss
Virginia, she breathe just fine." She pointed toward the glass
plate negative high up on the greenhouse wall. "You watch
that old moon. It gonna shine to beat all. Shine for Ginna, it
will."

"Neal?" Ginna moaned. "Neal, kiss me."

He leaned down and covered her lips with his. Would this
be their last kiss? She felt so cold.

"Ginna, please," he whispered, "don't leave me, darlin'. I
love you. I can't live without you."

Just as he leaned down to kiss her again, a great wind whipped
through the greenhouse, showering everyone with purple blossoms from the gnarled wisteria vine that Virginia Swan had
once carried as her bridal bouquet, then planted as a symbol
of her never-ending love for Channing McNeal.

The moon rose. The ghosts appeared. A great bolt of lightning
flashed.

"Neal!" Ginna cried. "Hold me tight!"

He tried to hold onto her. He really did.

Chapter Nineteen

With a jolt that almost took away what little breath she had left, Ginna Jones found herself once more inside Virginia Swan. By the brilliant green of the landscape, she knew it was early summer. She was alone—dusty and weary—walking up the path from the woods. She gazed toward the house on the hill, thinking how much she had missed the place and how wonderful it was to be home, after all this time. She paused at the swan pond and smiled. The old cob and his pen had their heads bowed together to form a perfect heart.

Looking back at Swan's Quarter, she thought she saw people on the veranda, rocking slowly, waving to her and smiling. But a moment later, they vanished.

A happy cry greeted her, as she drew nearer. *"Virginia?"* Her mother came rushing out of the front door, a pretty toddler clinging to her long, black skirt. "Virginia, can that really be you?"

She broke into a trot, eager to feel her mother's sheltering arms around her again, dying to hold her little daughter, Channelle.

"Oh, my sweet, dear girl!" Melora wept. "I never thought

I'd see you again. Where have you been? How have you survived all this time?''

Polly came bustling around the side of the house. ''I swannee, if it ain't Miss Virginia, in the flesh! You had us mighty worried, I can tell you, ma'am.''

Virginia, holding Channelle and kissing her sunlit curls, hugged Polly. ''You wouldn't happen to have some fried chicken on the place, would you? I'm starved!''

While Polly fried the chicken, Virginia bathed and changed clothes up in her bedroom, with Melora and Channelle by her side every moment.

Melora caught her up on all that had happened in their family since she left. Agnes and Roslyn were fine, still with her mother at the sulfur springs. The twins had gone all the way to California, where they were both married and raising families now. They had opened up a mercantile store in San Francisco. Most of the slaves had taken off for the North, but a few, who were ''family,'' had stayed on to work for wages.

''And Channing's family?'' Virginia asked, pulling on a frock that had been far too small for her before she left, but fit perfectly now.

''They arrived home from Paris a few months after the surrender,'' Melora said. ''Channing's father is in the wine business now. He brought cuttings back from France, and they seem to thrive in our rich soil.'' Melora beamed at her daughter. ''And Letitia is teaching me to paint. I've already done a portrait of Channelle, and I believe it's quiet good.''

Virginia reached for her daughter and drew her onto her lap. ''With such a pretty subject, how could it be anything but beautiful?''

The little girl, still shy with her mother, gazed up at her with Channing's dark eyes.

Melora took the girl from Virginia and said, ''Why don't you go down and ask Polly if that chicken is done yet, dear?''

With a wave and a smile, Channelle skipped out of the room. Melora hadn't wanted the child to hear her next question.

''What of Channing, Virginia? Did you find him?''

Her daughter's beaming face answered the question, even before she spoke. "I did. He was wounded at Petersburg, as we heard. I searched and searched, before I found him in a makeshift hospital. Had I not gone to nurse him, he would have died, Mother. The conditions were beyond deplorable. I don't want to think about it, much less talk about it."

"But where is he now? Why didn't he come home with you?"

"He will be here soon. He had to go to Washington to take care of some business first—something about a woman who was thought to have died, but is really alive. He didn't tell me all the details. It's army business, I suppose. We came most of the way together, then parted at Winchester. He said the sooner he got to Washington, the sooner he could come to Swan's Quarter to marry me in proper fashion."

Melora clapped her hands, then hugged her daughter. "Oh, I can't tell you how happy this makes me!"

"We both knew that you never considered our broomstick-jumping a proper ceremony. We want to make it perfectly legal."

"And perfectly lovely! Channing's mother brought you a beautiful gown from Paris. Polly and I will see to all the other arrangements."

Virginia soon discovered that there had been more changes at Swan's Quarter than she had suspected. Her mother had taken in several wounded veterans, and their wives had come to be with them. Some of the people seemed so familiar, yet she knew she had never met them before. There was one couple in particular, his name was Billy and his pretty wife was called Pansy. Many of the guests at Swan's Quarter joined Virginia, Melora, and Channelle for some of Polly's fried chicken, mashed potatoes, spring squash, and lemon-cheese cake.

This was a real homecoming. Virginia couldn't have been happier. The war was over and life, once more, was good at Swan's Quarter.

* * *

It wasn't Channing who had business in Washington, but Neal. He had a plane to catch; a wrong to right. Elspeth had provided the magic to make this possible. While the old woman went on to Swan's Quarter to be at the wedding, she sent Neal on another course, one not so far back in time.

"You do this thing, then you come on back and join the rest of us. You got a wedding to be at, remember?"

Before Neal could blink an eye, he found himself once more on the ill-fated flight 1862. Again, the awful fear gripped him, tearing and thrashing in the pit of his stomach.

The child beside him—Christine, she had told him her name was—clung to her mother, crying. Mrs. Henderson had said she was a teacher and a wife, with several other children. Now the woman was sobbing, even as she tried to soothe her terrified child.

"Don't worry, Mrs. Henderson. The emergency door is right here. I'll have it open, the minute we get down. You and Christine will be out and safe before you know it."

He tried to sound totally confident. He only hoped it would be that simple.

Their sickening descent seemed to last forever. All the passengers were screaming, moaning, or praying aloud. Neal Frazier was praying, too, but not for his own life. Silently, he said, *Dear God, let me do it right this time. Let me save the daughter and the mother. And then, please, God, send me back to my Virginia.*

The crash and the fire came so quickly that there was little time to think. What Neal did, he did by pure instinct. The door came off, and he turned to Christine and her mother. The woman tried to thrust her child into his arms.

"No!" Neal yelled. "Here, take my hand. I'll get you both out."

He was coughing, choking on the toxic fumes, as were the other passengers. Seconds slipped away—precious seconds, life-giving seconds. Somehow, he managed to extract the woman from her jammed seat belt. With a maximum of effort—he was dizzy and disoriented—he shoved the woman and her child from the plane to safety. He didn't try to follow them. He couldn't have anyway. The fumes and smoke overcame him, and he fell back into the flames. But he never felt the pain of death. Instead, he experienced a cool, fresh wind, scented with the flowers of spring. He felt weightless, as if he were now flying without a plane. Soaring through the clean air, happy, alive, and free.

The next thing he knew, he was astride a horse, riding up a familiar lane. There were people gathered on the veranda watching for him. He was home—home at last!

"Channing!" He heard her call, before he saw her. She stepped from the crowd on the porch and ran down the stairs, crying his name in joyful greeting. A little girl trailed behind, clutching her skirt.

"My wife," he breathed, "and my daughter."

Only when they were both in his arms could he really believe that this dream had come true, at long last.

"Oh, my darling, my darling," Virginia wept. "I thought you'd never come." After showering his face with kisses, she said, "Channelle, this is your father. He's a hero."

"Daddy!" the little girl said, reaching up to him with soft, dimpled arms.

Channing scooped her up, laughing, and rained kisses all over her pink cheeks.

Late that night, after all the excitement of his homecoming had subsided and they finally got a chance to be alone, Channing held his love in his arms for the first time in many months.

"I never thought I would live to see this day. I wouldn't have without you, darlin'."

"Let's don't talk of the past."

"Let's don't talk at all. I want to love you now, like you've never been loved before. And I want to think of the future—*our* future together, Virginia."

"It's going to be a long, lovely life," she said, with a happy sigh.

Soon, all conversation came to an end. Channing kissed Virginia's breasts, stroked her thighs, and finally came to her, offering all the love he had to give.

Virginia was right; it was a long, lovely life. The very next day, she donned the beautiful gown from Paris and came down the wide staircase at Swan's Quarter to join her love in holy wedlock, presided over this time by the Reverend Bulwer and witnessed by all their friends and Channing's family and the spirits of all those who would come to Swan's Quarter over a century in the future—those who had traveled through time to be at this wedding.

As Channing and Virginia stood together in the parlor, she forgot about all the others. She was aware only of the nearness of the man she had loved all her life and would continue to love through this life, and many others.

When the ceremony ended, Channing kissed her as though she were made of fragile china. Little Channelle came and hugged them both.

"Now we're a real family," Virginia said, through happy tears.

"Hallo! Anybody home?" The call came from the front door. No one had noticed the odd wagon coming up the lane past the swan pond.

"Who on earth could that be?" Melora said.

Beaming at his mother-in-law, Channing answered, "It's a surprise for my bride. I contacted Mr. Mathew Brady, while I was in Washington. He's come to make our wedding portrait."

Juniper showed the photographer in. He looked as Virginia remembered, with his blue-tinted spectacles and silver-headed cane. With him came the scent of Atwood's colonge.

"I've brought you a wedding gift, Mrs. McNeal." He handed her a photograph taken at Petersburg. "That's me there," he pointed to the figure in the canvas coat. "I had Gardner take the shot. And if you'll look very closely, I believe you'll see your husband, just there."

Virginia frowned, trying to remember. The photograph looked so familiar, but she knew she had never seen it before. Brady distracted her attention by insisting that the bride and groom come pose for him by the swan pond.

And to this day, if you happen to visit Swan's Quarter, you will see the "ghosts" in the greenhouse and the matching wedding portrait of Channing and Virginia McNeal, smiling into each others eyes, with a love and joy that transcends time.

For, indeed, it did, and still does.

Epilogue

Elspeth, Sister, and Marcellus Lynch sat on the veranda, rocking and drinking tea, which they poured from the old silver pot that had been wounded in the war.

It was a Monday, and it seemed odd not to be watching for Ginna, not to see the tulip poplar shimmering in the distance. They missed Pansy, too, but they all knew she was happier back in the past, back with her Billy and with Virginia and Channing.

"Tell us a story, Elspeth," Marcellus begged, about to sneak the last sugar cookie from the plate, before he decided to leave it for the two ladies to share.

She nodded and set down her blue and white flowered cup. "Well, as you may recall, Colonel Jedediah Swan rode off to the war at the head of his own cavalry unit, and all four of his sons went with him."

"Not *that* story," Sister fussed. "Tell us about later, after the war."

"Yes," Marcellus agreed, "tell the happy part."

Elspeth, who had only been teasing them, anyway, was more

than happy to tell the rest of the story. She rocked gently for a minute or two, gazing off into the distance before she began.

"There was once a girl named Ginna—a lonely girl, a girl with a sickly heart. She had no mama, no papa, no one but us. We loved her like our own. We made ourselves her family. And the best thing you can do when you love someone the way we loved our Ginna is to give her roots and wings. Her roots here at Swan's Quarter went down as far as the roots of that old wisteria vine in the greenhouse. And her wings have spread like a swan's to carry her to her love."

"Tell about Neal," Lynch said.

Elspeth took another sip of tea, and her eyes grew moist. "A sweet young man, but sad, so sad. He was a hero, you know. He saved little Christine and her mother in that plane crash. Gave up his own life, he did."

"But in return, he was rewarded, wasn't he?" Sister put in.

"That he was! With *love* everlasting. He made our Ginna happy with his love. We'll never forget him."

"Never!" Lynch agreed.

"And now our Ginna and her Neal are far, faraway, yet still right here at Swan's Quarter. Sometimes, in the late afternoon, 'twixt sunset and twilight, seems I see them down by the swan pond, holding hands or sharing a kiss. Yes, they're still here, all right, but in the fourth dimension. And I see their children— little Channelle and a boy named Jed, for his grandpa and his uncle, both heroes of our Cause. And then they'll fade, just like that. But they leave an afterglow in our hearts, a feeling that we'll meet again."

Sister wiped a tear from the corner of her eye. "Do you believe that, Els? Really, I mean—that we'll all meet again."

Elspeth reached over and gripped Sister's hand. "Oh, absolutely! As sure as a swan mates for life, we chose our friends for all time. For here and now, and for the hereafter."

The threesome fell quiet, thinking of all the loved ones who had gone before them, knowing in their hearts that their reunions would not be long in coming.

''Tomorrow's Tuesday,'' Sister said suddenly. ''Do you suppose Christine and Mrs. Henderson will come visit?''

''Of course, they will,'' said Lynch.

''Have they ever missed a Tuesday?'' Elspeth whispered with a smile and a wink.

ROMANCE FROM HANNAH HOWELL

MY VALIANT KNIGHT   (0-8217-5186-7, $5.50)

ONLY FOR YOU   (0-8217-4993-5, $4.99)

UNCONQUERED   (0-8217-5417-3, $5.99)

WILD ROSES   (0-8217-5677-X, $5.99)

PASSIONATE ROMANCE
FROM BETINA KRAHN!

HIDDEN FIRES   (0-8217-4953-6, $4.99)

LOVE'S BRAZEN FIRE   (0-8217-5691-5, $5.99)

MIDNIGHT MAGIC   (0-8217-4994-3, $4.99)

PASSION'S RANSOM   (0-8217-5130-1, $5.99)

REBEL PASSION   (0-8217-5526-9, $5.99)

Available wherever paperbacks are sold, or order direct from the Publisher. Send cover price plus 50¢ per copy for mailing and handling to Penguin USA, P.O. Box 999, c/o Dept. 17109, Bergenfield, NJ 07621. Residents of New York and Tennessee must include sales tax. DO NOT SEND CASH.